Love's
Faithful
Promise

Books by Susan Anne Mason

COURAGE TO DREAM

Irish Meadows
A Worthy Heart
Love's Faithful Promise

COURAGE TO DREAM
BOOK 3

LOVE'S FAITHFUL PROMISE

SUSAN ANNE MASON

BETHANYHOUSE
a division of Baker Publishing Group
Minneapolis, Minnesota

© 2016 by Susan Anne Mason

Published by Bethany House Publishers
11400 Hampshire Avenue South
Bloomington, Minnesota 55438
www.bethanyhouse.com

Bethany House Publishers is a division of
Baker Publishing Group, Grand Rapids, Michigan

Printed in the United States of America

Library of Congress Control Number: 2016938453

ISBN: 978-0-7642-1726-5

Scripture quotations are from the King James Version of the Bible.

This is a work of fiction. Names, characters, and incidents are products of the author's imagination and are not to be construed as real. Any resemblance to actual events or persons, living or dead, is entirely coincidental.

Cover design by Jennifer Parker
Cover photography by Mike Habermann Photography, LLC

Author is represented by the Natasha Kern Literary Agency.

16 17 18 19 20 21 22   7 6 5 4 3 2 1

To my brother, Greg, my sister-in-law, Tina, and my two nieces, Samantha and Madelyn, for their encouragement and support in my writing journey. And special thanks to Maddy for being my youngest number one fan! Love you all!

For I will restore health unto thee, and I will heal thee of thy wounds, saith the Lord.

Jeremiah 30:17

1

DEIRDRE O'LEARY strode down the wide corridor on the second floor of Manhattan's Bellevue Hospital, her stomach quivering with each step.

How many times had she walked these halls? Hundreds? Thousands?

Eagerly as a nursing student, and later with confident efficiency as a practicing nurse.

But never with such dread.

Barely a month had passed since she'd quit her position here, and now she was back for the worst possible reason.

In the pocket of her linen jacket, Deirdre's fingers closed around the slip of paper she'd read dozens of times on the train from Boston. Her father's telegram.

Your mother had stroke. Come quickly.

As a nurse, Deirdre knew all too well the dangers and the

complications that could arise. The odds were high that Mama would suffer a second and possibly fatal stroke. As soon as Deirdre had read her father's message, she'd left her medical studies at Boston University and boarded the next train for New York.

Now the heels of her shoes tapped a staccato rhythm that echoed off the sterile hospital walls. The familiar scents of antiseptic and pine cleanser brought her a small measure of assurance, reminding her of the healing that took place within these walls. She'd witnessed many miraculous recoveries during her time here as a nurse.

She would expect no less for her mother.

Deirdre passed the waiting room, surprised to see none of her brothers or sisters inside. She'd expected them all to be keeping vigil here. She slowed her pace as she came to the room number she'd been given and laid a hand on the doorframe while she paused to control her rapid breathing. For her family's sake, she must appear calm and in control.

Professional.

No matter how badly her heart was shattering.

She stepped through the doorway, and an unnatural hush met her ears. Right away her gaze flew to the metal bed that dominated the room. Her mother lay still beneath the bleached-white sheets. Beside the bed, her father sat hunched over the rail.

Deirdre's lower lip quivered. Mama looked so weak, just as she had when they'd almost lost her to typhoid fever. Deirdre and her brother Connor had also contracted the disease and had bounced back quickly, but not Mama. The illness had taken its toll, sapping much of her mother's vitality. The same panic Deirdre had felt back then returned to create a vise grip around her lungs.

She released a shaky breath and moved farther into the room. Against the far wall, her oldest sister, Colleen, sat with her head back, eyes closed. At least Daddy wasn't alone.

Her father looked up, the pinched lines in his forehead easing as he spotted her. "Dee. Thank heaven you're here."

He rose to embrace her. The fragility in his blue eyes, a direct contrast to his strapping build, tore at Deirdre's composure.

She kissed his cheek. "How is she, Daddy?"

"Stable for now. It's been more than twenty-four hours with no further episodes, which the doctor says is an encouraging sign."

"He's right." She lifted the chart from the end of the metal bed frame and scanned the notations. The word *paralysis* jumped off the page in several spots. She pressed her lips together. "Has the doctor said what treatment he recommends?"

Daddy's features hardened. He moved closer, his voice barely audible. "We'll discuss that later. For now, your mother needs to regain her strength."

Across the room, Colleen roused from her slumber, stretching her arms over her head. "Dee! Thank goodness." She pushed up from the chair, and Deirdre's gaze fused to her swollen abdomen. Another Montgomery baby on the way? How had she missed that piece of news?

Colleen grabbed Deirdre in a vigorous hug. "Now that you're here, we'll all feel better. If anyone can help Mama, it's our resident nurse." She pulled back. "Or should I say doctor-in-training?" Despite her obvious fatigue, a twinkle shone in her sister's violet-blue eyes.

"I'll do my best, no matter what title you give me." Deirdre smiled. "You look wonderful. Why didn't you tell me I'm going to be an aunt again?"

Colleen rested a hand on her belly. "With the size of our brood, I figured it must be boring by now."

"Nonsense. It makes what you do all the more amazing. Running the orphanage with Rylan, adopting two children, having two of your own, plus another on the way . . ." She tilted her head to one side. "You make medical school look easy. Besides, babies are never boring. Are they, Daddy?"

"Not my grandbabies." He gave a weak attempt at a smile,

his gaze straying to the bed as though he was worried Mama wouldn't be able to enjoy the anticipated addition to the family.

"Where is everyone?" Deirdre asked. "I expected the waiting room to be bursting with O'Learys."

Daddy resumed his place by the bed. "The others have been here and left. We're setting up a schedule so your mother is never alone."

A shiver of alarm wound its way along Deirdre's spine.

Colleen laid a hand on Daddy's shoulder. "Speaking of which, I need to get home before the children are out of school." She kissed his cheek and embraced Deirdre once more. "We'll talk soon."

As soon as Colleen left, Deirdre faced her father. "Have the doctors said if Mama's out of danger yet?"

He rose and motioned to the hallway. His tall frame seemed to eat up the space in the corridor. "The doctors won't say much. Only that her condition hasn't worsened."

Deirdre bit her lip. "Did they give any hope for recovering the use of her limbs?"

A nerve twitched in Daddy's jaw, a sure sign he was upset. He shook his head. "They say there's nothing they can do. Told me to prepare for permanent paralysis."

"But surely there's some type of therapy—"

Daddy made way for an orderly to pass with a mop and bucket. "I have people looking into the best facilities in the country."

Deirdre's throat seized, forcing her to swallow before she spoke. "Surely you're not thinking of putting Mama in a facility?" Her desperate whisper echoed in the hall.

"Of course not. I plan to bring in a specialist."

"Thank goodness." Her shoulder muscles went lax with relief. For a moment, she'd worried her father had taken leave of his senses.

Daddy draped an arm around her, and they started back

toward Mama's room. "Actually, your Uncle Victor has a doctor in mind. One who's making remarkable advances with injured limbs up in Toronto. He's going to speak to him and get back to me. In the meantime"—he turned to face her—"I need to know. Will you come home to look after your mother?" His expression became apologetic. "Brianna and Colleen have offered, but they both have young families. And you're the most qualified." A hint of pride sounded in his voice.

Deirdre paused to savor his words. He'd been far from thrilled when she'd first told him of her desire to become a nurse. And even less so once she'd decided to study medicine.

Visions of the campus at Boston's medical school flashed through her mind. After only a few weeks in attendance, she'd barely gotten used to her classes. Her professors had assured her they understood why she had to leave, but how long would they hold her spot when so many students clamored to get in?

Brighter, more promising students than she.

Her thoughts turned to Jeffrey and how much she'd already sacrificed to pursue this career path.

Yet one look at the pleading in her father's eyes and every trace of doubt vanished. "Of course, Daddy. There's nowhere else I'd be."

She only prayed that delaying her studies, even for a short while, wouldn't permanently derail her dream of becoming a pediatrician.

***

"That's it, Fred. One more repetition and you can stop for today." Matthew Clayborne guided the soldier's shriveled leg to a forty-five-degree angle and counted as Fred held the position for a full minute.

Sweat poured from the man's brow. He grunted when his leg finally dropped. "If you're trying to kill me, Doc, it's working."

Doubts crept in as Matthew unstrapped the iron weight and

removed it from Fred's shin. Had he pushed the man too hard for his second round of therapy this week?

Fred grinned, easing the lines of pain etched into his forehead. "Relax, Doc. I'm joking." He grabbed the crutch leaning against the wall next to him, pulled himself up, and hobbled over to his wheelchair. "Despite the pain, it actually felt good. Like the exercises are working."

A wave of relief rushed through Matthew's chest. "Glad to hear it. With continued hard work, you should be out of that chair in six months or less." Matthew turned to make a notation on the man's file.

Fred's story was much the same as most of Matthew's patients. Young and fit before he became injured in the war. Sent home a cripple.

As Matthew almost was.

Fred maneuvered his chair across the room. "See you next week, Doc. Unless a pretty girl makes me a better offer." He chuckled while retrieving his hat from a low bookcase near the door.

Rubbing the thigh of his own bad leg, Matthew marveled at Fred's ability to keep such a cheerful attitude. At least Matthew could walk, albeit with a slight limp.

"What's this about a pretty girl?" Marjorie, Fred's wife, appeared in the open doorway, holding a small boy's hand.

Fred's whole face changed, and the ravages of the pain he'd endured gave way to a laugh. "I'm talking about you, of course, honey. You're the only pretty girl in my life."

Marjorie's simulated scowl changed to a blinding smile that radiated her obvious affection for her husband. "Good answer, Mr. Knox." She bent to kiss him.

Matthew turned away, unable to squash a flare of envy. Even if Fred never walked again, Matthew doubted it would affect Marjorie's devotion. Did the man know how lucky he was? Unwelcome images of Priscilla wisped across Matthew's mind.

He would never forget her look of disgust upon seeing the ugly scar that traversed the length of his upper leg when he'd returned from overseas.

Fred's son, Harry, gave a loud whoop, snapping Matthew from his brooding. The child hopped onto Fred's lap and flung his arms around his neck. "Daddy, can we go to the candy store now?" His exuberance pulsed through the room like a current of electricity.

"That all depends, young man. Have you been good for your mama while you waited?" Fred regarded the boy who squirmed on his lap.

"Mostly good. Mama only had to call me 'Harrison' once."

Fred's lips twitched. "Well, I suppose that deserves some licorice and gumdrops. Don't you agree, Mama?" He winked at his wife.

Marjorie laughed. "As long as I get some as well."

The lad leapt up and raced across the room. Matthew contemplated the boy with bemused admiration, trying to imagine his frail Phoebe with so much unbridled energy.

Marjorie turned to Matthew. "How did Fred do today, Dr. Clayborne?" The note of hope in her voice was unmistakable.

Matthew gave a brief nod. "He's doing very well. If he continues to make progress, he might be out of that chair by late spring." There, he'd given himself—and Fred—more time than expected.

If Marjorie was at all dismayed by the length of time the therapy would entail, she hid it well. "I want to thank you again, Doctor, for everything you're doing. When I think of the years Fred wasted because no one was willing to work with him . . ." She bit her lip and broke off. "I thank God every day that we found you."

At the sheen of emotion filming her blue eyes, Matthew took a step back, fearing she might try to hug him. "Your husband is doing the work. He deserves your praise, not me."

She laid a hand on her husband's shoulder and smiled. "You both deserve credit. Good-bye, Doctor."

As soon as the young family left him in blessed solitude, a band of tension eased, allowing Matthew to breathe normally again. He moved to the counter and jotted a few more notes regarding the next therapy session. When he finished, he drew his watch from his vest pocket. Ten minutes until his next patient arrived. Unfortunately, Mr. Worthington was not nearly as receptive to treatment as Fred Knox.

A quick knock sounded on the door. Matthew looked up to see the medical director, Dr. Victor Fullman, enter the room. Victor had been his boss ever since Matthew had joined the staff of the Toronto Military Hospital almost four years ago.

"Good day, Matthew. Might I have a word with you?"

Matthew worked to keep the surprise from his features. It was highly unusual for Victor to come down to the therapy room. Normally, he would send word for Matthew to come to his office. "Of course, Victor. Is anything wrong?"

The big man crossed the floor. "I have a request I wanted to run by you as soon as possible."

From the hesitant look on Victor's face, Matthew imagined he was not going to like it. He removed his reading glasses and set them carefully on the counter. "What type of request?"

"I had a call from a good friend in New York." Victor crossed his arms over his barrel of a chest. "His wife has suffered a stroke and is paralyzed down one side of her body."

"That's unfortunate. I'm sorry." Matthew rose from the stool he was sitting on.

"The neurologist at Bellevue doesn't offer much hope for recovering the use of her limbs. James, however, is a stubborn Irishman and refuses to accept the prognosis." Victor smiled, creating fine wrinkles around his eyes.

Matthew waited, still not understanding what this had to do with him.

Victor straightened. "I'd like you to take on Mrs. O'Leary as a private patient. Consider it a personal favor to me."

Matthew frowned, the word *private* ringing all sorts of alarm bells. "Is Mr. O'Leary having his wife transferred here?"

Victor regarded him steadily. "No. I want you to go to him. He lives on a large estate on Long Island, and there'd be—"

"Absolutely not." Matthew stalked to the small rectangular window high on the wall that looked out at street level. He stared at the feet walking past on the sidewalk, his heart pumping unevenly in his chest. How could Victor suggest such a thing? He knew how much helping the soldiers meant to Matthew. The slightest delay in their therapy could set their progress back by weeks, even months. "I can't abandon my patients here."

"Dr. Marlboro can fill in until you return."

Matthew whirled. "Dr. Marlboro has no idea of the type of work I'm doing with these men."

Victor didn't blink. "You could fill him in before you leave."

Matthew opened his mouth, prepared to list all the reasons why that would be impossible. At the steely look in Victor's eyes, he stopped. No use wasting his breath on explanations when his boss would simply counter every one. "It's out of the question, Victor. Now, if you'll excuse me, I need to prepare for my next patient."

"Did you not mention just last week that the need for your services is dwindling? That you're considering a new direction for your practice? This could be your chance to test your techniques on someone paralyzed by a stroke."

It was true. The number of his patients had lessened. Most had reached the maximum benefit possible, while several still relied on their sessions to keep their muscles from atrophying. For Matthew's practice to remain vital, he would have to expand his clientele. Yet the thought of such a drastic change, of possibly having to move to another facility, made him shudder.

"I'm sorry, Victor. Perhaps if she were to come here, I would consider it, but I simply cannot leave the city right now." *Not with Phoebe in such a fragile state.* Perspiration gathered under Matthew's collar while he held Victor's stare.

At last, Victor inclined his head. "I understand this is a big decision. Especially given your personal circumstances. But I'm asking you to think it over. James O'Leary is like a brother to me. If I can do something to help him, I have to try."

Once the door closed, Matthew expelled a long breath. This was one battle his mentor wouldn't win. No matter how indebted he was to the man, Matthew would never leave Toronto, never leave Phoebe, to cater to one rich, entitled woman.

His daughter and his fellow soldiers needed him far too much for that.

2

DEIRDRE CHECKED her mother's vital signs one more time, compared the numbers to the last statistics on her chart, and let out a soft sigh. Mama had passed a peaceful night, and her condition remained stable. She'd seemed more alert this morning and even managed a few bites of breakfast.

Thank you, Lord!

Now if only Daddy would return from Colleen's with good news, things would indeed be looking up. Instead of going all the way to his Long Island home, Daddy had gone to Colleen's brownstone to call Uncle Victor and to take a short nap. But he should have been back by now.

With Mama asleep once again, Deirdre slipped out of the room to get a cup of coffee. She started down the hallway, but the sight of Daddy walking toward her dashed all thoughts of beverages from her mind. She went to intercept him, dismayed at the severe downturn of his mouth.

"How is your mother?" he asked without preamble.

"Resting comfortably. Did you reach Uncle Victor?"

His mouth formed a grim line. "I spoke with him, yes." With a touch to her elbow, he guided her into the empty waiting room.

"I'm afraid the news isn't good. Victor was unable to persuade Dr. Clayborne to come to New York."

"I'm sorry, Daddy."

"While the man's dedication to his patients is admirable, I wish he could set it aside for a few weeks to help your mother." He exhaled deeply. "But it seems nothing will sway the man."

"We'll find someone else. He can't be the only therapist."

Her father's troubled gaze met hers. "There are a few physicians doing this type of work, but they're in England. Which is where Dr. Clayborne learned the technique himself."

England? Even if they could get one of the therapists to agree to come, an ocean voyage would mean valuable time wasted.

Daddy's rough hand clasped hers. "Deirdre, I want you to go to Toronto. Persuade this doctor to change his mind."

Deirdre's stomach twisted with instant apprehension. "Oh, Daddy, I don't—"

"I'd go myself if I thought it would do any good. But you know the medical terms. You speak the same language. If anyone can get him to come around, it's you."

Tension squeezed her shoulders. She'd do almost anything to help her mother, but travel to Canada?

"Please, Dee." A film of moisture shone in his blue eyes. "You can charm the fish from the sea, as your mother says. Please say you'll try."

"Excuse me, Mr. O'Leary?" A nurse appeared in the doorway.

Deirdre's gaze locked on the wicker wheelchair at her side.

"We have the chair for your wife, sir. Perhaps when she wakens, we could get her to try it."

Her father's face turned ashen.

The nurse hesitated. "This chair will allow her to get out of bed. You might even push her out into the yard, if the doctor gives permission."

The image of Mama sitting in a chair for the rest of her life flashed through Deirdre's mind. Never being able to climb the stairs to her bedroom. Never able to walk in her garden. Never able to chase her grandchildren. Deirdre's throat constricted. If this Dr. Clayborne could save Mama from such a fate, didn't Deirdre owe it to her mother to use every means possible to persuade the man to help them?

Daddy thanked the nurse, who continued down the hall.

Deirdre gulped in a deep breath. "I'll do it, Daddy. I'll go to Toronto."

Relief flooded her father's features as he scooped her into a tight hug. "Thank you." The tremble in his whisper gave evidence of the depth of his gratitude. He pulled back and cleared his throat. "I'll find out when the next train leaves and let Victor know to expect you."

Deirdre nodded, firming her resolve. She'd do whatever it took to convince this man to come. And if he still refused, she'd take the opportunity to learn all she could about the type of treatments he was using and bring the knowledge home to help her mother.

One way or another, she'd make sure Mama regained the ability to walk.

Matthew exited the physical therapy room and headed down the hall to the cramped room that served as his office. He could have chosen a more spacious room on the second floor near Dr. Fullman, but from sheer practicality, it served Matthew to be near the area where he treated his patients. In between appointments, he could answer calls, swallow a mouthful of coffee, and retrieve his notes for the next patient. Plus, the isolation of this room suited Matthew better than Dr. Fullman's busy office.

He flipped on the electric lights and blinked as though seeing the space for the first time, mildly surprised at how messy the place had become. When had he last tidied up? He pulled out his chair and made a mental note to spend some time later that day filing his paperwork. He moved a stack of books to one side, found his spare reading glasses, and perched them on the end of his nose.

A light tap on his door caused a ripple of irritation. "Yes?"

The door opened. Matthew's eyebrows rose at the sight of the stunning young woman who entered. She was dressed in a blue skirt and matching jacket. Her hat hid most of her auburn hair, except for a tidy roll pinned at the nape of her neck. Eyes the color of summer grass held him in a bold stare.

Suddenly aware he was gawking, he pressed his lips together and gave her a fierce scowl, one that usually had the staff running for cover. "I'm afraid you have the wrong office, Miss. You probably want the physicians on the second floor."

She tilted her head. "You are Dr. Clayborne, are you not? Dr. Fullman told me where to find you."

Apprehension skittered along Matthew's spine. Why would Victor send a woman to see him? Surely he wasn't trying his hand at matchmaking again. After Victor's last attempt, Matthew had made his position crystal clear. Priscilla was gone, and he had no intention of ever marrying again.

Frowning, he removed his spectacles. "I am Dr. Clayborne."

The woman gave him a bright smile, one that created a dimple in both cheeks, and stepped forward, arm outstretched. "I'm Deirdre O'Leary. It's a pleasure to meet you."

Though manners dictated he shake her hand, Matthew scowled again. "What is it you need, Miss? I'm very busy, as you can see." He gestured to his overflowing desk, now glad for the extra piles.

A brief flicker of anger flashed in her unusual green eyes, but she quickly schooled her features into a frozen smile. "Might I sit down? I just got in from New York, and I'm a bit fatigued."

New York. Warning flares ignited in Matthew's mind. Victor wouldn't stoop so low—or would he?

"Suit yourself." He swept a hand toward the only other chair in the room, filled with books and journals.

Undaunted, the young woman picked up the stack and plopped the lot on the already teetering corner of his desk. With a gloved hand, she swiped the wooden seat before perching herself on the edge.

Her look of disdain chipped at Matthew's composure. "What can I do for you?"

She raised her chin. "I've come to implore your help, Doctor, for the sake of my dear mother, who is paralyzed due to a recent stroke." Moisture sheened her vivid eyes.

Matthew couldn't help but wonder if the tears were real or merely a ruse to evoke his sympathy. A favorite ploy of Priscilla's to get her way.

Miss O'Leary took out a handkerchief and squeezed it between her fingers. "Uncle Vic—that is, Dr. Fullman spoke very highly of your work. He's certain you can help my mother regain the use of her limbs."

The earnestness of her gaze caused a prick of sympathy in Matthew's surly armor. But not enough to entertain her request. "I'm afraid Dr. Fullman has wasted your time. I've already told him why I can't take on your mother as a patient. Surely there's a qualified therapist in New York who could treat her." *Someone who doesn't have to leave his child to do so.*

A slight frown puckered the area above her pert nose. "My father has tried, believe me, but there's no one doing the type of therapy you employ. Your name is known even in New York."

Matthew raised a brow. "Appealing to my ego will not sway me."

A pink hue infused her cheeks. "That's not—" She inhaled, then hissed out a breath.

Matthew stood and glanced at his pocket watch. It was

unlikely he'd get any paperwork done now. "While I'm sorry about your mother's condition, Miss O'Leary, I'm afraid it's impossible for me to leave Toronto. Now, if you'll excuse me, I have a patient scheduled." One of many he was not about to abandon, no matter what tactics this woman tried.

Miss O'Leary rose, her determined stare boring into him. "Very well, Dr. Clayborne. If you won't come with me, I will observe your techniques so I may apply them myself."

The audacity, not to mention the sheer lunacy, of this girl assuming she could duplicate his work herself almost made Matthew laugh out loud. He gaped at her. "What makes you think you could learn a therapy that has taken me years of practice to master?"

She shot him a haughty glare. "I happen to be a medical student myself, Doctor, with three years of nursing as well. I am fully capable of learning your techniques. Now, lead on or we'll be late for your appointment."

Of all the hard-headed, cantankerous doctors Deirdre had worked with, Dr. Clayborne surpassed them all. When he couldn't dissuade her from joining his session, his patient—a lovely gentleman by the name of Mr. Worthington—had given permission for Deirdre to observe, and Dr. Clayborne had no choice but to comply. However, he had pointedly ignored her as much as possible, barely answering her questions with a grunt.

Now Deirdre studied the doctor as he finished up. If the man wasn't so morose, he might be considered handsome. He wore his light brown hair combed back off a high brow, showcasing a set of piercing blue eyes. Yet there was a hardness to him that told of the wall he'd erected around himself. Even with his patient, he showed little emotion.

Once Mr. Worthington had left the room, Dr. Clayborne addressed her. "I trust you got the information you required.

Now, if you'll excuse me, I need to make some phone calls in my office."

"Very well." Deirdre picked up her handbag and made to follow him. "What time is your first patient scheduled tomorrow?"

He leveled her with a look of incredulity. "You're not seriously planning to attend all my sessions?"

"Not all of them," she said sweetly. "Only for the next week until I can manage on my own."

Red flags stained his cheeks. "Of all the—"

"Uncle Victor's orders, I'm afraid." She raised one brow and resisted the urge to wink, fearing an apoplectic outburst.

The man pinched his mouth shut tighter than a surgeon's clamp and stormed down the corridor toward the staircase.

As she followed him, her impulsive actions caused a wave of remorse. She was supposed to be charming the man, persuading him to help her, not antagonizing him. No matter how much she disliked him, she had to try to win him over—for her mother's sake.

"Dr. Clayborne, wait." She stopped to catch her breath at the top of the stairs. "I fear we've gotten off on the wrong foot. Could we perhaps share a cup of coffee and discuss the matter in a civilized fashion?" She flashed what she hoped was a winning smile.

His entire frame tensed. "No, Miss O'Leary. We cannot. I'm on my way to tell Dr. Fullman—"

"Matthew." Uncle Victor rounded the corner, his weathered features brightening. "This is a pleasant, though not entirely unexpected, visit."

"Might I have a word with you in private, sir?" Dr. Clayborne's clipped tone hinted at his displeasure.

Uncle Victor glanced at Deirdre and then back to Dr. Clayborne. "I can spare a few minutes, but I must insist Deirdre join us, since this most certainly concerns her."

Uncle Victor headed down the corridor, not giving Dr.

Clayborne a chance to argue. They followed him into a spacious reception area, where a woman sat at a large desk, hitting keys on an Underwood typewriter.

Upon seeing them, she rose from her chair. "Your messages, sir." She handed Uncle Victor several slips of paper.

"Thank you, Miss Howard. Please see that we are not disturbed."

He gestured for them to precede him into the office. Deirdre swept in and took a seat. She gripped her hands together on her lap and offered a silent plea for help to get through to this difficult man.

Perhaps with God's favor and Uncle Victor's encouragement, they would be able to make Dr. Clayborne see reason.

Matthew marched over to the window on the far side of the office. If Victor thought Matthew would back down because of Miss O'Leary's presence, he was sadly mistaken.

Victor's chair squeaked as he sat. "Well, Matthew, what's on your mind?"

Matthew turned to level a hard stare at his superior. With effort, he controlled the volume of his voice. "I'm dismayed at your audacity, sir. I expressly told you why I could not take on this patient, and yet you invited the woman's family here to sway me."

Miss O'Leary glanced at Victor, as though unsure of his reaction.

Victor simply studied him, his fingers steepled over his stomach. "I'm sorry to see you so aggrieved, my boy. When you refused my request, I invited Deirdre to come and observe your therapy techniques. As a medical student, she will be the primary caregiver for Mrs. O'Leary when she is released from the hospital."

Matthew remained silent, unconvinced by Victor's speech.

"I can't deny I hoped that when you met Deirdre and learned more about her mother's condition you might change your mind. Especially in light of the fact that you've mentioned your desire to one day apply your therapies to stroke victims." His mustache twitched. "But alas, I see I have only served to anger you. For that I apologize."

Matthew expelled a loud breath. Though he didn't fully believe the story, he did trust that the man's motives were well-intentioned. "I suppose it's possible that I . . . overreacted."

Matthew thought Miss O'Leary gave a snort, but he dared not look at her.

Victor pushed up from his desk. "So you'll cooperate with Deirdre and allow her to observe your sessions?" His tone was more command than question.

Matthew glanced over at the woman then and saw desperate hope shining in the depths of her eyes. "There's little point. Even with my medical training, it took me over a year to master this therapy. I'm afraid, Miss O'Leary, you'll never learn it in a week."

The woman rose with undeniable grace. "Anything I can do to benefit my mother will not be a waste of time."

Matthew knew when to concede. He exhaled and shrugged. "As long as you don't interfere with my patients, I suppose there's no harm in it."

A stunning smile spread across her features. "Thank you, Doctor. I appreciate it."

Before he could utter another word, a sharp knock sounded on the door, and Miss Howard poked her head inside.

"Sorry to interrupt, sir," she said, "but there's an urgent phone call for Dr. Clayborne." The woman turned, eyes swimming with sympathy. "It's about your daughter."

Panic knotted the air in Matthew's lungs. The nanny only called him at work if something serious had occurred. He charged out of the room, not even bothering to say good-bye, his only thought to get to his daughter before it was too late.

3

EARLY THE NEXT MORNING, Matthew quietly entered his daughter's bedroom. Miss Shearing sat dozing in the corner rocking chair. That alone gave Matthew a measure of relief, for it meant Phoebe must be faring better.

Matthew had checked on Phoebe several times during the night, and each time she seemed to be resting comfortably. Still, he'd barely managed to get more than two hours of sleep. He gazed at the sleeping child, wisps of blond hair lying across her cheek. His chest tightened as it always did at the remarkable resemblance she bore to Priscilla.

He laid a hand on her forehead, relieved to find it cool to the touch. Perhaps this time they would be fortunate, and the sniffles wouldn't turn into anything more serious.

Miss Shearing was right to have called him home when she had. She knew from previous experience not to take any chances. The mildest malady could turn deadly with little notice.

He arranged the quilt around Phoebe's shoulders, tucked her worn rag doll beside her, and straightened.

At the same time, Miss Shearing sat up in her chair. "Dr. Clayborne. What time is it?" She rubbed her eyes and patted a few stray hairs into place.

"A little past seven. No need to rush. Phoebe will likely sleep late this morning."

Miss Shearing rose and smoothed her wrinkled skirt. She peered at his suit. "You're going to work?"

He bit back an irritated sigh at the censure in her tone. "I planned to, yes. Phoebe passed a quiet night with no evidence of fever, and I have every assurance that if her condition worsens, you will let me know immediately."

A flush spread over the woman's plain features. "Of course."

"Very well, then. Good day, Miss Shearing."

She pressed her lips together and inclined her head.

Why did the woman's disapproval rankle so? She'd been with Matthew ever since Priscilla's death over two years ago and had proven invaluable to him. Yet lately, there had been a subtle shift in her attitude that Matthew couldn't begin to define.

Implied expectation? Thinly disguised disapproval?

Whatever it was, it made Matthew uncomfortable, and he found himself spending as little time as possible around the woman.

Thank goodness for his work. Without it, he had no idea what he'd do. Assisting his patients was the only thing that calmed the inner demons clamoring to take over his mind whenever he found himself idle.

Matthew made his way down to the front entrance of the grand home he'd shared with Priscilla. A wedding gift from his father-in-law, Dr. Terrence Pentergast. Matthew looked around at the enormous entry and held back a grimace of distaste. He'd never liked this house and had tried to move out after Priscilla's death, but her parents insisted he stay for Phoebe's sake. She needed the familiarity of her childhood home, they said. It would help her cope with the loss of her mother. And so he'd given in, even though the residence was far too grandiose for his taste. If only the house were the sole source of conflict between him and the Pentergasts.

Matthew shook off his morose thoughts and retrieved his hat from the hall stand. He checked his reflection in the mirror and prepared to head out to catch the streetcar. Would the irksome Miss O'Leary be on hand to annoy him again today? With the stubbornness she'd displayed so far, he imagined she would.

Footsteps sounded on the staircase. Miss Shearing appeared in the hallway.

"Might I have a word with you, Doctor?"

Matthew held back a sigh. "What is it, Miss Shearing?"

She took a hesitant step closer. "Couldn't you call me Catherine?"

Matthew startled at the emotion evident in her brown eyes—a combination of sympathy and . . . affection? Goodness, had the nanny developed feelings for him? That might explain her odd behavior of late, but he prayed it was not the case, since he in no way reciprocated. After his wife's death, Matthew had vowed he would never again be responsible for a woman's unhappiness.

"That would be highly inappropriate. Now what is it you wish to discuss?" Perhaps if he made himself as surly as possible, it would dissuade any wrong notions.

Color rose in her cheeks. "I'm concerned with the lack of progress in Phoebe's recovery."

"If you're talking about her lungs, I am well aware of their weakened condition."

"I'm referring to her emotional state." She frowned. "Phoebe's taken to hiding in her closet again. In addition, she's stopped speaking. I thought I was making headway with her, but something has rendered her mute again."

Matthew's muscles seized, her words confirming the relapse he'd begun to notice in Phoebe as well. He'd rather face an injured soldier with an amputated leg than speak of crippling emotions. He kept his own scars buried so deep that he need never speak of them. Only in his nightmares did they surface. How could he help his daughter with her demons when he was powerless to overcome his own?

Miss Shearing gripped her hands together in front of her plain brown skirt. "Do you know of anything that might have triggered a setback?"

He searched his memory for anything out of the ordinary in the past few weeks and could think of nothing. "I'm afraid I have no idea."

She moistened her lips as though nervous. "Seeing that I'm not qualified in matters of the mind, I'd like permission to call in a psychiatrist to treat Phoebe."

Matthew's stomach muscles clenched. "Absolutely not. I will not subject my daughter to . . . *that*. Am I clear?"

Miss Shearing's mouth puckered as if she'd tasted something unpleasant. "Very. I'm sorry for wasting your time." She turned, her skirts flaring behind her, and walked away.

On that sour note, Matthew left the house, anxious to be out in the cool morning air, away from his home fraught with problems. He would never subject Phoebe to a psychiatrist. Not after the one he'd endured when he had returned from overseas. Electric shock treatments. The endless barrage of questions that dredged up horrid memories from the war.

No. Much better to forget the past and move forward.

He'd managed to do so, and his daughter would do the same.

Deirdre paused in the dimly lit corridor outside Dr. Clayborne's physical therapy room to shore up her courage. No matter how surly the man was, she would ignore his attitude and concentrate on acquiring the skills to help Mama.

Clearly the doctor was not inclined to change his mind about coming to Long Island, and Deirdre was beginning to think that was a good thing. Mama did not need such a disagreeable man around her. She deserved someone cheerful and optimistic, and if no such person existed, then Deirdre would become that for her.

She opened the door and entered the empty room, surprised to discover she'd arrived before Dr. Clayborne. Finding the switch for the overhead lights, she illuminated the space, then stood to marvel once again at the equipment he employed to treat his patients. A series of ropes and pulleys to test the endurance of withered muscles, parallel metal bars at hip height, as well as a variety of iron weights, straps, metal braces, and crutches. They seemed like instruments of torture, but if the doctor was seeing results, they must be doing the job. How would she duplicate such equipment at Irish Meadows? She made a note to discuss that with Dr. Clayborne.

"You must be an early riser, Miss O'Leary."

Deirdre's spine stiffened at the deep voice behind her. Pasting on a smile, she turned to face Dr. Clayborne.

He removed his hat and set it on a hook before casting his cool blue gaze on her. Determined not to be intimidated, she crossed the room. "I am up early most days," she said. "How is your daughter faring today?"

A flicker of surprise lit before the mask settled into place. "She is stable for the moment. Thankfully, no fever developed overnight."

Deirdre noticed then the lines of fatigue around his eyes and mouth. He must have spent a nearly sleepless night watching over his daughter. Despite her dislike of the man, she couldn't help but soften a little at the idea of him as a worried father. "Who is with her now?"

"Her nanny, as usual." He removed his jacket and took a white coat from the tree stand.

Sensing the conversation had come to an end, Deirdre removed her own overcoat and smoothed the white apron of her nursing uniform. At least today she felt more professional, not dressed in her street clothes. If the doctor noticed the change, he didn't mention it.

"Who is the first patient?" she asked brightly, exchanging her cloche hat for her nursing cap.

Dr. Clayborne picked up a file. "Samuel Pickett. Age twenty-two, left leg amputated at the knee. He's recently been fitted with a wooden leg and is having trouble adjusting to it."

Deirdre held back a sigh. Normally such a case would interest her, but she didn't see how working with an amputee would help her mother's paralysis.

"My next patient may be of more interest to you." The doctor speared her with a knowing glance.

Had her dismay shown? She usually hid her emotions well, as she'd been trained in nursing school. But with Mama, she seemed to have lost her objectivity.

"Mr. Rockford has a spinal injury from a bullet and is paralyzed. The techniques I use with him may be of benefit to your mother." He said the words begrudgingly, as though he didn't want her there.

Which clearly he didn't.

"Thank you. I'm most eager to see it."

Dr. Clayborne placed the file on the counter and exhaled wearily. "My refusal to treat your mother is in no way personal, Miss O'Leary. I am simply unwilling to leave my patients and cause a setback in their progress. As well, I have my daughter to consider. Her delicate condition dictates many of my actions."

For the first time, Deirdre understood his deep reluctance. He didn't want to abandon his patients or his daughter. She could respect that. "I understand. I had little expectation I would be able to change your mind." She smiled. "As long as I can bring back some tools to help my mother, I will be grateful."

His shoulders relaxed slightly from their stiff posture. "I'll do my best to help with that."

His features softened ever so slightly, allowing Deirdre to imagine what he might look like if he ever smiled. The effect might be . . . breathtaking.

The arrival of Dr. Clayborne's patient erased such silly musings.

For the most part, Deirdre did nothing but observe Dr. Clayborne with Mr. Pickett, a bright young man with a shock of blond hair and deep brown eyes. Though his stump obviously pained him, he remained cheerful throughout the rigorous exercises.

"If I'd known you'd have such a pretty nurse helping you today, I would have worn my best suit and combed my hair." The man's charming grin made it impossible to take offense, and Deirdre merely laughed.

"Nothing like some incentive to inspire you." She gave him a bold wink, earning a blush in the process. "You're doing very well, Mr. Pickett."

"Please call me Sam." He dropped onto a stool to rest.

Deirdre brought him a towel and a glass of water, ignoring Dr. Clayborne's frown. "Do you have a family, Sam?"

He drained the glass, handed it back to her, and wiped his chin with his sleeve. "No, ma'am. I had a girl before the war, but when I came home like this"—he gestured to his leg—"she couldn't handle it. Found herself a new beau."

"I'm so sorry." Deirdre kept her features impartial, though inwardly she railed at such fickleness. If the man she loved had returned from the war minus a leg, Deirdre would have been happy just to have him alive.

"That's enough for today, Sam," Dr. Clayborne said. "I'll see you on Friday."

"Thanks, Doc." Sam rose from the stool and limped to the door, where he grabbed his cap. "Nice to meet you, Nurse O'Leary."

"Likewise, Sam." She smiled as he exited the room, the sound of his wooden leg thumping down the hall.

"Do you always flirt with your patients, Miss O'Leary?"

Deirdre turned to find the disagreeable scowl back on Dr. Clayborne's face.

She lifted her chin. "I use whatever means I can to lighten my patient's mood. Be it a joke, a smile, or a wink."

Heated sparks seemed to light his blue eyes. "We are here to help our patients, not entertain them."

"I disagree, Doctor. In my opinion, healing is much more effective when a person is in good spirits. A patient's physical well-being is directly tied to their emotions."

"Hogwash. If your hypothesis was correct, then a morose or depressed person would never get better. I have seen numerous instances to the contrary. In fact, I am living proof of it." He flushed and turned away.

Deirdre bit back the retort on her lips. Obviously he'd let something slip he normally wouldn't discuss.

She joined him at the counter. "I simply meant that healing occurs far quicker in a person with a cheerful disposition. Have you not noticed this in any of your patients?" She kept her tone gentle, non-inflammatory.

His hand stilled on the papers he'd been sorting. "There are one or two who might fit that description."

"Then why not try to lift their spirits while healing their physical ailments? It makes the work so much more enjoyable."

He looked at her with such incredulity she almost flinched. Uncle Victor had told her a little of Dr. Clayborne's participation in the war. Clearly, the poor man did not realize how emotionally wounded he was. Perhaps there'd been no one to lift his spirits when he'd been injured.

A knock on the door drew their attention across the room, and Uncle Victor entered. From the grim set to his jaw, Deirdre steeled herself for bad news.

Oh, Lord, no. Please don't let it be Mama.

"Matthew, I'm afraid your nanny called. She's taken Phoebe to the Hospital for Sick Children."

4

THE NEXT DAY, Matthew exited the private hospital room where Phoebe now rested and walked down a long corridor to a bank of windows overlooking College Street. He stared at the people passing on the sidewalk below, the autumn wind blowing their overcoats out behind them. How he wished he could join them and let the fresh air clear the cobwebs from his mind.

Phoebe had spent an uncomfortable night, yet thankfully her condition hadn't worsened. But after enduring the endless snipes and disapproving looks from Miss Shearing, Matthew had finally sent the irritating woman home. She acted as if he were to blame for Phoebe's illness. How could he have known she would develop a high fever as soon as he left for work yesterday morning?

Still, guilt and fear held him in a chokehold as memories of Priscilla and Phoebe, stricken with tuberculosis, rose up to haunt him. Matthew had resisted sending them to a sanatorium, believing his skills were enough to cure them. His arrogance had cost Priscilla her life—and nearly Phoebe as well.

Now, exhausted after another sleepless night, his mind swirled with doubt. Had he once again waited too long to seek proper treatment for his daughter? He rested his forehead against the cool windowpane in an effort to soothe the ache in his brow.

The sound of footsteps on the tiled floor didn't register until they stopped beside him. He lifted his head and startled at the sight of Miss O'Leary's clear green gaze.

What was she doing here?

She gave him a tentative smile. "Uncle Victor wanted to check on Phoebe. He's gone to find her specialist." She laid a hand on his arm. "How is she doing?"

The sincere sympathy on her expressive face was almost his undoing. He stiffened, desperate to gain control of his emotions that were far too near the surface. "Her fever remains high, which in her condition is less than desirable."

"I daresay." In an almost unconscious gesture, she rubbed her hand over his forearm.

Warmth radiated up to his elbow. He pulled away as though scalded and strode down the hall. Did the woman know no boundaries?

Clearly not, for she followed him like a stray puppy.

"Matthew, wait."

He halted out of sheer shock, hearing her use his Christian name as if . . .

She came around in front of him. "You're exhausted. You won't do Phoebe any good if you get sick as well." Her eyes widened in earnestness. "Uncle Victor and I will stay with her. Go and get a few hours of sleep."

He stared down into her face, noting the tiny beauty mark beside one eyebrow. Warmth suddenly surrounded his hands as she took hold of them and massaged his stiff fingers.

"Your hands are freezing. Have you eaten anything lately?"

Had he? He couldn't remember.

She peered down the hall. "Ah, here he is. Uncle Victor, can your driver take Matthew home? He needs to rest."

"Of course. My car is parked near the front entrance."

Matthew seemed to have lost the ability to speak. Exhaustion weighted his limbs like the iron dumbbells in his therapy room.

Victor motioned for him to follow. "I'll walk you down. Deirdre, will you sit with Phoebe?"

"Certainly."

A cold breeze seemed to envelop Matthew the moment she took her hands from his and headed toward Phoebe's room.

Matthew blinked. Perhaps he did need sleep. *A lot of sleep.*

He walked with Victor to the end of the corridor, where Phoebe's specialist stood waiting.

Victor shook hands with the other doctor. "I hope you don't mind, Matthew. I asked Dr. McElroy to join us."

Matthew tried to focus his thoughts. "Do you have any news on my daughter?"

Dr. McElroy fingered the stethoscope around his neck. "I can't deny I'm concerned. This is Phoebe's third serious episode in the past six months." He shook his head. "I hate to say it, but her lungs have deteriorated further, and if things continue in this manner . . ."

An ache spread through Matthew's chest. He'd suspected as much, but hearing it spelled out so bluntly made it all the worse. "I've done my best to keep her isolated, away from potential germs. I don't know what else I can do."

Victor laid a hand on his shoulder. "Dr. McElroy has suggested a possible move to the country, where the air is cleaner and the population less congested."

Dr. McElroy nodded. "I believe this is the best way to improve her condition. Take some time and think about it. But not too long. The sooner you act, the better. Now if you'll excuse me, I have rounds to make."

Matthew attempted to process the man's advice. How would he ever be able to move to the country when his work kept him in the city?

Victor clapped Matthew on the shoulder. "Come on. My car is outside."

They made their way down two flights of stairs and exited out the main door.

Victor halted on the walkway below, his brows drawn together. "I hope you'll give Dr. McElroy's suggestion serious consideration. The timing of this can't be coincidental."

"What do you mean?" The breeze whipped Matthew's hair across his forehead, and he realized he'd forgotten his hat in Phoebe's room.

"The O'Learys' estate on Long Island would be the perfect place for Phoebe. Irish Meadows is surrounded by acres of meadows and woods. It would do her a world of good to get away for a while. I've already mentioned to James that you have a daughter, and he was more than willing for her to accompany you."

Matthew's shoulders slumped. "What about my patients here?"

They'd reached Victor's automobile, and the driver hurried over to await his instructions.

Victor gave Matthew a frank stare. "Most of your patients are long-term ones who know the exercises by heart. Would you be willing to apprise Dr. Marlboro of some simple procedures he can use while you're gone? They may not make huge strides, but at least their progress won't be set back."

Matthew released a weighty sigh. If it were simply a matter of Mrs. O'Leary versus his own patient load, he wouldn't consider leaving. But how could he pass up this opportunity to help his daughter? Surely his patients would understand. "I will give it serious thought and have an answer for you soon."

The tension in Victor's brow released, and he smiled. "I'll

be praying God guides you to make the right decision. Now go and get some rest. Things are bound to look brighter when you're feeling refreshed."

"Thank you. And please thank Miss O'Leary for me as well." Matthew realized how much it helped to have someone share his burden, if only for a few hours. He couldn't say why—perhaps it was Miss O'Leary's fierce devotion to her mother, or the fact that Victor held her in such high esteem—but he trusted her implicitly with his daughter's well-being.

He got into the car and sank back against the seat. As the driver navigated the crowded streets of the city, Matthew drifted into a quiet dream in which his daughter ran over green meadows and played amid an array of wildflowers, laughing and twirling, with sunlight dancing off her hair.

"And how is little Phoebe faring today?" Seated beside Uncle Victor at the long dining table, Aunt Maimie addressed her husband with a look of concern.

Deirdre leaned forward in her seat, eager to hear the answer as well. After taking turns sitting with Phoebe for the better part of the previous day, she'd grown attached to the frail child. The few times the girl had awakened, she'd stared at Deirdre with wide blue eyes, communicating with nods and head shakes. Deirdre had wondered if the child was too weak to speak or if being in the hospital had filled her with fear.

Uncle Victor's features brightened. "You'll be pleased to know there's been a marked improvement. Her fever has lessened, and the cough is much better."

"Oh, I'm so glad." Aunt Maimie heaved a great sigh and poured some coffee into Uncle Victor's cup.

The tension eased in Deirdre's shoulders as well. "Dr. Clayborne must be greatly relieved."

"He is. Though they'll keep Phoebe in the hospital until the danger of a relapse has passed." Uncle Victor patted a napkin to his mouth. "I offered our services to share the watch again tonight, but he insisted he'd be fine on a cot in the room."

Deirdre admired Matthew's devotion to his daughter, yet it seemed at odds with his often brusque manner. "Tell me more about Dr. Clayborne," she said as she sipped her after-dinner coffee. The rich flavor burst onto her tongue, a welcome complement to Aunt Maimie's apple pie, which topped off their meal.

Uncle Victor set down his cup and glanced over at her. "You know most of his history. Matthew was a medic in the war. He was wounded and sent to England for treatment before being shipped home. He became passionate about helping injured soldiers and started working for me about four years ago." Uncle Victor released a sigh. "Such a shame. The war changed Matthew. He hasn't been the same since."

Deirdre sensed there was far more to the story. "What about his wife?" she asked.

Uncle Victor pressed his lips into a firm line. She thought he was about to reprimand her for her question, but then Aunt Maimie laid a hand on his arm. The robust woman's pale blue eyes glowed with a mixture of sympathy and love as she gazed at her husband. They seemed to share an unspoken message, and he nodded as though giving permission.

She turned to Deirdre. "Priscilla Clayborne died of tuberculosis two years ago. She and little Phoebe both contracted the illness, and despite Matthew's efforts, Priscilla succumbed. Thankfully, the Lord spared their daughter, although Phoebe spent quite some time in a sanatorium before they finally released her."

"And her lungs now bear the permanent scars," Deirdre murmured. "What a worry it must be for Dr. Clayborne."

When he'd returned from his brief respite yesterday, Deirdre had sensed a shift in the doctor's demeanor. A deep resignation—as though the fight had gone out of him.

Aunt Maimie sighed. "Phoebe's health is a constant burden for him. I don't know what he would do without the nanny to keep such close watch over her."

"Did Mrs. Clayborne receive treatment in a sanatorium as well?" Deirdre kept her tone casual.

"She did, near the end, but by then it was too late." Aunt Maimie's gentle features were wreathed in sorrow. "I fear Matthew blames himself for not getting her treatment sooner."

"Hush, Maimie. You don't know if that's the case." Uncle Victor's rebuke of his wife surprised Deirdre.

But Maimie didn't seem fazed by it. She merely smiled. "I see it whenever Priscilla's name is mentioned."

From the front area of the house, a bell rang. Seconds later, the butler appeared at the dining room entrance.

"Dr. Clayborne to see you, sir."

Uncle Victor's eyebrows rose, mirroring Deirdre's surprise. "Send him in."

Deirdre concentrated on her pie, attempting to ignore the flutters in her stomach. She wished she could continue her dislike of the man—much safer than this unsettled feeling he provoked in her.

Uncle Victor rose from his chair. "Matthew, come in."

Dr. Clayborne hesitated in the doorway. "I'm sorry. I didn't realize you were eating."

"Nonsense. Join us for a slice of Maimie's apple pie."

He bowed to Aunt Maimie. "Good evening, Maimie." His glance slid to Deirdre. "And you, Miss O'Leary."

Aunt Maimie jumped up to retrieve a cup from the sideboard, not even bothering to summon a maid. "Please sit down, dear." She poured his coffee and added a generous slice of pie to his plate.

With apparent reluctance, Dr. Clayborne pulled out a chair at the far end of the table. "I can't stay long. I just wanted to apprise you of a decision I've made." He directed his focus to

Deirdre. "I'm glad you're here, Miss O'Leary, since this concerns you as well."

Deirdre set her fork beside her plate, lest she choke on a bite of pie.

"If you're willing to have Phoebe and her nanny accompany me"—he paused as though the words had lodged in his throat—"I will come to Long Island and treat your mother."

Deirdre hesitated, unsure how to process this sudden turnaround.

Matthew's blue gaze did not leave hers. "Miss O'Leary? You don't seem pleased."

She lifted her chin. "May I ask what changed your mind?" Obviously it had nothing to do with her powers of persuasion. Yet something must have brought about this change of heart.

He gave a sheepish shrug. "I must confess to an ulterior motive. One that concerns my daughter."

Deirdre waited for him to explain.

"Phoebe's specialist recommended a move to the country, where the air would be better suited to her condition." His expression became almost apologetic. "Victor told me your farm might be the perfect location."

So his motives were not entirely altruistic. Still, if it helped her mother, did the reason for his coming really matter? "As long as you are as committed to restoring my mother's health as you are your daughter's, then I know my family will be most grateful."

His hand stilled on his coffee cup. "Fair enough. I propose a trial period of one month, during which time I promise to do my utmost for your mother. At that point, we can reassess and determine the next course of action."

The sincerity in his voice allowed Deirdre to relax. She had no doubt that once Dr. Clayborne committed to something, he would give it his all. "I look forward to working with you, Doctor."

A measure of relief oozed through Deirdre's tense frame. Her mother would get the therapy she needed after all. *Thank you, Lord.*

Dr. Clayborne lifted his head and exchanged a pointed look with Uncle Victor, who gave a subtle nod.

Matthew expelled a soft sigh. "There's something else you should know . . . about Phoebe. My daughter suffers from several phobias related to the death of her mother. She sometimes hides in her closet for long periods, and most times, she barely speaks."

Deirdre pressed her lips together, sympathy welling for the taciturn doctor. No wonder his disposition was less than sunny with so many worries to consume him. "I'm sorry to hear that. Let me know if I can help."

Matthew shook his head. "I'm only telling you so you will treat Phoebe with sensitivity. She's unused to strangers, due to being shielded for most of her life. I'm not sure how she will handle traveling to another country."

Deirdre's heart broke for the girl. "I'll do whatever I can to make this a fun experience for her."

He frowned. "I'm not sure Phoebe even knows the meaning of the word."

Deirdre set down her cup. "Well, then it's time she found out."

Aunt Maimie laughed. "That's our Deirdre for you. Ever the optimist. You'd do well to listen to her, Matthew. She's very wise for her age." She leaned back in her chair. "And for what it's worth, I believe God has brought you together for a reason. Deirdre just might be the one to help Phoebe recover."

Matthew rose from his seat, his pie almost untouched. "Thank you, Maimie, for your hospitality. Victor, I will see you tomorrow. I'll take the next few days to apprise Dr. Marlboro about my patients."

"Very good, my boy. I believe you're making the right decision."

From the pinched expression on Dr. Clayborne's face, Deirdre feared he did not agree. Yet she couldn't stop a prickle of excitement. Not only for her mother, but for Phoebe, too.

For the first time in a week, Deirdre's spirits lifted. She wanted to become a pediatrician not only to treat children's bodies, but their minds and hearts as well. Had God brought Phoebe into her life to show Deirdre where her true vocation lay?

If so, she vowed she would do her best to listen to the Lord's gentle nudging during the brief time she would be associated with the Claybornes. She'd do everything in her power to heal little Phoebe's emotional scars as well as her physical ones.

5

DEIRDRE STRAINED FORWARD in the front seat as Gil guided Daddy's Model T up the road with Dr. Clayborne, Miss Shearing, and Phoebe in the backseat. Deirdre had been pleased to find her brother-in-law waiting for them at the Long Island train station, his presence making her more anxious than ever to get home to the rest of her family. As they turned onto the long drive, the peaks of the house came into view.

Irish Meadows.

Equal measures of delight and trepidation rushed through her system. In what condition would she find her mother? When Deirdre left for Toronto, Mama had been barely conscious. Would she be more cognizant now? She must be improved enough for the doctors to allow her to come home, albeit with assistance from the round-the-clock nurses Daddy had hired.

Still, Deirdre wouldn't rest until she assessed Mama for herself.

She turned to the passengers in the backseat. "We're almost

there. You can see the house up ahead. The stables are over to the right."

The sight of her brother Connor working with the horses in the paddock brought about a giddy sense of homecoming. She'd missed her family more than she'd realized.

When the auto stopped, Deirdre pushed out the door and waited for Dr. Clayborne and his entourage to alight.

Phoebe looked around with undisguised curiosity. Miss Shearing clutched the girl's hand in a death grip. Matthew settled his hat more firmly on his head and stood, as rigid as a fencepost, staring at the house.

What was going on behind those shuttered blue eyes?

"Welcome to Irish Meadows," Deirdre said, unable to contain the rush of pride that accompanied her words. Not even the dour Miss Shearing could dampen her spirits. "Come in and meet my family."

The ornate front doors opened, and her sister Brianna hurried across the porch.

"Bree!" Deirdre rushed into her older sister's waiting arms. She squeezed her tight, happy tears brimming. "I've missed you so much."

Brianna pulled away and sniffed. "Me, too. I couldn't believe Daddy sent you all the way to Toronto."

"How is Mama?" Deirdre braced herself for the worst. Gil had told her Mama was doing fine, but Deirdre wanted her sister's opinion.

"She's coping as best she can. Daddy's set her up in the small library so she won't have to contend with the stairs."

Deirdre straightened her spine, determined that when she and Dr. Clayborne were through, Mama would walk out that front door on her own. Better yet, they'd have her working in her beloved garden by spring.

Gil moved up beside Brianna. "I don't suppose you have any hugs left for your husband?"

Bree swatted his arm with a laugh. "I see you every day."

"That's okay. You can save mine for later." Gil winked and dropped a kiss on her nose.

Deirdre smiled at the unmistakable bond between Brianna and her husband. After eight years of marriage and three children, their love shone as brightly as ever.

Deirdre linked arms with her sister and steered her toward their guests who stood at the side of the car. "Brianna, this is Dr. Clayborne. He's come to treat Mama."

Brianna stepped forward, hand outstretched. "Nice to meet you, Doctor. You've already met my husband, Gil."

Dr. Clayborne gave her hand a solemn shake. "A pleasure, Mrs. Whelan."

Bree laughed. "Please call me Brianna." She bent to smile at Phoebe. "Well, hello. I didn't know Dr. Clayborne had such a pretty little girl. What's your name?"

Phoebe's blue eyes, so like her father's, widened. Deirdre practically begged the girl to say her name. But she remained silent.

"This is Phoebe," Dr. Clayborne finally said.

"Welcome, Phoebe. I hope you'll be good friends with my children. They're off visiting their cousins today, but you'll meet them soon."

Brianna stood and encompassed Miss Shearing with a welcoming smile. "You must be Phoebe's nanny."

"Yes, ma'am. Miss Shearing."

"Welcome. I'm sure you'd all like to freshen up after your journey. Follow me."

Deirdre and her fellow travelers followed Brianna into the house. After they removed their coats, Brianna led Miss Shearing and Phoebe upstairs, while Deirdre and Dr. Clayborne stayed behind to wait for Daddy.

An odd quiver of nerves swirled in Deirdre's stomach as she watched Dr. Clayborne observe the grand foyer. His gaze moved upward from the mahogany railing of the curved staircase to the crystal chandelier above. Did he think them ostentatious—or was he used to such luxury?

Before he could comment, their housekeeper came down the hall.

"Miss Deirdre. Welcome home."

"Thank you, Mrs. Johnston. This is Dr. Clayborne, come to help Mama with her recovery."

A shadow lifted from the tall woman's brow. "We're most happy to have you here, sir. I pray you can bring Mrs. O'Leary back to good health."

"I'll do my best, ma'am."

Deirdre removed her hat and laid it on the hall table. "Mrs. Johnston, will you tell Daddy we've arrived? And could you ask Mrs. Harrison to have some tea and sandwiches sent to the parlor?" She glanced in the gilded mirror and patted her hair into place.

"Right away, Miss."

"The parlor is this way." Deirdre gestured to the double doors across the foyer. She entered, inhaling the familiar scents of lemon furniture polish and the faint remains of Daddy's pipe tobacco.

The doctor followed and stood somewhat awkwardly in the center of the room, taking in the marble fireplace and the piano by the French doors. "You have a beautiful home, Miss O'Leary."

"Thank you. We're quite fond of it. Please have a seat." She gestured to the sofa and chairs surrounding the fireplace.

"If you don't mind, I'd prefer to stretch my legs."

Deirdre bit back a sigh as he walked to the French doors and stared out over her mother's garden. Why did conversation with him feel so stilted and unnatural? Was it the man's taciturn nature, or did he find her so distasteful that he couldn't put out the effort to make small talk?

Daddy's entrance seconds later came as a welcome relief.

"There's my daughter, home at last." His booming voice, always too loud for the indoors, filled the room with energy.

"Hello, Daddy." She stepped into his embrace, and for the first time in over a week, allowed the tension to seep away. Safe in the shelter of his strong arms, she once again felt secure and protected.

If only she could stay there forever.

In no way had Matthew been prepared for the luxury of the O'Leary estate. For some reason, he'd pictured a rustic dwelling out in the country with a weathered barn for the livestock. Nothing like this stunning mansion and magnificent-looking stables.

Matthew turned from his view of the impressive gardens to see a large, broad-shouldered man enveloping Miss O'Leary in a warm embrace.

The man pressed a kiss to the crown of her head before focusing his attention on Matthew. "You must be Dr. Clayborne. Welcome to Irish Meadows." He moved forward to pump Matthew's hand. "I can't tell you how grateful I am you agreed to come." Lines crinkled around his weathered face. Threads of silver invaded the dark hair at his temples.

"Thank you, sir. I hope I can be of help to your wife."

"Please call me James. We don't stand on formalities here. I'll give you a chance to settle in, and then you can meet Kathleen." His voice caught on the woman's name, giving Matthew a good indication of the burden that lay on the man's heart.

A maid pushed a tea cart into the room. "Your refreshments, Miss."

"Thank you, Nora." Miss O'Leary smiled. "And please thank Mrs. Harrison for such speedy service."

The maid gave a quick curtsy.

"Oh, and could you please have some sandwiches sent upstairs for Dr. Clayborne's daughter and her nanny?"

"Right away, Miss." She curtsied again and retreated from the room.

Miss O'Leary seemed to treat her staff with an easy familiarity, almost as if they were family. Matthew couldn't help but make a comparison to his late wife's wealthy parents. The Pentergasts used their social position as a means of manipulation to get what they wanted, as though their wealth entitled them to satisfy their every whim. *Like when they tried to gain custody of Phoebe after Priscilla died.*

Matthew's stomach twisted. He truly hoped the O'Learys weren't cut from the same cloth as his elitist in-laws, who at this moment were touring Britain. They certainly wouldn't approve of his decision to take Phoebe out of the country, but the fact that they weren't expected back until sometime in December made Matthew's decision easier to bear. What they didn't know wouldn't hurt them, especially since he'd be back long before they returned.

Pushing aside his negative musings, he joined the others at a low table while Miss O'Leary poured the tea into delicate china cups.

Weary from the journey, Matthew forced himself not to sink back into the soft cushions. "So, James, could you tell me a little about your wife's history? It might offer some insight into what method of treatment would work well for her."

Miss O'Leary's hand stalled as she handed him his cup, and her eyes widened as if in surprise.

"You find my inquiry unusual, Miss O'Leary?" he challenged.

She held his gaze. "Frankly, yes. I thought you would take a more clinical approach."

"On the contrary, I like to get to know my patients on a personal level before I treat them."

A slight flush rose in her cheeks. "I'm glad to hear it."

Matthew sensed she was holding back what she really thought, perhaps because her father was studying them intently.

"Has Mrs. O'Leary enjoyed good health until now?" Matthew prompted while choosing a selection of triangle-shaped sandwiches.

"For the most part, except for a bout with typhoid fever several years ago when we almost lost her." James paused as though the memory pained him. "After that, she never regained her full strength."

Though his focus was on James, Matthew was acutely aware of Miss O'Leary's scrutiny. "Did your wife's physician have any theory as to what might have brought on the stroke?"

"Not really." James leaned back in his chair. "They ran several tests while Kathleen was in the hospital, but the results haven't come back yet."

Matthew nodded. "Was she under any undue stress?"

"Not that I'm aware of."

"Were there problems in the family"—Matthew hesitated—"or in the marriage?"

James's expression remained unchanged. "None."

Miss O'Leary set down her cup with a clank. Sparks flashed in her eyes, making them appear almost emerald. "What are you trying to insinuate, Doctor? That my father caused my mother's stroke?"

"Deirdre." James's instant rebuke surprised Matthew. "The doctor isn't asking anything that Dr. Shepherd and the neurologist haven't already asked me."

Her anger seemed to fade. "I'm sorry," she murmured. "I'm a little defensive when it comes to my family."

Matthew found himself wondering what it would be like to be championed with such fierce loyalty. "No offense taken." He paused to wash down a bite of sandwich with a swallow of tea and held back a grimace, wishing for a cup of strong coffee instead.

The three sat in silence for several moments before another question occurred to him.

"Brianna mentioned she has children. Does Mrs. O'Leary help look after her grandchildren?" The exuberance of several youngsters could take a toll on a frailer person.

James set his cup on the table. "Brianna and Gil have their own house on the property. They're over quite often, but Kathleen isn't involved in rearing the children." He chuckled. "Though that doesn't stop her from giving advice."

Miss O'Leary laughed as well.

"Well, then I must assume the cause was a physical weakness in an artery. I will proceed with the utmost caution." Matthew set his plate aside. "May I meet my patient now?"

James rose from his seat. "Certainly. Right this way."

As they moved out into the hallway, Miss O'Leary followed. From the determined set of her jaw, Matthew feared the stubborn woman would plague him his entire stay.

He gave an inward sigh. In order to keep his sanity, he'd better find a way to work with her. Perhaps if he kept her busy, she wouldn't end up being a thorn in his already prickly side.

6

ONNOR O'LEARY LOOPED the length of rope over his shoulder and stood back to survey the obstinate horse that tossed his mane and snorted his outrage to the skies. Excalibur, it seemed, was in no mood to cooperate with his trainer today.

Connor slapped his work gloves against his denim pants, causing a cloud of dust to rise. "You may have won this round, boy, but I'll wear you down yet."

"This fellow giving you trouble?" Gil came up to lean on the top rail of the fence.

"Nothing I can't handle."

"Good to hear. Do you have a minute? I need to talk to you about a new hand starting tomorrow."

Connor gave the ornery beast another glare. "I think I'm done for now." He opened the gate and came out to meet his brother-in-law and boss. Connor hoped he hadn't done anything to make Gil regret giving Connor this promotion.

Despite his being an O'Leary, Daddy had made Connor start

at the bottom and work his way up through the business, like every employee. Although it chafed at Connor's pride, he realized that Daddy couldn't entrust his clients' prize-winning steeds to an untried trainer, and Connor had worked all the harder to prove his worth.

Recently, Sam Turnbull, their head trainer and stable manager, had gone out West to visit an ailing brother, and Gil had given Connor the job of overseeing the stable hands. If Connor handled it well, the position might become permanent—especially with Sam hinting he wanted to lessen his workload now that he was getting on in years.

Connor joined Gil at the fence. "So there's a new hand starting tomorrow?"

"Yes, Seth Miller. Sam hired him before receiving word about his brother being so ill. I wanted you to know so you could look out for him."

"Sure." He studied Gil. "Anything special I need to know?"

"Sam mentioned the kid seemed edgy. Like he was desperate for the job. Sam felt bad he wouldn't be here to help him settle in."

Connor pulled off his cap and swept his sleeve across his forehead. "Thanks for the warning. I'll be sure to keep an eye on him."

Gil slapped Connor on the back. "I was hoping you'd say that. Now, if you've got things under control, I think I'll head home for dinner with my family."

Connor straightened away from the fence. "Give Bree my love. And tell young Sean I'll give him another roping lesson as soon as I have some spare time."

Gil grinned. "He'd love that. Thanks, Connor."

Early the next morning, Connor headed out to the secondary barn to talk to the hands already at work. He wanted to alert them about the new hire expected today. Two of the men, Tim and Mac, were busy feeding the horses.

"Good morning," Connor greeted them.

"Hello, Mr. O'Leary." Tim nodded as he poured out the oats.

Connor frowned. "Call me Connor. Mr. O'Leary is my father." Only a few years older than these fellows, Connor had been their peer until a week ago. Now it seemed strange to be their supervisor.

Tim shot a glance at Mac, who lugged a pail of water over to the trough, but neither spoke.

Connor leaned against a stall door and absently patted a horse's nose. "We're expecting a new stable hand today," he told them. "I want you to make him feel at home and help him learn the ropes."

"Yes, sir," they said.

"His name is Seth Miller. Let me know when he arrives."

They nodded.

Connor paused, wishing they'd tell a joke or regale him with some inside stories. But the lines had been drawn, and he was now firmly on the other side. "Okay, then. Carry on."

Shaking off the last vestiges of regret, he strode outside and breathed in the clean air of fall—his favorite time of year, when the summer's heat had dissipated and the trees had started to change color. He walked to the white fence surrounding the track and paused to watch one of the trainers exercising a stallion.

"Excuse me, sir. I'm looking for Mr. Turnbull."

Connor turned to see a boy standing on the path behind him, his features partly hidden by an oversized floppy hat. He wore a plaid shirt under denim overalls, which sagged on his slight frame.

"Are you Seth Miller?"

"Y-yes, sir."

"Mr. Turnbull had to leave to deal with a family emergency.

I'm Connor O'Leary. I'll be filling in while he's gone." Judging by the lad's lack of facial hair, Connor doubted he was much past puberty. "How old are you, son?"

"Nineteen." The boy stuffed his hands in the pockets of his overalls.

Connor scratched his head. He didn't look a day over sixteen. Why had Sam hired this kid still wet behind the ears? "Have you had much experience with horses?"

"Yes, sir. I've worked with my pa since I was young."

"Okay, good. I'll give you a brief tour and then introduce you to the other men. They'll fill you in on the rest." Connor started back toward the barn, and the boy fell in step beside him.

Under the overlarge hat, beads of sweat stood out on the boy's forehead. Connor bit back a sigh. The kid looked terrified. Connor stopped him. "No need to be nervous, son. You'll know your way around soon enough."

The kid nodded, a hint of relief crossing his features.

They entered the barn, and Connor acquainted him with the thoroughbreds. Seth remained unusually silent, yet his connection to horses became evident in the way the animals responded to his touch and low murmurs.

Geesh, had the boy's voice even changed yet? Sam didn't usually hire them quite so young.

"Seth?"

No answer.

"Mr. Miller?"

The boy stiffened. "Sorry, sir."

"You hard of hearing, son?" Connor suppressed a sigh, suddenly feeling ancient at twenty-three.

"No." The lad squirmed and stuck his hands in his pockets. "It's just . . ."

"What?"

Distress shone in his blue eyes. "Everyone calls me Joe. My brother gave me the nickname, and it stuck."

A sense of protectiveness rose in Connor. Something about this boy affected him in a way he'd never expected. Maybe Sam had felt the same way and that's why he'd hired him. "Fair enough, Joe." Connor slapped a hand on the boy's rather bony shoulder. "Let's go meet the other hands."

Josephine Miller rode her old nag across the meadow as fast as Mabel could go. As soon as they reached a good pace, Jo let out a long sigh of relief.

Freedom at last. She'd thought the day would never end. Seth owed her in a big way for this. She peered over her shoulder to make sure no one was watching before slowing Mabel to a walk and guiding her under the overhanging branches. They picked their way through the underbrush until they came to a clearing and the log cabin on the outskirts of Mr. Sullivan's property. Only then did the muscles in her shoulders begin to loosen. Only then did Jo whip her father's hat off, pull the netting off her hair, and let her long tresses fly out behind her.

Skirting to the far side of the structure, Jo dismounted and tied Mabel to the post. An outdoor water pump stood between the cabin and the small lean-to that served as shelter for Mabel. Jo pumped a bucketful of water, poured some into a trough for the horse, and lugged the remainder up to the front door of the cabin, where she quietly opened the door. She paused, hoping her father would be asleep, since Seth would no doubt still be at work.

Once inside, she immediately wrinkled her nose, praying not to detect any scent of whiskey. A slight chill hung in the air, which meant the fire must have gone out.

Jo set the pail of water beside the woodstove and moved into the main room. Pa lay slumped on the sofa, one arm draping the dusty floor. A loud snore echoed through the room.

Relieved, she tiptoed to the fireplace and patiently stirred the embers back to life. Then she went to the woodstove and lit a fire, ready to cook whatever Seth brought back for their supper.

She still couldn't shake the sense of dread over this whole deception her brother had talked her into. If only Pa hadn't started drinking again right when he was about to start the first real job he'd managed to get in a long time. Instead, he'd gotten involved in a drunken tavern brawl and severely injured his leg. The bad swelling and deep gash on his shin made it impossible to start work as the Sullivans' farm manager.

While Jo waited for the fire to heat the stove, she went into the bedroom, changed back into her cotton dress, and braided her blond hair. Once again, she felt like Josephine Miller, not the pretend Joe that she'd had to fake the entire day.

Seth had better come up with a new plan. From the intelligent look in Connor O'Leary's eyes, Jo doubted she could pull off the deception for long. At least the other stable hands had left her mostly to herself.

The door to the cabin opened, and Seth entered, bringing a gust of cool air with him. His dark hair sat in a tangled mop over his forehead, his plaid shirt open to reveal a white under-shirt beneath.

Pa stirred on the couch, moaning as he changed positions.

Seth set a skinned rabbit carcass on the rough wooden table. Looked like they'd be having rabbit stew. "Sorry I'm late, but it took me a while to catch this guy."

He scanned her dress and hair. "How did it go at the O'Learys'? Did they believe you were me?"

Jo pulled out the cast-iron pot and dumped some water from the pail into it. "It went just as you said it would. Mr. Turnbull has gone out West, and Connor O'Leary showed me around."

"He didn't seem suspicious?"

"I caught him staring at me a few times. I think he wondered why Mr. Turnbull hired someone so young."

Seth frowned. "You're not that young."

She rubbed her fingers over her chin. "I don't exactly look like a man. But don't worry," she hastened to add, "I'll prove myself soon enough, and it won't be an issue." She took out an onion and began to slice it. "Tell me this won't have to go on for long."

Seth plopped onto a chair. "Sorry, Jo, but until Pa sobers up and his leg heals, I have to keep filling in for him, and you have to fill in for me." He let out a long breath. "I'm just glad Mr. Sullivan is being so reasonable."

Jo peeled a carrot with more force than necessary. "What then? How are you going to take my place at Irish Meadows?"

Seth shrugged. "I'll figure something out when the time comes. I'm sure if I explain I'm your older brother and you were filling in for me, they'll understand."

"Then why didn't you tell them that in the first place?"

"Couldn't take the chance they'd say no. Once it's over and done, they'll be more likely to forgive us, especially if you're a good worker." He gave a tired grin. "Who knows? If they like your work, they might keep us both on."

Jo swallowed her disappointment. Pa's injury could take weeks to heal. Weeks she'd have to pose as a boy. Could she pull it off?

She'd have to. Staying in this cabin hinged on one of them working for the Sullivans. Without it, they'd have nowhere to live. And Jo couldn't go back to living in a tent—not with winter fast approaching.

She chopped a potato and two more carrots, slid them into the water, and added the rabbit. Once it had boiled for a while, she'd take it out and cut the meat off. Maybe she'd get a pot of soup out of it as well.

Seth scrubbed a hand over his face and pushed to his feet. "I've never worked so hard in my life. I'm going to lie down for a while before dinner. Wake me if you need me."

Seth climbed the rickety ladder to the loft where he'd fashioned a bed out of straw.

A faint twinge of guilt hit Jo anew that she had the bedroom to herself while their father had the worn couch. The one advantage to being the only girl in the family. Perhaps she deserved it, since she now had a full day's work to put in at Irish Meadows on top of the cooking, cleaning, and laundry. The chores just went on and on, like they had for years.

In some ways, it seemed she'd been trying to atone all her life for being responsible for her mother's death. Flora Miller had died giving birth to Jo, leaving a newborn girl at the mercy of a rough father and an older brother, neither prepared to raise an infant on their own. Never mind a female one at that.

Jo set the lid on the pot to let the contents simmer and went to sit in the rocker by the fireplace. Her body ached from the extra physical work she'd done today. She hoped the first few days on the job would pass quickly so she would cease to be a novelty and simply blend into the background.

She would do her job and nothing more—nothing that might earn her notice.

The key to surviving this deception, she decided, was to keep all attention away from her.

Especially attention from the handsome Connor O'Leary.

7

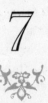

FAR FROM THE FRAIL, emaciated woman he had expected, Matthew found Kathleen O'Leary surprisingly robust. In a main-floor room, which, judging by the wall of bookcases, used to be a small library, Mrs. O'Leary sat propped up in a raised hospital bed near the window. A late-afternoon sunray brushed the ends of her fading auburn braid. Matthew studied her face, relieved to find no facial drooping. Her bright blue eyes, good bone structure, and clear skin made her seem years younger than her age. The only visible indication of her infirmity was her left arm, which sat at an odd angle against her body. Near the bed, a brown wicker wheelchair bore further evidence of the woman's disability.

Upon spying the three of them, a nurse rose from a chair in the corner. "Good afternoon, Mr. O'Leary."

"Good afternoon, Nurse Cramer. This is Dr. Clayborne from Toronto. And my youngest daughter, Deirdre."

"Nice to meet you both." She smiled at Matthew. "You'll find all the pertinent information on Mrs. O'Leary's chart.

Now, if you'll excuse me, I was about to take these dishes to the kitchen."

Once the nurse left, Miss O'Leary rushed over to embrace her mother.

"My baby girl." The woman's eyes squeezed shut.

"Mama, it's good to see you sitting up." A hint of tears colored Miss O'Leary's voice.

They clung together for a moment, then Miss O'Leary brushed the moisture from her mother's cheeks and, with a light laugh, swiped the wetness from her own face.

James approached the bed. "Kathleen, this is Dr. Matthew Clayborne."

Matthew gave a slight bow. "A pleasure to meet you, ma'am."

"Please call me Kathleen." Her eyes seemed lit from within. "Thank you for coming, Doctor."

Matthew shifted his stance, trying to dispel a sense of shame at his initial reluctance to come. "Please don't thank me until we see if I can help you." The fact that there was no slur to her speech was a good sign. From what Matthew could tell so far, the paralysis had affected only her left arm and leg, which would make it easier to determine the type of exercises he would use with her.

Everyone seemed to regard him expectantly. He turned to James. "If you don't mind, I'd like to talk to your wife alone."

James raised a questioning brow. "Is that all right with you, Kathleen?"

"It's fine."

James bent to kiss her cheek. "I'll be in my study if you need me."

He left the room, but Miss O'Leary lingered. "Maybe I should stay, since I'll be helping with Mama's therapy."

Matthew tensed, prepared for conflict. "I'd like to talk to your mother alone. It won't take long."

She shot Matthew a withering glance as if in warning. "Fine. I'll wait in the parlor."

When she'd gone, Matthew scanned the nurse's notations on the clipboard attached to the foot rails. Then he moved the chair closer to the bed and took a seat. "I like to know a bit about my patients before I begin treatment. If you become fatigued, just let me know."

Kathleen settled back against the pillows. "That sounds fine."

He proceeded to ask her the same questions he'd asked James, relieved to find her answers matched her husband's. From all accounts, the family situation was as blissful as the others had indicated. No hint of any strife or tension that might have contributed to her condition. It had been almost two weeks since the stroke, so the worst danger of reoccurrence had passed.

"How hard are you willing to work to regain the use of your limbs?" he asked. "The exercises I employ can be grueling. I've been known to make grown men cry." He regarded her for any subtle change in her demeanor.

She didn't blink. "If you're trying to scare me off, Doctor, it won't work. I'm determined to get back to normal, no matter what I have to do." She tilted her chin in a way that reminded Matthew of her daughter. "Now, when do we begin?"

"Is tomorrow too soon?"

"Tomorrow is perfect."

"Good." He rose and moved the chair back. "I should tell you I've committed to stay for a period of one month, which should be enough time to give us a good indication as to whether the exercises will be beneficial or not. After that, we'll reassess and go from there."

"Fair enough." Mrs. O'Leary's smile exuded kindness and peace, something he rarely experienced with his patients. Most liked to rail at the fates for dealing them such ill fortune. Much like the cheerful Fred Knox, Mrs. O'Leary promised to be a refreshing change.

Matthew's thoughts turned to Phoebe, and he paused near

the doorway. "I don't know if Mr. O'Leary told you, but my daughter and her nanny have come with me."

The woman's whole face softened. "Oh, I didn't realize . . . How old is your daughter?"

"Four and a half." He hesitated, but for everyone's sake, she needed to know about Phoebe's issues. "Phoebe is somewhat frail. She had tuberculosis when she was two."

"I'm so sorry."

"You should also know that she suffers from several phobias related to her illness and to her mother's death."

Matthew shrank from the stark sympathy on Mrs. O'Leary's face.

"I'm glad your daughter is here," she said. "God has a reason for it, I'm sure. I'll pray she receives His healing grace."

Matthew clenched his hand into a fist, willing himself not to react. He gave a quick nod and pushed out of the room before his skepticism became evident in his eyes.

If the woman wanted to waste her time praying, he wouldn't stop her. But based on past experience, he held no assurance of its success.

Besides, if prayer brought about healing, what need would the world have for doctors?

❦

The next day, after observing Dr. Clayborne's session with Mama, Deirdre felt the first stirrings of hope. The doctor was patient with her mother, and didn't push too hard. Of course, it could be because he wanted to start off slowly. But Deirdre hoped it boded well for their future sessions.

At noon, everyone gathered for the midday meal in the dining room, all except Mama, who was napping and would take a tray later in her room. Looking down the long table, Deirdre couldn't help but feel sorry for Miss Shearing. The woman seemed decidedly ill at ease, her eyes cast down at her plate for most of the meal. Phoebe, on the other hand, watched everyone with unconcealed interest, like a curious baby bird. Deirdre took it as a good sign, hoping that the child wasn't as introverted as she'd feared. The fact that the girl's father sat at her immediate left probably helped her feel secure.

When the dishes had been cleared, Connor headed back to the stables, and Daddy went to sit with Mama, leaving Deirdre with the Claybornes and the nanny.

As Miss Shearing prepared to usher Phoebe back upstairs, Deirdre rose from her chair. "Would anyone care to take a walk outside?" she asked. "I could show you the grounds and the horses." Children needed fresh air and exercise, and from the look of things, little Phoebe had been sorely lacking in this area. Did Miss Shearing ever take her outside at home?

Phoebe tugged on her father's sleeve, a pleading expression in her eyes.

He hesitated, and Deirdre feared he would refuse, but then he nodded. "I believe a walk would be enjoyable."

Deirdre turned to Miss Shearing. "You're welcome to join us if you wish."

The nanny stiffened. "Thank you, but I could use some time to unpack my things."

Dr. Clayborne nodded. "That's fine." He seemed almost relieved. A strange sort of tension existed between the doctor and his employee.

Once they had donned light wraps, Deirdre led them outside. She inhaled the crisp autumn air, containing the faint scent of manure that drifted over from their neighbors' farms, a scent that always reminded her of the changing seasons. Deirdre directed her guests along the path to her mother's renowned gardens.

"You should see Mama's roses in the summer," Deirdre said. "Their perfume alone is breathtaking."

"I'm sure they're lovely."

Dr. Clayborne's automatic response threatened to steal

Deirdre's enjoyment of the day. Did the man ever show any enthusiasm? Phoebe's wide eyes, however, expressed her delight. She seemed in awe of everything, as though she'd never experienced a simple garden before.

Deirdre led them to the main stables where Daddy housed his clients' thoroughbreds. She gave a small commentary about the more noteworthy horses that had run in the Kentucky Derby. Dr. Clayborne remained as mute as his daughter, leaving Deirdre somewhat unsettled. What was he thinking behind that stoic façade?

Deirdre peered at Phoebe, wanting to ensure the large animals weren't frightening the child. Thankfully, she showed no fear, only curiosity.

Deirdre continued on to the secondary barn where the workhorses and ponies resided, eagerly anticipating one particular animal. Twizzle's familiar whinny sounded before she even caught sight of him over the stall door.

"Phoebe, this is my pony, Twizzle. My daddy bought him for my brother and me when we were just a little older than you. I learned how to ride on him." Her beloved Twizzle was getting old and stiff, but he still provided much entertainment for her nieces and nephews.

Phoebe stood on her tiptoes, attempting to peer over the door.

"May I lift you to see better?"

When Phoebe nodded, Deirdre lifted her until her feet found a slat to rest on. Deirdre kept her arms around the child to make sure she didn't fall. Twizzle came forward for his expected snack. She pulled the small pieces of carrot from her pocket where she'd hidden them earlier.

Phoebe watched in fascination as the pony's lips closed around a piece.

"That's my good boy," Deirdre crooned. She rubbed the area between his ears and he gave a delighted snort, blowing air across Phoebe's arm.

The girl gasped, and Deirdre laughed. "It's all right. That means Twizzle's happy."

Under Deirdre's palm, the stiffness left Phoebe's back. She reached out a tentative hand.

Immediately, Dr. Clayborne moved in. "I don't think that's a good idea."

Deirdre looked up. "Don't worry. Twizzle loves children. He would never hurt her."

She took Phoebe's hand and ran it over the pony's nose. Then she gave the girl a piece of carrot. "Would you like to give him a treat? Twizzle loves carrots almost as much as we love ice cream."

A giggle escaped the girl's upturned lips. Deirdre thought she'd never heard such a lovely sound. "Hold your hand flat."

Twizzle's lips found the carrot, and he gave another soft snort of triumph.

"You did it." Deirdre hugged her, grinning at the look of wonder on the girl's face.

And then Phoebe laughed out loud, an expression of unrestrained joy on her face.

Deirdre pushed back a swell of emotion. "Maybe one day, if your father agrees, you can ride Twizzle. Would you like that?"

She nodded vigorously, her blond braids bobbing. Deirdre glanced at Dr. Clayborne, unsure of his reaction.

A muscle worked in his jaw. "We'll see," he said, his voice gruff.

Deirdre's spirits tumbled, thinking him displeased. But as they headed outside toward the racetrack, Dr. Clayborne halted her. "Thank you, Miss O'Leary. I haven't heard my daughter laugh since . . ." He swallowed, and his Adam's apple bobbed. "In a very long time."

Deirdre considered his serious face. How long had it been since he'd laughed himself? Did the man ever relax? Even his speech was clipped and formal. "Don't you think you could call me Deirdre?" she asked softly.

He seemed to study her, then nodded. "Very well, Deirdre. And you may call me Matthew."

Matthew stared into the green depths of Deirdre's eyes and, for a second, forgot to breathe. She had a way of looking at him that seemed to peer right through to his soul.

"Matthew," she repeated. "I've always liked that name." She smiled again, and the engaging dimples appeared.

The sound of children's voices tore Matthew's focus away. A boy and two girls raced up the path near the white fence that surrounded the track.

Phoebe, who had initially run on ahead, now came back and leaned against his leg. He laid a protective hand on her shoulder.

"Aunt Dee-Dee! You're home!" The older girl ran straight at Deirdre, who instead of bracing herself reached out and grabbed the girl under the arms, swinging her into the air.

The red-haired child bellowed out a laugh.

"How's my Rosie?" Deirdre set the girl on the ground and gave her a loud kiss.

"I lost another tooth." She pointed to a gap in her upper teeth.

"My goodness. You're getting old, aren't you?" Deirdre's exaggerated expression made the girl laugh again. "Why aren't you at home doing your lessons?"

"Mama let us out of school early so we could come and see you."

The other two arrived, kicking up a cloud of dust with them. Deirdre embraced them both at once.

Matthew had never seen such an exuberant greeting. At most, his family had only ever given each other a polite peck on the cheek or a handshake. Phoebe seemed as taken aback as he, for she just stared at the energetic children.

Deirdre gestured to them. "This is Phoebe, and her father,

Dr. Clayborne. They're guests staying with Granddad and Grandma. Matthew, these are Brianna and Gil's children, Sean, Rose, and Betsy."

"Hello." Matthew shifted his weight, unsure what to say to the three pairs of eyes staring at him. Phoebe remained silent, clutching his leg.

Betsy, the younger girl, came to stand before Phoebe. "I'm four. How old are you?"

A quiver went through his daughter. Just when Matthew thought her silence would drown them both, Phoebe held up her free hand, showing four fingers.

"You're four, too?"

Phoebe nodded.

"She'll be five soon," Matthew added, feeling the inexplicable need to speak for his daughter.

Wisps of Betsy's light brown hair had sprung from the pigtails that hung over her shoulder. She frowned at Deirdre. "Can't she talk, Aunt Dee-Dee?"

Matthew sucked in a sharp breath. This was why he'd kept Phoebe away from other children, fearing their insensitivity would only scar her further.

Deirdre bent down between the girls. "Of course Phoebe can talk. She's just shy. I'm counting on all of you to make her feel at home."

The older girl, Rose, looked at her brother, who bore an unmistakable resemblance to Gil. "She can play with us anytime, Aunt Dee-Dee."

Deirdre rose and dropped a kiss on her head. "Good girl."

Betsy grinned and grabbed Phoebe's free hand. "My mama teaches us at home. She's a real good teacher. Maybe you can do lessons with us?"

Phoebe smiled back and nodded, which Matthew took as a good sign. Yet the thought of letting his daughter go off to a strange house without him sent chills up his spine.

"We'll talk about it later," he said in answer to her inquiring gaze. Matthew would speak to Deirdre first and find out more about this home schooling.

"Our dog had puppies," Betsy told Phoebe. "When they're bigger, Papa says we have to give them away." The sorrow on her face would have rivaled a mourner at a funeral. "Do you want to see them?"

Phoebe nodded so fast, strands of hair slipped from her braid.

Matthew's head swam. Horses, ponies, children, and now puppies. He wanted to scoop up his daughter and carry her back to the staid Miss Shearing, who never exposed Phoebe to anything more dangerous than a tepid bath.

As if mirroring his fears, a child's scream tore through the air. The hair on Matthew's neck rose at its intensity.

"Sean!" Deirdre flew toward the fence surrounding a pasture.

Inside, a large, black horse snorted and pawed the ground.

Sean Whelan stood barely a foot from the imposing beast, his face ashen, apparently frozen in fear.

The horse reared, its hooves slicing the air.

Adrenaline surged through Matthew's system, springing him into action. He raced forward, madly searching for a way to save the boy from certain injury.

In front of him, Deirdre scaled the fence and jumped to the ground. Lifting her skirts, she sprinted toward the animal.

Matthew's heart leapt into his throat, clogging his airway. The foolish woman was risking her life. He vaulted over the fence after her.

Deirdre threw Sean to the ground, covering his body with hers. The hooves came down, missing them by inches. With a loud trumpet, the horse reared again, its eyes wild.

Matthew dove on top of them, shielding them both with his body. His last thought as he waited for the hooves to descend was of Phoebe.

8

CONNOR RAN FROM THE BARN, his heart thumping in his chest. He thought he'd heard the high-pitched sound of a child screaming. As he neared the fence, the blood drained from his head so fast he had to blink to make sure he was seeing right.

Good Lord! What was Sean doing in the pen with Excalibur?

Connor's boots kicked up dirt as he charged toward the enclosure. Before he could reach the fence, Deirdre had tackled Sean to the ground. Then right behind her, Dr. Clayborne threw himself over both of them.

Sweat pooled under Connor's hat and trickled down his temple. From the wildness in the stallion's eyes, Connor gauged the animal to be beyond reason. It would take too long to calm the beast down. Still, he had to do something. He'd hurdled the fence, mentally planning his strategy, when a figure shot past him.

The new stable hand slowed his pace as he neared the still-bucking horse. Connor bit back a shout of warning, not wanting to spook the animal further and endanger Joe's life.

The lad spoke in a low, lilting voice, almost singing to the beast, and to Connor's utter astonishment, Excalibur's hooves remained on the ground. He snorted, air coming out in puffs, yet his attention remained riveted on Joe Miller.

Connor approached cautiously, afraid to set the horse off again.

Joe held up a hand to halt Connor. Though it galled him to remain motionless, Connor had little recourse. He tensed, clenching his hands into fists at his sides, unable to do anything but watch.

Slowly, Joe reached up and grabbed the reins. Connor's muscles seized, ready for the horse to panic. To rear and strike the lad. If the horse injured him, Connor would never forgive himself. He was responsible while Sam was away.

But Joe continued to talk to the animal, which, for some unknown reason, quieted.

From the corner of his eye, Connor saw the doctor move Deirdre and Sean to safety.

Joe rubbed his hand over Excalibur's neck. The tension seemed to leave the animal, and its muscles relaxed.

"It's all right. No one's going to hurt you." Joe stroked the stallion's flank.

Connor pulled off his cap and scratched his sweat-soaked head, unable to believe what he was seeing. The boy led the subdued horse across the pasture, now as docile as a lamb.

Connor thrust his cap back on and strode to the opposite side of the fence, where the group of onlookers huddled around his nephew. Deirdre had her hand on the boy's shoulder. The doctor knelt beside his daughter, whose cheeks dripped with silent tears. Betsy and Rose held hands, their faces as white as Sean's.

Fear, relief, and a snarl of annoyance balled up in Connor's chest, releasing in an angry snort. "Sean Whelan!" he bellowed. "Come here right now."

A flash of fear crossed the boy's features, but Connor held firm.

Deirdre came toward him, pinning Connor with the same glare she'd used when they were kids. "Can't this wait?"

"No, it can't." Connor gestured to Sean. "In the barn. Now."

The boy threw his aunt a desperate look.

She shrugged. "I'm sorry, honey. Uncle Connor's in charge. You'll have to do as he says."

Sean hung his head and trudged toward the barn.

Connor regarded his sister's disapproving face. "It's for his own good, Dee. He could've been killed. I can't let that slide."

He stalked over to the barn, dreading having to punish his nephew. But someone needed to teach Sean respect for the rules, and if it had to be him, then so be it. His parents would thank him in the long run.

Connor glanced briefly at the far edge of the pasture where Joe stood with Excalibur, and a begrudging sense of admiration crept over him. A talent for horses like he'd just witnessed was rare indeed, and he fully intended to make the most of Joe's gift.

Once Jo managed to get the great stallion back into the barn, her heart rate finally slowed to near normal. She offered a quick prayer of gratitude that God had allowed her to soothe the agitated animal. Excalibur wasn't purposely trying to harm the boy, she was sure. Clearly not used to being around children, the stallion had panicked. Now, back in his stall where he felt safe, the animal remained quiet.

Jo rubbed a hand over his nose. "There's nothing to fear. No one is going to hurt you, I promise."

What a magnificent animal. She'd never seen a horse so fine. How she wished she could work with Excalibur. But a mere stable hand would not be allowed to interfere with the training of a champion racehorse.

Though she'd love to find out how receptive Connor O'Leary

might be to any advice from her, she didn't dare try. Best not to draw any undue attention to herself.

Quietly, she exited the stables and made her way into the secondary barn. As she rounded a corner, a childish voice halted her stride.

"Are you gonna whip me, Uncle Connor?"

Jo froze, every vertebrae stiffening at the ring of fear in the boy's voice. Her muscles tensed as she waited for an answer, prepared to intervene if need be. She would not allow any child to be harmed if she could prevent it.

"Don't you think you deserve a whipping for what you've done? Disobeying your granddad's rules. Almost getting yourself killed, not to mention endangering your aunt, Dr. Clayborne, and a valuable racehorse."

Jo inched closer to the edge of the wall, stopping when a tiny voice answered, "I guess so."

Jo peered around the edge of the last stall. Connor sat on a wooden stool, his back to the wall. The boy stood directly in front of him, toeing the dirt.

Connor picked up a long, thin piece of wood lying across his lap and tapped it lightly against his palm.

Jo tensed. Surely he wouldn't use that stick on the child. She shuddered, recalling the many objects her father had used on her, some of which had left a lasting reminder.

"Lucky for you, young man, I don't believe in whippings. However . . ." He paused, seemingly for effect.

Jo wished she could see Connor's face.

"However, your actions must have a consequence. I think one fitting the crime is in order."

The boy's head flew up, his expression half relieved, half tentative.

"You will muck out all the stalls in both barns for one week."

The boy's freckles stood out on the bridge of his nose. "But that's—"

"What? Not fair?" Connor leaned forward, his face inches from the boy's. "Would you prefer a whipping, then?"

"No, sir." The youngster's chin touched his plaid shirt.

Connor leaned the stick against the wall and rose. "Good. You can start tomorrow morning."

The boy remained unmoving.

"Go on home now and tell your parents what happened."

"Yes, sir." The boy took two steps and then turned back, his lip quivering. "I'm sorry, Uncle Connor." A tear escaped from the corner of his eye.

Connor gave a gusty sigh, then caught the boy up in his arms. "You have to be more careful, Sean. We all love you very much. If anything ever happened to you . . ." He cleared his throat and set Sean back on the ground.

"Will you still teach me how to rope?"

He rested a hand on Sean's shoulder. "Once your punishment is over, we'll discuss it again."

The boy nodded. "Papa's going to be mad."

Jo stiffened. Would Mr. Whelan beat his son for his crime?

But Connor chuckled. "Yes, he will. You may have more chores to do at home as well."

As the boy scampered out of the barn, Jo let out her breath. Sean would be fine, in the stable and at home. And with any luck, Connor O'Leary would treat his employees as fairly as he did his nephew.

Thinking to make a quiet retreat, she took a step back. Her foot landed in a metal pail. She squeaked as cold water flooded her boot and sloshed onto the dirt floor. With a groan, she pulled out her foot and gave it a shake.

"That's one way to clean your boots."

She looked up, horrified to find Connor grinning at her.

"Sorry." She bent to right the bucket and set it on a nearby bench.

"Relax. It's only water."

She started walking, and he followed her through the barn. "I wanted to thank you for what you did out there with Excalibur. How did you get that horse to settle?"

Jo kept going, trying to ignore the wetness squishing between her toes. "I just talked to him. He was more afraid than the boy." She glanced up. "What happened to him, anyway?"

Connor's brows rose. "To the horse?"

She nodded.

"There was an accident during a race. Excalibur was injured and—" Connor swallowed—"his rider was killed. No one's been able to ride him since."

Jo fought the sting of tears. "That poor thing. No wonder he's so spooked."

"Yeah, well, you sure saved the day, so thank you."

"You're welcome." Jo's heart thumped hard at his scrutiny. A rush of heat invaded her cheeks. This was exactly what she didn't want—fuss and attention.

Especially from this man who did funny things to her insides.

"One more thing." Connor's command halted her departure.

She kept her eyes trained on her saturated boot.

"My nephew will be working in the barn for the next week as punishment. I'd like you to supervise him while he works. He won't be as intimidated by you as the others."

Jo swallowed. "Yes, sir." She dared to look up, only to find Connor's steady gaze on her. Intriguing flecks of gold in his eyes mesmerized her.

"Make sure you don't go too easy on him. He needs to feel the punishment."

"Got it."

"Joe?"

She stopped again and waited.

He laid a hand on her shoulder. "There's no need to be nervous around me—or anyone else here. But if someone gives you trouble, you come to me. Understand?"

Warmth from his hand spread down her arm. The fact that he was willing to protect her, even though he thought her to be an adolescent boy, made her throat tighten. "Thank you, sir."

"Call me Connor. See you tomorrow, Joe."

She nodded and set off before he could say anything else, painfully aware of him watching her walk away.

She would have to do her best to avoid him for the next few days until the curiosity she sensed in him faded. She only hoped that working with his nephew wouldn't mean he'd need to talk to her on a regular basis.

The less time she spent around Connor—and those amazing hazel eyes—the better.

9

DEIRDRE ATTEMPTED TO BRUSH the dirt from her dress, but with her hands as dusty as her skirt, her efforts were useless. Somewhere in the midst of saving Sean, her hairpins had fallen out, and her unruly tresses now spilled over her shoulders. She swiped a curl from one eye and attempted to gather her wits about her.

With the danger past, delayed nerves danced in her stomach. She couldn't quite believe Matthew had jumped into the enclosure and thrown himself on top of her and Sean, risking his life for theirs.

She owed him a big debt of gratitude.

With a sigh, she turned to see where he'd gone. Betsy and Rose were nowhere in sight, likely scampering home to tell their mother about their brother's bad behavior. She found Matthew crouched by the fence, his arms around a tearful Phoebe.

Deirdre's heart sank. That must have been scary to witness. Her idea of getting Phoebe to ride Twizzle faded with the scowl Matthew gave her as she approached.

"Are you all right?" she asked, taking note of the dirt on his trousers and the tear in his sleeve.

He rose, leaving one hand on Phoebe's head, the other pulling a handkerchief from his pocket. He handed it to her. "I'm fine. And you?"

She dabbed at her cheeks with the piece of linen that smelled like sandalwood soap. "A little dirty but otherwise fine. Thank you for what you did back there."

His glance slid away. "No need for thanks. If you'll excuse me, I'll take Phoebe back in to Miss Shearing."

Where she's safe. He didn't need to say the words for his meaning to be clear.

As he led Phoebe toward the house, Deirdre hurried after him. "Matthew, wait. That was a highly unusual occurrence. Sean knows better than to go into the pen with a stallion."

Matthew turned livid blue eyes on her. "Unusual or not, Miss O'Leary, I do not want Phoebe near any of the livestock—your pony included. Understood?"

So we are back to formalities again.

Deirdre glanced at Phoebe and bit her lip to keep from arguing. It would serve no purpose to confront Matthew in the aftermath of the incident. She would wait a few days until things had calmed down, then she would broach the topic again.

"I understand." She pressed the handkerchief into his hand.

He stuffed the cloth into his pocket, then leaned closer, lowering his voice. "And I do not want my daughter associating with the Whelan children. She's far too delicate for such . . . shenanigans."

His warm breath fanned her cheek, doing nothing to cool her rising temper. Once again she held herself in check, biting back a scorching defense of her nieces and nephew. "You are entitled to your opinion, Doctor."

Then, with as much dignity as she could muster with her hair askew and dirt everywhere, she marched back to the house.

There was more than one way to get around Matthew Clay-borne. And for Phoebe's sake, Deirdre was determined to find it.

❧⟡☙

"Is something troubling you, Matthew?"

Kathleen's voice snapped Matthew's attention away from the window where he'd been staring out at the manicured grounds.

He schooled his features. "Not at all. Are you ready for your next round of exercises?"

She wheeled her chair toward him, using her good hand and foot. "Forgive me, but you were scowling out that window as though witnessing a murder." Her light laugh took the sting from her words.

"It's nothing." Matthew crossed to a table where he'd set out an assortment of rubber balls and weights, all designed to aid with finger dexterity in the hopes that she'd be able to play the piano again. He picked up a small weight and handed it to her.

"Does it have anything to do with Sean and that horse yesterday?"

He struggled to keep the surprise from his face. "You heard about that?"

"Of course. I know everything that happens around here." She laid the weight on her lap. "I'm sure it must have been frightening, especially for someone not used to high-spirited horses."

"Yes. Phoebe was quite upset by the whole thing." Matthew wished for the hundredth time she hadn't had to witness him almost being trampled to death.

"I wasn't referring to Phoebe."

He clenched his jaw together and moved back to the table.

Kathleen rolled closer. "What you did for my daughter and grandson was very brave."

"It was nothing. Now if you don't mind, let's continue our work."

"Matthew." She reached out her good hand and laid it on

his sleeve. "Please don't let one unfortunate incident color the way you view my family. Sean is a good boy, though he can be rambunctious. Betsy and Rose are darling girls who would be wonderful companions for Phoebe—"

"Thank you for your opinion," he bit out. "However, I think I know what is best for my daughter." He pointed to the weight. "Shall we continue?"

"Of course." She put the iron into her gnarled left hand.

Matthew helped her close her fingers around it. Kathleen grimaced but kept on. As Matthew worked with her, guilt over his sharp words consumed him. He realized she only wanted to help, yet no one seemed able to fully understand the depths of his fear. The fact that one small illness could bring Phoebe to the brink of death.

"I hope I didn't offend you, Kathleen," he said when they paused for a brief rest.

"Not at all. I know how hard it is to be a parent." Her gaze held no judgment, only sympathy.

Matthew didn't know which was worse.

"Did you know I had another son?" she said.

The sadness around her eyes made his breath hitch. "*Another* son?"

"Besides Adam and Connor, and of course Gil, who we raised as our own." She took out a handkerchief and dabbed at the perspiration on her forehead. "My darling Daniel drowned in the back pond when he was eight years old."

Matthew swallowed the bitter taste of fear, as though hearing the story could make it happen to him. "I'm very sorry."

"Of all my children, Daniel was the happiest. He seemed lit with joy from the inside out." Her smile trembled. "He had such an exuberance for life. Much like our Sean."

Unable to think of an appropriate response, Matthew remained silent.

"Do I wish we'd paid more attention to Danny that day?

Certainly. But would I change the way I raised him? Keep him cocooned in the house so no harm would ever befall him?" She shook her head. "No, because then he wouldn't have really lived, would he?" Tears glistened at the corners of her eyes.

Matthew set his jaw, then released it with a long exhale. "I've already lost my wife. I can't—I *won't*—lose Phoebe, too."

Kathleen touched his arm. "There's a difference between being cautious and smothering a child."

Outrage slammed through him in a hot wave. "I am not smothering Phoebe. I'm protecting her."

Her features softened. "Oh, Matthew, don't you see? We can't protect our children from everything. The best we can do is entrust them to God."

Matthew jerked away from her. His limbs shook with the force of repressed rage that broke loose inside him. "God?" he all but shouted. "Where was God when I begged Him for my wife's life? Where was God when thousands of men died in that infernal war?"

"What is going on in here?" Deirdre stood inside the door, staring at him in horror.

His chest constricted with such force that his lungs seemed to collapse. He couldn't get any air in or out, and for a second he imagined he must look like a fish with its mouth flapping open. Finally he managed one huge gulp of air. "Excuse me," he sputtered and pushed past her out the door.

Stunned, Deirdre crossed the room to her mother and knelt in front of her chair. "Mama, why was Matthew so upset?"

She peered at her mother's reddened eyes, evidence of the recent tears she'd shed. If Matthew had bullied her, Deirdre wouldn't hesitate to give the man a piece of her mind.

Mama sighed. "I'm afraid I may have pushed him too far."

Deirdre could not begin to fathom how her fragile mother

could have pushed Dr. Clayborne, although when a look of steely determination replaced her sadness, Deirdre began to understand. Mama could be relentless when trying to get her point across.

"What happened?"

"I told him he was being too overprotective of his daughter. And I told him about Danny."

"Oh, Mama." She clasped her mother's hand. No wonder she'd been crying—reliving the loss of her child. Deirdre had been too young to remember much about her brother, but she recalled going to the cemetery every year to visit Danny's grave. "It appears Matthew didn't appreciate your advice."

Mama smiled. "Not at all." She straightened her back against the chair. "Not to worry. I'll apologize when he returns, and in the meantime, the seeds have been sown. It's up to the Lord to see them to fruition."

Deirdre's lips twitched. "I may have an idea how to nudge God's timing along. I asked Bree to bring the children over to do their lessons here for a few days. If Matthew sees how well-behaved the children are and how civilized the schooling is, then maybe he'll relent. And this way Phoebe will be nearby, so he won't worry."

Mama patted Deirdre's cheek. "Such a clever girl."

"I want to help her, Mama. I know Phoebe must want to live a normal life—with friends, and fresh air, and playtime."

"I'm sure you're right." Mama's eyes brightened. "Why don't you bring her to visit with me for a while?"

Deirdre's spirits lifted. If anyone knew how to reach children, it was her mother. "That's a wonderful idea. Then she'll be here when Brianna and the kids arrive."

Matthew stood at the white fence, staring blindly over the far meadows. His hands clenched the top rung of the railing so hard that tiny slivers of wood pricked his skin.

As his breathing evened out, he attempted to sift through the layers of anger to find what was really disturbing him. Fear for Phoebe sat at the heart of it, yet it was more than that.

Everything about this place unsettled him. The open air and large spaces. The animals, the unstructured way of life with people coming and going, and the exuberance of the O'Leary family.

But most of all, Deirdre O'Leary unsettled him with her passionate, fearless approach to life. She hadn't hesitated for a second before racing to save her nephew.

Matthew shivered, recalling the feel of her beneath him as he'd shielded her body with his own. And afterward, the way her hair had come free in waves to her waist. Even with her face streaked with dirt, she'd never looked more beautiful.

He'd have rushed to protect any woman, any child. But the instant he'd perceived Deirdre was in jeopardy, he realized he felt something . . . more.

And that realization now sent a rush of terror through him.

He thought longingly of his safe office in the basement of the hospital, where he saw the same patients week in and week out. Where no one challenged him on his methods and certainly not on his parenting.

"There's a difference between being cautious and smothering a child." Kathleen's reprimand echoed in his head.

Matthew banged a fist on the fence until it rattled. He never should have come here. Never should have exposed Phoebe to the type of carefree life she couldn't lead.

And now he was committed to seeing it through. Maybe he should send Phoebe back to Toronto with Miss Shearing. Yet the thought of his daughter so far away—without him nearby to make sure she was all right—choked the air from his lungs.

No, he could never allow that. He'd have to stick it out for the next few weeks, then return home and try to forget this whole unfortunate episode.

A pair of spring-green eyes, auburn hair, and enchanting dimples rose in his mind to mock the very idea. It would be impossible to forget Deirdre O'Leary.

The sound of children's laughter drifted toward him, penetrating his haze of self-reflection.

Brianna Whelan and two of her children strolled down the path toward the house. Matthew stiffened. What were they doing here at this time of day? He searched for somewhere to step out of sight, but Brianna had already spied him.

She waved in his direction. "Hello, Dr. Clayborne. How are you this lovely day?"

With an inward sigh, Matthew joined them on the path. "Fine, thank you."

She smiled brightly. "The children wanted to see their grandmother, so I thought I'd combine their lessons with a visit. Perhaps Phoebe might like to join us?"

Matthew's muscles tensed. "I'd have to check with her nanny to see what she has scheduled for today."

Brianna's smile dimmed. "Oh, I see. Well, they're both welcome to do lessons with us. We'll be in the dining room, after saying a brief hello to Mama."

They entered the house together, and the girls scampered down the hall. Matthew and Brianna followed.

"Grandma is likely in the sitting room, girls," Brianna called. "Check there first . . . quietly."

"Yes, Mama."

Brianna's brow wrinkled. "You don't think they'll be too much for my mother, do you?"

"On the contrary, I believe they'll do her a world of good."

When Matthew looked into the room, his jaw went slack. Phoebe was seated on Kathleen's lap, while the Whelan girls clamored about the wheelchair.

Matthew checked the urge to pluck his daughter out of the

melee, yet she seemed to be enjoying the excitement. A definite glint of interest lit her pale eyes.

"I hope you don't mind." Deirdre's voice came from behind him. "Mama wanted to see Phoebe, and I thought a small break from . . . upstairs would do her good. Though I don't think Miss Shearing was too pleased."

Matthew squared his shoulders. One more example of how things concerning his daughter were spiraling out of his control. "In the future, I wish you would consult me—"

"Mama, can Phoebe do her lessons with us?" Betsy hopped from one foot to the other, tugging on her mother's arm. "Please?"

Brianna glanced at Matthew. "That would be up to Dr. Clayborne."

The unspoken question hovered in the room. Matthew felt all eyes on him, but it was the pleading in his daughter's that almost broke him. "I suppose it wouldn't hurt for a little while."

A blinding smile broke out over Phoebe's face. She pushed off Kathleen's lap and went to stand by Betsy, who clapped her hands in glee.

"Say good-bye to Grandma, girls," Brianna said. "Then wait for me in the dining room. I have to make sure Sean has finished his chores so he can join us." Brianna winked at Deirdre.

Matthew frowned. Why did it feel like he'd just been duped?

The children trooped out of the room behind Brianna. Phoebe didn't look back once.

Deirdre laid a hand on his arm. "Relax, Matthew. It's only a spelling lesson. Nothing to worry about."

The teasing glint in her eyes lessened the sting of her comment, yet words of defense raced to his tongue. "Phoebe's not used to being around other children . . ." He trailed off, realizing how inane he must sound.

"Which is exactly why this is so good for her," Deirdre said gently. "You can't keep her in a cocoon forever."

A fresh surge of anger spiked through him. "If it keeps her healthy, I will."

Kathleen wheeled over. "I tried that with Deirdre after she survived typhoid fever as a child."

Matthew blinked. "I thought *you* had typhoid."

"Deirdre and Connor contracted it as well. For some time after, Deirdre was quite frail, and I'm afraid I was guilty of being overprotective myself. Losing one child made me more fearful about the others." She gave a sad smile. "But because Deirdre was already used to her freedom, she didn't let me get away with coddling her."

"And believe me, Mama tried. Good thing I inherited the O'Leary stubborn streak."

"I'll say." Matthew's eyes widened when he realized he'd spoken aloud.

Kathleen and Deirdre both laughed.

"The point is," Kathleen continued, "once I relented and let Deirdre play outdoors and ride her horse again, she became even stronger."

Deirdre turned to address him. "I know Phoebe's condition is not the same. But a little fun can go a long way toward healing."

Matthew released a weary breath. "I guess I can try to be less . . . rigid."

The women beamed at each other, and Matthew fought back a scowl. These O'Leary women were more tenacious than some of the most difficult doctors he worked with. However, he supposed he could let the women win this one.

Because when it came to more important issues concerning his daughter, he would not be swayed.

10

THE NEXT DAY, Deirdre wrapped her shawl around her shoulders and let herself out the back door. While Mama rested and Dr. Clayborne talked with Daddy, she allowed herself a rare moment alone, grateful for the opportunity to walk around her beloved grounds.

All these years, she'd taken her home and her large family for granted. But now, seeing them through Phoebe and Matthew's eyes, Deirdre realized how truly blessed she was to be surrounded by such love.

Brianna had shown up again this morning with her children so Phoebe could participate in the lessons without worrying Matthew. The joy on the girl's face as she'd joined Betsy, Rose, and Sean at the table made Deirdre's heart sing. These children could be the key to Phoebe coming out of her shell; Deirdre felt certain of it.

She shivered, pulling her shawl closer around her, and wandered through the garden toward the far enclosure where Connor worked with the stallion. Excalibur seemed much calmer today, allowing Connor to lead him around the pen with little fuss.

"Hello, Deirdre."

She whirled around to see a familiar man on the path. He wore a wool jacket, tan pants, and scuffed boots. Brown hair peeked out from a flat cap.

She squinted. "Caleb Sullivan? Is that you?"

When he gave her his trademark crooked grin, she knew for sure.

"Glad you remember your old friend."

She rushed over to embrace him, then pulled back. "What are you doing here? I thought you moved to Montana."

"You mean after you broke my heart?"

Deirdre gave him a playful swat. "I did no such thing. You always knew I would never marry a farmer."

She and her siblings had grown up with the Sullivans, their nearest neighbors, and Connor and Caleb had been best friends all through school.

Caleb sobered. "Instead, you picked a lawyer—or so the family wrote to tell me."

The mere mention of Jeffrey brought a wave of heat to Deirdre's cheeks. "Unfortunately, that didn't work out, and I've sworn off marriage altogether." She pasted on a wide smile. "But what are you doing here? Visiting your family?"

"Actually, I'm back for good. Dad can't keep up with the farm anymore, so I'm taking on a large share of the workload." He moved closer to her. "I heard about your mother. How is she doing?"

Deirdre stilled. Would she ever get used to answering that question? "She's gradually regaining her strength. We're hopeful in time she'll be able to walk again."

He rubbed a hand down her arm. "If anyone can help her, you can, Dee."

Sudden memories of the time Caleb had professed his feelings for her came rushing back—along with the recollection of the hurt she'd inflicted when she'd told him she was leaving Long Island.

Deirdre carefully stepped away. "Thank you, Caleb. I'm sure Connor will be thrilled to see you. If you'll excuse me, I'd best get back to Mama."

A flash of disappointment crossed his features. "Of course. See you around, Dee."

Only after she'd gone back inside the house did she pause to consider whether Caleb had come to see her brother—or her.

Matthew climbed the sweeping staircase to the second floor and made his way to the room where Miss Shearing had been tutoring Phoebe. The nanny had asked to see him, and Matthew had a sinking feeling he knew what she wanted to speak to him about.

On a deep inhale, he gave two sharp raps.

"Come in."

Matthew opened the door and looked in. At the far side of the cheerful room, Miss Shearing stood staring out the window.

She turned to face him, her features pinched. "Thank you for coming. I wanted to speak to you in private."

Matthew entered the room, taking note of the welcoming décor—chintz chairs, breezy curtains, and a large white fireplace. "I've been meaning to speak with you as well." He gestured to the upholstered chairs. "Would you care to sit?"

"I'd prefer to stand."

"Very well. What is it you wish to discuss?" Matthew braced himself for her complaints.

She walked over to the desk and picked up a book, holding it in front of her like a shield. "If Phoebe is to take lessons with the Whelan children every day, then what is my role to be?"

So his assumption had been correct—she didn't like being

usurped by Brianna Whelan. Phoebe, however, was enjoying her sessions with them, and Matthew wouldn't deny her happiness simply to please the nanny. He braced for unpleasantness. "Actually, I believe the timing is fortuitous. We agreed you would stay until Phoebe had grown accustomed to her new surroundings. Now that she's settled, I feel it's time for you to return to Toronto. I'll happily pay your salary while you take the next few weeks off until we return."

Instead of appearing grateful for the chance at a paid holiday, Miss Shearing frowned.

"Is there a problem?"

She lifted her pointy chin, nostrils flaring. "As a matter of fact, there is. I see what's happening, and I cannot remain silent."

Matthew forced his shoulders to relax as he waited for her to continue.

Miss Shearing moved away from the desk. "I would appreciate your honesty, Doctor. Do you intend to marry Miss O'Leary?"

Every muscle in Matthew's body went rigid. "Where did you get that ridiculous idea?"

Red blotches spread across the nanny's thin cheeks. "I'm not blind. When she's in the room, no one else commands your attention. You act . . . differently around her." She paused, squeezing her hands together.

Matthew stilled, unable to dispute her claim. He *was* attracted to Deirdre—not that he would ever act on it. However, the fact that Miss Shearing had noticed was unsettling at best.

"You indicated when you hired me that you had no intention to remarry," she continued. "If you've changed your mind, I believe I have a right to know, especially given the way Miss O'Leary tries to undermine my authority with Phoebe."

"I haven't changed my mind," he said stiffly, ignoring the comment about Deirdre.

The woman came closer, intensity bringing life to her eyes.

"If you ever do, please know that you have other . . . options . . . available to you."

Matthew blinked, certain he must have misconstrued her meaning. "I assure you, Miss Shearing, I have no such intention. Now, getting back to the matter at hand, I will arrange your transportation home as soon as possible."

He stared at her until she lowered her gaze.

"As you wish." She crossed the room but stopped at the door. "I cannot leave, however, without a word of warning. Earlier today, I saw Miss O'Leary with a man near the garden, involved in a seemingly intimate conversation. You should know you're not the only man she's flirting with."

An uncomfortable sensation moved through Matthew's chest—part irritation, part guilt. After leaving James's study that morning, Matthew had gone for a walk outdoors where he, too, had witnessed Deirdre talking with a stranger. At their seeming familiarity, a flare of something akin to jealousy had twisted Matthew's stomach. A sense of unease had plagued him ever since.

Now he fought to remain logical. "That type of character assassination is uncalled for, Miss Shearing. You have no idea who that man was. Perhaps an old friend or a neighbor."

Hadn't he tried to convince himself of the same thing?

Miss Shearing's expression told him she didn't believe his theory for a minute. "Nevertheless, it would pay to be cautious. Good day, Doctor."

When the door shut firmly behind her, Matthew sank onto a nearby chair. Emotions churned through his system like thick oil through a clogged engine. How had his life become filled with such drama? Ever since Priscilla died, he'd tried to live a quiet existence, focused on his daughter and his work. But since meeting Deirdre O'Leary, everything had turned upside down, including his staid nanny.

As Matthew headed downstairs to make arrangements for

her train ticket, his shoulders slumped with the weight of a new worry. He would have to find a replacement for Miss Shearing since he could no longer ignore the fact that she hoped for a personal relationship with him—something that would never happen.

He released a weary sigh. The next time he hired anyone—be it nanny, governess, or housekeeper—he would make sure the woman was old enough to be his grandmother.

<hr />

The next afternoon, Deirdre breezed into Mama's therapy room with a wide smile. "It's a beautiful day, possibly the last one before winter sets in. I suggest we take advantage of the weather." She hoped to get Matthew and Phoebe outdoors today for something other than work.

Seated behind the desk, Matthew lifted his head from the paperwork, a frown wrinkling his brow. "But we haven't finished our session."

"I'm sure Mama wouldn't mind a break." She gave her mother a playful wink.

"Not at all. I'd love to spend some time with my husband."

Matthew removed his reading glasses and set them on the table. "I suppose it wouldn't hurt. And I could catch up on my reading."

Deirdre walked over and flipped his book closed. "Oh no. You will not waste this day indoors poring over medical journals. We're taking Phoebe for a walk to my sister's house."

Ignoring his glower, she moved then to help her mother back into her wheelchair. "I'll take you into the parlor, Mama, and send Daddy over."

"Thank you, honey. This is a wonderful idea. Little Phoebe could use an outing."

Still frowning, Matthew rose. "Why are we going to the Whelans'?"

Deirdre slipped a pillow behind her mother's back and arranged the shawl over her knees. "Because you've been promising to let Phoebe see the puppies, and it's the perfect day to enjoy the walk over."

Matthew's mouth formed a hard line, one Deirdre had come to know all too well. She stifled a grin. If she had her way, he might actually loosen up and enjoy himself.

She grasped the handles of the chair and wheeled Mama out into the hallway toward the parlor, leaving Matthew little choice but to follow.

Twenty minutes later, after collecting Phoebe from the kitchen where Mrs. Harrison had been letting her help bake sugar cookies, the trio set off on their adventure.

In direct contrast to Matthew's staid demeanor, Phoebe's eyes sparkled with excitement. She skipped ahead of them across the pastures, stopping to pick an array of late-blooming wildflowers, leaving Deirdre and Matthew in awkward silence.

Matthew walked stiffly, his arms clasped behind him. "So, Miss O'Leary—"

"Deirdre."

"Yes, Deirdre. What made you decide to become a doctor after earning your nursing degree?"

She plucked a long strand of grass and twirled it between her fingers. "Ever since I survived typhoid fever, I wanted to work with children. While nursing is satisfactory in some regards, the amount of influence I had over a patient's care was minimal—always having to defer to the doctor's decisions." She quirked a brow. "No offense."

"None taken."

"As a pediatrician, I would wield more power. Be a more effective healer." She grinned. "I'd also be much nicer to the nursing staff."

He gave a small chuckle. "We doctors do earn a bad reputation in that regard."

The sound of his light laughter sent tingles along her arms. Was this the first time she'd heard him laugh? His arm brushed hers as they walked, and her pulse rate jumped. She focused her attention back to a safe topic of conversation. "How about you? What made you go into physiotherapy?"

Even though she knew the answer, she wanted to hear his explanation.

He glanced over at her. "I presume you know I was injured in the war."

"Uncle Victor mentioned it."

"I ended up in a hospital in England. The doctor who treated me specialized in new therapy techniques. He worked with me to overcome my lameness."

She paid more attention to his gait. "Obviously it worked well, since you walk with barely a limp."

"Thank you. It did prove quite successful."

"So you decided to bring those techniques back to Canada?"

"Precisely."

"But the war ended years ago. Surely the number of soldiers needing treatment must be decreasing."

"True, which is why I'm hoping to expand my practice to polio and stroke victims. There may also be advantages to using therapies on accident victims suffering from paralysis— to keep the muscles from atrophying if nothing else." He grew more animated as he spoke, and a flush of color infused his face.

"So in a way, my mother's case could prove timely for you."

He raised a brow. "That was never in question. It was the necessity to leave my other patients that worried me. It still does."

Her admiration for Matthew swelled, thinking of how much he'd sacrificed, albeit reluctantly at first, to come to Irish Meadows. "I'm sure they're all doing splendidly."

They walked in silence for several minutes, content to watch Phoebe run after the leaves blowing across the grass.

Finally Deirdre gathered her courage. "If I ask you something, will you give me an honest answer?"

He turned his piercing gaze on her. "I am always honest, Deirdre."

Her heart did a slow roll in her chest. "Of course you are." She hesitated. "Do you think Mama will ever walk again?"

He pursed his lips. "I can't guarantee anything, but there's been definite improvement in motor function and strength. I see no reason why she won't eventually regain the use of her leg and hand."

Deirdre let out a slow breath. "That's a relief to hear."

Brianna and Gil's house came into view—a simple brick home with a wraparound porch. Betsy and Rose flew out the front door and across the grass with Sean close behind. Once they reached Phoebe, the chatter of her nieces along with Phoebe's giggles warmed Deirdre's heart.

Would she ever be fortunate enough to have children, or would caring for her young patients have to suffice?

Her longing must have shown on her face, for Matthew peered at her in a quizzical manner. "Given your apparent love of children, are you prepared to sacrifice having a family of your own for your career?"

Her footsteps slowed as she stored her emotions back into place. "It has already cost me a fiancé, but I still hold out hope that I might meet a man who's willing to accept a working wife."

Furrows etched Matthew's brow. "You were engaged?"

"For a time. Jeffrey studied law at Columbia. He didn't seem to mind my nursing, but when he learned I wished to pursue a medical degree, he was furious. He'd accepted a wonderful job in Philadelphia and expected me to follow him."

"Why not study at the university there?" Matthew asked. "They have an excellent medical program."

She shrugged. "Jeffrey expected me to quit my job, and I wasn't willing to give up my dream just to become Mrs. Atcheson.

So he broke our engagement and left. That was five months ago." A familiar pang squeezed her heart, an echo of the immense sense of betrayal she'd felt at the time. Yet now, after the hurt had faded, she could see that she had never really loved Jeffrey.

Matthew remained silent, as though pondering his response. "I can sympathize, believe me. At first my wife appeared to support my career, but she soon began to resent my long hours at the hospital. It became a thorny issue in our marriage."

"I'm sorry. That must have been difficult."

"It was. I was constantly torn between my duty as a husband and my duty to my patients. Which is why when Priscilla died, I decided I would never remarry."

Shock spurted through Deirdre's system. That seemed wrong on so many levels. Despite his gruff demeanor, Matthew was kind and loyal. He would make a fine husband for someone. And the thought of Phoebe never having the love of a mother, of growing up with the dour Miss Shearing, made Deirdre's heart ache. "Being Phoebe's only parent must be difficult as well. Surely you've had to make time for her?"

He pressed his lips together. "I've tried. Finding a balance has been . . . problematic."

For the first time, Deirdre understood more behind Phoebe's emotional issues. Before she could respond, the children came running toward them.

Sean and Rose reached them first. "Aunt Dee-Dee! Mama said we could skip our lessons this afternoon to play with Phoebe and the puppies."

Betsy and Phoebe followed, their faces mirrors of delight.

Deirdre's spirits rose, buoyed by the children's infectious joy. "That's wonderful! I'm dying to see the puppies." She took Betsy by the hand and held out the other to Phoebe. The girl smiled and slipped her hand into Deirdre's.

She grinned at them. "Come on, girls. Let's race to the barn."

Matthew watched Deirdre dash across the meadow, the children doing their best to keep up with her. Her laughter blended with the childish giggles that floated on the air. How he envied her zest for life, the uncomplicated manner in which she put her all into every moment.

Matthew followed at a more sedate rate, surprised when Sean appeared beside him, mimicking Matthew's stride.

"Dr. Clayborne?"

"Yes, Sean."

"I'm sorry for making you have to rescue me and Aunt Dee-Dee from the horse. And for scaring Phoebe." Sean's words sounded stiff, as if his mother had prompted the apology.

Matthew glanced at the boy, whose gaze stayed glued to the ground. "You gave us all quite a scare. I hope you learned something from the incident."

"I learned a lot about cleaning up after horses."

Matthew coughed to cover a snort of laughter. "I was thinking more about respecting the rules."

"Oh yeah. Papa gave me a lecture about that. He said I have to set a good example for the other kids." The lad peered up at Matthew. "I hope Phoebe won't be too scared to ride our pony. She'll love Twizzle. He's really gentle."

Matthew's insides twisted at the thought. "We'll see."

"Do you ride horses, Dr. Clayborne?"

Matthew repressed a shudder. "I learned when I was young, but in the city, we use autos now."

Sean's expression of sorrow was almost comical.

They reached the Whelans' barn and entered through a door the others had left open. Inside, Matthew found a tidy space containing stalls, a work area, and a ladder to the loft. The pleasant scent of hay filled the area.

High-pitched squeals drew Matthew's attention to the far

corner where the girls knelt in the straw. Deirdre peered over their shoulders.

Rose and Betsy each clutched a ball of fur. Matthew moved closer, muscles tightening in fear that the mother might be protective of her pups.

But the black and white dog lay contentedly on the straw with three babies nursing.

Deirdre picked up a black pup with white markings and held it to her face. "Aren't you the sweetest thing?" She kissed the top of the animal's small head.

"That's Patches, Aunt Dee-Dee," Rose informed her. "Phoebe, do you want to hold one?"

His daughter raised her head, eyes imploring him for permission.

He forced his muscles to relax. "Go ahead."

"Here, take Patches." Deirdre placed the squirming puppy in Phoebe's arms.

Almost immediately, the animal nestled against her neck, and Phoebe's eyes grew round.

Matthew kept a close watch for any sign that Phoebe's breathing might be affected, but she seemed fine.

Deirdre turned to Matthew. "Your turn. Come and hold one."

"Oh no. I'm fine right here."

She grabbed his hand, tugging him forward. "No one can resist puppies. Am I right, kids?"

Rose and Betsy snorted as though they had trouble picturing him with one.

Matthew had only a second to nurse his indignation before Deirdre plopped a wriggling ball of fur in his arms.

"What's this one's name?" Deirdre asked.

"Rufus." Sean reached up to pat him. "He's my favorite."

The tiny body snuggled into Matthew's chest. Never having had a pet of his own, he was unused to animals, yet he found the rapid heartbeat and tiny whimpers oddly endearing.

Deirdre moved in close to stroke its ears. "He's a handsome boy. Aren't you, Rufus?"

She raised her head and smiled at Matthew, her face inches from his. The air seemed to congeal in his lungs. For several seconds, he couldn't catch his breath. All he saw were the startling green eyes, brimming with life, and the dimples that seemed to wink at him.

"Papa? Can I have a puppy?"

Every muscle in his body froze. Deirdre's astonished expression proved he hadn't imagined Phoebe's sweet voice. A voice he hadn't heard in ages.

Slowly, he crouched beside her, still holding the pup. "What did you say?" he whispered.

"Can I have a puppy?" Hope brightened her gaze.

He wanted to answer, but his mouth wouldn't cooperate. Hot prickles stung the backs of his eyes.

A warm hand squeezed his shoulder.

Deirdre leaned down to Phoebe. "Why don't you give your father time to think about it? The puppies are too young to leave their mother yet anyway."

Phoebe nodded, but the spark left her eyes and her bottom lip trembled.

Matthew's stomach clenched. He couldn't be responsible for any more disappointment in her young life. He cupped her chin with his free hand. "When the puppies are old enough, you may pick one for your own."

Pure joy beamed from her face. "Thank you, Papa. Thank you."

She launched herself into his arms, puppies and all. He gathered her to him, careful not to squish Rufus or Patches.

"Why are you crying, Aunt Dee-Dee?" Sean asked.

Tears glistened on Deirdre's cheeks as she leaned forward and kissed Phoebe's face. "I'm just happy Phoebe's going to get a puppy. I remember when I got my first pet."

Matthew set Phoebe on the ground, the dog still clutched in her arms.

Beside them, Betsy plopped down in the bed of straw. "Which one is your favorite, Phoebe?"

"I like Patches."

The whisper was the sweetest thing Matthew had ever heard. "Well, then," he said, "if no one minds, we'll choose Patches to become part of our family."

Family. It was time to remember that he and Phoebe were still a family, even if a rather unconventional one.

His daughter's smile and Deirdre's approving wink loosened the tightness in Matthew's chest.

Perhaps coming to Irish Meadows hadn't been a mistake after all.

11

CONNOR WATCHED JOE lead Excalibur around the enclosed pen and scratched his head. In a matter of days, the boy had transformed the unmanageable stallion into a creature as docile as a pet—an accomplishment Connor hadn't been able to achieve in the months he'd been working with the animal.

Connor lifted his boot from the fence and fought the pinch to his pride. He needed to see Joe as an asset, not as a source of competition. "Nice work, Joe," he called out.

Joe raised his head and nodded. Beneath the large hat, Connor couldn't quite determine the boy's expression, yet his cheeks turned a deeper shade of red.

For a boy, Joe certainly blushed a lot.

And spoke very little.

Not that there was anything wrong with the strong, silent type, but Connor sensed a source of angst within Joe, as if his silence hid a dark secret. Joe's home life was really none of his business, yet Connor couldn't simply ignore his suspicions. If the boy was in some kind of trouble, he wanted to help. Sam Turnbull would do no less, nor could Connor.

Connor followed Joe into the barn and down to Excalibur's stall. "Can I speak with you a minute, Joe?"

A look of fear leapt into the boy's eyes before he lowered his head. "Yes, sir." He continued unhooking the halter from Excalibur.

"How's everything going?"

Joe frowned before turning back to his task. "Fine."

Connor curbed a sigh of frustration. It would take a crowbar to pry any information out of this kid. He leaned against the stall door, trying not to feel like a complete idiot, poking into an employee's personal affairs. "I meant . . . are things all right at home?"

Joe's hand stilled on the straps. "Yes, sir."

All Connor's instincts screamed that the boy was lying. Connor forced himself to speak in a gentle manner, sensing Joe was as nervous as this high-strung stallion. He entered the stall and laid a hand on Joe's shoulder. "If you ever need anything, you can come to me. No questions asked."

Under Connor's palm, a tremor went through the boy's frame before he stepped away. "Thank you, Mr. O'Leary."

"Why don't you call me Connor? *Mr. O'Leary* and *sir* make me feel ancient."

A faint twitch lifted Joe's lips. "Okay," he said.

"Well then, I guess I'll leave you to your work." Connor walked out of the barn, his gut churning with unnamed emotions. Something wasn't right; he could feel it. Was the boy a runaway, maybe living in some abandoned hut? Or worse yet, camping out under the stars? With winter fast approaching, he had to be sure the boy had a proper roof over his head.

Connor tugged his hat down over his forehead with firm resolve. One way or another, he was determined to find out what the boy was hiding.

Later that day, at the time when Joe normally headed home, Connor sat astride his buckskin, Dagger, in the far pasture behind an oak tree, waiting for Joe to pass. If nothing else, maybe seeing where Joe lived might ease Connor's mind. He prayed the boy lived with his parents in a respectable house, and that Connor's imagination had been working overtime.

Right on schedule, Joe left the stables. He guided his horse down the road toward the neighboring farms.

Keeping back far enough not to be seen, Connor trailed the boy. About half a mile later, Joe slowed his horse. Connor quickly moved Dagger behind a thicket of bushes to remain out of sight. The boy looked right and left and then guided his mount across the grass toward a grove of trees.

Connor followed him through the wooded area, his heart thrumming. Why was Joe taking this strange route? When the boy exited into a clearing, Connor waited in the woods until he crested a small rise, then followed once more. He hoped he hadn't lost Joe's trail, but as he got to the top of the hill, Connor saw the old log cabin—Joe's obvious destination.

Joe rode his horse to the rear of the structure and, after several minutes, appeared on foot. He opened the door and entered the cabin.

Connor tried to make sense of the puzzle. From what he could tell, there was no evidence of anyone else living there. No wash hanging on a line, no flowers to brighten the windows, no remnants of a garden where the family grew their vegetables. Was Joe poaching on someone's land?

Connor mentally calculated the distance to the Sullivans' farm, then straightened in the saddle. Though they'd come around it by a different route, Connor was sure this cabin belonged to the Sullivans—that it usually housed the farm manager and his family.

Did Joe's father work for Mr. Sullivan? If so, why hadn't he mentioned it?

Connor set his jaw as he turned Dagger around. Seemed it was time to pay his friend Caleb Sullivan a visit and see what he could tell Connor about their foreman.

⚜

Once inside the cabin, Jo pulled off her father's hat, removed the annoying netting, and shook her long hair loose. In her bedroom, she threw the hat on her bed and grabbed her hairbrush. With hard strokes, she pulled the bristles through her hair, not even minding the snags. Anything was better than the infernal itching.

She quickly braided her hair, changed into a dress, and went to check on Pa. He awoke as she entered the main room.

"About time you came back," he groused. His unruly salt-and-pepper hair sprang up in all directions and a slight beard hugged his jaw.

Jo would have to get Seth to give Pa a bath and a haircut soon. "Can I get you anything before I start dinner?"

"Yeah, some whiskey."

Jo stiffened. Not this again. She'd hoped after this long without alcohol, Pa's cravings would wane. "How about some coffee?"

He snarled. Jo took that as a yes.

In the kitchen, she set the pot on the stove, then pulled a larger pan from the icebox and lifted the lid to examine the leftover soup. Barely enough to stretch for one more meal. Jo sent up a quick prayer that Seth would bring some food home with him.

When the coffee was ready, Jo filled a tin mug and brought it to her father.

"Feeling any better, Pa?" She set the cup on the rickety table beside him.

"My leg feels like it's on fire. You got any more salve?"

She went to the shelf in the kitchen and retrieved the tin of salve, as well as a basin of water and a cloth. She'd been trying her best to keep the wound on his shin clean, but the fact that it wasn't healing as fast as it should worried her. The swelling from the sprain had started to lessen, but the long gash seemed to be getting worse instead of better.

She knelt by the sofa and rolled up his pant leg, holding back a grimace of distaste. Not only did the wound look terrible, but it smelled bad. A sinking sensation settled in her stomach. This cut needed more than her meager skills.

Her pa needed a doctor.

Jo sighed. If she dared even mention it to her father, he'd bellow louder than the Sullivans' bull. But the angry redness, along with the putrid odor, told Jo that an infection had taken hold. Without treatment, Pa might lose his leg.

Jo lifted her head. She met her father's worried gaze. If only Pa didn't have such a distrust of doctors. She focused back on his leg, determined that this time she wouldn't give him a choice.

As she bathed the wound, her thoughts churned. Connor's sister was a nurse and the man staying at Irish Meadows was a doctor. Surely they would help if she asked.

She applied the salve as gently as possible. Pa sucked in a hard breath and swore. Jo could no longer sit by and do nothing. Pa might not be the best father in the world, but he was the only one she had.

She took the basin of dirty water to the door and flung it outward, a decision firming in her mind. Tomorrow she would ask Miss O'Leary if the doctor could come and examine Pa.

Jo cringed at the thought of having someone come here, of having to keep up the deception within these walls. What if they figured out she was lying? That she was really a girl?

They'd surely report back to Connor, who would send her packing faster than a flea off a dog. He might even warn the Sullivans about them.

What would they do if both she and Seth lost their jobs?

Jo swallowed hard and straightened her spine.

For the sake of her father's health, it was a risk she'd have to take.

Per Matthew's instructions, Deirdre had started giving Mama a massage every morning to limber up her muscles prior to Matthew's grueling exercise routines. The therapy definitely seemed to work better that way. This morning, Deirdre took special note of the way Mama's arm and leg reacted to the massage. Her muscles seemed looser, taking less time to become agile.

A flutter of joy moved through her. Mama was indeed showing small but significant signs of improvement.

She set her mother's heel gently on the floor. "How's that, Mama?"

Her mother gave a soft sigh. "Wonderful. I do believe the circulation is improving in my hand and foot."

"Your observation is correct, Kathleen." Matthew breezed in the door, looking crisp and efficient in his doctor's coat. "I see definite improvement in the overall condition of your muscles, and your grip is much better than when we started."

"Does this mean I can play the piano?" Mama quipped.

Matthew's lips twitched. "Soon, I hope."

A sudden rush of tears hit Deirdre with unexpected intensity. She moved to the far side of the room on the pretense of arranging the equipment, biting her bottom lip to gain control. Up until now, she'd managed to contain all trace of emotion, giving in to tears only when she was alone in her room. But this time was different. These were tears of pure gratitude. For the first time, Deirdre saw proof that her mother would make a full recovery.

She slipped a handkerchief from her pocket and tried to dab unobtrusively at her cheeks.

"Is everything all right?" Matthew whispered near her ear.

The small hairs on the back of her neck rose. "Fine." She stuffed her handkerchief back into her pocket.

"Then why are you crying?"

She glanced sideways at him and, noting his concerned expression, managed a smile. "I'm just so grateful Mama's getting better. I don't know how to thank you." On impulse, she gave him a quick hug. "Thank you for allowing me to assist with the therapy. It feels good to be able to do something to help her." She smiled again through her tears. "I think we make a pretty remarkable team."

Matthew cleared his throat. "That we do. Now, if you'll pass me the rubber ball, we'll continue our work."

She handed it to him. "I think I'll get some fresh air. I don't want Mama to see me upset."

He gave her a long look and nodded. "We'll be right here when you get back."

Deirdre walked out to the foyer, pulled her shawl from the hook, and draped it around her shoulders. As soon as she stepped outdoors, her tension seemed to fade away. A few minutes in the crisp autumn air would certainly restore her equilibrium, though she wasn't sure what had thrown her more, Mama's improvement or Dr. Clayborne's nearness. She only hoped her hug hadn't offended him. She really must learn to curb her enthusiasm.

Deirdre strolled along the path leading to the pastures and paused to appreciate the landscape.

"Excuse me, Miss O'Leary?"

A stable hand—the one who had saved them from the stallion—came up behind her. The boy's shoulders were slouched forward, his eyes almost hidden beneath the brim of his overlarge hat.

"It's Joe, isn't it?"

"Yes, ma'am."

At a sudden gust of wind, Deirdre pulled her shawl closer around her. "Please call me Deirdre. What can I do for you?"

"I understand you're a nurse." The boy's voice seemed forced lower than what was natural.

"I am." She peered at him. "Are you sick?"

"Not me . . . but my father is." He lifted his head to reveal vivid blue eyes shadowed with anxiety. Fresh-faced, with no hint of stubble on his jaw, the boy couldn't be more than sixteen.

"I'm sorry to hear that. What's the matter with him?"

"A leg wound. I think it's infected." Joe shuffled his feet, the worn boots seeming too large for him.

"I could give you some salve—"

"I've already tried that." He stopped and seemed to collect himself. "Could you . . . Would you ask the doctor if he'd come and examine my father?"

"That won't be necessary. I can do it."

"No offense, but I really think Pa needs a doctor."

Deirdre swallowed her ego and managed a nod. "I'll ask Dr. Clayborne. Where do you live?"

Joe bit his lip and looked around as though making sure they wouldn't be overheard. "In a cabin on the other side of the woods. It's kind of hard to find."

She stared at the boy. Something about him—about the whole situation—seemed odd, but she couldn't put her finger on what exactly bothered her. "We'll meet you by the stable when your shift ends." She had no doubt Matthew would agree to see the man.

Relief stole over Joe's face. "Thank you, ma'am."

Deirdre watched the nervous lad stride back toward the barn and made a mental note to speak to Connor about him. She trusted her brother's instincts about people. If anything was amiss, Connor would have noticed it, too.

Still, she didn't want to make trouble for the boy. To be fair, she'd wait until she'd seen the father. Then if her senses still told her something was wrong, she'd have to involve her brother.

"I have a favor to ask."

At the sound of Deirdre's voice, Matthew set the silver coffee-pot on the sideboard in the dining room. He'd been trying his best to forget the hug she'd given him. Forget the flowery scent of her hair beneath his nose and the feel of her warm figure in his arms.

"What type of favor?"

She reached for an apple from the bowl on the table. "You remember that young stable hand—the one who calmed the stallion?"

"Of course. He likely saved my life."

She cocked her head to one side, exposing the long line of her neck. "He asked if you would come and examine his father. Joe fears a leg wound has become infected."

Matthew stiffened. "I'm sure you're more than capable of handling it."

She smiled. "Thank you. I thought the same thing, but Joe insisted his father needed a doctor."

With deliberate care, Matthew stirred a spoon of sugar into his coffee, willing his breathing to remain even. The thought of treating a stranger's wounds unleashed a flood of anxiety, as well as a rush of unpleasant memories—dying soldiers on the battlefield, Priscilla wasting away before his eyes, his utter helplessness at not being able to save them. Perspiration beaded on his forehead as he grappled for a suitable excuse. "I promised Phoebe we'd spend time together . . . later today."

Deirdre swallowed a bite of apple. "It won't take long. You'd still have time for Phoebe." She studied him. "Is something wrong?"

He sighed. How did the woman manage to see right through him? "Of course not."

"Good. I'll come with you, and once you assess the situation,

I can do the treatments. I think Joe just needs the assurance that a doctor has seen the wound."

Matthew took a quick sip of coffee, attempting to steady his nerves. How threatening could a leg wound be? And he did owe the boy. "Very well."

"Thank you." The brilliant smile she gave him almost made it worthwhile.

She crossed to the door and paused to look back, mischief gleaming from her expressive eyes. "You do ride, don't you, Doctor?"

"Ride? As in horses?" His anxiety level shot skyward.

"Yes, unless you'd prefer a pony like Twizzle." She grinned, apparently enjoying his discomfort.

"I haven't ridden since I was a boy." He frowned. "Can't we take the car?"

She shook her head. "Not through the woods we can't."

"Oh." He drew himself up, trying to preserve some dignity.

Her laugh echoed through the room. "Don't worry. I'll find you our most docile mare. You'll be fine."

Matthew held back a sigh. This day was getting worse by the minute.

12

HOURS LATER, as Matthew struggled to remember how to sit in a saddle, he found himself wishing for the bustling streets of Toronto, where he could drive his car or catch a streetcar with equal ease. The only saving grace was that Joe's swayback horse, which appeared older and stiffer than Matthew's mount, was setting the pace, so at least Matthew didn't have to worry about holding up the entourage.

Deirdre, on the other hand, looked perfectly at ease on her brown and white mare. Matthew focused on keeping an appropriate distance from her horse, ducking low-hanging branches as they plodded through the woods. The weather had turned decidedly colder, making Matthew wish he'd worn a scarf and a heavier coat. At last, they came to a clearing, and when they crested a hill, a log cabin came into view.

"This is it," Joe called over his shoulder.

They followed him around the side of the cabin to a wooden lean-to, where they dismounted and tied the horses to the posts.

Matthew struggled to find his footing with legs that quivered like jelly.

Joe led them to the front of the cabin. "Give me a minute to prepare my father. He doesn't know you're coming." He paused. "I should warn you my pa is kind of cranky. Don't take it personally."

When the boy slipped inside the door, Matthew turned to Deirdre. "Does something about Joe seem odd to you?"

Her eyes widened. "I thought the same thing." She rubbed her hands together and blew on her fingers. "I'm not sure what to expect in there."

Matthew clenched the handle of his bag, suddenly glad he hadn't allowed Deirdre to come alone. Heaven only knew what conditions they might find inside.

Joe appeared and waved them forward. "He's not happy, so please excuse anything he might say."

They followed Joe inside and found themselves in a kitchen with wooden cabinets, a table, and a woodstove. Joe led them across to the living area where a man lay on a faded sofa near the stone hearth. Immediately, an unpleasant odor hit Matthew. From the man's unkempt appearance, it became evident he hadn't partaken of a bath in quite some time.

Joe stood nervously beside the couch. "Pa, this is Dr. Clayborne and Miss O'Leary."

He glared at them. "I don't need no doctor."

"Why don't you let me be the judge of that?" Matthew set his bag on the warped floor. "Since we've come all this way, I might as well take a look."

The man shifted, attempting to sit up. "My leg is fine."

Joe shook his head. "No, it's not. The wound's not healing."

"Unless you're willing to lose your leg, sir, I suggest you let me examine it."

The man scowled but finally lifted his foot onto the low, rickety table in front of him. Matthew bent to peel back the material, which had been cut to allow him access. The stench made Matthew's eyes water.

As soon as he lifted the makeshift bandage, Matthew understood why the smell seemed familiar. Gangrene had set into the wound. His stomach churned at the realization that he'd have to do more than just clean and apply salve.

He glanced at Deirdre. She gave a nod to indicate she understood the severity of the condition.

Matthew turned back to the patient. "I'm afraid there's evidence of gangrene in this wound. It would be in your best interest to go to the nearest hospital so they can treat you properly." And relieve Matthew of the duty.

"Gangrene." A flicker of fear passed over the man's scruffy face. "That's bad."

"Yes, it is. If you don't take care of this, you'll likely lose your leg from the knee down." Matthew would not sugarcoat the issue for the man. He needed to know what was at stake.

"I ain't going to no hospital. Can't you do something?"

"I don't have the necessary—"

"Either fix me here or leave. I don't care."

Joe knelt beside his father. "Pa, please." Tears stood out in the boy's eyes.

Matthew's gut clenched at the boy's apparent fear. Was Joe alone in the world except for this man? Was that why he was working at Irish Meadows? To support his ailing father?

"No hospital. That's final."

Once again Matthew faced a situation where his actions could affect a man's life. Did he have the right to force him into a facility for proper treatment? Matthew scanned the crude living quarters, which likely didn't even include a lavatory. Out in the middle of nowhere, what chance did this man have? Yet how could they get him to leave if he didn't want to?

Matthew exhaled, willing his anxiety to lessen. He'd have to do his best with what he had. "What's your name, sir?"

"Clayton Miller."

"Clayton, if I treat you here, I will have to excavate the wound in order to eradicate the infection before it spreads. But I warn you, it won't be pleasant."

The man's hard gaze pinned him. "Do it."

Matthew nodded. He opened his bag and took out a clean towel and his instruments. "Do you have any alcohol in the house?"

A sharp intake of breath sounded. Matthew looked up to see Joe's pinched expression.

"No alcohol."

Clayton seemed to perk up. "Come on, Joe," he wheedled. "I could use a little whiskey to help with the pain."

The man was practically begging. Perhaps he had issues with alcohol.

"It's not to drink," Matthew put in calmly. "It's to sterilize the wound."

Clayton's face fell. "A swallow or two wouldn't hurt."

"Yes, it would." Joe remained adamant. "In any case, we have nothing in the house."

Deirdre came forward. "I have some rubbing compound that may serve." She set her own small bag on the table.

"That will do. Thank you, Nurse."

Clayton squinted at her. "You're a nurse? I thought you were one of them rich O'Learys."

Deirdre straightened. "I am both, sir." She turned to Matthew. "Shall I get water to wash the area first?"

"Yes, thank you."

"I'll help." Joe hurried to the kitchen area, where he grabbed a basin from the rough shelf. "The pump's outside."

Deirdre shot Matthew a concerned glance, then followed Joe out the door.

Clayton grabbed Matthew's arm, his bony fingers pinching. "Doc, you gotta get me some whiskey. I need it, for medicinal purposes like you said. And my . . . boy's got a thing about alcohol."

Matthew studied the desperation on the man's features. His suspicions appeared correct. "I'm afraid I can't do that. Once you're back on your feet, what you do is your own concern."

The door opened, saving further debate. Deirdre brought over the basin of water and a cloth and set about cleaning the wound. Despite her pallor, she worked without complaint.

Matthew moved to the hearth, glad to find a small flame glowing, and sterilized his scalpel.

"You might want something to bite down on." He flicked a glance to Deirdre. Her face was pale, but Joe's was worse. "If anyone is going to faint, I'd appreciate it if they would leave now."

"Just get it over with, Doc." The man gripped the arm of the sofa and closed his eyes.

"Here goes." Matthew paused for a second to inhale and make sure his hand was steady. If he were inclined to pray, now would be the time. Relying on his training, he steadied his hand and made the first cut. As quickly as possible, he removed the affected areas, thankful to note the gangrene hadn't spread through to the bone.

Sweat poured from Clayton's brow, dripping down the sides of his face.

Matthew was vaguely aware of Joe rushing from the room but couldn't concern himself with the boy. Without flinching, Deirdre held the man's leg steady, and despite the groans of protest, Clayton held up well.

Matthew had saved the worst cut for last, knowing it would be painful, going so near the bone. "Hold on. Almost done."

Clayton's scream of agony jarred everyone.

"Cleanse the area please, Nurse O'Leary."

She obeyed quickly. Then Matthew applied a healthy dose of salve and proceeded to bandage the entire shin.

Deirdre used a wet cloth to mop the man's face.

"Your ankle is swollen and has residual bruising," Matthew observed. "Did you injure it at the same time?"

Clayton opened one eye. "I had a bad fall a couple of weeks ago. Sprained my foot and got this gash."

"Why didn't you seek medical help?"

"Don't put much stock in doctors ever since one let my wife die. Figured Joe could take care of me."

One let my wife die. Just as Matthew had let Priscilla die. He wiped a bead of sweat from his forehead and forged on.

When he finished, Deirdre rose, collecting the waste and the basin. "I'll clean this up and be back in a minute."

Once she left, Matthew snipped the gauze and pulled the pant leg back in place. "Clayton, I suggest you take a sponge bath and get some fresh clothes. It's essential to keep everything around you clean to avoid further infection."

Clayton slumped back against the sofa. "Gotcha, Doc. Do you think you can save my leg?"

Matthew exhaled softly. "I've done the best I can under the circumstances, but I can't make any guarantees." He repacked his bag, snapped it shut, and then rose. "I'll come back in a couple of days to check on you."

"Thanks, Doc. I appreciate it."

Deirdre dumped the contents of the basin into the grass and pumped in fresh water. Using one of the clean rags, she washed out the bowl. As she worked, she took a minute to let her system settle and attempted to discover what was niggling at her. Something about Joe's mannerisms—his voice, his nervousness—bothered her.

And this place. A remote cabin with only Joe and his ailing father.

Deirdre scanned the trees and the land surrounding them.

If she didn't know better, she'd say this was part of the Sullivan property. This cabin might belong to one of the workers on their farm. Was Clayton Miller working for Mr. Sullivan?

When she finished drying the basin, she rose and walked past the lean-to. A retching sound drew her attention. Joe was bent over in the grass, one hand holding the ever-present hat to his head.

Poor kid must have a weak stomach. He should have left the room when Matthew gave him the chance.

"Are you all right, Joe?"

The boy's head jerked up. "I—I'm fine. Just queasy."

Why was he always so nervous? An unwelcome suspicion arose. Did Mr. Miller abuse the boy? Was that why he seemed so skittish?

A breeze blew strands of Deirdre's hair about her face as she approached the still-kneeling boy. "Don't feel bad. That was an unpleasant procedure, even for me." Deirdre handed him a handkerchief from her pocket.

He wiped his face and the back of his neck.

"Why don't you take off your hat? Pouring water over your head might help the nausea pass more quickly."

Joe shot to his feet. "I'm fine." He looked like a spooked horse ready to bolt.

Deirdre took a step forward. "Joe, is it only you and your father living here?"

He swiped a sleeve across his face. "And my older brother."

Deirdre began to piece the puzzle together. "Does your brother work for Mr. Sullivan?"

Again the wariness crept across Joe's features. "Yes."

"What does your father do?"

One of the horses let out a loud neigh in the lean-to.

"Pa was supposed to work on the farm, but he got injured." Joe set off toward the cabin, forcing Deirdre to follow.

As they rounded the corner, a strange man came charging

into view, carrying a rifle. The minute he spied Deirdre, he skidded to a sudden halt. His gaze ricocheted from Deirdre to Joe and back again.

"What's going on here, Joe?"

From the way Joe's expression turned to guilty surprise, Deirdre braced herself for yet another twist in the mystery surrounding the Miller family.

13

MATTHEW WALKED OUT of the cabin and froze, his intended words flying straight from his mind.

A stranger in a bulky overcoat and with shaggy hair and a scruff of beard stood scowling at Deirdre and Joe.

Immediately, the man swiveled toward Matthew, raising the rifle. "Who the devil are you?"

Matthew held up his free hand in a gesture of surrender. "I'm Dr. Clayborne, here to treat Mr. Miller."

Joe moved forward. "It's okay, Seth. I asked them to come to look at Pa's leg."

Ah, so this was Joe's brother. Now that Matthew looked closer, he could see the family resemblance.

The furrows in Seth's brow eased a fraction as he lowered the weapon. "You're a doctor?"

"Yes." Matthew stepped quietly in front of Deirdre in case Seth changed his mind about shooting something. "I'm afraid I found gangrene in your father's leg."

"Gangrene?" Seth gave Matthew a hard stare. "Will he lose his leg?"

Matthew eyed the rifle. "If you put the gun away, I'll explain everything."

Seth leaned it against the outer cabin wall. "Sorry. I was out hunting but didn't have much luck."

Matthew's stomach muscles unclenched, and he took a breath. "Nurse O'Leary and I did a minor surgical procedure on your father's leg. If you can keep the infection away, he should be fine, but I'm not making any guarantees. He should be in a hospital." Matthew shifted to stand at Deirdre's side. "I'd like to come back in a day or two to check on him." He waited, still not sure how this man would react.

Seth shot another glance at Joe, then nodded. "Okay. That would be good." He squinted at Deirdre. "Did he say your name was O'Leary?"

Deirdre tilted her chin. "That's right. Joe works at our stables. Why?"

Seth shrugged. "Just curious why a woman like you would be out here."

"Joe knew I was a nurse and asked us to come. It's a good thing we did."

Despite her defensive tone, Matthew sensed an undercurrent of nerves. He didn't blame her. The Miller family was definitely an odd bunch. He'd have to make sure Deirdre didn't come back here alone. Joe seemed harmless enough, but Matthew didn't trust the two older Millers for a minute.

"Miss O'Leary and I have to get back," Matthew said. "Joe, we'll talk later about a follow-up visit." He took Deirdre by the elbow and gave a slight squeeze, prompting her to hand the empty basin to Joe.

"Thank you both," Joe said. "Can you find your way back?"

"I believe so," Deirdre said. "See you tomorrow, Joe."

Matthew guided her toward the lean-to where the animals

were tied. Never did he think he'd look forward to getting back on that horse. But he didn't think he'd take a full breath until they were back on O'Leary property. Those Millers were as cagey as a family of outlaws. Judging from Deirdre's pale features, she seemed as unsettled as he.

When they arrived back at Irish Meadows, one of the hands came to take the animals from them. Even as Deirdre handed over the reins, she remained silent.

He fell in step beside her as they made their way across to the house. "You're very quiet. Is anything the matter?"

She looked at him with worried eyes. A few freckles stood out on her pale face. "I'm not sure. Something seems wrong about that family."

"I got the same feeling."

"It's clear Joe is terrified. Do you think his father could be abusing him?"

Matthew considered her question. "It's possible. Though my initial feeling is that they may be hiding from the law." He stared out over the windswept meadows. "I do believe Clayton has a problem with alcohol, which may be contributing to Joe's troubles."

"That poor boy. What can we do to help?"

One thing about Deirdre—she had a heart the size of Irish Meadows itself, always wanting to help someone in need.

He paused at the porch stairs. "All we have are theories. Let's wait until the follow-up exam and see what we can find out then."

The breeze tugged at her hair beneath her hat, pulling strands across her cheek. "I don't know, Matthew. Waiting is not my strong suit." She sighed. "But I'll leave it for today."

Matthew could tell by the set of her jaw it was the best he was going to get. A distraction might be in order.

He held the front door open for her. "Why don't we take Phoebe over to see her puppy again?"

A bright smile was his reward. "That sounds wonderful."
Indeed it did.

On Sunday morning, Matthew followed the congregation
out of the small country church, nodding politely at the various
members who paused to welcome him and his daughter. At the
base of the stairs, the reverend stood greeting his parishioners,
despite the less-than-ideal weather. Gusty winds tore at the
man's robes and whipped the gray hair about his head.

Matthew pulled his coat collar tighter, keeping one hand
firmly around Phoebe's fingers. He hadn't been to church with
any regularity since he was a boy—since before his mother
died—and never imagined he'd go back. Even his marriage
to Priscilla had taken place outdoors on her parents' estate.
He'd only agreed to come today to please Phoebe, who'd
wanted to join the Whelan children. Yet he'd found the com-
munity atmosphere, as well as the reverend's sermon, pleasantly uplifting.

He stood in line to greet Reverend Filmore. The stout man
laid a hand on Phoebe's head and murmured a blessing, which
made Phoebe smile. Something warm curled around Matthew's
heart. He could count on one hand the number of times she'd
laughed since her mother's death, but since coming to Irish
Meadows, she gave her smiles freely. More important, she'd
started talking again.

Phoebe broke away from him and ran to join Betsy at her
mother's side. The two girls giggled and skipped down the
walkway toward another group of children.

Matthew's heart clutched, grieving for a fraction of a second
the fact that his daughter was becoming more independent and
less reliant on him. Then he released a quiet sigh. Kathleen and
Deirdre were right. Phoebe needed to be around other children,
to laugh and play and enjoy her childhood.

Deirdre's distinctive laugh sounded over the buzz of conversation. Matthew spotted her standing beside the man he'd learned was a neighbor. Caleb Sullivan. The same man he had seen Deirdre talking with at Irish Meadows.

Sullivan leaned in to speak to Deirdre, his head almost touching hers.

She said something in response, smiling up at him.

Matthew shoved his clenched fist into his coat pocket. It was obvious Sullivan was smitten with her. Did Deirdre feel the same? The very idea made Matthew squirm in his shoes.

Connor and Gilbert joined the pair, and the tension in Matthew's shoulders eased. He needed to put Deirdre's romantic interests out of his mind. They were no concern of his. He set his jaw and turned his attention to Brianna, who was headed his way with a woman beside her.

"Dr. Clayborne, I'd like you to meet my friend Clara Baldwin. She is most interested in the work you're doing with my mother."

Matthew bowed to the attractive blond woman. "A pleasure, ma'am."

She smiled. "Please call me Clara."

"Very well then, I'm Matthew."

"Clara's father, Mr. Sullivan, is having health issues due to crippling arthritis. Her brother, Caleb, has had to come back to help with the farm."

Caleb. There was that name again.

Clara came closer. "I wondered if the therapy you're using on Mrs. O'Leary might help someone like my father."

Glad to focus on a subject he loved, Matthew smiled. "Back home I've been reading about such cases, though I haven't had the opportunity to conduct any clinical trials."

He detailed a few of the cases he'd read about.

Clara seemed to hang on his every word. "Could I bring my father over one afternoon? I'd appreciate your opinion on whether it might be worth our while to seek treatment."

He hesitated. What could it hurt to meet the man and give a quick assessment? "I'd be happy to."

She beamed at him. "Thank you so much, Doctor. I'll be in touch soon."

As the women excused themselves to find their husbands, Matthew's thoughts spun. Perhaps there was more call for physical therapy than he'd imagined. Perhaps he could make the transition from treating soldiers to treating civilians without too many problems.

"Matthew. We're leaving now." Deirdre's voice cut through his musings.

His heart sped as he turned, steeling himself to guard his emotions. "I'll get Phoebe."

"No need. Brianna said she could come back with them." Deirdre fell in step beside him as they made their way to James's auto. "I saw you talking with Clara Baldwin. I hope none of her children are ill?"

"No. She wanted to ask me about her father, whether I thought therapy might help him."

Instant concern filled her eyes. "Caleb told me how bad his father's arthritis has become." She gave him a questioning look. "Are you going to treat him?"

"I agreed to meet with him to see if I felt therapy might help him. There's no point in my beginning treatment if I'm leaving soon."

A shadow crossed her features. "I don't think Mr. Sullivan would agree to go into the city for treatment. It's a shame that there's nothing around here." Her eyes brightened with enthusiasm. "Would you ever consider opening a clinic on Long Island? Phoebe's doing so well here. It would be wonderful if you could stay."

For an instant, excitement rose in his chest. What would it be like to open a clinic here, away from the mistakes of his past, where his daughter was thriving? Then reality hit like a cold splash of water. "I'm afraid that would be impossible. Phoebe's grandparents would never allow it."

Deirdre came to a halt, her brows pinched. "Why not? If it would benefit Phoebe's health?"

James was busy talking with a man on the other side of the car. Matthew lowered his voice. It wasn't something he wanted everyone to hear. "I'm afraid I have a rather strained relationship with Priscilla's parents. They harbor a great deal of resentment toward me due to Priscilla's death. When Phoebe was released from the sanatorium, they . . ." He gulped in a breath. Best just to tell her the whole sordid affair. "They tried to get custody."

Horror bled over her face. "Oh no. How terrible." She grasped his arm. "Did they take you to court?"

"It didn't get that far. I can't be certain, but I believe Victor intervened on my behalf. The Pentergasts did, however, make me promise to keep Phoebe close by and allow weekly visits."

"Did they give permission for you to bring Phoebe here, then?"

A flash of guilt surfaced. "They don't know we're here. They're in England and won't be back until December. Since we'll be home long before then, I didn't see the need to bother them."

"I'm so sorry about your in-laws, Matthew. That must be such a strain for you."

"I try not to let it bother me. For Phoebe's sake. She adores her grandparents."

Deirdre's face softened. "I'm sure she does. I always wanted grandparents when I was a kid."

"You didn't have any?"

"No, they died before I was born." She smiled. "But my sister-in-law Maggie's mother has been like a surrogate grandmother ever since she moved here from Ireland."

Matthew couldn't keep his eyes from her vivacious face, reminding him of another benefit to moving here. Of being able to explore these feelings that he was growing tired of fighting.

"How about you?" she asked. "Do you have grandparents?"

He swallowed and let his gaze drop. "I have no family left, except Phoebe." Which was why he couldn't allow anything or anyone to jeopardize their relationship.

Any thought of moving here vanished like a puff of air.

Besides, as soon as Kathleen regained her strength, Deirdre would be returning to her medical studies in Boston. Studies that would take many years to complete.

Even if he gained the courage to act on his attraction, there'd be no point. Nothing could come of it, since their futures were obviously headed in very different directions.

Matthew tugged the brim of his hat down tighter to combat a gust of wind, at the same time attempting to secure his wayward thoughts back to the practicality of his usual existence.

Nothing to be gained from useless fantasy.

On Monday morning, Connor skipped breakfast in the dining room, wanting to be in the barn the moment Joe arrived. Deirdre had told him about her visit to the Miller cabin and expressed some concerns about Joe. Connor promised to try once more to get Joe to talk to him. Now that he knew a bit more about the situation and that Joe's brother was filling in as the Sullivans' foreman, Connor hoped that Joe would confide in him.

He jammed on his hat and braced against the cold morning air. His breath created white puffs that lingered in front of him. Winter was definitely on its way here a little earlier than usual. They might even have frost tonight.

He'd started down the path toward the barn when a movement in the enclosure caught his attention. Connor's heart chugged to a halt in his chest.

Joe was attempting to mount Excalibur.

A chill of foreboding raced through Connor's veins. Joe had made progress with Excalibur in recent days, but was the stallion ready for a rider?

Connor quickened his pace to the fence. "Joe, wait!"

His warning came too late. Joe hauled himself up into the saddle.

Excalibur's whole body shuddered.

Connor clenched the top fence rail and held his breath, bracing for what was to come.

Sure enough, the horse gave a loud trumpet and reared, front hooves slashing the air. Joe clung like a burr to the horse's mane and managed to stay in the saddle. The stallion bucked and jumped, leaping around the enclosure like a jack rabbit. Any minute now, Joe would lose his grip and be flung off.

Connor ran to pull a length of rope from the corner post and leapt over the fence into the pen. He twirled the lasso and raced toward the animal, keeping to the rear as much as possible to avoid the hooves. He let the rope fly, momentarily relieved when it landed over Excalibur's head.

But then, to Connor's horror, the horse did a vicious twist in midair, attempting to dislodge both the rope and the rider. A scream sliced through Connor's nerves as Joe hurtled through the air, landing with a sickening thud.

Excalibur pulled the rope from Connor's fingers and streaked to the opposite side of the enclosure.

Connor ran to Joe's side and carefully rolled him over. "Joe, are you hurt?"

The boy groaned but didn't open his eyes.

Fearing a broken limb or worse, Connor ran his hands over the boy's limbs. Immediately, Joe flailed and attempted to rise.

"Whoa. Stay put for a minute." Connor leaned in to pin him down, then stilled as the feel of distinct curves beneath the boy's clothing registered in his brain.

Joe's eyes flew open. He stared for no more than a second, then raised up and pushed Connor hard. Pain shot through Connor's chest, and with a surprised grunt, he fell backward.

Joe half limped, half ran out of the enclosure. By the time Connor got to his feet and dusted himself off, Joe was nowhere in sight.

Connor's mind swirled with doubts. In the heat of the moment, had he imagined the feminine figure? If not, then why did Joe shove him and bolt?

Anger rushed up in a hot wave. Connor had had enough of all the secrets. He was getting to the bottom of it—now.

He glanced over to make sure Excalibur had settled. Then he stormed out of the pen and across to the working barn. Inside, he scanned the main aisle, which was empty. He stopped and listened, finally hearing some labored breathing.

"Come out, Joe. Right now."

Connor waited. Two seconds later, Joe stepped out of one of the stalls, eyes cast down at the ground. His hand clutched his midsection. Dirt streaked his cheeks.

Connor marched toward him, attempting to curb his temper. "What possessed you to do something so foolish? Clearly Excalibur's not ready for a rider."

Joe lifted his head. "I thought he was."

Connor paced several feet away and back. "You were supposed to consult me before any drastic measures were taken. That was our agreement."

"I'm sorry. I—"

"You could have been killed." The truth of his words sank in, and a spasm clutched Connor's chest.

"I'm sorry," Joe repeated.

Connor blew out a hard breath, hoping to expel the remaining anger with it. "Come up to the house. I want the doctor or my sister to make sure you're okay."

Joe's eyes widened. "That's not necessary. I'm fine."

"No arguments. Let's go."

Connor stomped out of the barn, banking back his frustration. Why didn't he just yank Joe's hat off and be done with it? But he couldn't bring himself to do that. What if his suspicions were correct and Joe was indeed a female?

It would be too humiliating—for both of them.

No, it would be better to have Deirdre examine the boy and see if she could determine the truth.

Later that day, Connor guided Dagger along the path to the Sullivan property and attempted to ignore the prickle of irritation that crept up his spine. When he'd finally had a chance to talk to Deirdre, she'd told him Joe had refused to let her examine him, insisting he was fine—a fact that only made Connor more suspicious. Was Joe worried that Deirdre would want to check for bruises and, in doing so, determine he wasn't really a male?

The situation had been eating away at Connor all afternoon. Short of confronting Joe, which could prove horribly embarrassing for all concerned, Connor decided his best course of action was to once again follow him home—and this time get closer to the cabin to see what he could find out.

When he reached the wooden structure, Connor waited for Joe to enter the cabin, then moved Dagger to a spot in the trees that afforded him a good view of the door. He was prepared to wait as long as necessary to find out what was going on with the Miller family.

The wind picked up, and even though the trees sheltered Connor from the worst of it, the cold started to creep into his bones. He pulled up his wool collar and breathed in a lungful of frigid air. If this cold kept up, it wouldn't be long before the first snowfall.

The door to the cabin squeaked open. Connor squinted to

see who would emerge. A girl came out, dressed in a plain skirt and a bulky coat, carrying a pail. Her long, fair hair bounced as she walked toward the pump.

Connor's heart beat furiously in his chest. He wasn't close enough to make out the girl's face. He'd have to get nearer. Slipping from Dagger's back, he made his way through the thicket toward the girl.

Intent on filling her pail, she didn't notice him approaching. "Joe?"

Her head flew up. She gave a startled cry, and the bucket slipped from her hand, splashing water over her skirt.

Connor moved closer until the sight of familiar blue eyes cemented his feet to the ground. Even in her simple attire, her hair loose about her shoulders, she was one of the prettiest girls he'd ever seen.

His chest churned with unnamed emotions as he stared at her. "Why?" he croaked out at last. "Why are you pretending to be a boy?"

She bit her bottom lip. "You wouldn't understand."

He hardened himself against the tears that bloomed in her eyes. "I think you owe me an explanation."

She stared at him for several seconds, then turned to retrieve the pail. Her fingers shook on the handle. "My father got injured, so my brother had to take his place as foreman at the Sullivans'." She swiped some hair from her face. "I was supposed to fill in at Irish Meadows just until Pa got better—but instead he got worse."

Ignoring a tug of sympathy, Connor allowed his anger free rein. "And then what? Your brother would show up and take your place—no questions asked?" He threw out his hands. "You didn't think I'd care that you'd been lying to me for weeks?"

She cringed and stepped back. "We were just trying to survive."

"And that made it okay to betray my trust?"

Her expression hardened. "Would you have hired me if you'd known I was a girl?"

Connor clamped his mouth shut. "No."

Her slim frame shook. "I knew I could do the job, if I was given the chance. I'm good with horses."

"You almost got yourself killed by one." Again Connor's temper flared, thinking of her being thrown by the stallion, the jolt of terror he'd felt when her body had hit the ground.

"I'll be more careful from now on." She placed the pail beneath the pump and yanked on the handle, sending a flood of water into the container.

He gave her an incredulous stare. "You really think I'd allow you to come back after this?"

The color bled from her face. "No one needs to know I'm a girl."

Connor snorted, so consumed by her betrayal he couldn't see straight.

"Please, Connor. We need the money."

"Why?" he snarled. "You have Seth's salary and a free roof over your head."

She dropped her gaze to the pail at her feet. "Work's been scarce for my father these past few years. He has a lot of debts to repay—"

"Josephine. Where in tarnation are you?" A man's voice bellowed from the open door.

Panic flitted across her features. "Coming, Pa," she hollered, then turned to Connor. "I have to go. Can we talk about this tomorrow? Please?"

Connor hesitated, calling himself every sort of fool for letting her pleading chip away at his anger.

"Josephine!"

Desperation brewed in her eyes. "You're a man of integrity, Connor O'Leary. I know you'll do the right thing." She picked up the pail and hurried toward the cabin, throwing him one last anxious look before disappearing inside.

He stood staring at the door for several seconds, then slowly headed back to his horse, his mind swirling. How could he allow Joe— *Josephine*—to continue working for him, now that he knew she was a girl? Her gender shouldn't matter, since he knew she could do the job even better than some of their current hands. But her talent wouldn't matter to the others.

The reality remained that he would be the laughingstock of Long Island if word got out. Just thinking about Daddy's reaction made Connor shudder. He'd worked hard to earn his father's respect, and now with a promotion hanging in the balance, there was no way Connor could allow a slip of a girl to destroy his reputation.

No matter how pretty she was.

No, Josephine Miller would have to find herself another job.

14

MATTHEW STOOD at the French doors in the O'Learys' parlor, staring out at the barren landscape. As much as he tried, he couldn't shake the insidious sense of foreboding that had plagued him since he'd awakened. Perhaps it had something to do with the drastic change in the weather—the almost oppressive gray clouds that hung in the sky, the fierce wind that whipped the last leaves from the nearly bare branches.

More likely, it had something to do with the time of year. November was the month when his younger brother, George, had succumbed to polio, and then—one year later—in a haze of grief, his mother had taken her own life, leaving Matthew and his father alone.

Matthew turned away from the window. Phoebe had started going to the Whelans' every day to do her lessons with them, a fact he'd gradually gotten accustomed to. But today, he hadn't wanted to let her go, fearing the bitter weather would prove detrimental to her health. To allay his concerns, Deirdre had made sure that when the Whelan children arrived to walk with Phoebe, she was bundled up warmer than an Arctic explorer.

"It might snow today, Papa," she'd said, her eyes bright with excitement beneath a borrowed red beret and matching scarf. "Betsy says we can make snow angels."

Faced with such childish joy, Matthew found he couldn't deny Phoebe the opportunity for such an adventure. "That sounds fun." He'd kissed her cheek before the children had scurried out the door.

Now, in the waning afternoon light, Matthew fought the urge to rush over to the Whelan house and carry his daughter back here where he could ensure her safety. Would he ever overcome this paralyzing fear of losing her?

"There you are, Doctor."

Matthew turned to see Deirdre wheeling Kathleen into the room.

Deirdre's beaming smile could almost chase away the gloom of the day. "I'd hoped you'd be able to join us. Mama wants to try a few notes on the piano."

Determined not to let his despondent mood affect them, Matthew forced his features to lighten. "I'm glad I'm here, then."

Deirdre moved the bench away and wheeled her mother over to the keyboard. She lifted Kathleen's affected arm and laid her fingers on the ivory keys. Kathleen flexed her good hand and placed it in position.

Matthew couldn't help but worry at the impact this might have on his patient. If Kathleen failed to accomplish what she hoped, the disappointment might set her progress back. Still, he had no right to stop her from trying.

Kathleen raised tentative eyes to him. "Well, Matthew, let's see if all our hard work has paid off."

Words of encouragement froze on his tongue. He couldn't seem to do or say anything.

Sudden warmth encompassed his hand. He looked down at

Deirdre's fingers entwined with his. His gaze moved to her face, where he found a subtle anxiety in the shadows of her eyes and knew he wasn't alone in his concern for Kathleen.

Keeping her hand discreetly linked with his, Deirdre peered over her mother's shoulder. "Whenever you're ready, Mama."

Kathleen inhaled and let out her breath. At first, only her right hand moved, eliciting lovely notes from the magnificent instrument. Matthew wished he knew more about music, for he had no idea when to expect her injured hand to join in.

Finally, the bent fingers shifted on the keys. Matthew held his breath. Would she have enough strength to make the notes sound?

Her fingers slid in silence over the instrument, only the keys under her right hand making any noise. Still Kathleen played on. The tense muscles in her back and shoulders spoke of the effort she was making. After several excruciating minutes, her left hand struck a note. She continued as though filled with renewed purpose, and a few more notes became audible. Some of her fingers had more strength than others, but the fact that she could move them at all thrilled Matthew.

When at last her fingers stilled, Kathleen turned her head. Tears streamed down both cheeks.

"You did it, Mama!" Deirdre swooped over to embrace her mother.

A smile bloomed, followed by a laugh of triumph. "It needs a lot of improvement, but it's a start." Kathleen reached out a hand to Matthew. "Thanks to you, Doctor."

Matthew swallowed a lump of raw emotion and squeezed her hand. "It's all your doing, Kathleen. You put in the time and effort. I merely guided you."

"Mama's right. We owe her success to you." Moisture glistened in Deirdre's eyes, making them shimmer like leaves in a summer rain.

She threw her arms around his neck and pressed a kiss to his cheek. "How can we ever thank you?"

Her whispered words fanned his ear, sending a thrilling vibration through his torso. The intoxicating scent of vanilla surrounded him. As his arms tightened around her, the overwhelming urge to kiss her rose through his chest.

The discreet clearing of a throat broke the spell, and Deirdre pulled away, her cheeks flushed. "I'd better take Mama back to her room for a rest before dinner."

Matthew clasped his hands behind his back, certain they must be shaking. "Congratulations again, Kathleen."

Kathleen's answering smile made her appear years younger. "Thank you, Matthew."

He remained in the parlor for several minutes, willing his system to settle. Never had he experienced such a powerful reaction to a woman, and indeed the force of his longing for Deirdre had shocked him.

He walked to the window once again, not entirely surprised to see fat snowflakes falling over the dormant garden beyond. He glanced at the clock on the mantel. Surely Phoebe would be back any minute. If the weather worsened, he'd ask Deirdre about going to the Whelans' home by horse to retrieve her.

Still unsettled, not only by his reaction to Deirdre, but by the impending snowstorm, he headed out into the hallway. Perhaps some fresh air might restore his sense of equilibrium. He could start walking toward the Whelans' and perhaps meet the children halfway.

In the front hall, he retrieved his coat from the closet. As he started to don it, the door burst open. Rose, Betsy, and Phoebe piled into the foyer, snowflakes clinging to their hats and coats. The look of terror on Rose's face stilled Matthew's hand.

"Dr. Clayborne," she gasped out. "We need help."

Content that Mama was settled in her bed, Deirdre stepped out into the hall and closed the door with a quiet *click*.

Immediately noise from the front of the house drew her attention. Deirdre hastened to the foyer to caution the children not to disturb their grandmother, but the wide-eyed fear on the girls' faces chased all reprimands from her mind.

Deirdre frowned and rushed forward. "Rose, Betsy, what is it?"

Tears spilled down Rose's cheeks. "Aunt Dee-Dee! Sean's hurt. You have to come and help him."

Betsy nodded, biting her lip as she often did when agitated.

Deirdre glanced at Matthew, who bent to pick up Phoebe. He met Deirdre's gaze, his brows tugged together over turbulent eyes.

Forcing herself to remain calm, Deirdre bent down before her nieces. "Tell me exactly what happened."

"Sean took us on a shortcut through the woods," Rose said. "He saw a fox, and we tried to follow it." She paused to wipe her nose with her mitten. "But Sean slipped and fell all the way down to the creek." More tears brimmed. "He's stuck on a branch in the water."

Alarm shot through Deirdre's system. In this cold, the boy's life could be in danger. She kept her tone even. "Where did this happen?"

"At the cutoff. Where Papa takes us fishing in the summer."

Deirdre straightened. "I know the place." She reached into the open closet for her overcoat. Today of all days, the men were away from home. It would be up to her to rescue Sean before the cold claimed him. She stuffed her arms into the sleeves and addressed her nieces. "I want you to go into the kitchen and ask Mrs. Harrison for some hot chocolate. Wait there with her until your daddy comes to get you."

The girls nodded, more tears flowing. "We're sorry, Aunt Dee-Dee."

She bent to kiss them each on the cheek. "You did the right thing coming straight here. I'll find Sean. Don't worry."

Matthew set his daughter on the ground. "Phoebe, go with the others. I'll be back soon."

When the girls scurried off, Matthew began to button his overcoat. "I'm going with you."

A rush of relief nearly buckled her knees. She wouldn't be alone, and if Sean was badly hurt, she'd have a doctor with her.

Wordlessly, Deirdre fastened her coat. They grabbed boots, hats, and gloves, and moments later they dashed out into the snow toward the stables.

Deirdre ran inside the tack room. She weighed the option of foregoing saddles, but given the fact that Matthew was so inexperienced, coupled with the weather conditions, it would be safer to take the few minutes necessary to equip the horses. She grabbed two saddles and bridles and headed to her mare's stall, where Ginger peered out over the door as if expecting her.

Matthew came up beside her and without a word lifted one of the saddles from her.

"Take the same mare you used last time," she said. "Cinch the saddle under her belly. I'll put on the bit."

Within minutes, they had mounted and were heading across the far pasture. The heavy snow forced Deirdre to keep blinking the flakes from her lashes. She tried not to think about how long Sean had already been out in this weather and the length of time it would take to reach him.

Cold talons of fear gripped her heart. *Please, Lord, protect Sean. Let us be in time.*

She glanced over her shoulder every few minutes to check on Matthew. He seemed to be managing, though riding at a slower rate than she. The pond came into view, and Deirdre veered hard to the right, toward the opening in the trees she remembered. With her vision obscured by the falling snow, she prayed she could locate it.

She waited until Matthew was close enough to see where she entered the woods, then ducked beneath the branches and guided the horse in. She kept her head tucked low over Ginger's back, impatient at the slower pace she was forced to endure. But she couldn't chance an injury on the slippery, uneven ground.

Behind her, Matthew's horse moved even slower, and other than the *clop* of hooves over the ground, a hushed silence filled the space. At last, the trees thinned out and she could hear the faint sound of trickling water.

Deirdre slid from Ginger's back and looped the reins over a branch. Moving forward on foot would be safer. She couldn't wait for Matthew, so she forged on alone, knowing he'd find Ginger and figure out where she'd gone. Her feet made little sound as she hiked through the trees to the slope that led to the creek below.

At the top of the incline, she stopped. "Sean! Can you hear me?"

She waited but received no response. Looking down the steep slope, Deirdre inhaled sharply. With the added impediment of slick snow, the descent would be treacherous. If only she'd thought to grab a length of rope before leaving.

She'd have to navigate as best she could.

Grasping bare tree branches, Deirdre slowly inched her way down, her skirts making the descent even more treacherous. She called out again, then waited, praying Sean would answer.

Still no response.

She searched the terrain as she approached the flowing water, looking for anything out of the ordinary—a color, a fabric— anything to let her know Sean was near. When she reached the edge of the rushing creek, she scanned the bank and called out again.

A whimper came from somewhere downstream. Was that Sean or an animal?

"Sean, where are you?" she called.

A heartrending cry was her only reply. Relief filled her chest. At least he was still alive and conscious.

"I'm coming!" she yelled, but the wind snatched her words.

Deirdre scooted toward where the sound had originated, heedless of the branches and brambles tearing at her face. At last she spotted a flash of color—Sean's blue knitted hat. She scrambled toward it as quickly as possible.

Sean laid on the edge of the creek, part of his body pinned under a tree trunk.

Dear God, let him be all right.

She kept moving until she reached him. "Sean, it's Aunt Dee-Dee."

He opened his eyes. The pallor of his face and the blue tinge to his lips caused Deirdre's heart to hammer hard against her ribs. She laid her gloved hand on his shoulder. "Where are you hurt?"

"My leg," he moaned.

She inched farther down the slope. The lower part of his body was submerged in the freezing water, his left leg trapped beneath the tree. To release him, she'd have to lift the heaviest portion of the trunk. She bit her lip against a rush of hopeless despair.

It would take a miracle.

Matthew's thighs burned from clamping his legs against the horse beneath him, but his injured leg pained him worst of all. Bent low over the creature's neck, he gripped the reins with frozen fingers, concentrating every ounce of his attention to stay on the beast, not letting his mind stray to the alarming idea that he might be required to save Sean Whelan's life.

All Matthew could do was pray the boy would be found unharmed, suffering nothing more than a mild case of frostbite. Yet no matter how much he dreaded this journey, he could never have let Deirdre come out here alone.

Wiry branches whipped his neck and face as the horse plunged on. He'd lost sight of Deirdre and only hoped his mount knew enough to follow her trail. Finally, when the trees thinned, Matthew lifted his head. Deirdre's horse stood alone—riderless—on the path before him.

Where had she gone?

His own horse slowed to a stop, as though one animal had conveyed a silent message to the other. Matthew uncurled his stiff fingers, unclamped his thighs, and slid off the horse's back. His bad leg almost buckled beneath him, but he grasped the saddle to steady himself.

He took a moment to find purchase for his unsteady limbs, then forged onward, following the trail of footsteps in the snow, which led to a small rise that overlooked a running creek. The footprints continued down a steep incline to the water.

Matthew inhaled a deep breath, the cold searing the insides of his lungs, and started down.

Three feet from the creek, he heard his name.

"Matthew, I need help. Over here." Deirdre's voice held a touch of panic.

He picked his way over snow-covered tree roots until he saw Deirdre beside a fallen tree. His heart stuttered like an engine deprived of gas. Deirdre stood knee-deep in the icy gray water, her overcoat billowing out around her. She looked up, her forehead pinched.

"Sean's trapped. I need help to lift this tree."

Matthew stiffened his spine, steeling himself for the task at hand. He'd do whatever necessary to get this boy safely back to his mother.

He half-slid down the slope toward them, skidding to an awkward stop at the sight that met him. Wedged under the tree, Sean's legs were submerged in the creek. A cold lump of dread formed in Matthew's gut.

The boy has been in the water all this time.

Matthew held out his hand to Deirdre. "Here, you get on the other side of the trunk." He wanted her feet out of the numbing water.

She grasped his hand, and when he pulled her up, she landed against his chest, staring up at him with anguished eyes.

"It's going to be okay," he said, as much to reassure himself as her.

She swallowed hard, nodded, and stepped away.

Matthew gritted his teeth and plunged into the frigid water, keeping his attention glued to the boy's fear-filled face. The icy sting of the water threatened to steal his breath.

"Okay, Sean, we're going to lift this tree. When we do, I need you to pull your leg out. Can you do that?"

The boy gave a slight nod, his teeth chattering. Matthew glanced up, dismayed to note the snow was falling faster and thicker now. They'd have to hurry.

When Deirdre was in place, Matthew gripped the tree. "On the count of three. One, two, three." He grunted and heaved with as much strength as he could muster. With Deirdre's efforts, the tree surged upward.

"Sean, pull your leg out." Matthew couldn't release a hand to help him or the tree would fall. "You can do it."

"I—I can't feel my legs."

Matthew caught Deirdre's eye and shook his head. His muscles burned under the weight, and they had to lower the tree. He fought to ignore the sharp needles of pain in his feet and calves in order to devise another plan. Sean's legs were numb, whether from the cold or a spinal injury Matthew didn't know, but he would need help to get out.

"Deirdre, the next time I lift the trunk, you pull Sean out."

Her brow furrowed, but she positioned herself closer to the boy's trapped leg.

Matthew took two deep breaths and found himself praying for God's help to shift the weight of the tree on his own. "Ready?"

At her nod, he thrust all his might into his arm muscles,

straining to raise the trunk. His arms shook, but finally the tree moved. "Now!"

Deirdre yanked hard. Nothing happened.

Matthew groaned, his arms shaking from the exertion. His fingers burned. The wet gloves slipped a fraction, and he feared he wouldn't be able to hold on. "Hurry."

Deirdre wrenched harder. This time, Sean's pants tore and his leg came free.

The tree fell from Matthew's grip and crashed back into the water, spraying him with icy droplets. He crawled onto the creek bank, his lungs heaving. The piercing wind bit at his face and neck. Wet snow seeped through his pants, adding to the hot stab of pain in his bad thigh.

With Sean's head on her lap, Deirdre stared at Matthew, an anxious question in her eyes.

He made his way over to them and peeled off his sodden gloves to run his fingers over the boy's near-frozen limbs. Nothing appeared to be broken. He paused to gauge his next actions. If the boy had a spinal injury, he shouldn't move him, but it wouldn't matter if Sean didn't get warm. He'd die of exposure.

As gently as possible, he lifted Sean into his arms. "We're going to take care of you, Sean. Hang on a while longer."

The boy's eyes had fluttered closed. Was he even conscious?

By unspoken agreement, Matthew and Deirdre began to ascend to the path above. Deirdre kept a supporting arm under Matthew's elbow as they climbed, pulling on branches and pieces of brush sticking out from the snow to assist them.

"Is there any type of shelter nearby?" Matthew asked when they reached the top, hoping she understood the urgency of his message.

Deirdre looked around as though she might find something amid the trees, then nodded. "There's the old hunting cabin." She frowned. "I think it's a bit farther to the west. But it hasn't been used in years."

"It will have to do."

When they reached the horses, Deirdre grabbed the reins and swung up onto her mare's back. "Give me Sean. I can handle the horse better holding him than you can."

Matthew knew there was no point in arguing. He handed the boy up to her and mounted his own horse. His thigh and arm muscles screamed at him, while his extremities burned with the beginnings of frostbite.

As the horses plodded forward, Matthew prayed they could find this cabin quickly.

It was their only chance to survive the encounter with the icy creek.

15

THE HORSES PLODDED ALONG the snow-covered path that Deirdre hoped led to her father's old hunting cabin. She and Connor used to play there as children, but in the swirling snow, her sense of direction was not at its best.

Icy fear chilled her more than the biting squalls. What if she led them the wrong way and they became lost in the woods? In this storm, no one would find them and they'd all freeze to death.

She pushed back the claw of panic. She had to keep her wits about her, for everyone's sake. Most of all for Sean. Deirdre would not let anything happen to her sister's firstborn child.

Her arm tightened about the boy. God had been with them so far. She had to trust He'd see them through this crisis.

Branches tore at her face, catching her hat and jerking it from her head. The wind whipped her hair, tearing it from the pins to blow across her eyes. She bent over Sean to shield him from the brunt of the storm's onslaught.

At last, they came into a clearing. Looking up, Deirdre's

pulse quickened. Even under the weight of snow, she recognized the oddly-shaped tree that marked the area near the cabin. It should be around the next bend.

"We're almost there!" she shouted over her shoulder, hoping her words made it back to Matthew.

Seconds later, relief bloomed as the familiar structure came into view. *Thank you, Lord.* Deirdre guided Ginger to a post beside the cabin and waited for Matthew to come and take Sean from her. She slid to the ground and led the mares to the shelter Daddy had made for the animals. As much as she'd like to tend to the horses properly, she didn't have the luxury of time. Sean's well-being had to take priority.

She climbed the rickety stairs to the door Matthew had left ajar and stepped inside. Other than being dirty, the cabin remained untouched by time. The great stone hearth dominated the main area. A wooden table and two chairs sat in one corner.

While Matthew laid Sean on the dusty sofa, Deirdre went to the fireplace and pulled a box of matches off the mantel. With stiff fingers, she opened the container. A flood of relief loosened her muscles. They had matches to start a fire. The woodbin beside the fireplace brimmed with logs and kindling. Thank goodness Daddy always left basic supplies ready for anyone who might come upon the shelter.

She handed the matches to Matthew and went into the bedroom in search of blankets or quilts. Grabbing the linens off the bed, she lugged them out to the front area.

Matthew had pulled the sofa closer to the hearth, where the beginnings of a fire glowed. "Help me get Sean out of these wet clothes."

Deirdre dropped the bedding, tugged off her cold-stiffened gloves, and began to unbutton Sean's coat while Matthew worked at getting the soggy boots off. A slow burn invaded Deirdre's fingers as she fought to unfasten the buttons. Eventually she succeeded and pulled off the sodden coat. Matthew removed Sean's torn pants and woolen socks. Blood oozed from a long gash on his left thigh, likely where the tree had landed. Shivers now wracked the boy's slight frame.

"Shivering is a good sign," Matthew said. "When the body can't shiver, a person is in serious trouble."

Deirdre nodded, trying to ignore the increasing discomfort in her own extremities. "If I remember my studies, we have to warm the torso first."

"Correct." Matthew unbuttoned his own coat and removed his wet scarf. "I'll treat the wound while you dry him off."

Using one of the blankets, Deirdre pressed it to the boy's body, careful not to rub the delicate skin. Matthew picked debris from the wound and used some melting snow to wash it, then tied his scarf around the leg. Once finished, he chose another dry blanket and wrapped the boy in an almost mummy-like fashion, leaving the material loose around his feet.

"How are his toes?" Deirdre tried to quell her anxiety over the fact that Sean hadn't stirred during the entire process.

"I'll check them now." He spared her a stern glance. "But you need to get dry yourself."

"I'm fine. Sean needs—"

"Deirdre."

His stern voice seemed to drain all the fight from her. "All right. I'll change in the other room." She pushed the hair off her face, suddenly aware of the shivers coursing through her body. Ignoring the pain in her feet, she grabbed one of the blankets and started across the room, but after two steps, her legs gave out beneath her and she crumpled into a heap.

Through the haze in her brain, she felt Matthew lift her and carry her to a chair by the fire. Then he knelt and started tugging off her boots.

Deirdre couldn't make her fingers move to help him. The adrenaline had seeped from her body, leaving her as weak as a newborn.

Matthew set her boots aside and raised his head to meet her gaze. "I have to remove your stockings now."

She nodded and closed her eyes. He reached beneath her skirts, still crusted with snow, and peeled back the woolen stockings. As Matthew gently dried her legs and feet, hot prickles of pain shot through her toes. Deirdre clamped her lips together. At least the discomfort kept her from feeling embarrassed by the situation. Only her absolute trust in Matthew made the incident bearable.

He peeled off her overcoat and laid a thick blanket around her shoulders. "Can you stand up to get out of your skirt?"

"I think so."

He helped her to her feet, and once assured she was steady, he turned away to tend the fire.

Beneath the cover of the blanket, she dropped her waterlogged skirt to the floor and sank back onto the chair, wrapping the coverlet around her. She'd only been up to her knees in the water, and thankfully her undergarments were dry. She inhaled and attempted to gather her strength. Matthew and Sean needed her. She wouldn't let them down.

The door creaked open. She looked over to find Matthew poised at the opening, a metal pail in hand.

"I'm getting some snow to melt. I'll be right back," he said and disappeared outside.

The cold dissipated as the warmth from the fire bathed her cheeks. If it weren't for the pain in her extremities, she might have been lulled to sleep. Wearing the blanket like a cloak, Deirdre walked over to her nephew, so innocent and vulnerable. She crawled behind him on the sofa and wrapped her arm around him, willing her body to infuse him with her warmth and vitality.

Please, Lord, help us to know what to do for Sean. Cover him with your healing grace.

Her thoughts turned then to her brother Danny who had

drowned when only a little older than Sean. They couldn't lose another child.

Her family would never recover.

Amid a swirl of wind and snow, Matthew entered the cabin and shut the door behind him. He stomped the slush from his boots and carried the pail over to the fire, where he hung it on a hook above the flames so the snow could melt.

He rose and turned to the sofa. Deirdre had crawled in behind the sleeping boy. She lay with her eyes closed, one arm over her nephew in a protective gesture that made Matthew's throat tighten.

The fate of these two precious people rested with him. And he had none of his medical supplies with him. He had nothing but a dirty shelter, a fire, and the snow. A tidal wave of powerlessness and fear engulfed him. How would he keep them alive with only these rudimentary elements?

With my help.

The words entered his mind like a whisper, shaking him to the core. Would it do any good to pray? He'd tried when Priscilla and Phoebe were so sick. And still his wife had died. He'd tried to pray on the battlefield for the gravely injured soldiers, yet the majority didn't make it. He, himself, had barely gotten away with his life.

So why would God help him now?

Matthew knelt before the sofa. Deirdre and Sean's even breathing gave him momentary comfort. He opened Sean's blanket to check his toes. Still stiffened with cold, Matthew enclosed one foot within his hands and blew gently on it to warm it. Taking care not to rub the skin, he repeated the process with the other foot, then checked the boy's hands. They were much nearer to normal temperature, so he repositioned them against Sean's stomach and wrapped the blankets around the boy once more. He then repeated the same process with Deirdre's feet before tucking the covers around her. As a further precaution, he laid another quilt over them both. He knew it would take time to warm the body, that it was crucial to be patient and not heat the core too quickly.

Matthew pushed up from his knees, the sharp stinging in his toes reminding him he needed to take care of himself as well. He removed his boots and socks, placed them near the fire with the others, rolled up his soggy pant legs, and dried his feet. Then he dragged a chair over to the hearth and stretched out his feet toward the warmth.

Matthew's mind whirled with helpless frustration. The only thing left for him to do, whether it helped or not, was pray. He closed his eyes and poured out heartrending entreaties to the Almighty.

Please, Lord, don't allow this boy to die because of me. Guide me to do what is best for him, whatever will help him recover. Grant peace to his parents and to all who are worried about him. And please cover Deirdre with your healing power as well.

He must have dozed off—for how long Matthew didn't know—but the fire had all but burned out when he awoke. Quickly he added more wood and struck another match to get the blaze going once again. Their survival depended on this source of heat.

Once Matthew had repeated his ministrations to Sean, re-washing the wound with the melted snow, he turned his attention to Deirdre. Carefully he unwrapped her feet and repeated the same process to warm them. Holding her delicate foot in his now-warm hands seemed impossibly intimate. He only prayed she didn't awaken to find him in this awkward position.

Once he'd tucked the blanket back around her, he picked up one of her chilled hands. Cocooning it within his own, he breathed onto their joined fingers to warm them. As he did, he stared down at her beautiful face—the long lashes against her skin, the tiny mole beside her brow. He reached over to brush a lock of hair from her forehead, attempting to ignore the fear that choked him. His worst nightmare had come roaring to life. Once again, a woman he cared for, as well as a vulnerable child, relied on his skill to keep them alive.

Would he fail this time, too?

Sheer determination stiffened his spine. Even if God chose not to answer his prayers, Matthew would not—*could not*—fail again.

A new truth wisped through his mind and wound its way around his battered heart. Feelings so strong they could not be denied bled through every pore of his being. Although Matthew had cared for his late wife, he'd never been in love with her. And though he'd been incredibly saddened by Priscilla's passing, his grief was for Phoebe, that she would grow up without a mother. He knew from bitter experience nothing could replace that bond.

Now, as his fingers brushed the satiny paleness of Deirdre's cheek, he knew he'd never before experienced this type of connection with another person. Only his devotion to his daughter came remotely close, a bond that had been strengthened thanks to this amazing, fearless woman who gave her all to those she loved.

Once again, he took her hand in his, but when she stirred, he quickly released it.

She blinked at him, squinting in the dim light from the fire. "Matthew." She attempted to rise, her attention going immediately to Sean. She caressed the boy's cheek with her hand. "How is he?"

"Still asleep. But he seems to be gradually warming up." He couldn't keep his gaze from the rich spill of hair across her shoulders. "How do you feel? Any pain in your hands or feet?"

Her nose wrinkled. "My toes are burning."

"You have a mild case of frostbite, but you should be fine."

She flexed her fingers and peered at him. "Were you holding my hand?"

Heat crawled up his neck, and he made a point of stoking the fire. "Just checking your fingers." He dared not look at her for fear his feelings might be written across his face.

He rose then and walked to the window. In a poor attempt to gauge the time, he peered outside, but the dark overhang of trees and the dense falling snow made it impossible to tell anything. It could be early evening or the middle of the night. If only he'd worn his pocket watch today.

In the blackened pane of glass, Matthew's disheveled reflection stared back at him, the glow of the fire providing a backdrop of light.

They were alone in the woods, and it appeared they'd be here until the storm ceased. Unless the O'Learys sent out a search party, which, given the weather, seemed unlikely.

Matthew stared at his somber image in the darkened glass. The one thing he prided himself on above all else was his integrity. He was a man of honor, and he would do what he had to, as a doctor and as a man, to protect this woman and child. No matter the consequences to himself.

"Matthew?"

He startled, jarred from his thoughts.

Deirdre stood beside him, wrapped in the blanket, worry etched in the lines around her mouth. "You're not keeping anything from me, are you?" With her hair loose about her shoulders, she seemed much younger than her years.

A wave of tenderness shot through him, and he attempted a smile. "Everything's fine. Except the storm isn't letting up. I'm afraid we're trapped here until it lessens."

"I don't mind—as long as you're here. I know you'll keep us safe." She gazed at him with such trust that the air stalled in his lungs.

At that moment, he wanted nothing more than to kiss her.

To reaffirm they were both alive, that they had survived. He moved closer and brushed a knuckle down her cheek. Her pupils darkened, her breath caught. The scent of wood smoke and ashes swirled around them. He closed his eyes on a sigh. No matter how much he wanted to, it wouldn't be right. Not with them virtually alone in the woods.

Matthew prided himself on being a gentleman, and a gentleman would never take advantage this way.

He gave her a soft smile. "Come and have something to drink." Taking her hand, he led her to the pail he'd removed from the fire. Earlier, he'd found a tin cup, a ladle, and a spoon in a cabinet. He ladled some of the melted snow into a cup and handed it to her.

She took a sip, then drained the contents. "Thank you." She set the cup on the table and began to rummage in the cupboard. "I wish there was something to eat."

"There isn't. I checked earlier. You should try to stay off your feet to protect the skin."

He guided her back to the sofa, only to find Sean had shifted to take up most of the space. Instead, Deirdre sat on a chair by the fire.

Matthew ladled out more water and took it over to Sean. He lifted the boy's head and managed to get a few sips past his cracked lips. Even a tiny amount would help keep him from becoming dehydrated.

He checked Sean's body temperature, wishing mightily for a thermometer. The boy seemed warmer than the last time he'd checked, and Matthew offered a prayer of thanks. He bundled him back up in the coverings, then retrieved another chair to sit beside Deirdre near the fire.

"Daddy, Connor, and Gil will be out searching for us. If they made it back from the city." Deirdre stared into the flames in front of them. "I wish there was a way we could let them know we're all right."

Matthew nodded. "I'd hoped to be able to head back once Sean was out of danger, but we'll have to wait until the storm lets up."

Matthew longed to ease Deirdre's worry. He needed to find a way to divert her attention.

Anything to distract her from agonizing about her family.

Anything to distract *him* from thinking about the two of them in this intimate setting—alone.

16

D EIRDRE SETTLED BACK in her chair, allowing the warmth from the fire to ease the chill in her body, though nothing seemed to chase the apprehension from her heart. Things could have so easily gone wrong for them. Only by the grace of God had they found this cabin.

Otherwise they'd have certainly perished.

She thanked God for the hundredth time that she wasn't alone, that Matthew was with her, steadying her with his calm demeanor.

"So, when do you plan on returning to your studies?" Matthew's deep voice had a soothing quality about it. She allowed it to lull her away from her worries. Away from the discomfort in her body.

She glanced over at him on the chair beside her. "Not until Mama's back on her feet and able to function without assistance."

"That could take months. Will they hold your place at the university?"

The question was one that had plagued Deirdre of late. She'd been away for nearly six weeks now. How could she even begin to catch up on all the material she'd missed?

"I don't know. I'll likely have to start over next semester." She lifted her chin, determined not to think in negative terms. "But it will be worth it to have Mama's health back."

"She's lucky to have you." Matthew's voice was gruff. "I know what it's like to be incapacitated, far from home and family. I wouldn't wish that on anyone."

Deirdre hated the thought of him badly injured in a foreign land. "Your wife must have been frantic."

A log shifted in the hearth, causing a shower of embers to fly out. Matthew reached over to slap at a spark that landed on her blanket. "Priscilla's letters indicated she was worried, as well as angry. She hadn't agreed with my decision to enter the war and held a great deal of resentment."

"It must have been hard to leave, knowing how she felt."

"It was." He paused. "Especially when she told me she might be expecting. Though I confess I thought she was lying to keep me from going."

Deirdre tried to imagine how she would feel if the man she loved, her husband, was going off to war. "She didn't understand that going to war was important to you?" Deirdre asked quietly.

"She didn't even try. Priscilla didn't like any deviations from the life she had planned." Matthew winced. "Still, I should have been more sensitive to her fears."

Deirdre shifted on the hard chair, her curiosity getting the best of her. "Forgive me for saying so, but your marriage doesn't sound like a happy one."

The muscles in his jaw tightened.

"I'm sorry. That's none of my business."

He released a weary breath. "Your statement is accurate. I married Priscilla because it seemed logical at the time. Unfortunately, I didn't live up to her expectations for a husband."

Deirdre's heart ached for Matthew. A wife was supposed to be a source of comfort and support. Priscilla Clayborne sounded like anything but. "That must have been a terrible time for you."

He nodded, staring into the fire, and rubbed a hand over his thigh. "When I returned from England, I tried to make amends, for Phoebe's sake, but nothing helped. Then Priscilla took ill."

Deirdre reached over to cover his hand with hers. "I can't imagine the heartache you've had to endure."

When he turned to her, his eyes swam with agony. "I'd rather face ten years on the battlefield than to endure my daughter being sick again." He remained silent for several minutes. Then suddenly a whisper croaked out. "Priscilla's death was my fault. I waited too long to take her to a sanatorium. Her parents still blame me."

Helpless frustration seized Deirdre as she absorbed the grief Matthew had endured. She recalled how surly he'd been when they'd first met, and for the first time she understood the immense pain that had shaped him. The rare glimpses of hesitancy with his patients now made sense. She'd heard of other doctors losing their confidence after feeling responsible for a patient's death.

She gripped his hand tighter. "Don't let them make you doubt your skills, Matthew. I've worked with many physicians and I can tell you're a wonderful doctor."

He shook his head sadly. "I wish I could believe that." He rose and went to check on Sean again, as if to prove he wasn't shirking his duty.

Deirdre's heart grew heavy as she watched him. How could Matthew not realize his own worth? If it weren't for him, Sean would be dead.

He returned to the chair beside her. "You should rest. I don't want you to become ill from this mishap."

"If I do, it's my own fault." The guilt that had been sitting like a weight on her shoulders now bubbled to the surface.

His confused gaze swung to her. "How is this your fault?"

"I acted without thinking, ready to rush off on my own. If I had, Sean would have perished." Admitting her recklessness aloud caused the burn of tears.

"That's not true—"

"It is. I couldn't have lifted the tree alone. I would've had to go back for help, and it would have been too late." She swiped her fingers across her eyes. "You saved Sean's life."

He studied her, the firelight glowing on his face. "You were the one who knew about this cabin. If I'd had to bring Sean home in that storm, we'd be looking at a very different outcome."

Foolish tears brimmed again. "I didn't think the situation through. I'm far too impulsive. It's one of my worst traits."

This time Matthew took her hand and engulfed it in his. "Acting quickly is not a bad thing. I, on the other hand, am too cautious, which can be equally detrimental."

She attempted a shaky smile, relishing the warmth of his fingers surrounding hers. "Perhaps we balance each other's flaws."

"Perhaps we do." He lifted her hand to his lips, his eyes trained on her face.

The intensity of his gaze made her heart flutter. The air seemed to thicken and grow warm around them. Light from the fire danced in the hearth, casting shadows against the wooden walls behind Matthew's head. A look of regret passed over his features before he pulled back. Releasing her hand, he grabbed his boots and stuffed his feet into them.

"What are you doing?"

He rose, then reached out to brush a strand of hair off her cheek with a sad smile. "A little cool air might do me good right now."

As the door closed behind him, Deirdre attempted to regulate her breathing. If she weren't careful, she might easily fall in love with Matthew Clayborne—a turn of events that could put her plans for the future in serious jeopardy.

She would have to take better care to guard her heart, no matter how appealing the man had become.

The morning light seeped through the grimy windows, alerting Matthew to the fact that the night had passed. He rose from his blanket in front of the hearth and stretched his back muscles. Despite the hard floor, he'd managed to get an hour or two of sleep. He hoped Deirdre and Sean had fared better on the sofa.

He rose, tended the fire, and then went to check on his small patient, still slumbering under his aunt's arm. Carefully, he unwrapped Sean's feet, relieved to find they were warmer to the touch. Sean stirred as Matthew opened the blanket around his torso. Matthew inspected the boy's hands, finding them at a good temperature, then laid his hand on Sean's stomach. His core was still cooler than normal, but improving.

Sean blinked and stared at Matthew. "Dr. Clayborne?"

The tension in Matthew's shoulders seeped away. He released a long breath. "Hello, Sean. How are you feeling?"

"Thirsty."

"I'll get you some water."

When he came back with the tin cup, Deirdre had also awakened.

"Good morning," he said. "Can you help Sean sit up?"

"He's awake?" A wide grin creased her sleepy features.

Matthew smiled in return. "Awake and thirsty."

Deirdre pressed a kiss to the crown of Sean's head, then shifted to raise him up against her.

Matthew held the cup to his cracked lips until the boy drained its contents.

"I'm hungry," Sean announced sullenly.

Deirdre laughed out loud. "So are we, honey. Hopefully we can get home soon to have some of Mrs. Harrison's oatmeal."

She looked over at Matthew with such joy that his heart

seemed to expand in his chest. *Thank you, Lord, for Sean's recovery.*

The boy rubbed his eyes. "Where are we?"

"In Grandpa's hunting cabin. Do you remember what happened?"

He thought for a moment, and his eyes widened. "I slipped down the hill and crashed into a tree. It fell on top of me."

Matthew marveled again that they had managed to find the boy in time.

Deirdre hugged Sean. "Your sisters came to tell us. Dr. Clayborne and I got you out."

Matthew checked the dressing on Sean's thigh. "How does your leg feel, Sean?"

"It's sore, and my toes burn."

Matthew pulled the blanket back over him. "You got frostbite on your feet from being in the cold water. But they'll get better."

Matthew got himself and Deirdre a cup of water. The ache in his belly had him wishing for some scrambled eggs and bacon.

Deirdre picked up her clothing she'd spread out to dry. "I'm going to get dressed in the other room."

Matthew nodded. "I'll check on the horses. Clear some of the snow."

Anything to keep from picturing Deirdre putting on her stockings—and remembering taking them off. He shoved his feet into his boots and tugged on his overcoat, then exited the cabin, sweeping snow off the stoop as he went. The cold bite of wind stung his cheeks, and he quickly closed the door to keep in the warmth. Matthew took a moment to survey the pristine expanse of white before him. Above the treetops, slices of gray sky cast shadows over the mounds of snow. How could something so beautiful be so deadly?

He cleared the stairs with his boots and waded through the deep snow toward the lean-to where the horses still stood.

Thankfully, the rough structure seemed to have sheltered the beasts from the worst of the storm. He patted their necks and murmured soothing words before heading back inside.

He found Deirdre fully dressed, her hair in a long braid down her back, helping Sean get into his clothes.

"Good news," he said. "The snow has stopped, and the horses appear fine. I think we can set out for home."

Deirdre's smile illuminated the room. She tucked Sean's feet into his socks. "Are you ready, honey? Your mama and daddy could probably use some good news about now."

"Do you think Mrs. Harrison will make me pancakes?"

She laughed. "I'm sure she'll make you anything you want."

Without warning, the door crashed open.

Matthew's heart jumped into his throat as three men entered the cabin, dressed in large overcoats with hats and scarves covering most of their faces. He immediately stepped between Deirdre and the intruders.

But she surprised him by rushing forward with a squeal of glee. "Daddy! I knew you'd come."

James O'Leary caught her in a huge hug. "Are you all right, sweetheart?"

"I'm fine. And Sean is, too." She pulled away, beaming at him. "Thanks to Matthew."

Three pairs of eyes turned to him. One of the men rushed past them to the sofa.

"Papa!" Sean tumbled into Gil's arms.

Gil buried his face in the boy's neck, his frame shaking with emotion. "Thank you, Lord."

Deirdre crossed the room to lay a hand on Gil's shoulders. "He's okay, Gil. Other than a nasty gash on his leg and a mild case of frostbite."

Matthew turned his attention to James and Connor. "We were just preparing to leave now that the snow has stopped. I hope you haven't been out searching all night."

"No." James pulled down his scarf. "The storm forced us back home until this morning."

"I'm sorry you were worried. If there were any way we could have made it back, I would have tried." Matthew leaned in to lower his voice. "But Sean's condition was precarious at best. If Deirdre hadn't known about this cabin . . ." He trailed off, letting the meaning sink in.

"Thank heaven I didn't tear this place down. I knew it might come in handy."

"It certainly did." Matthew let out a breath. For the first time in hours, a huge burden lifted from his shoulders. "If you'll excuse me, I'll get the rest of my things and we can be off."

Connor nodded. "I'll prepare the horses."

James clapped a hand on Matthew's back. "You'll never know how grateful I am for you keeping my daughter and grandson safe." He gave him a pointed look. "However, when we get home, you and I might need to chat about exactly what went on in this cabin all night."

Matthew froze, his muscles seizing like an ice-covered tree limb. Images of removing Deirdre's stockings blazed through his mind, and heat streaked up his neck.

Deirdre came over and linked her hand through James's arm. "Daddy, don't scare him like that. You know very well Matthew was a perfect gentleman."

"If you say so, daughter." James gave her a wink. "Now let's get this boy back to his mama and grandmother before they wear themselves out with worry."

17

DEIRDRE HAD NEVER BEEN HAPPIER to see her home. When the bedraggled party entered the parlor where the family had gathered to pray for everyone's safe return, her throat tightened in gratitude.

Gratitude for their survival, and gratitude for the love and prayers of her family.

Thank you, Lord, for keeping us alive and allowing us to bring Sean safely home.

Brianna leapt up from the sofa and rushed toward them. Tears flooded her cheeks as Gil delivered Sean into her waiting arms. She rained kisses over her son's face and head and squeezed him until he squawked in protest.

Deirdre swiped the dampness from her own eyes.

"How can we ever thank you, Dr. Clayborne?" Brianna gathered Matthew in a fierce hug.

He stepped back, brow furrowed. "Actually, the greater thanks must go to your sister."

At his admiring look, heat infused Deirdre's cheeks. "I only did what anyone would do in the same circumstances."

Standing behind his wife, Gil placed a hand on Brianna's shoulder. "Let's take the children home. I can have the horses hooked up to the sleigh and ready to go in no time."

Lines of concern marred Brianna's forehead. "I don't think we should take Sean out again so soon. I'll give him a bath here and see how he feels after he's had some of Mrs. Harrison's chicken soup."

Gil scratched his head, a bemused expression on his face. Deirdre figured that even if he didn't agree with his wife, he wasn't about to argue after the ordeal she'd been through.

"Very well, Mrs. Whelan," he said with a gentle smile. "I'll collect the girls from the kitchen and take them with me to feed the animals." He kissed her cheek, patted Sean's head, and then strode out.

Once Brianna took Sean upstairs, Connor went back to the barn to see to the horses. Mama claimed fatigue and, after more hugs and kisses, Daddy took her to her room—leaving Deirdre alone with Matthew.

"I'd better go and change," she said, suddenly at a loss for words. "Then I think I'll take a long nap." Her muscles groaned in protest as soon as she moved.

Matthew shifted his stance by the door. "I'll do the same once I let Phoebe know I'm okay."

Deirdre paused, oddly reluctant to leave his presence. Sharing the ordeal of rescuing Sean and then being holed up in the cabin together had forged a bond she didn't wish to lose. Matthew had opened up to her in a way he never had before, and she feared that come the morrow, he'd revert back to his reserved self, safely concealed behind the walls he'd erected.

Her feelings for him didn't make sense, didn't fit with her goals for her life, yet she couldn't seem to shake them.

She moved closer and laid a hand on his arm. "Thank you

again, Matthew. We couldn't have gotten through it without you."

"You're welcome." He stared down at her, the blue of his eyes more vivid than ever.

Her pulse sprinted at the intensity darkening his gaze. Did she sense a similar longing in him? She'd never know if she didn't act.

Deirdre reached up and laid a soft kiss on his lips. His whole body tensed, his muscles solidifying. But he didn't move. Didn't take her in his arms as she'd hoped.

Had she been mistaken the times she'd thought he meant to kiss her?

She pulled back an inch to peer at him. He stood still, eyes closed, a pained expression pinching his features. Deirdre's heart squeezed. Once again she'd given in to impulse—and done the wrong thing.

Matthew opened his eyes. The agony shining within them seized her breath.

"I'm sorry, Matthew. I had no right—"

He cut off her apology by crushing his mouth to hers. Strong arms wrapped around her, pulling her so close she didn't know where her heart ended and his began. After several seconds, his lips gentled on hers, caressing her with exquisite tenderness. His mouth moved to her eyelids, her cheek, her temple, and back to claim her lips once again. She clutched his shoulders, fearing the storm of emotion rioting through her would cause her to swoon.

This was the sensation she'd dreamed of. *This* was how she'd imagined love would feel. Just when she thought she might burst with the enormity of the heady sensations coursing through her, Matthew gently drew away.

"Deirdre." He breathed her name with such sorrow that her chest constricted. "Forgive me. I shouldn't have done that."

"Please don't apologize." She blinked at the moisture gathering in her eyes.

His tousled hair fell over his brow. "It wasn't fair to you. Not when I can't give you what you deserve."

She longed for him to sweep her back into his arms and kiss her again. Yet the lingering pain that haunted his features told her he wouldn't. No matter how much he might care for her, he was trapped by memories of an unhappy marriage.

She shook her head. "I have no one to blame but myself."

He smiled sadly and reached out to brush one finger against her cheek, a world of regret in his eyes.

And then without another word, he walked away.

Later that afternoon, Connor hefted a bale of straw into an empty stall and attacked it with a pitchfork in the hopes that some hard physical labor would calm the turmoil in his mind.

Now that Deirdre and Sean had returned home unharmed, Connor could no longer avoid the other matter haunting him. What was he to do about Josephine Miller?

Yesterday she'd arrived in her male get-up and continued to work as though nothing had changed. Though he admired her tenacity, it didn't change the situation. If Connor hadn't had to leave with Daddy and Gil for the city, he would've raised the issue of her needing to find new employment. However, there hadn't been time for a proper conversation.

Then when they'd returned from the city, concern over Sean and Deirdre had taken top priority. A long, cold search in the dark, followed by a sleepless night and a fresh trek in the morning, had left Connor exhausted and cranky. He knew enough not to confront the girl in his present state. He'd need a clear head to tackle that problem, and to keep his reaction to her in check.

No doubt about it—Jo was a distraction he didn't need.

Connor worked until the straw was spread evenly across the floor, then continued on to clean a few saddles in the tack room.

Once he'd run out of mindless chores, he realized the sun had started to dip behind the trees to the west.

Good. Jo would already have headed home, so he wouldn't have to worry about running into her today.

Coward.

He strode out of the barn and over to the fence surrounding the racetrack, inhaling the crisp air. Leaning his elbows on the top rung, he gazed out at the serene landscape. Everything lay still beneath the new blanket of snow.

The crunch of footsteps sounded and a figure came up beside him.

"Thought I might find you out here."

Connor smiled at the sound of his friend's voice. "Caleb. What brings you by?"

"Heard about Sean, and I wanted to . . ." He trailed off.

Connor took his attention from the pasture and squinted at his friend. "Wanted to what?"

Caleb's brown eyes held a hint of embarrassment. "Ma made cookies to bring over." He gave a sheepish shrug and lifted the basket he held. "I thought I'd pay a call on Dee to make sure she was all right."

Connor took in the fact that Caleb's usual messy brown hair was combed neatly over his forehead and he'd exchanged his overalls for his Sunday clothes. "Don't tell me you still have it bad for my sister."

"What if I do?" The challenge in Caleb's voice rang out.

"Then I'm afraid you'll be disappointed all over again, my friend. Dee hasn't changed her mind about becoming a doctor."

"You never know if you don't take a chance. A friend gave me that sage piece of advice long ago."

"Yeah, well, he was wrong." Connor started down the path toward the house, his footsteps crunching over the snow. "See how far it got me with Clara. She married Silas Baldwin anyway."

"You got over Clara years ago." Caleb kept an easy pace with him. "So what else is stuck in your craw?"

Connor stopped at the base of the porch stairs. One thing about his friend, he could always tell when Connor had a problem. He exhaled in a cloud of white. "It's one of our hands." He hesitated. "Can you keep something to yourself?"

"You know I can."

"Turns out this particular hand"—he lowered his voice—"is really a girl." Connor wouldn't mention Jo's name, seeing as Seth Miller was working for Caleb. "Now that I've found out, I don't know if I should keep her on."

"That *is* a quandary." Caleb shifted the basket.

"If the other guys knew, they'd refuse to work with a woman. But she seems desperate for a job. I don't know what to do."

Caleb scratched his jaw with his free hand. "Maybe see if your mother knows of any positions in the area. I can ask around, too, if you'd like."

A trickle of relief wound through Connor's tight muscles. He clapped Caleb on the back. "That's a great idea." If Mama was able to find Jo another job, Connor wouldn't feel so guilty for having to fire her.

Caleb grinned at him. "Thanks. In the meantime, how about you invite me in to warm up before I head back?" He lifted the basket. "We can bribe your mother with these."

18

MATTHEW ATTEMPTED to concentrate on the notes before him, but the words blurred on the page. He had too much on his mind, his thoughts shifting and twisting in numerous directions at once. The attention he'd received from the O'Learys and the Whelans for saving Sean, while wonderfully validating, chafed at him. Everyone had made him out to be a hero. But heroes, he'd learned long ago, soon fell off their pedestals.

To make matters worse, Matthew could not stop thinking about the intoxicating sweetness of Deirdre's kiss. Nor her look of devastation when he'd realized what a mistake it had been. That soul-stirring embrace had changed things between them, and he had no idea how to get back to their former relationship.

"Is everything all right, Matthew?"

Kathleen's quiet question jarred him from his thoughts.

"Yes. Why do you ask?"

"You've been sitting with your pen poised in midair for over ten minutes now." Her faintly amused expression matched her tone.

He straightened his back and laid the instrument down. "I suppose I haven't been able to get Sean's misadventure off my mind."

She released a ragged sigh. "Thankfully, the Lord brought you safely home."

Matthew looked away, not willing to enter a religious debate. Especially since this time he couldn't quite refute her claim. He still remembered the feeling that he wasn't alone in the cabin when Sean and Deirdre had been most at risk.

Kathleen rolled her wheelchair over to the desk. "Matthew, may I ask you something?"

"You may." He closed his logbook.

"How do you feel about my daughter?"

He sucked in a sharp breath but forced his expression to remain neutral. The last thing he wanted was to discuss his feelings for Deirdre. But he couldn't ignore the woman. "I admire Deirdre very much," he said carefully. "Her spirit, her kindness, her loyalty." And her impulsive nature, so different from his own.

Kathleen's shrewd gaze held his. "Do you have a romantic interest in her?"

Matthew jerked up from his seat. "Where would you get that idea?"

"I've seen the way you look at her."

Matthew's heart thudded in his chest, the air seeming overly warm. "I don't know what you mean." He moved to the other side of the room, as though he could escape her questions.

"I'm asking because I'm fairly certain Deirdre is interested in you as well."

Matthew banked down a rise of panic and turned to face her. "This conversation is pointless, Kathleen. After my wife died, I vowed I'd never marry again. So I'd be obliged if you'd let the matter drop."

She studied him quietly. "You must have loved your wife very much to make such a vow."

Matthew's spine cinched with tension. He needed to get off this hero's pedestal—before he fell off and shattered. "You couldn't be more wrong. My marriage was an unmitigated disaster, which is why I'm not willing to enter another. I've come to learn I will never be enough for any woman. Not my mother and not my wife. I only pray I don't fail Phoebe as well." His rib cage pinched on a loud exhale.

"That's a lonely way to live," she said sadly.

"Not really. I've been alone most of my life." The ache that spread through his chest mocked him. He clenched his hands into fists. "Please excuse me, Kathleen. I need some air."

He marched from the room and exited the house without even stopping for an overcoat. The biting wind pierced his shirt while drifts of snow swallowed his feet. Matthew welcomed the discomfort. Far easier to bear physical pain than to relive the emotional pain of his past.

Matthew kept walking in a desperate attempt to outrun his demons. Yet he feared it was too late. That his outer shell—the one he thought so tough—had begun to crack.

Panic clawed up his throat. He needed to leave Irish Meadows as soon as possible, before he broke wide open, never to be whole again.

With the wet snow seeping through his shoes, he turned back to the house, wishing it was as easy to numb his heart as it was his feet.

Matthew was avoiding her.

Deirdre rose from the dining table with an audible sigh. He'd started taking his breakfast before she even rose, for the sole purpose, she was certain, of not having to eat with her. He'd also taken great pains to make sure they were never alone, leaving a room if she were the only one present.

All because of one silly kiss. *One silly, heart-stopping kiss.*

By acting on feelings better left alone, she'd ruined their close relationship and frightened Matthew away—probably for good. Never again would he let his guard down around her. The wall around his heart would be fortified with a layer of cement, one she'd never be able to break through.

When would she ever learn to curb her impulsive nature?

Deirdre took her empty coffee cup and set it on the sideboard. Then she raised her chin and stepped out into the hallway. Whether Matthew liked it or not, she would join Mama's therapy session again, and he'd be forced to interact with her—no matter how uncomfortable it made him.

Mrs. Johnston intercepted her before she reached Mama's room, waving an envelope. "Miss Deirdre. A letter arrived for you. It looks official."

A chill of unease swept through Deirdre as she accepted the mail. "Thank you, Mrs. Johnston."

The return address of Boston, Massachusetts, seemed to jump off the envelope. Deirdre sighed again. Mama's therapy would have to wait. Deirdre needed privacy to read whatever the university had to tell her.

Taking advantage of the fact that her father was busy outdoors, Deirdre entered his study and crossed the room to sit in one of the wingback chairs by the hearth. She ran the envelope between her fingers and tried to calm the roll of nerves in her stomach. Perhaps it was simply some routine correspondence. Or perhaps they were inquiring about her return. Gathering her courage, she opened the letter.

Dear Miss O'Leary,

We regret to inform you that due to your lengthy absence, we have no choice but to revoke your place in our medical program.

We realize your personal circumstances had to take precedence over your academic career; however, holding your spot is depriving other students of the opportunity to study.

If you desire, you may reapply for the next academic year beginning in September 1923.

Sincerely,

*Josiah Q. Abernathy,
Dean of Boston Medical
Sciences*

An invading numbness spread through Deirdre's body. The stationery fluttered from her fingers to the floor. After everything she'd sacrificed to get into the medical school at Boston, she'd been expelled.

How would this look when she reapplied in the future? Would they risk offering her another place after this?

Not likely.

The thought of having to fight all over again to find a new placement was almost too daunting to consider.

Sorrow and anger crashed through her in equal measure, spearing her chest with a ripping spasm of pain. She snatched the paper from the carpet, crumpled it into a ball, and heaved it into the fire.

The flames curled around the offering, twisting and burning until nothing remained but the smoldering ashes of her dreams.

Deirdre walked to the window of her father's office and stared out at the bleak terrain. She laid her forehead against the cold pane of glass and allowed the pent-up tears to fall.

Matthew wheeled Kathleen back to her room and assisted her into bed. The therapy session this morning had been more grueling than usual. Today, for the first time since her stroke,

Matthew had helped her get to her feet. He'd supported her weakened side, while Kathleen bore most of her weight on her good leg. Once she'd gotten the feel of standing again, Matthew had helped her put a little pressure on her bad leg, triumphant when she'd managed to take two steps without buckling. The beads of perspiration that streaked her face, however, told him of the huge toll it had taken. He'd insisted on cutting the session short so she could rest until later in the day when they would continue with the hand weights.

Kathleen's elation over her progress had been most gratifying. Matthew only wished Deirdre had been there to experience her mother's victory. Remembering their shared joy when Kathleen had managed a few notes on the piano, he swallowed a sigh of regret. Perhaps it was better to avoid such temptation.

Matthew closed his logbook and removed his reading glasses. He and Phoebe had become too entwined in the O'Learys' lives here at Irish Meadows. It was time for them to think about returning home—to reality.

Yesterday had marked the end of the one month trial period he'd agreed to. Now that Kathleen's recovery seemed certain, he could leave without guilt. Having fulfilled his promise, there was nothing to stop him from booking his return trip to Toronto.

He rose from the desk, resolution steeling his spine. He would make the telephone call right away—before he had a chance to put it off.

Matthew headed straight for James's study and closed the door behind him. He'd taken a few steps into the room, inhaling the pleasant odor of pipe tobacco, when an unexpected sound met his ears—one resembling stifled weeping. He stopped in surprise, scanning the room for its source. In the far corner, he recognized Deirdre's dejected figure. She stood with her back to him, head bent against the windowpane. Her shoulders shook with near-silent sobs.

A sense of alarm crept through him, and he immediately crossed to her side. "Deirdre? What's the matter?"

She jerked and swiped a hand across her cheeks. "Matthew, you startled me."

The look of devastation on her face chilled his insides. "Tell me what's wrong."

She clasped her fingers around a bunched-up handkerchief. "The university has rescinded my place in the medical program."

He paused to take in her meaning. "You've been expelled?"

"Yes." More tears bloomed. "I won't be able to go back unless I apply all over again."

Without thinking, he wrapped his arms around her trembling frame and drew her to him. "I'm so sorry. I know how much your studies mean to you."

It shocked him how much he wished he could fix the situation for her. Every sob, every sniffle, seemed to resonate through his chest to echo in his heart. He held her for several minutes, relishing her nearness, grateful he could provide some small comfort.

When at last the tears subsided, she stepped back and looked up at him, her eyes washed in sorrow. "I don't want Mama to know about this. She'd only feel terrible—as though it was all her fault."

His mind whirled for any possible way he could help. "I know a few doctors on the board at the Boston hospital. Perhaps I could make a few calls. See if there are any strings they could pull at the university."

She gave him an incredulous look. "You'd do that for me?"

"Certainly. I can't guarantee a positive outcome, but it couldn't hurt."

Deirdre gave him a tremulous smile. "Thank you, Matthew. Just the fact that you would go to the trouble means a lot." She squared her shoulders. "Perhaps this delay is for the best, though. Mama will need me for a long while yet. This way I won't be tempted to return to my studies too soon."

Matthew marveled at Deirdre's inner fortitude. She'd just lost her deepest desire and all she worried about was her mother's welfare.

"I'm sorry," she said. "What did you come in here for? Not to console a weeping woman, I'm sure."

He glanced at the telephone on the desk, then shook his head. "Nothing that can't wait."

If Deirdre could set aside her dream for a whole year to help Kathleen, surely he could spend another week or two at Irish Meadows—long enough to speed up Kathleen's recovery and ensure she was able to walk on her own. It wasn't much, but it was one tangible way he could help Deirdre get on with her own life.

He gazed down into her lovely face. Wisps of auburn hair feathered over her flushed cheeks. Her lips trembled in another attempted smile, and he had to quell the overwhelming urge to kiss her. Instead, he took a painful step away from her.

Matthew's career might survive an extended stay at Irish Meadows, but could his heart?

He was afraid to find out.

19

J O FINISHED BRUSHING two of the workhorses and wiped the perspiration from her forehead. It had been three days since Connor O'Leary had followed her home. Three days since he'd discovered her gender—and he hadn't spoken to her since.

Was that a blessing or a curse?

Jo took the brushes to the tack room and replaced them neatly on the shelf. Every day now, she performed her tasks with the threat of disaster looming over her head. Would Connor allow her to stay, or would he tell her she must go?

With each day, her hope grew that his compassionate nature had won out and he'd decided not to fire her.

And each day, she fought harder to ignore that compassionate nature—among Connor's other amazing qualities. His strength and his gentleness. The hazel eyes that twinkled with mischief one minute and warmed with affection the next.

Utter foolishness. A man like Connor was not for her.

Footsteps sounded in the barn. Jo stiffened and poked her head out of the room.

Mac, one of the other stable hands, strode toward her. "Hey, Miller. The boss wants to see you. He's outside by the track."

Jo froze, her stomach churning. It appeared Connor had made a decision. "Thanks, Mac."

She stepped outside the barn, tugging her hat down more firmly against the pull of the wind.

Connor leaned against the white fence, watching her approach with wary eyes.

"You wanted to see me?"

"Yes." His intense gaze did nothing to appease the swarm of buzzing bees inside her.

She forced herself to remain still and wait.

"First of all, I have a message from Dr. Clayborne. He and Deirdre will be going back to see your father today. They got sidetracked with the snowstorm and all."

Jo shifted her focus to the slush at her feet. "I heard about your nephew. I'm glad he's all right."

"Thank you. We were pretty worried for a while."

A few seconds of silence followed, and when Jo couldn't stand it any longer, she raised her head. "Have you decided what you're going to do?" she blurted out.

He crossed his arms. "I'd like you to talk to my mother before I make my decision."

Her mouth gaped open. "You told your mother about me?" She couldn't begin to fathom what was going on in his mind.

"There's no one whose opinion I trust more than hers."

She tilted her chin. "And if I refuse?"

His eyes narrowed. "It will make my decision a whole lot easier."

Her heart hammered against her ribs. "I guess I don't have much choice then."

"Good. I'll tell the housekeeper to expect you." He gave a tight nod and strode away.

Connor had practically worn out the carpet, pacing his father's study until he could stand it no longer. He'd asked his mother for help, thinking that Jo might talk more freely to another woman. More specifically, he'd asked Mama to find out what other type of work Jo might be qualified for and to suggest possible places to seek such employment. Then when he broke the news that Jo had to leave Irish Meadows, he could do so knowing he'd tried his best to help her.

Connor exited the study and headed toward Mama's room, fairly certain the conversation must be over. He looked forward to learning his mother's opinion on Jo's situation.

Hearing feminine voices coming from the sitting room, Connor slowed his approach. It seemed his timing was off once again.

Instead of retreating, however, curiosity overcame his sense of propriety. He approached the door, which stood slightly ajar, and peered inside. Mama had her arm around a hunched-over Jo, who was still wearing that detestable hat. Jo sniffed into a handkerchief held to her nose.

Was she crying?

Connor pressed his back against the wall. He could deal with almost anything except a woman's tears.

"I'm so sorry to hear about your father." Mama's voice drifted out to Connor. "Addiction to alcohol is a dreadful disease. Once it gets hold of a person, it's difficult to shake."

"It's gotten worse over the last few years. My brother tries to keep everything going, making excuses for Pa and filling in when he can. But even Seth is worn out." A loud sniff punctuated her remark. "I had hoped Prohibition would make it harder to get whiskey, but Pa always seems to find a way."

"I need to ask you something, dear, and I hope you'll trust me with the truth."

Connor held his breath. A twinge of guilt flared over the fact that he was eavesdropping on a private conversation. Yet part of him felt justified after the deception Jo had perpetrated.

"Does your father mistreat you when he's . . . overindulged?"

Several seconds passed, and then a small voice answered. "Mostly he just yells, but sometimes, if he gets really riled, he . . . hits me."

Connor balled his hands into fists at his side. A streak of anger roared through him. He wanted to ride over to that cabin and make sure the man never laid a finger on Jo again.

"But Pa's always sorry afterward."

Unable to contain himself, Connor shoved away from the wall and barged into the room. "Apologizing doesn't mean a thing if he doesn't change his behavior."

Jo's head flew up, tears streaking her cheeks. Very feminine cheeks and very beautiful blue eyes. How had he ever believed she was a boy?

"Connor!" Mama's stern expression told him she didn't approve of his interruption, nor his eavesdropping.

But he couldn't sit by and say nothing. He needed to know Jo wasn't in danger at home. "What about your brother? Does he hit you as well?"

Jo shook her head. "Seth would never hurt me. Pa only gets violent if Seth isn't there to protect me."

Exasperation flooded Connor's system as he paced the carpet in front of her. "Why do you stay with a father who abuses you?"

She gave a tiny shrug. "I suppose I feel responsible. Pa didn't start drinking until my mother died giving birth to me. He couldn't cope with losing her."

"That's ridiculous. You weren't—"

Mama reached out to touch his sleeve, giving him a pointed stare. "I'm sure Jo loves her father, despite his flaws."

Jo nodded. "Pa and Seth are all I've got."

Connor burned with the need to save her from such a sorry

life. But there was little he could do. A decision solidified in his mind. At least he could ease her mind in one respect. "I want you to know you have a job with us for as long as you need it."

Relief spread over Jo's face. "Thank you, Mr. O'Leary."

"It's Connor, and you're welcome. If your father gives you any trouble, I want you to come here for help. Promise me."

She bit her lip and nodded.

"Good. You don't have to go through this alone."

"Thank you," she whispered again as she rose.

The tension in Connor's gut eased a notch. It wasn't much, but it was the least he could do to protect her.

For the moment.

Seated on Ginger's back, Deirdre flexed her fingers to get the blood flowing to her chilled hands, wishing she knew what Matthew was thinking. She'd been pleasantly surprised when he'd asked her to accompany him on his follow-up visit to Mr. Miller. Ever since he'd found her crying in the study, he'd reverted to a reserved politeness around her. Better than avoiding her, yet she couldn't help but yearn for the closeness they'd shared at the cabin.

She released a long breath, which puffed out in the cold air. She was sure the only reason he'd put up with her company was his unfamiliarity with the land and his unease with horses.

Deirdre slid from Ginger's back, and once Matthew dismounted, they trekked across the snow-laden ground to the cabin door. She gave a loud knock and waited for a response. When no one answered, she knocked again.

After several seconds of silence, Matthew gave her a sharp look and pushed the door open.

"Mr. Miller? It's Dr. Clayborne." He stepped inside. "I'm here to check on your leg."

An eerie silence filled the space. Matthew motioned for Deirdre to stay back and walked farther into the room.

With a frown, she followed him in. She wasn't about to let him go in alone.

The sofa was empty except for a tangled sheet. A tin cup and plate lay scattered on the table.

Where was Mr. Miller? Had he perhaps felt well enough to venture outside?

Deirdre opened the bedroom door. She found the area tidy, the bed made, a hairbrush the only adornment on the plain dresser. Matthew checked the loft, which he announced was empty as well.

"Where could he be?" Deirdre fisted her hands on her hips. "Surely Jo would have warned us if her father was up and about."

Connor had confided in her and Mama that Jo was a girl, but had asked them not to say anything. However, Deirdre had told Matthew, feeling it only fair since he was treating her father. He had a right to know the true situation.

"Let's have a look outside. Maybe there's an outhouse nearby." Matthew strode out of the cabin.

Deirdre followed him to the water pump, where a bucket lay overturned within a large area of melted snow. With a grim feeling of foreboding, she headed to the rear of the cabin and stopped sharply when she spied a prostrate form in the snow. "Matthew! Come quickly."

Matthew's grim features gave little away as he dropped down beside the man and felt for a pulse. "He's alive. Help me get him up."

She wedged her shoulder under Mr. Miller's arm, holding her breath against the foul stench of body odor and alcohol, as Matthew hefted the other side.

"We need to get him to a hospital right away," he said.

Deirdre didn't need him to tell her Mr. Miller was near death. Together they lugged the man's body over to the horses.

Matthew frowned. "What's the best way to do this?"

"If you drape him over your horse, we can double up on mine."

"Okay. Help me lift him."

It took some effort, but they managed to get the unconscious man across the back of Matthew's mare, then tied the horse to the rear of Ginger's saddle.

Deirdre took hold of the reins. "I'll get on first, then you climb up behind me."

While she pulled herself into the saddle, Matthew secured his leather bag on the side.

She looked down into his grave face. "It's okay. I've done this many times with Connor." She removed her foot from the stirrup and gestured. "Put your foot there and I'll help." She held out her hand.

Matthew exhaled, grabbed her hand, and swung up behind her.

Deirdre stilled as his solid chest met her back. "Hold on to me. You don't want to fall off."

A beat of time passed, and finally Matthew's arms wrapped around her waist. She closed her eyes and drank in the heady feeling of his strength surrounding her.

Then she gave Ginger a quick kick, and they set off.

A hundred sensations swirled through Matthew as the horse plodded on. Fear for the well-being of the man behind them, discomfort at being back on a horse yet again, and unease at his proximity to Deirdre.

Holding her within the shelter of his arms was proving to be a mix of torment and bliss. He forced himself not to think about the passionate kiss they'd shared, not to appreciate the curves leaning back against him, and not to inhale the scent of her perfumed hair, lest he give in to temptation once again.

Instead, he gazed ahead at the maze of trees and planned the best way to get Mr. Miller to the hospital. James's auto would be the quickest means of transport, far faster than waiting for an ambulance.

The trip back seemed agonizingly slow, probably due to the delicious torture of being so close to Deirdre. At last, the Irish Meadows stables came into view.

"I'll need to borrow your father's car," he announced as they slowed. "Can you arrange that?"

She twisted to glance over her shoulder. Matthew caught his breath at the heated look in her eye. Was she feeling the same pull of attraction as he?

"Daddy's car is parked beside the barn. You get Mr. Miller inside, and I'll find someone to drive us."

"I can drive."

One brow lifted. "All right. Then I'll get Jo. She'll want to come with us."

He dismounted and gave a long exhale, allowing the tension to slowly seep from his body. He turned his attention to Clayton Miller while Deirdre headed into the barn.

The stench of his unwashed body could not disguise the distinct odor of alcohol as Matthew lifted the man into the automobile. Somehow Mr. Miller must have found a supply of whiskey—a large quantity, judging by his present state. If Matthew had thought it was merely a matter of the man sleeping off the effects of drink, he would have left him in the cabin. But he feared something far more serious was endangering his health.

This time, Matthew would take no chances. Since the man was unconscious and could offer no objection, Matthew would take him to the hospital for a thorough examination.

Once Deirdre and Jo were settled in the auto, Matthew followed Deirdre's directions and steered the vehicle toward town. Faint sniffles coming from the backseat alerted Matthew to Jo's distress. He only prayed her father would make it.

Matthew carried Mr. Miller into the hospital, where several attendants rushed to help him. They whisked the man onto a gurney and wheeled him off.

Matthew turned to Deirdre. "I'll go and apprise them of Mr. Miller's condition."

She nodded, keeping an arm around Jo. "We'll be in the waiting room."

Acid churned in Matthew's stomach as he strode down the corridor. Once again, he found a prayer on his lips for Clayton Miller's life. He couldn't help feeling that if he'd only gone back sooner to check on the man, he wouldn't be in this situation.

A nurse pointed to a curtained area where they had taken the patient. Already a team of professionals was working on him.

A doctor lifted his head and stared at Matthew. "Were you the one who brought this man in?"

"That's right. I'm Dr. Clayborne." Matthew removed his hat. "I was treating Mr. Miller for a leg wound. When I came back to check on him today, I found him unconscious in the snow."

"The man smells like he's been doused in alcohol." The doctor pressed a stethoscope to Mr. Miller's chest. "His vitals are weak. Any idea how long he was outdoors?"

"No. But judging from his condition when I found him, I'd say no more than ten to twenty minutes."

"I agree. Which leads me to suspect his problem has more to do with the alcohol than the cold." The man straightened. "I'm Dr. West. Is there a family member I could speak with?"

"His daughter. I'll get her for you." Matthew paused. "I did a procedure on this man's leg to remove an infection that had turned gangrenous. Could you check to see if it's worsened?"

Dr. West threw him a sharp glance. "I'll take a look."

Matthew swallowed the lump of dread in his throat. What if the infection had spread through the man's system and caused his collapse? Could Matthew be responsible for his condition?

He clamped his jaw shut and went in search of Deirdre and

Jo. When he reached the waiting room, he was surprised to find Jo without her hat for once, her long, blond hair neatly plaited.

The women rose as he entered.

"How's my pa?" Jo asked.

"The doctor is examining him now. He'd like to speak with you."

Deirdre put her hand on Jo's shoulder. "I'll come with you."

Matthew led the way back and introduced them to Dr. West.

The man brightened when he spotted Deirdre. "Nurse O'Leary. How nice to see you again."

"And you, Dr. West."

His smile faded. "Why are you here?"

"I was helping Dr. Clayborne treat Mr. Miller."

"I see. Well, I'd like to speak to Miss Miller about her father, but first, Dr. Clayborne, let me commend you on the excellent job you did on the man's leg. The infection is healing nicely. Clearly not the source of the present problem."

The weight of two boulders released from Matthew's shoulders. "Thank you. That's good to know."

Deirdre squeezed his arm, as though she understood the demons that tortured him.

For the first time since Priscilla's death, Matthew felt a fragment of his former confidence returning. Perhaps he was a better physician than he thought.

Now if only they could keep Clayton Miller alive. Because even though his leg was healing, Matthew could tell something far more serious was wrong with the man.

Hours later, Jo paced the empty waiting room of the Long Island hospital. Dr. Clayborne and Miss O'Leary had stayed with her for a while, but when it started getting late, Dr. Clayborne had insisted on driving Miss O'Leary back to Irish Meadows.

He'd promised, however, to return to keep Jo abreast of her father's condition.

If only Seth could be here. But other than riding over to the Sullivan farm, Jo had no way of letting him know about Pa's situation. She supposed she could ask someone to call the Sullivans and get a message to him, yet she doubted Seth would jeopardize his job just to come and hold her hand.

Jo wrapped her arms around her waist. At the mercy of her nerves, she couldn't seem to sit more than five minutes in the uncomfortable chairs. Instead, she recited every prayer she could remember over and over as she paced.

At last, footsteps sounded in the corridor. Jo rushed to the door, hoping for news on her father.

Instead of a doctor, however, Connor O'Leary came into view. Her pulse took off like a bucking bronco. How did he always manage to look so good? Fresh snowflakes glistened on his hat and shoulders. The lamb's-wool collar of his coat was pulled up around his ears. He whipped off his hat, walking directly toward her.

"Jo, Deirdre told me about your father. I'm so sorry." His hazel eyes appeared almost green in the overhead lights.

"Thank you. But you didn't need to come." Anxiety made Jo's palms moist. She pushed her braid over her shoulder, suddenly conscious she must look a mess.

"I drove back with Dr. Clayborne. I wanted to make sure you were all right."

She straightened her spine. As much as she valued his kindness, she'd been dealing with her father's drinking her whole life. She couldn't afford to start depending on Connor O'Leary. "I appreciate your concern, but I'm not your responsibility."

Connor shook his head. "I disagree. I have a vested interest in the outcome of this situation, since it affects you doing your job."

She peered at him, sure this was an excuse to appease her. But since anything was better than waiting alone, she didn't argue.

"Why don't we sit down?" Connor gestured to the row of chairs. "Dr. Clayborne said he'd come back with an update."

Jo nodded and took a seat. Connor sat beside her, so close their thighs touched. She squirmed over an inch, disturbingly aware of his solid frame.

She twisted her fingers together on her lap. "My brother will be worried when he gets home and we're not there."

"Already taken care of. We stopped by the Sullivans' on the way here. Caleb is going to let your brother know what's happening."

She bit her lip. His thoughtful gesture cemented her view that Connor O'Leary was indeed a good man. "Thank you."

Sudden warmth enveloped her hand. "You're not alone, Jo. We'll get you through this. You'll see."

Jo's stomach fluttered. She stared into his eyes and fought to corral her emotions, not wanting to become unglued in front of him.

"This isn't the first time, is it?" Connor's quiet question seemed overly loud in the empty room.

Her gaze fell to the speckled floor tiles. "No. After Pa's last . . . episode . . . we left Illinois and moved here, hoping for a fresh start. When Pa got this job as a foreman, it seemed things were finally turning around." Jo let out a shuddering breath. "Guess I was wrong."

She was so tired of running, tired of hiding Pa's secret, tired of trying to scrape together the money to pay their debts and still have enough to eat.

Connor's arm came around her shoulders and pulled her close. She stiffened, her heart battering her ribs.

"It's okay to share the burden for a while." Connor's low voice near her ear sent a wave of warmth down her back. "I want to do that for you. Will you let me?"

With another tug of his arm, she let her head fall to his shoulder. The dam holding back her emotions crumbled, and hot tears flooded her cheeks. She cried until it seemed her insides had hollowed out. Though ashamed of her weakness, she couldn't deny how good it felt to have someone share her troubles.

The next thing she knew, male voices woke her. Dr. West and Dr. Clayborne stood in front of them.

Jo blinked and pushed away from Connor's shoulder. "How is my father?"

Dr. West's face was grave. "I'm afraid the prognosis isn't good."

The words floated on the air, not penetrating her mind. "What does that mean?"

"Your father's in a coma. It's doubtful that he'll ever regain consciousness."

Shudders coursed through her body. Connor's arm slipped around her waist, holding her up.

"What's wrong with him?" she finally asked.

The two doctors shared a look, then Dr. West exhaled. "Years of drinking have taken their toll. His organs are wearing out. And . . ." He paused. "It seems your father indulged in a large quantity of alcohol. He has severe alcohol poisoning."

She struggled to comprehend. "So it wasn't being out in the snow?" The smell of whiskey on her father's coat had been strong, but she was so used to it, she didn't pay much attention anymore.

"No." Dr. Clayborne's grim expression said it all.

She pressed her lips together. How had Pa gotten ahold of alcohol? Surely Seth wouldn't have brought him any.

Dr. Clayborne gestured to the hall. "You can sit with him for a while if you'd like."

She swallowed and nodded. The only thing she could do now was keep Pa company and pray for a miracle.

20

AFTER A DELICIOUS SUNDAY DINNER of roast beef with mashed potatoes and gravy, topped off with apple pie, Matthew pushed his chair away from the O'Learys' dining table and laid a hand over his stomach. If he kept eating this well, he'd have to start engaging in regular exercise to keep his weight under control. A deep sense of contentment lulled him into a state of total relaxation, a feeling so foreign, he almost didn't recognize it.

Beside him, Phoebe tugged on his sleeve. "Papa, when is my birthday?"

Matthew pulled himself from his food-induced stupor, allowing the thrill of her sweet voice to raise his spirits. "Very soon. Why?"

"Mrs. Harrison says she'll make me a special cake." Her blue eyes danced with excitement.

He marveled at how easily children found happiness.

Deirdre leaned across the table, seeming as excited as Phoebe. "We should have a birthday party to celebrate. Betsy, Rose, and Sean will want to come."

Phoebe's eyes widened. "A party for me?"

"That's right. We'll have cake and presents and games. It's just what we need around here."

"I agree." Kathleen clapped her hands, looking in that instant like a young girl herself. "Brianna can help us arrange it. And we'll invite Colleen and Adam and their families, too."

Matthew's relaxed state vanished. He did a mental tally of how many people that would involve and fought an ensuing surge of alarm. As usual, any time he pictured Phoebe in the midst of a large group of people, his anxiety level shot skyward. Even though Phoebe's health had improved significantly since coming to Irish Meadows, he still couldn't get rid of the inherent worry. Both Adam and Colleen lived in the city. Colleen and her husband Rylan worked in an orphanage, where they'd be exposed to numerous germs on a daily basis. What if they brought an illness into this house?

Matthew wanted to put an end to all talk of parties, but the look of awe on Phoebe's face melted his objections.

He would have to figure out a way to overcome his fear and cope with the situation because disappointing Phoebe was not an option.

<hr />

Deirdre followed Matthew into the parlor, wanting to find out why he'd suddenly gone quiet and left the table. She hoped he wasn't mad about her suggestion for a birthday celebration. She really ought to have discussed it with him first, but the idea had just sort of burst forth on its own.

He stood at the French doors overlooking the snow-covered balcony, his hands clasped behind his back.

She came up beside him. "Is having a party for Phoebe a problem?" she asked. "You didn't seem very enthusiastic about the idea."

He turned his head, and the distress in his gaze caused her heart to flop in her chest.

"Phoebe's never had a birthday party before," he said.

"Never?"

He shook his head. "Priscilla took sick around the time Phoebe turned two, and Phoebe was in the sanatorium for her third birthday. Afterward . . . well, with her health so fragile, I didn't want her around a lot of people."

"Is that why you're anxious now? You fear there will be too many people?"

He gave a wan smile. "Old habits die hard, I suppose. I still find it difficult to let Phoebe . . . be a child. My first instinct is always to hide her away where no harm can come to her."

Sympathy spread through her, and she laid a hand on his arm. "It will get easier in time, I promise." She smiled, grateful that Matthew seemed to have gotten past the lingering awkwardness in her presence and could confide in her once again.

His gaze locked with hers, drawing her to him. Foolish as it was, she longed for him to kiss her again. The thrill of their last embrace still resonated inside her, making her yearn for more than just friendship. Would he ever let down his guard again?

A throat cleared behind them. "I hope we're not interrupting." Mama's amused voice lilted across the room.

Heat flared in Deirdre's cheeks as Connor wheeled her mother into the room with Phoebe beside them.

"Not at all," Deirdre replied. "We were just discussing the party."

"Must be some discussion." Connor threw her a cheeky grin. "If you'll excuse me, Daddy wants to see me in his study."

Phoebe skipped across the room to seize Deirdre's hand, her fingers slightly sticky from the pie. "Miss Deirdre? Could we invite my grandma and grandpa to the party?"

Deirdre brushed a wisp of blond hair from the girl's cheek.

Looking into the earnest little face, her heart swelled with love. "You'll have to ask your father about that."

Matthew bent to the girl's level. "Your grandparents are away on a trip. And even if they weren't, Toronto is far away."

Phoebe frowned, and then her face brightened. "They could take the train like we did."

He shook his head. "I don't think they'll be able to come. But don't worry, we'll see them again very soon. Once we finish Mrs. O'Leary's treatment, we'll be going home."

Deirdre had a fair idea Phoebe thought they'd be staying at Irish Meadows indefinitely, and braced herself for the girl's reaction.

Sure enough, tears filled Phoebe's eyes. "I don't want to go home. I like it here. Why can't we live here?"

The torment on Matthew's face tore at Deirdre's composure as much as Phoebe's distress. She swung the girl up in her arms. "Maybe you could come for a visit in the summer and learn to ride Twizzle." She hoped her false cheeriness would lift the girl's spirits.

The tears seemed to vanish. "I could go swimming with Betsy and Rose."

"That would be fun. But for now, let's think about your party. You must tell Mrs. Harrison your favorite kind of cake."

Her ploy worked. Phoebe's eyes lit up, and she began to describe the flavors she loved.

Deirdre met Matthew's grateful gaze over the girl's head.

"Thank you," he mouthed.

Deirdre nodded, very glad she didn't have to speak. Phoebe wasn't the only one who'd have trouble coping when it came time for the Claybornes to leave.

Connor knocked on the door to his father's study, then pushed into the room. As usual, Daddy sat behind the massive mahogany desk, a ledger in front of him.

"I'm here. What did you want to see me about?" Connor plopped down in the leather chair facing the desk.

Daddy removed his reading glasses and rubbed the bridge of his nose. "I need to discuss something with you."

Connor's spirits instantly nose-dived. "Is this about Excalibur?"

"As a matter of fact, it is. The McCreadys are coming by next weekend to see what type of progress you've made with him." His eyes narrowed. "Should I be worried?"

Connor stiffened. He hadn't spent as much time as he should have with the animal. Ever since he'd discovered Jo's connection with the horse, he'd left Excalibur to her. "We're getting close. My stable hand, Jo, managed to ride him around the enclosure the other day."

His father's brows dipped. "That's a far cry from being ready to race."

"I'm aware of that."

"How do you plan to remedy the situation? If he's not ready by spring, the McCreadys will expect a full refund."

Connor ran a hand over his jaw. "I'll make it my priority for the rest of the week. Jo has been doing some great work with him. We should be ready for a trial race soon."

"Which brings me to my next topic."

Connor swallowed hard and waited.

"Gil tells me you've allowed the new hand to take over Excalibur's training." His father's piercing stare had the same effect on Connor as it had when he was a child. Suddenly he was ten years old again, waiting for punishment for one of his many pranks.

He met his father's gaze. "Jo's assisting me, yes."

"Gil says this kid is still green, and while I admire your attempt to mentor the boy, the McCreadys are paying for *your* services, not those of a rookie stable hand." Daddy closed the ledger. "As of today, I want your undivided attention on this horse. Leave the boy out of it."

Connor scowled. In a matter of minutes, all his hard work had trickled away and only Gil's opinion mattered. He stood, arms crossed, staring at his father. "Fine. I'll devote all my time to Excalibur," he said stiffly.

"Good. I'll check with you in a few days to see how you're progressing."

Connor gave a curt nod and strode out the door. Tomorrow he'd have to figure out how to get Excalibur to respond to him without Jo around.

Connor feared that might be an impossible task.

Matthew pillowed his head on his arms and stared at the ceiling of his bedroom, all thoughts of sleep far away. Down the hall, his daughter had fallen into a peaceful slumber, thanks to Deirdre and Mrs. Harrison's talk of parties and birthday cakes.

Matthew sighed, replaying the night's unsettling events. His daughter's dependency on Deirdre and the O'Leary family was worse than he'd imagined. Even the addition of a puppy to their Toronto household might not be enough to ease Phoebe's sorrow at having to leave Irish Meadows. Matthew needed to start preparing her for the reality that very soon they would be going home.

His thoughts turned to the dour Miss Shearing and the need to secure a new nanny. It seemed unfair to leave the woman believing she had a job to return to. In the morning, he would pen a letter of termination, as well as one to his housekeeper to begin interviewing candidates for the position. With any luck, by the time they arrived home, she'd have it narrowed down to the best of the lot.

He shifted to his side and punched his fist into the pillow. The real reason he couldn't sleep churned in Matthew's chest like a bad case of indigestion. Phoebe wasn't the only one who'd be miserable to leave Irish Meadows. The thought of never seeing Deirdre again caused a deep ache inside him that nothing could alleviate.

This unwelcome longing continued to wreak havoc on his sanity, shaking his perceived control over his life. He felt trapped in a state of limbo. For even if he found the courage to take a risk and voice his feelings, Deirdre's career stood in their way. Becoming a doctor required years of schooling and long hours as an intern. She would have no place in her life for a husband or stepdaughter. No matter how much Matthew and Phoebe might wish it.

Somehow, over the next few weeks, he'd have to learn to accept that fact—and say good-bye.

21

CONNOR STARED IN DISBELIEF as Jo led Excalibur into the corral. She was supposed to be at the hospital with her father. Connor had counted on her absence to give him time to come up with a plan—a way to tell her she would no longer be able to work with the stallion.

He made his way over to the fence. Conscious of the other workers nearby, he called out, "Jo, can I speak to you a minute?"

She patted Excalibur's side and started toward him. "Good morning, Mr. O'Leary." The infernal hat hid half of her face.

If only she didn't have to wear that horrible get-up, but the other men would refuse to work alongside a woman. Not to mention his father's reaction should he find out.

Yet he couldn't seem to ignore the part of him that wished she could release her beautiful blond hair from its hideous prison and uncover that pretty face.

Connor leaned over the fence. "Why aren't you at the hospital?"

She frowned. "I can't sit at Pa's bedside for weeks on end.

Besides, some of the other hands said Excalibur's owners are coming to check on his progress. I didn't want us to lose momentum in his training."

"Us?"

She tilted her chin. "That's right. If you're going to make any progress, you need my help."

He clamped his mouth shut. Despite his father's orders, Connor knew Jo was right. He would never have the stallion ready before the owners arrived unless she assisted him.

Jo pushed up the brim of her hat and smiled at him. "If we work as a team, I'm sure we'll see results."

He jerked at the realization that he'd never seen her really smile before. The effect was . . . disconcerting . . . to say the least. He took a deep breath to rein in his emotions and focus on the task at hand. Working together was a risk Connor was going to have to take. "Fine. Let's get started."

He pulled his work gloves out of his jacket pocket and entered the enclosure, praying his father wouldn't come out to check on the horse today.

Over the course of the next few hours, Connor and Jo developed a rhythm. They worked in tandem, each taking turns walking Excalibur and trying to ride him. By the end of the morning, the horse had actually allowed each of them in the saddle.

When they broke for lunch, Connor ate at his father's desk while finishing up some paperwork, yet he found his thoughts drifting to Jo. She was right about one thing—without her help, Excalibur would never be ready for inspection. He closed the ledger with a smile, surprised to be so eager to get back to work.

Back to Jo.

He admired so many things about her. Her strong work ethic, her love for the animals, her loyalty to her family. Not to mention her flawless blue eyes that gazed at him as if he were some sort of hero.

He shook his head as he rose. He needed to keep that type of thinking far away from his work.

On his way to the stables, a burst of male laughter rang out in the barn. Connor's feet halted on a wave of regret. He missed the camaraderie he'd once enjoyed with the men. Instead of continuing on, he entered the barn in the hopes of joining the fun.

Several hands were huddled around the tack room door. The sound of scuffling came from inside.

Connor's light mood vanished.

Mac hung on the outskirts, his brow furrowed. "Leave the kid alone, why don't ya? Can't you see he's scared?"

The tallest hand—Lanky Luke, as they called him—shoved at Mac's shoulder. "We're just having a little fun. He's gotta learn to be a man somehow."

"It's about time we see what's under that hat," a voice drawled from inside the room, "or under those baggy overalls."

Another round of guffaws rang out.

Connor's gut tightened. On a surge of adrenaline, he pushed forward. "What in the blazes is going on here?"

The men parted like ants scurrying from the hill, leaving Connor access to the open doorway.

Inside, Jo sat huddled on a bench, both hands clutching her hat.

Eugene Jones had his fist around the shoulder straps of her overalls.

A red haze clouded Connor's vision. He leapt into the room, grabbed Gene by the shirt, and shoved him against the nearest wall. Tightening his grip, he lifted the man until his toes barely skimmed the ground. "If I ever catch you manhandling Jo again, you'll be finding yourself unemployed. And I guarantee you won't get another job around here." He let his hard gaze swing to the other men in the room. "Have I made myself clear?"

With Connor's fist at his windpipe, Gene could only nod.

Slowly, Connor relaxed his grip until the man's boots hit the ground. "Now get back to work—all of you."

Eugene glared at Connor, tugged his shirt back into place, and stalked out of the tack room. The others followed, muttered oaths the only evidence of their dissent.

Connor took a breath to get his temper under control and turned to face Jo. "What was that about?"

She swiped her sleeve across her face. "Nothing."

"Don't give me that. Something made them go after you."

She lifted her head, her eyes luminous with unshed tears. Connor's heart stalled like an automobile with no gasoline.

"They've never liked me since the day I started. Called me a baby and made fun of my clothes. All except Mac. He's always been sweet."

An irrational annoyance toward Mac itched at Connor's neck.

"Now they're jealous because I'm allowed to work with one of the racehorses." Jo shrugged. "They call me the 'boss's pet.'"

Connor paced the small area. "Of all the small-minded, immature . . ."

Jo stood and adjusted the straps of her overalls. "Let's forget it and get back to work. I want to finish on time so I can go to the hospital."

She squared her shoulders as though willing herself to be strong, yet a sweep of sadness passed over her features.

A horde of emotions slammed through Connor's system—emotions he didn't care to examine too closely. "Fine. But if anything like this happens again, I expect you to come and find me. I won't tolerate bullying on my watch."

"All right." She slipped by him into the main corridor.

Connor remained behind to clear his head. He needed to focus on Excalibur, not on a certain female who was creating more problems by the minute.

And not only with his staff.

After one last workout on Saturday morning, Jo brushed Excalibur's coat until it shone. The McCreadys were expected in less than two hours, and Connor had asked her to be on hand to keep the stallion calm. She couldn't help the nerves that jangled her system, wishing for some way to predict the outcome of the day's events. All she could do was pray things would go well—for Connor's sake.

Her heart quivered at the mere thought of the man. A man who'd allowed her to keep working here despite her deception. A man who treated her like an equal and who valued her opinion with Excalibur. A man who defended her against the bullying of the other hands.

How was she supposed to guard her heart against someone like that?

She sighed and ran her hands over Excalibur's flank. No point in wishing for the impossible. She was the uncultured daughter of an alcoholic drifter. He was the son of one of the richest families in the county.

And on top of it all, he was her boss. One more reason to keep her emotions in check.

"Hey, Jo. How are you doing?" Connor's head appeared over the stall door.

She gave a small start, then resumed her brushing. "A little nervous."

"That's only natural." He lifted his hand to reveal a package. "I figured you might like a change of clothes, something more suitable for a champion horse trainer."

Panic rushed in. "But I can't—"

"I got trousers, a shirt, and a large vest. Plus a riding cap. All very masculine." He handed the package to her. "Try it on and see what you think."

"Where?" She couldn't exactly just take off her clothes in front of him.

"In Sam's quarters. I'll show you."

She followed him to the far end of the secondary barn, where Connor stopped in front of a door that apparently led to the trainer's private quarters.

"Don't worry. Sam won't mind," Connor said as he opened the door. "There's a mirror above the sink."

Jo entered and closed the door behind her. Though small, the room was cozy, with a single bed, a chair, and a bedside table. On the far wall, she found a chest of drawers and a sink with a rectangular mirror above it.

Jo quickly changed into the clothing Connor had brought and pulled the riding cap on. She secured the chin strap and squinted in the mirror to make sure all of the netting was covered. Without the floppy sides of her usual hat, Jo felt naked. She tugged her kerchief from the pocket of her overalls and knotted it around her neck. Thank goodness the weather was cold. If it were summer, she'd look ridiculous wearing all these layers of clothes buttoned up to her ears.

She walked to the door and opened it an inch. Connor, who'd been standing guard, whirled around. "Let's see."

He pushed the door wider and scanned her from the hat to her boots. "Big improvement." He grinned.

"But do I still look like a boy?" she whispered anxiously.

"Sure. Unless anyone gets too close, which they'll have no cause to do."

"What about the other guys? They'll notice right off and . . ." She gulped. What would Eugene do?

"You can change back right after the race. The guys won't even notice."

Jo swallowed her nerves and laid her things on the wooden chair beside the bed. "Won't your father be expecting *you* to ride Excalibur?"

Connor had been strangely vague about his father's view of her work with the stallion.

"Let me worry about my father. Come on. Let's show these folks what their horse can do."

Half an hour later, Jo sat astride the great stallion at the starting position of the racetrack and willed her heart rate to lessen. Her nerves would not help Excalibur perform his best, even if it was only a mock race. They'd opted not to use the gates, since they hadn't had a chance to reintroduce the horse to that yet. Today was simply about running.

Connor had chosen three other horses with even temperaments to race against them. The best-case scenario, he explained, was to show the owners that Excalibur could run the track in a competitive manner. Winning wasn't a requirement yet. All the McCreadys needed was a show of good faith that their money wasn't being wasted and that Connor was making progress.

Please, God, just let Excalibur finish the race cleanly.

As if in answer, the stallion let out a whinny and tossed his head. Jo leaned forward to give him a rub of encouragement. "We can do this, boy," she whispered.

She pulled her cap down as tight as it could go and leaned forward in the saddle, crop in hand, though she would never use it.

The starter's pistol rang out, and the horses shot forward. Jo kept her hands loose on the reins, giving Excalibur his lead. And he did not disappoint. He surged around the track as though flying. After rounding the second bend, Jo finally relaxed and relished the sheer joy of the ride. They kept a steady pace back from the second horse. At the last turn, Jo gave Excalibur a light kick, and he responded with a burst of speed. He reached the first-place stallion, inching forward just past his tail. But in the end, the other horse crossed the finish line before them.

Jo released a breath as she gradually slowed their pace. They hadn't won, but she hoped the owners would be pleased with a solid second place.

From the corner of her eye, she saw Connor, Mr. O'Leary, and the McCreadys watching them ease to a stop. Her heart still thundered in her chest. She'd done what she needed to do—and now she had to quietly disappear.

Before anyone could question her.

Still glowing in the aftermath of Excalibur's triumph, Connor whistled his favorite tune on the way to find Jo. Without her assistance, Excalibur would never have been ready to race, never mind come in second. That talented girl had saved his pride and his reputation—and he owed her a big debt of gratitude.

Thankfully, his father hadn't said a word about Connor not riding the horse, likely due to the McCreadys' ecstatic reaction.

Connor couldn't keep the grin off his face as he practically ran into the barn. Jo should be finished changing her clothes by now. He hoped she hadn't left for home yet.

His grin widened when she emerged from Sam's quarters and closed the door behind her. Why did he suddenly find that ugly hat so endearing?

"We did it!" Connor swooped her up in a bear hug, twirling her around until her feet left the floor.

Her eyes widened and she let out a squeak. "Put me down."

But he didn't release her. "Do you know how amazing you are?" He swung her around in another circle.

A few seconds later, he slowly set her feet on the ground, not letting her go. She felt too good against his chest. "You saved my life. How can I ever thank you?"

A rosy blush invaded her cheeks as her lashes swept down. "You're exaggerating."

He tipped up her chin. "You have no idea how much was riding on this. If Excalibur had done badly, it would have cost me my pride, as well as my father's respect. More importantly, you saved us from losing a valuable client."

Her lips lifted in a soft smile. "It's the least I could do after you let me continue to work here. Not to mention what you've done for my father, paying his hospital bill."

A burst of irritation momentarily dampened his euphoria. "That's not—"

"Don't deny it, Connor O'Leary. Dr. West told me what you did."

He frowned, incensed that the doctor hadn't kept that information to himself.

"I don't know where I'd be right now if not for you. I'm only glad I could do something to repay your kindness."

She looked at him with such admiration, such affection, such . . . longing, that Connor labored for breath. His pulse pounded like a hundred hooves in his chest. Before he could think, he lowered his head and pressed his lips to hers. She gave a small gasp. He pulled back, his mouth hovering over hers, waiting for her to push him away . . . or not.

"Connor," she whispered.

Taking that as permission, he captured her mouth again. She wrapped her arms around his neck pulling him closer until he thought he would explode with the sensations rioting through his system. She tasted like honey and smelled like the outdoors. Her lithe figure melded perfectly with his. The world shrank to the feel of her lips, the caress of her hand on his neck, the warmth of her body.

"What in tarnation am I looking at here?"

His father's bellow sliced through the haze in Connor's brain.

With a gasp, Jo jerked out of his arms. An expression of horror flashed over her face.

With no other recourse, Connor came forward to face his father. "Dad, this is Josephine Miller, the person responsible for Excalibur's amazing progress."

His father's brows slammed together. "Josephine? You mean to tell me you have a girl working here? Training one of the most expensive horses this side of the country?"

Nerves trembled in Connor's stomach, but he would not give in to his father's intimidation tactics. He lifted his chin. "That's right. And she's done a fantastic job, as you saw today."

Daddy grunted. "Stand aside."

Every instinct in Connor wanted to protect Jo, but he moved to one side, ready to jump in if needed.

Daddy reached out to raise the brim of Jo's hat. "You rode in the race?"

"Y-yes, sir."

"Why were you pretending to be a boy?"

Connor expected her to shrink back against the verbal barrage, but instead she squared her shoulders. "Folks don't hire girls as stable hands, and I needed the job."

He turned to Connor. "So you didn't know she was a girl?"

"Not at first, no."

A nerve ticked in his father's jaw. "As much as I appreciate what you've done for Excalibur, I'm afraid we can't have a female working here. It will cause too much dissension among the men." He raised a brow at Connor. "Among other things."

Heat blasted up his neck, but Connor refused to cower. "No one needs to know she's a girl. The disguise has worked so far."

A slight flare of sympathy crossed Daddy's features. "I'm sorry, but I can't go along with this. I'm afraid you're out of a job, young lady."

Jo's gaze slid to the floor. "I understand, sir. If you'll excuse me, I need to be going." She jammed her hat down and dashed toward the door.

"Jo, wait!" Connor went to chase after her, but his father grabbed him by the arm.

"Let her go. We need to talk."

Connor watched Jo's retreating back and sighed. He'd talk to

210

her later, in private, when things had calmed down. He turned and steeled himself for his father's reaction.

Sure enough, anger simmered in his father's eyes. "Have you taken leave of your senses, boy? Kissing a stable hand?"

Connor's stomach sank to his boots. It sounded so demeaning when Daddy said it out loud. "I didn't mean to. I came to congratulate her and . . . got caught up in the moment."

The vein in his father's temple pulsed. "You're lucky the McCreadys weren't with me. They certainly wouldn't appreciate knowing some unqualified adolescent girl was training their prize racehorse." He raked a hand over his face. "You went against my express instructions concerning Excalibur and compounded that by acting inappropriately with an employee. It's clear I can't trust your judgment right now." Daddy straightened to his full height, as if firming a decision. "Until further notice, I'm removing you from your training duties. You can take the vacant stable hand position—if you think you can handle that." He gave Connor a long look, disappointment shadowing his eyes, and then walked away.

Stunned, Connor sagged against the barn wall, as deflated as a punctured tire. How had everything gone so wrong? One minute, he'd been riding high on a wave of victory. The next, he'd lost his father's respect and approval.

One lapse in judgment had cost Jo her job and derailed Connor's future.

And he had no idea what to do to fix it.

22

T HE DAY OF PHOEBE'S BIRTHDAY PARTY dawned cold but sunny. Deirdre leapt out of bed, full of purpose and excitement for the day ahead, ready for the preparations that needed to be done.

But first she had a mission. She rummaged in the back of her closet, pulled out her floral hat box, and opened the lid. Inside sat her treasured china doll dressed in blue velvet. Angelina had blond ringlets, blue eyes that blinked, and red lips. Deirdre stroked the hair with reverent fingers, waves of nostalgia making her smile. Angelina had been her favorite toy as a child. Deirdre only hoped the doll would bring Phoebe half as much joy.

Carefully, she returned the toy to the box and, using some ribbon she had in her top drawer, tied a bow on the top. Then she set the gift on the dresser for later.

After a quick breakfast, Deirdre found the bag of decorations in the hall closet and headed into the living room. She'd only started to sort through the contents when Brianna breezed in, armed with her own supplies.

"This is a wonderful idea." Bree kissed Deirdre's cheek in greeting. "My children are almost as excited as if it were their own birthday. Gil's keeping them busy until it's time to come over."

Deirdre paused from sorting rolls of ribbon. "I can't believe Phoebe has never had a birthday party."

Brianna set her bag on a chair. "Never?"

Deirdre shook her head. "She lost her mother, then lived in a sanatorium for over a year. She's hardly been around anyone but her nanny ever since."

"That poor child. I can't imagine what she's been through." Tears welled on Brianna's lashes. She sat down hard on the sofa and pulled out a handkerchief.

Deirdre laid the ribbon down with a frown. Brianna had always been the sister most prone to tears, but this display seemed unusual—even for her.

Deirdre crossed to sit beside her. "Is everything all right, honey?"

Bree dabbed her eyes. "Everything's wonderful." She gave a light laugh, her cheeks pinkening.

Deirdre's mouth fell open. "You're not?"

Brianna grinned. "I am."

Deirdre grabbed her sister in a hard hug. "When?"

"In the spring." She pulled back to dab at her cheeks. "Oh, Dee. I've been longing for another baby, but I felt so guilty. After all, we have three beautiful children already. How greedy is it to want more?"

"It's not greedy to love children. You're a wonderful mother. And I'm so happy you'll get to welcome another child into your family." Deirdre's own eyes grew damp with happy tears, yet her delight was mixed with a twinge of regret that she would likely never experience this joy herself. "Looks like you and Colleen will have babies together again."

Brianna beamed. "I must admit to feeling jealous when I

heard she and Rylan were expecting. But now our children will have more playmates." She leaned in to whisper, "And if my instincts are correct, I believe Adam and Maggie might be expecting as well."

A spurt of envy twisted Deirdre's heart. It seemed all her siblings, except she and Connor, had been blessed with large families. She took in a deep rasp of air and forced a smile. "That's wonderful."

As if sensing her sadness, Brianna squeezed her hand. "Don't worry, honey. Your turn will come."

She sighed. "I don't think so, Bree. I believe God wants me to dedicate my life to my patients." Resolutely, she pushed her regrets aside and got to her feet before her sister could argue with her. "We'd better get this room decorated before a certain birthday girl comes down."

Matthew sat on a wingback chair in a corner of the O'Leary's parlor and surveyed the mayhem surrounding him.

Children chased one another around the room, shouting and squealing, while the adults seemed able to carry on normal conversations around them. Surprisingly, Phoebe seemed unperturbed, right in the thick of it all.

Matthew tried unsuccessfully to remember the names of all Deirdre's nieces and nephews. He had a hard enough time getting her siblings and their spouses straight. Rylan and Colleen, he'd learned, ran an orphanage in Manhattan and had two adopted children plus two boys of their own. And judging from Colleen's expansive middle, they expected their next child very soon. Deirdre's oldest brother, Adam, and his wife, Maggie, lived in the city as well with their three kids. Brianna and Gil's were the only children he could tell apart.

Deirdre walked to the middle of the room and gave a shrill

whistle. Amazingly, everyone stopped, and for two blessed seconds, silence reigned.

"All right, it's time for cake and presents."

A loud whoop went up, followed by another ear-splitting whistle.

"We'll only have cake if everyone is seated quietly." Deirdre paused to look pointedly at her nephews elbowing each other. "Find yourselves a chair or a spot on the floor. Phoebe, come here, sweetheart."

While the other children raced to find seats, Phoebe approached Deirdre with a hint of trepidation on her face.

Deirdre pulled over a fancy chair and motioned for Phoebe to sit. "The chair of honor goes to the birthday girl."

Phoebe gave Deirdre a blinding smile before she climbed onto the seat and arranged the folds of her dress.

Kathleen had insisted on making Phoebe a special outfit, saying she could still sew with her right hand and it gave her good practice using her left one to assist. The bright blue fabric looked suspiciously like the gown Deirdre was wearing.

Everyone had gone out of their way to make this day special for his daughter, and Matthew had no idea how to show his appreciation for all they'd done.

Mrs. Harrison came in wheeling a cart containing the most amazing cake he'd ever seen. It had multiple layers covered with chocolate icing and what appeared to be swirls of roses, as well as five lit candles.

Phoebe's eyes grew as round as the top layer of the cake.

The piano sounded, and everyone began to sing. Matthew blinked, vague memories stirring from one of his own birthdays when his mother had done something similar.

The cart stopped in front of his daughter.

Deirdre laid her hand on Phoebe's shoulder. "Okay, sweetie, make a wish and blow out the candles."

Phoebe nodded, taking the instructions very seriously it seemed.

"I wish for—"

Betsy grabbed her arm. "You can't tell anyone or it won't come true."

Phoebe clapped a hand over her mouth and giggled. Then she blew until all the flames were extinguished.

Everyone clapped and hollered. Mrs. Harrison came forward. "I'll cut the cake, and Miss Brianna will serve all the children who are seated quietly."

Matthew marveled at the adults' ability to control such a motley crowd. Though boisterous, the youngsters were remarkably obedient.

"From the expression on your face, Doctor, I assume you haven't been to many birthday parties."

Matthew looked up to see Deirdre grinning at him.

"Not really."

She laid a hand on his shoulder, still smiling. Her enticing perfume enveloped him like a hug. She leaned down, and for one crazy moment, he thought she might kiss him. Instead, she whispered in his ear. "Do you have a gift for Phoebe?"

He stiffened on his chair. "I never thought of it."

He made the mistake of turning his head and found wide green eyes much too close to his.

"Don't you exchange birthday gifts?" The incredulous tone of her question made him feel like the worst sort of heel.

"It's not a practice I'm accustomed to, no." He didn't tell her that after his mother died, there had been no more celebrations of any kind in his house.

Stark sympathy washed her features. She gave his shoulder a slight squeeze. "Don't worry. You can share mine."

Once they had partaken of the most delicious chocolate cream cake Matthew had ever sampled, the children came forward with small wrapped packages. It appeared each child had chosen one of their own toys to share with Phoebe. She opened every one with equal glee.

Kathleen wheeled her chair closer to Phoebe. "I know I said your dress was my present," she told her, "but I have another little something as well."

She handed Phoebe a book. Phoebe flipped open the pages and Matthew made out some colorful illustrations.

"It's a picture Bible. It used to belong to my son . . . before he died. I thought you might like it." Kathleen's sad smile matched the sheen of tears in her eyes.

Matthew sprang to his feet. "Kathleen, this is too generous. Are you sure you don't want to keep it?" He knew how much her son had meant to her, and how much this Bible must mean as well.

She smiled at him. "I'd rather someone enjoy the stories as much as Daniel used to."

As though sensing the enormity of the gift, Phoebe came forward to hug Kathleen. "Thank you, Mrs. O'Leary. I like it very much."

"You're most welcome, sweetie."

The women around him dabbed hankies to their faces. Even James appeared moved.

Deirdre turned to pick up a large hat box with a bow on top. "Happy birthday, Phoebe. This is from your daddy . . . with a little help from me." She winked and handed the gift to his daughter, now back in her special seat.

Phoebe looked up in awe. "It's very big."

Deirdre laughed. "Go ahead and open it."

Carefully, Phoebe removed the lid and pulled out a doll with blond curls. Phoebe's mouth fell open, and then she gasped. Clutching the gift to her chest, she jumped from the chair and threw herself at Matthew. "Thank you, Papa. I've always wanted a doll like this."

Matthew froze for a second, then bent to kiss the top of her head. "You're welcome. But you should really thank Miss Deirdre. It was her idea."

Deirdre knelt beside Phoebe and fingered the doll's curls. "She used to be mine when I was your age. I hope you love her as much as I did."

Phoebe wrapped her arms around Deirdre's neck. "I do. Thank you, Miss Deirdre."

The two clung together for a second, then Deirdre kissed Phoebe's cheek. Blinking, she rose. "Well now, how about we ask Aunt Maggie to play the piano for us and we can sing some songs?"

A loud chorus of cheers went up, and the children scrambled to find positions near the piano.

When the rousing voices raised the volume level of the room to near blistering, Matthew came up behind Deirdre and touched her elbow. "Join me outside for a moment?"

She raised a brow in question but nodded and followed him out into the hallway. In search of privacy, he led her to the therapy room and flicked on the lights.

"Is everything all right?" Concern shadowed her frank gaze.

He smiled. "Everything is perfect—thanks to you."

A blush spread over her cheeks. "It wasn't only me."

"You came up with the idea of a party and arranged all the details—down to the perfect gift for Phoebe." He moved closer. "I've never seen my daughter happier, and I have you to thank for it." For the first time, he truly understood what Phoebe had been missing by living such a sheltered existence.

Deirdre's eyes reflected the glow from the overhead lights. "I was happy to do it. She is such a special girl, Matthew. All she needs is a little love and attention to truly blossom."

Matthew swallowed a giant lump in his throat. This woman had enriched his relationship with his daughter in ways he could never express.

"Promise me something," she said, her expression earnest. "Promise you'll try to find Phoebe a mother who will love her."

A dagger of pain pierced his heart. "You know my views on marriage."

"Then promise you'll find a new nanny for Phoebe. One who will love her and not stifle her like Miss Shearing."

"Actually, I'm planning on replacing Miss Shearing as soon as I get home."

She tilted her head. "You are?"

"Yes. It became apparent that she's quite unsuitable." *In more ways than one.* He sighed. "If only you would take the job."

"What?"

Heat blasted up his neck. Had he said that aloud? "It's just that you're so good with Phoebe, and she adores you. But I know you have plans for your future."

A soft sigh escaped Deirdre's lips. "The good of the one versus the good of the many."

"I beg your pardon?"

"Something you said to me back in Toronto, about abandoning your patients for one stroke victim. I understand now what you meant." She pushed a strand of hair behind her ear. "Though I'd love to dedicate myself to Phoebe, I can help so many more children by becoming a pediatrician." She gave a weak smile. "I know you'll find the right woman to help raise your daughter, Matthew. I'll keep you and Phoebe in my prayers. Always."

Matthew's chest muscles tightened to the point of pain. Of course she couldn't waste her talents as a mere nanny. "Thank you, Deirdre, for everything."

He bent to kiss her cheek. She turned her face, and his breath clogged in his lungs. The irresistible urge to pull her closer and taste her lips again swept through him. But he held himself firm, knowing it wouldn't be fair. Wouldn't be right.

They stared into each other's eyes for several seconds, until a wave of sadness overpowered him and, with great reluctance, he stepped back. "I'd better see how the birthday girl is faring."

As he left the room, he tried to brush aside the foolish notion that Deirdre could ever join their family. Clearly she wanted no part of such a future, and Matthew could not in good conscience ask her to sacrifice her dreams for his daughter.

He'd have to trust God to help him find the right person for Phoebe.

Engulfed in his thoughts, he didn't see the housekeeper emerge from James's study and almost walked right into her.

"Excuse me, Mrs. Johnston. I wasn't paying attention."

"Dr. Clayborne, I was about to come and find you." Confusion etched the older woman's face. "There's someone on the telephone asking for Miss Phoebe."

Matthew went completely still. "Did they give their name?"

"A Mrs. Pentergast."

Matthew's stomach dropped to his shoes. His in-laws were supposed to be in England. How had they found out Phoebe was here? "Thank you, Mrs. Johnston. I will handle this."

With grim determination, he entered the study and closed the door.

23

JO SAT AT HER FATHER'S BEDSIDE, watching the shallow movement of his chest beneath the white sheet, and fought the despair that crept over her like a fog.

Please, Lord, let Pa wake up. I promise to take better care of him if you just let him come back to us.

Despite what the doctors said, Jo had to believe her father would recover. He'd been in worse situations and pulled through. She was sure he'd do it again this time.

Jo still couldn't believe Pa had fooled her into thinking he was weaker than he was, and while she was at work, he'd got out to find some alcohol. Seth had discovered the empty bottle in the snow near the outhouse and followed Pa's footsteps all the way to the Sullivans' bunkhouse where the stable hands lived. Seemed Pa had snuck in while the men were at work and snitched a bottle of bourbon. He must have drunk the whole thing on the way back and passed out before he reached the cabin.

Resentment bubbled through her. Resentment at having to

constantly monitor her father's every move, as if she were the parent and he the child.

Yet a persistent tug of guilt ate at her conscience. Could she have prevented his self-destructive behavior if she hadn't been so wrapped up in her job at Irish Meadows? She couldn't wait to escape that dreary cabin every morning. Couldn't wait to spend time with the horses. And with Connor.

Now, with her father's life hanging in the balance, she'd been fired. Her shoulders sagged. She'd have to find another job, perhaps cooking or cleaning, since no one would hire a female to work with horses. Mr. O'Leary's reaction proved that.

She laid her head back and attempted to find a bearable position on the hard chair. With little to occupy her mind, Jo's thoughts circled back to Connor and the kiss they'd shared in the barn. Her pulse sprinted, recalling the feel of his lips on hers, his strong arms around her.

But the question remained—why had Connor kissed her?

Surely he couldn't be interested in the poor daughter of an alcoholic—a girl who, up until recently, he'd thought to be a boy. No, he must have just lost his head in the thrill of the moment.

Footsteps sounded as someone entered the room. Maybe Seth had finally come to visit, as he'd been promising.

Jo opened her eyes and blinked. Connor stood at the foot of the bed.

Her pulse stuttered to life as she straightened on the chair. "Connor, why are you here?"

"I wanted to see how you . . . how your father is doing."

She willed her breathing to return to normal as she rose and smoothed her clothing. "The same. But at least he's no worse."

"That's good, I guess." Connor's usual jovial personality seemed to have disappeared. Lines bracketed his mouth.

"I'm sorry about earlier with your father," she said. "I hope he didn't give you a hard time for . . ." Heat rushed into her cheeks. She hadn't meant to mention the kiss, but the issue rose up larger than life between them.

"For kissing a stable hand?" Connor's lips twitched. "Yeah, he wasn't thrilled about that. I think he was just relieved you were a girl."

"Oh." She bit back a nervous laugh, for the first time realizing what it must have looked like to Mr. O'Leary.

"I owe you an apology, Jo. I was out of line, kissing you like that. I hope you can forgive me."

Forgive him? She wished he'd repeat the crime. "No need to apologize," she said. "I didn't exactly beat you off with a stick." Again her cheeks burned, recalling how brazen she'd been in her response. She moved to straighten the pillows behind her father's head.

Connor cleared his throat. "So what will you do for work now?"

"I'll find a job—somewhere. I always do." She fussed with the bedsheets.

He came up and took her arm, turning her to face him. "Jo, I care what happens to you." His hazel eyes burned with intensity. "What can I do to help?"

Silly tears pricked the backs of her eyes. "You've already done more than enough. But once I collect my last pay, I'm no longer your problem."

"I can't accept that. I *won't* accept it."

He pulled her close and lowered his mouth to hers. Gone was the sweetness of their first kiss. This kiss tasted of desperation, of trying to prove something to her. She grabbed his jacket and held on, her heart bucking harder than Excalibur on the day he'd thrown her.

When at last Connor pulled away, he gave her a heated stare. "I care too much about you to let you walk out of my life."

For a moment, her heart soared. She couldn't believe what he was telling her. If only . . . "Your father would never accept our relationship, Connor. My family works for rich people like you. We barely have food on the table each night." She shook her head. "There's no point in starting something that can never be."

His brows thundered together, causing him to look, in that instant, exactly like his father. "I don't give two figs about that. I know your heart. You're kind and loyal, and you love your family—whether they deserve it or not. You sitting vigil here, despite what your father's done to you, proves that." He cupped her face between his hands, his callused thumbs caressing her cheek. "Jo, I—"

A strange gurgling noise came from the bed behind them. Jo pushed past Connor to her father's side. His lips were blue, his face a ghastly gray. He couldn't seem to breathe.

"Get a doctor!" she screamed.

Connor raced from the room.

"Pa! Can you hear me?" She shook his arm, but the eerie noise continued to rattle in his chest. She had no idea what to do to help him. "Don't leave me, Pa. Please." Panic swirled in her lungs.

A doctor and two nurses rushed into the room and immediately started working. One of the nurses moved in front of Jo. "You'll have to leave, Miss."

Jo's feet seemed rooted to the floor, her eyes glued to the flurry of arms and equipment. Someone jabbed a needle into her father's arm. Jo bit back a cry, her legs suddenly refusing to hold her weight.

"Come on, Jo." Connor's arm wrapped around her, gently pulling her from the room.

The air seemed trapped in her lungs. She clawed at Connor's sleeve.

He stopped in the middle of the hall and held her in his arms. "It's going to be okay. Hang on a bit longer."

She laid her head on his shoulder. The warmth of his body cocooned her, and slowly her tense muscles began to relax. She focused on the steady beat of Connor's heart and the simple act of breathing.

How long they stood there she couldn't tell, but when footsteps sounded on the tiles behind them, Jo's muscles seized once more.

"Miss Miller?"

The cautious tone of the nurse's voice made Jo tremble. She didn't need to hear the words to know what the woman was about to say.

The nurse shook her head. "I'm terribly sorry, but there was nothing the doctor could do. Your father's gone."

Connor felt the jolt travel straight through Jo's body. Her muscles seized and then suddenly went lax. If he hadn't had his arm around her waist, she would have crumpled to the floor.

A keening sound oozed from her throat.

He pulled her closer and rubbed a hand over her back. "I'm so sorry."

Sobs wracked her frame, and hot tears dampened his shirt. He held her for several long minutes, until the weeping subsided and she straightened.

Connor pulled a handkerchief from his pocket and handed it to her.

Jo looked up at him with wooden eyes. "I have to tell Seth. Would you be able to take me?"

"Of course."

She stepped back. "First, I want to see my father."

Connor remained in the waiting room, giving Jo privacy to say good-bye. The need to protect her pulsed through him with helpless impotence. When she finally emerged, she seemed beaten down by the world, her eyes rimmed in red.

"The doctor said his heart gave out." She gave a tiny sniff. "I really thought he'd pull through. He always has before."

227

Connor held out his hand to her. He'd give anything to ease her pain. "Come on. I'll drive you to the Sullivans'."

Twenty minutes later, they pulled up in front of the sprawling ranch.

Jo peered out the window. "I had no idea the place was this big."

Connor got out of the auto and came around to open the door for her.

She ran a hand over her hair. "I don't even know where Seth would be."

The late-afternoon sun had already begun its descent. "Let me find Caleb. He might know."

He led Jo over to the barn. Before they reached the door, Caleb came out, his welcoming smile tinged with confusion. "I thought I heard a car. What brings you here at this time of day?"

Connor ushered Jo forward. "This is Josephine Miller. We're looking for her brother, Seth."

Caleb frowned. "He's in the barn. Is there a problem?"

"Would you mind getting him for us?"

"No need. I'm right here." A man about Connor's age walked out of the barn, wiping his hands on a rag. His gaze snapped right to Jo. "It's Pa, isn't it?"

Jo bit her lip and nodded.

Seth went still for an instant, then rushed forward to clasp Jo in his arms. "It was bound to happen sooner or later," he said. "Don't worry, kid. We're going to be all right."

Caleb leaned toward Connor. "Mr. Miller died?"

Connor exhaled. "Yeah. Not more than an hour ago."

"What a shame." Caleb removed his cap and ran his fingers through his messy hair.

Seth approached them. "Mr. Sullivan, I'd like to be considered for the foreman position. I've been filling in for my father for several weeks, and I believe I've been doing a good job."

Caleb glanced from Seth to Jo. "Perhaps we should discuss this at another time."

"No need. I don't hide things from my sister."

Caleb released a slow breath. "I'm afraid my father is looking for someone older to take the foreman job. But I'll see if we might have another position available."

Jo had grown even paler. "Would the position come with housing?" she asked.

"There's a bunk for the stable hands, but"—Caleb shot her an apologetic look—"it's for males only."

Connor could almost read the question swirling in Jo's eyes. *Where will I live?*

"There's no rush to vacate the cabin," Caleb added. "I won't need it until I find a new foreman, which could take a while."

"Thank you," Jo whispered.

Caleb nodded and turned to Seth. "In the meantime, you might as well take the rest of the day off. I'm sure there are things you need to attend to."

A muscle in Seth's jaw pulsed. "I'd just as soon finish out my shift if it's all the same to you." He turned to Jo. "I'll see you back at the cabin. We'll talk then."

Connor's thoughts churned as he drove Jo down the lane to the foreman's cabin. What if Seth didn't want to stay under Caleb's terms? What if he and Jo up and left after they buried their father? Would Seth even stick around long enough to do that? From his dry-eyed response to his father's passing, Connor figured there wasn't much love lost between the two.

And what about Jo? Would she blindly follow her brother wherever he went, as she had with her father all these years? That was no life for her. She needed a place where she could put down roots, make friends, establish relationships.

No, there had to be a better solution. If it took all night, Connor would come up with something. He had to—because he wasn't ready to let Josephine Miller just walk out of his life.

24

AFTER ALL THE GUESTS HAD LEFT the party and Mrs. Johnston had taken Phoebe upstairs, Matthew approached James and Kathleen in the foyer. "May I speak with you both before you retire?"

Kathleen wheeled over. "Is everything all right, Matthew? You look pale."

"I'll explain inside." He gestured to the parlor door.

Deirdre appeared in the hall and came toward them. "Whenever you're ready, Mama, I'll help you into bed."

"In a few minutes, dear. Matthew wants to speak with us."

Deirdre's eyebrows rose and her gaze swung to him.

He gave a slight bow. "Please join us. This concerns you as well."

They entered the parlor, watching him with expectant yet slightly wary expressions.

"Well, Matthew, don't keep us in suspense. What is this all about?" James's deep voice boomed out over the room.

Matthew steeled himself. "I'm afraid I must leave Irish Meadows immediately."

Shocked silence hovered in the room. Against his will, Matthew's gaze snapped to Deirdre, perched regally on her chair. In her eyes, he saw the disappointment he'd always dreaded.

He turned to Kathleen. "If I wasn't so certain of your recovery, I could never leave. But you've come so far in such a short amount of time, I know you'll continue to improve on your own."

She wheeled her chair over and took his hand. "Matthew, dear. My therapy is not important. You and that sweet girl of yours are. What has happened to make you leave so suddenly?"

Looking into her concerned face, it took immense effort to contain his emotions. "My former in-laws have recently returned from England. They weren't happy to discover I had taken Phoebe out of the country."

Kathleen bristled. "You have the right to take your daughter wherever you wish."

"That's not entirely true." He moved to stand by the fireplace, staring into the flames. "As I told Deirdre, when my wife died, the Pentergasts tried to take Phoebe from me. After some unpleasant negotiations, we came to an understanding about their access to Phoebe. I had mistakenly assumed that since they were abroad, I didn't need to inform them where we were. It seems I was wrong. And now they've threatened to seek custody again if I don't return home immediately."

He shook his head in an attempt to dislodge the memory of the hostile telephone exchange. Apparently, Miss Shearing, bitter over her dismissal, had taken it upon herself to inform his in-laws that he'd taken Phoebe to New York. The Pentergasts had been so upset they'd cut their trip short, returning to Toronto with one plan—to get their granddaughter back home.

Allowing Phoebe to speak to them had momentarily appeased

their anger, but it hadn't stopped their threat at the end of the conversation. *"We will be speaking with our lawyer."*

James stalked across the room. "I don't understand. Why would they do such a thing? There must be more to the story."

A band of tension seized Matthew's throat. "We've been at odds over Phoebe ever since Priscilla died. The Pentergasts hold me responsible for their daughter's death."

"Oh, Matthew. That's so unfair." Kathleen reached out to squeeze his arm.

James nodded. "I agree. And making sure your daughter stays with you must take priority now. Go with our blessing and our thanks." He clapped a beefy hand to Matthew's shoulder. "And if there's anything we can do, please let us know."

"Thank you." Matthew released a breath, relieved they both understood his plight. Only Deirdre remained unusually silent, her gaze focused across the room. Was she as bereft as he at the thought of never seeing each other again? "If you don't mind, I think I'll turn in. It's been a long day."

Matthew hoped Deirdre might follow him out and give them a chance to speak privately. But she made no move to join him, and as Matthew started upstairs, he forced his thoughts away from her. Right now, the Pentergasts had to be his sole focus. What would he do if they weren't bluffing—if they followed through and tried to get custody?

His heart seized in his chest. He could not lose his daughter. No matter what he had to do, he'd make sure of that.

Deirdre rose from her seat and moved to the window. Her thoughts churned like water tumbling over rocks. Matthew and Phoebe would be leaving tomorrow. This was the last night she'd spend in their company. The last time she would gaze into Matthew's eyes, or hear Phoebe's sweet laughter. A shaft of pain pierced her heart.

But even worse than their leaving was the potential threat that Matthew could lose custody of his daughter. Deirdre clasped her hands together to keep them from shaking. How would Phoebe ever cope with being separated from her father? Would she revert back to the frightened, fragile child Deirdre first met in the Toronto hospital?

Deirdre set her jaw. She couldn't allow that to happen.

"Could you help me to my room now, dear?" Mama's voice pulled Deirdre's attention back to the parlor.

She turned to find her mother alone, her father no longer in the room. How long had she been staring out the window? "Of course, Mama."

Deirdre wheeled her from the parlor and down the front hall to her room. "I'm sorry you're losing Matthew, Mama. But I promise to continue working with you until you're completely recovered." Deirdre flipped on the light and pushed her mother inside. "I'll set out your nightclothes."

"Not yet. Come and sit with me a minute."

Deirdre paid closer attention to her mother. Far from seeming fatigued, Mama seemed filled with purpose.

"I want to talk to you about something." Mama gestured to the chair beside her bed.

"What is it?"

Mama rolled closer, a steely glint in her eye. "I want to discuss your feelings for Matthew and what you intend to do about them."

Deirdre's mouth fell open, shock rendering her speechless.

"Don't bother to deny it. I know you care for Matthew, and I suspect he feels the same, only he's too stubborn to do anything about it."

Despair clawed at Deirdre's throat. "Mama—"

"Listen, please." Mama's stern voice brought back childhood memories of being scolded for some transgression. "I believe God brought Matthew to us for a purpose—one greater than just my therapy. You've seen the way Phoebe has blossomed here. She's a completely different child than the one who arrived mere weeks ago. And you, my darling, are a large reason why."

Deirdre blinked back sudden tears and dropped her gaze to her lap.

"Matthew has changed as well. Again, mostly due to your influence."

Deirdre shook her head, vigorously denying the truth of her mother's words.

Mama reached out to squeeze her hand. "I understand your desire to become a doctor, to heal sick children. But what about this one precious child you could do so much for? Matthew and Phoebe need you in their lives."

Deirdre sighed. "Even if that were true, Matthew doesn't want a wife. He's told me so on more than one occasion. I need to respect that and focus on my career."

"What about love? And a family?"

The quiet question pierced the shell around Deirdre's heart. "I don't think that's what God intends for me," she said quietly.

Mama laid a palm against Deirdre's cheek. "Are you sure? Could it be you're so determined to follow this path that you haven't really listened to make sure it's in accordance with God's plan?"

Deirdre shook her head. "I don't know, Mama. I wish I had the answers."

"What if Matthew changed his mind and proposed to you tonight? What would your answer be?"

Deirdre's hands fluttered to her throat. Would she really give up her vocation to satisfy her own longings?

"If Matthew were engaged, or better yet married, he'd stand a much better chance in any legal battle that might ensue. Will you at least think about it? Pray about it?"

Deirdre swallowed her doubt and confusion. "I'll pray, Mama, but I doubt the answer will change."

Mama gave a serene smile, her eyes seeming lit from within. "That's all I ask, sweetheart. God will take care of the rest."

After a nearly sleepless night, Deirdre rose at dawn and quickly washed and dressed. As she'd promised her mother, she'd prayed on and off all night, reading her Bible in between.

And she'd come to a decision, one she hoped Matthew would be open to. But she needed to talk to him—alone—before he left for the train. And the only way she could think of was to seek him out in his room.

Her palms damp, she raised her hand to give three hard raps on his door.

"Who is it?"

"Deirdre. I need to speak to you."

Her heart hammered in her chest so hard she could barely catch her breath. She prayed for guidance to help her through this conversation.

The door swung open. A frown pulled Matthew's brows together. Dark shadows gave his face a hollow look. Deirdre wished she could ease his pain and worry. If only he'd let her . . .

"Deirdre. Is something wrong?" He tugged his vest into place, having obviously donned it in haste.

"I'm sorry to bother you so early, but I've been up most of the night thinking and . . ." She paused. "May I come in? I don't wish to be overheard."

His eyebrows rose to his hairline. "All right, but we leave the door ajar."

"Fine."

She entered what had once been her brother Adam's bedroom, amazed to find it almost identical, save for a new quilt covering the bed.

Matthew turned to her. "So you were saying?"

She clasped her hands together. "The thought that you could

lose Phoebe . . . of what that would do to her . . ." She struggled to contain her emotions, determined not to break down in front of Matthew. She needed to state her idea in a calm, logical fashion. "We can't let that happen."

Matthew walked to the desk. It appeared he, too, had been reading his Bible. He clutched the back of the chair until his knuckles turned white. "Believe me, I don't intend to."

"What are you going to do?"

He faced her. "Once I'm home, I'll ask Victor's help to procure a lawyer. I'll concentrate on my job, hire a new nanny, and do the best I can to provide a good home for my daughter." He pointed to the Bible. "And pray God sees fit to let me keep her."

Deirdre advanced toward him. "What if there was something you could do to give you an advantage? Would you be willing to consider it?"

His gaze hardened. "I'd do almost anything if it would help."

"Even . . ." She hesitated and attempted to control her rapid pulse. Once she verbalized her idea, there'd be no going back.

"Surely you're not suggesting something illegal?"

"Certainly not. Although kidnapping did cross my mind at one point." A nervous laugh bubbled up.

"I considered that myself, but only as a last resort."

She was relieved to see a slight glint of humor in his eyes.

He quickly sobered. "But what is your idea?"

She released a quiet breath. "You may recall my ex-fiancé is a lawyer. Last night, I called him to ask his advice on what you could do to gain the upper hand against your in-laws." She gripped her hands together. "He was very clear. The best thing you could do is . . . find a wife."

Matthew went rigid. "Out of the question."

Expecting that response, she was prepared with a counter-proposal. "I agree. Too drastic. But what if we got engaged?"

He stared at her as though she'd sprouted wings and was

about to fly around the room. A host of emotions flashed across his features before he clamped his mouth shut. "No."

She pressed forward, laying her palm on the desktop. "I've given this a lot of thought. If we got engaged temporarily, it would convince a judge about the stability of your home life." She let the words hang in the air.

Matthew closed the distance between them. "Why, Deirdre? Why would you do this?"

The undeniable truth reverberated through her soul. Not only did she love Phoebe, she loved the girl's impossible father as well. But she was nowhere near brave enough to lay her heart and her emotions bare.

Instead, she straightened, unflinching under his gaze. "Because I love Phoebe, and I'll do whatever it takes to ensure her happiness."

⁂

Matthew stared into Deirdre's vibrant green eyes, alight with the passion of their heated conversation, and fought to control tremors of repressed emotion.

How he wished she'd given a different answer.

Because it had become painfully clear to him, after a sleepless night plagued with thoughts of leaving here forever—of leaving *her* forever—that he cared very deeply for Deirdre.

So much so that his heart nearly ripped from his chest at the idea of saying good-bye.

She moved away from the desk. "We could announce our engagement with the intention of marrying next year. And once matters were settled, we could quietly end the engagement before I apply to another university. That way, we both get what we want and no one gets hurt in the process."

The lie vibrated between them as surely as a caress. Did she really believe they could both emerge from a fake engagement without their emotions becoming involved? Without hurting Phoebe?

He sighed. "I can't let Phoebe believe you're going to be her mother, only to crush her down the road. It wouldn't be fair."

The spark drained from Deirdre's features. "I didn't think of that." She gave a sheepish shrug. "There I go again, being too impulsive."

"You're trying to help. And I appreciate that more than you know. If only . . ." He clamped his lips together before he blurted out something he shouldn't, then paced to the window to stare out at the landscape below. His packed bag sat by the bed, ready to leave for the station. His mind raced to come up with a solution.

He turned to face her. "What if you came with me as Phoebe's nanny—on a temporary basis until the custody issue is settled?"

She stared at him. "How would that help your case?"

"It would prove I have a dedicated, caring woman in my daughter's life. One whom Phoebe adores." He took a step toward her. "It would show she's well taken care of when I'm at work. That she's a happy, confident little girl. For she would be . . . if you were living with us."

As the words left his mouth, he saw the error in his thinking. Realized the torture it would be to have Deirdre living under his roof as part of the family, but not really belonging.

The agony in her eyes mirrored his regret. She blinked and moved to the desk to finger the pages of his Bible. After several seconds, she straightened, seeming to regain her poise. "All right, Matthew. I accept your proposition." A determined light shone in her eyes as she waited for him to respond.

"You're certain you're willing to do this?"

"Absolutely." She didn't waver for a second.

Relief pulsed through his veins. "Thank you, Deirdre."

Her lips trembled into a smile. "I won't let you lose her, Matthew. No matter what it takes."

She moved toward the door, but he stopped her with a hand to her arm.

"There's one more thing. We'll have to make sure Phoebe understands this is a temporary arrangement until I can find a new nanny I don't want her getting the idea that you're staying permanently."

A flash of sorrow shadowed her eyes, but she nodded. "Agreed."

His gaze held hers, hoping it was enough to convey his undying gratitude at her generosity.

At last, she stepped away. "I'd best go and pack my things if we want to make the train."

25

MATTHEW ALLOWED the *clickety-clack* of the train to lull him into a stupor. Anything to keep from obsessing about the strange turn his life had taken. Phoebe slept with her head pillowed on his lap, exhausted from her tears at leaving Irish Meadows. The Whelan children had come to the house to say their good-byes, with hugs and assurances that they'd look after Patches until he was old enough to bring home. Only the fact that Deirdre was accompanying them, as well as Matthew's promise to return and pick up the puppy before Christmas, had calmed Phoebe.

In the seat across from them, Deirdre stared out the window, her brow creased in a frown. Was she already regretting her decision?

A trainload of guilt weighed on Matthew's conscience. First, for leaving Kathleen, although she had assured him she would continue her exercises under the supervision of Nurse Cramer, whom James had hired again until Deirdre returned. And second, for allowing Deirdre to get caught up in his drama. She was too talented a nurse not to use her skills. Matthew set his jaw. As soon as the situation with his in-laws was resolved, Matthew would gently send her back to New York.

Back where she belongs.

"Matthew, can I talk to you about something?" Deirdre leaned forward in her seat, her voice low. "Before Phoebe wakes up?"

He pulled his thoughts back to the present. "Of course."

"I've been thinking about our plan."

Matthew curbed a smile at her use of the word *our* and the way her nose scrunched up when she was deep in thought. "Oh?"

"It concerns our living arrangement." Her gaze dropped to the sleeping Phoebe. "I know you expected me to live at your house. However, I think it would be better if I stayed with Uncle Victor and Aunt Maimie."

Matthew frowned. "But sometimes I don't get home until quite late. I wouldn't want you to have to find your way home at that hour, only to come back early the next day."

"I'm sure it won't be a problem. Uncle Victor will send his driver whenever I need him."

Matthew studied her. "Why don't you want to stay with us?"

She bent her head to fidget with her gloves. "I think we need to keep everything aboveboard, so the Pentergasts don't have any added ammunition to use against you."

Matthew shook his head. "I don't understand. Many people have live-in nannies. Miss Shearing had no qualms about living across the hall from Phoebe."

The blush in her cheeks deepened. "I think it's prudent that we avoid . . . temptation."

Sudden images of Deirdre dressed in a nightgown, her hair long and loose, rose in his mind to taunt him. *Temptation indeed.* He swallowed hard. "Very well."

"Thank you." She sank back against her seat as though relieved of a great burden. After a few beats of silence, she leaned forward again. "Tell me more about your family. Did you grow up in Toronto?"

"Yes."

"What about your parents? Where were they from?"

"My father was born here. My mother came over from England as a child."

"Were both of them only children?"

Matthew frowned, giving her a look that he hoped would quell her questions. His family was not a topic he ever discussed.

"You said you have no relatives other than Phoebe. No aunts, uncles, cousins?"

"No."

Deirdre's features softened. "When did your parents die? Was it an accident?"

Matthew ground his teeth together, wishing he could escape her probing gaze. But he supposed she deserved to know. Might as well get it over with. "My mother died when I was eight. My father passed away during the Spanish flu epidemic."

Her eyes widened. "I didn't realize. How sad to grow up without a mother. You and Phoebe share that in common."

His muscles tightened at the stark sympathy on her face.

"How did she die?" Deirdre asked softly.

Pain sliced through his chest. Why did it hurt so much even after twenty years? He released a pent-up breath. Perhaps it was time to talk about it—allow the festering wound to heal. Keeping silent all these years certainly hadn't worked. "After my brother died, my mother fell into a deep depression—one she never recovered from." He paused for several seconds, steeling himself to say the words. "On the first anniversary of George's death, she . . . hung herself. I found her in George's bedroom . . ." He closed his eyes to push the image from his mind, trying to forget the pain of an eight-year-old wondering why he hadn't been enough for his mother to want to live.

Sudden warmth encompassed his hand. He opened his eyes to find Deirdre in front of him, tears standing in her eyes.

"I can't imagine the pain you've endured, Matthew. I'm so sorry."

His throat closed up. He looked away from her, not knowing what else to say, feeling like he'd just ripped out his soul.

She squeezed his hand and resumed her seat, almost as if sensing his inability to continue the conversation. Or perhaps realizing how truly damaged he was.

Thankfully, she remained silent for the rest of the trip, which passed in relative peace. By the time the train arrived at Union Station, he'd managed to regain his emotional equilibrium.

Half an hour later, the taxicab pulled up in front of Matthew's house. He paid the driver, who then hauled their bags onto the walkway. Matthew stared at the brick building, trying to dredge up some excitement to be home. Instead, nausea churned in his stomach, a sensation he didn't wholly attribute to the train ride. This house held many unpleasant memories that resurfaced every time he returned.

They no sooner entered than his housekeeper rushed to the door to greet him. "Welcome home, Dr. Clayborne. It's good to have you back."

"Thank you, Mrs. Potts." He removed his hat and gloves and set them on the hall table.

The older woman bent to greet Phoebe. "And look at you, missy. I believe you've grown two inches since you've been away."

Phoebe giggled. "Do you know we're getting a puppy, Mrs. Potts? He's too little to come home right now, but Papa said we'd go back later and get him."

Mrs. Potts's eyes widened.

Matthew chuckled. "I guess you haven't heard Phoebe talk this much before."

"I certainly haven't. It's a lovely sound indeed."

Matthew gestured to Deirdre. "Allow me to introduce Miss Deirdre O'Leary, Phoebe's temporary nanny."

"A pleasure to meet you," Deirdre said.

Mrs. Potts beamed. "And you as well. If I can do anything for you, please ask."

Matthew helped Phoebe with her coat. "Some refreshments would be welcome, if you don't mind," he said.

"Of course, sir. I'll get the cook to prepare them right away." She bobbed a curtsy and disappeared down the hall.

"Papa, where is Miss Deirdre going to stay? In Miss Shearing's old room?"

Matthew blinked. How was it Phoebe suddenly had more energy than the rising sun, when he seemed completely drained? The fatigue of the journey, coupled with the stress of the whole unfortunate custody situation, threatened to swamp him. He needed to recoup before Victor and his lawyer came by later as scheduled.

Deirdre took Phoebe's hand. "Phoebe, how would you like to show me your room before we have our snack?"

Phoebe's ringlets bobbed. "Can I show you my toys?"

"I'd love that. We can introduce Angelina to her new home." Deirdre winked at Matthew.

Relief coursed through him. Bringing Deirdre into his home would either be the best thing he'd ever done . . .

Or the worst.

Once her vivacious essence permeated this dull abode, he may never be able to face it without her.

"Deirdre, my dear. How lovely to see you again." Uncle Victor walked into Matthew's parlor later that day, a wide smile creasing his cheeks.

Deirdre found herself encompassed in a welcoming hug. A wave of pleasure rushed through her. "It's good to see you, too, Uncle Victor."

He pulled her back to peer into her face. "Your father called to ask if you might stay with us for a while, and I told him we'd be delighted to have you. But is it true you've come here as Phoebe's nanny?" His tone told Deirdre he thought she'd taken leave of her senses.

"It's true." Deirdre smiled. "I did suggest a betrothal, but Matthew turned me down."

A thud sounded from across the room. Deirdre looked over to see Matthew frowning as he retrieved a book he'd dropped.

She'd hoped a touch of levity would relieve the seriousness of the situation, and both men would relax.

Instead, Matthew's scowl deepened, and Uncle Victor remained silent.

"Actually," an unfamiliar voice said from the doorway, "the young lady makes an excellent point."

Uncle Victor turned. "Oh, William, do come in. I'm sorry I left you in the foyer."

An attractive blond man around the age of thirty approached, carrying a leather case.

"William, this is Dr. Clayborne and Miss O'Leary. William Bancroft, my lawyer. He's agreed to advise you and, if necessary, take your case."

Matthew stepped forward to shake Mr. Bancroft's hand. "Thank you for meeting us here. I appreciate it."

Mr. Bancroft bowed to Deirdre, and the men all chose a seat. Matthew closed the parlor doors, likely to make sure that Phoebe, who was helping the cook bake cookies, wouldn't overhear them. He then took a spot on the settee near Deirdre.

Mr. Bancroft set his briefcase on the floor beside his chair. "All joking aside, Dr. Clayborne, marriage is your best bet at ensuring you win custody. The judge will be looking for evidence of a stable home life for the child, a decent house, a loving family."

Matthew shifted marginally away. "As I explained to Miss O'Leary, marriage is not an option."

246

Uncle Victor leaned forward. "What about a betrothal, Mr. Bancroft?"

Apparently unflustered by the tension in the room, Mr. Bancroft stared calmly at Matthew. "An engagement is the next best option. If a judge sees you plan to bring a suitable woman into the home, one who would create a loving family environment, then yes, it would go a long way toward tipping the scales in your favor."

Matthew frowned. "Miss O'Leary is here as my daughter's nanny. She's a qualified nurse, someone Phoebe adores. Surely this will suffice?"

Mr. Bancroft spared Matthew a pitying glance. "Unfortunately, a paid nanny would never trump a set of doting grandparents. I'm sorry."

Matthew jerked to his feet and paced the carpet. "But I've done everything to guarantee Phoebe's comfort and safety. Mrs. Potts runs the household. The cook and the maids take care of the rest, and now Miss O'Leary will be looking out for Phoebe's well-being. What more can a judge expect from a man who has lost his wife?"

Deirdre's breath caught. Matthew made it seem that he was so bereaved he couldn't conceive of marrying again. But Deirdre knew better.

"You're talking logistics, Doctor." Mr. Bancroft crossed one leg over his knee. "The court will see a man dedicated to his profession, who spends a great deal of time outside the home. They'll see a young girl left in the company of paid servants. To be blunt, you'd be handing the Pentergasts your daughter gift-wrapped with a bow on top."

Matthew stopped pacing, his back rigid. The clenched fists and the tick in his jaw bore witness to his immense frustration.

From the moment they'd boarded the train, Deirdre had watched Matthew slip back into the closed-off man she'd first met. One who kept his daughter at home, away from the world.

It was as if he'd never been to Irish Meadows, never watched his daughter come out of her shell, play with other children . . .

Her stomach dipped. Drastic measures were needed so Phoebe wouldn't lose that valuable connection with her father. But what?

"I have one other suggestion." Mr. Bancroft swung his regard to Matthew. "What about a temporary engagement until the custody issue has been resolved? The Pentergasts' lawyer may even recommend they drop their suit if he thinks you intend to marry. If not, it will still help with the judge."

Deirdre's heart sped up. "We could keep it quiet. You wouldn't even have to tell Phoebe."

Matthew threw her a skeptical look and focused on Mr. Bancroft. "Even if I won, what's to stop the Pentergasts from going back to court when they find out the engagement has been terminated?"

Mr. Bancroft shifted on his seat. "Once a judge makes a ruling, he won't be inclined to reopen the case."

Uncle Victor, who had been quietly observing the exchange, slapped a hand to his knee and chuckled. "For once Maimie's gossip might have come in handy. I do believe she mentioned hearing something about the Pentergasts' other daughter, the one who married that investor from California."

Matthew frowned. "What about her?"

"Rumor has it she's expecting twins. Apparently Helen is planning to go out and help her closer to the due date. So she might not be around to pay much attention to the state of your engagement."

Trying to bank her excitement, Deirdre rose and went to Matthew by the fireplace. "This could work, Matthew. But it's up to you."

He dragged a hand across his jaw, lines of despair bracketing his mouth. At last, he released a long breath. "If this will allow me to keep my daughter, then so be it. I'll announce the engagement to my in-laws when they come to see Phoebe tomorrow."

Mr. Bancroft cleared his throat and rose. "Well, I'm glad that's settled. May I make one other suggestion, Dr. Clayborne?"

"What is that?"

"It would be prudent to procure a ring to make the betrothal look official. And"—he leaned forward—"try to act as if you're actually happy about the upcoming nuptials." With an amused chuckle, he clapped Matthew on the shoulder and turned to Deirdre. "Good to meet you, Miss O'Leary. I'm sure we'll see each other soon."

Deirdre's spirits sagged. If Mr. Bancroft had noticed Matthew's near-abhorrence at being engaged, what would the Pentergasts think?

Uncle Victor joined Mr. Bancroft. "I'll walk you out, William. Deirdre, I'll see you later this evening. Just ring when you want Davis to pick you up."

"Thank you." Deirdre forced a smile until the three men had left the room.

As soon as she was alone, her shoulders slumped with a release of tension. She crossed to the mantel, where a group of photos caught her attention. One of Matthew graduating from medical school, and another of Matthew in his soldier's uniform with a beautiful young woman and an infant. A third depicted Phoebe alone, seated on a high-back chair, her face wreathed in sadness. Deirdre ran a finger over the frame and let out a sigh.

Lord, help me to focus only on that sweet girl and ignore anything hurtful Matthew might say or do.

Despite everything, part of her wished the circumstances were different. That by some miracle, Matthew might suddenly declare his affection for her and ask to make the betrothal real. But he'd made it clear that would never happen.

"We need to talk." Matthew's deep baritone echoed across the spacious room.

She steeled herself and slowly turned. Judging by his expression, the discussion wouldn't be pleasant.

He crossed the room to stand before her. "I think we need to outline the terms of our new . . . arrangement."

A log shifted in the fireplace and the flames jumped, casting a wavering shadow over the area. She waited for him to continue.

Finally he cleared his throat, not quite looking at her. "As you indicated, we will enter into a temporary engagement until the custody issue is resolved. After that, once I hire a new nanny, you will be free to resume your life, and I mine."

Did he worry she might have designs on him? That she might refuse to release him from the betrothal when the time came? She sighed. "Would you like me to sign an agreement? Or is my word good enough?"

He raised his chin. "I only want to make sure you understand I'm doing this for Phoebe. And for no other reason."

"Don't worry. You've made your position very clear." She started to cross the room but stopped. "Mr. Bancroft is right about one thing, however. In order to make this engagement appear real, we will have to act like a couple who want to be married. Do you think you can do that?"

"Of course I can. I used to be quite good at pretending to be happily married." With that, he turned and strode out of the room.

Oh, Matthew. Her annoyance drained away as understanding dawned. He was terrified to risk being vulnerable again.

She longed to ease his pain. To hold him until he let go of everything keeping him from fully embracing life. But only a higher power could make that happen. It would take God's healing grace to set Matthew free from a prison of his own making.

The only thing Deirdre could do for him now was pray.

26

TERRENCE AND HELEN PENTERGAST arrived promptly at one o'clock the next afternoon. Mrs. Potts ushered his in-laws into the parlor while Matthew waited a few extra minutes in his study, mentally preparing to enter the fray. Not since the Great War had he felt so besieged, so unsure of himself—as though the earth were shifting beneath him with every step.

Phoebe's excited little voice drifted into the hallway as she regaled her grandparents with stories of life at Irish Meadows. Matthew paused, drinking in the sweet sound. He could almost imagine Helen's pinched features as she heard about the horses and puppies, the snowstorm, and Sean's perilous escapades. To the Pentergasts—who viewed Toronto as the only truly civilized city this side of the ocean—Irish Meadows probably seemed like the Wild West.

He drew his pocket watch out of his vest to check the time. Half an hour before Deirdre would arrive. Victor had assured Matthew his driver would drop her off at precisely one-thirty—

long enough to give Matthew a chance to speak to the Pentergasts alone. Somehow in the next thirty minutes, he would have to find a way to announce the fact that he was engaged.

His lunch churned in his stomach at the very thought.

With a loud exhale, he straightened his tie and entered the parlor.

"Papa! Grandma and Grandpa are here." Phoebe dashed across the carpet to throw her arms around his legs.

Matthew laid his hand on her shoulder, his gaze glued to the man and woman seated on the sofa. As usual, the two were impeccably dressed, as though ready for a night at the opera.

Terrence and Helen rose as one. Terrence stepped toward him, hand extended. "Matthew. You're looking well."

"Thank you, sir. As are you." He shook the man's hand, then bent to kiss Helen's cheek. "I take it you had a pleasant trip."

Helen's pencil-thin eyebrows shot toward her nose. "Hardly pleasant with my dear sister so ill."

"I'm sorry. I didn't realize." Matthew clamped his lips together. How did he always manage to say the wrong thing to her?

Terrence rested a hand on his wife's arm. "Thankfully, Edith is greatly improved. And the rest of our stay was quite pleasant." His apologetic expression allowed the tension radiating up Matthew's spine to ease a notch.

"Please have a seat. Can I offer you some refreshments?"

"Tea would be lovely." Helen resumed her spot on the sofa. Phoebe instantly snuggled up beside her.

Matthew rang for Mrs. Potts, then took a seat on one of the armchairs, suddenly feeling like a guest in his own home. The fact that the Pentergasts owned the deed to this property could account for that.

"Phoebe was telling us about this place you took her." The disdain in Helen's tone fortunately went unnoticed by Phoebe.

"You'd love it, Grandma." Phoebe pushed away from Helen's arm to perch on the edge of the sofa. "They have puppies and horses and a pony. When I go back in the summer, Sean is going to teach me to ride Twizzle." Eyes sparkling with enthusiasm, Phoebe prattled on, oblivious to the horror on Helen's face. "Maybe you and Grandpa can come and visit us there. Mrs. O'Leary said—"

"My dear child, you won't be going back, so we needn't worry about that."

Matthew held back a groan at the instant glower that darkened his daughter's face.

"But Miss Deirdre promised—"

Matthew rose. "Phoebe, would you ask Cook to get out those special cookies? The ones you helped her make?"

The frown lifted, and Phoebe beamed at Terrence. "I baked cookies for you, Grandpa, 'cause I know you love them."

Terrence's features softened like melted butter. "That was very thoughtful of you, Phoebe. I'd love to try them."

"I'll be right back."

As she dashed out the door, Matthew released a slow breath, grateful for the diversionary tactics Deirdre had taught him in dealing with Phoebe's outbursts. Schooling his features, he turned back to face his in-laws.

Terrence chuckled. "My goodness, the child has become a regular chatterbox. It's wonderful to see her opening up this way."

"I'm glad you noticed." Matthew took a few steps across the room. "Living for a short time in the country did Phoebe a world of good. Not only her health, but her whole demeanor, improved—thanks in large part to Miss O'Leary."

In the silence that followed, Matthew moved to his chair but couldn't bring himself to sit. Instead, he gripped the curved back, as though to gain strength from the solid wood. "Before Phoebe returns, there is something I must tell you."

Helen rose from her seat like a queen might rise from her throne. "If this has anything to do with you taking our granddaughter off to some godforsaken—"

"Now, Helen." Terrence stood and took his wife's arm. "You don't know what Matthew was about to say."

She gave him a haughty glare and resumed her seat. "Very well. What is it you wish to tell us?"

Matthew's tongue seemed pasted to the roof of his dry mouth. "Miss O'Leary has accompanied us to Toronto. She is . . ." Matthew swallowed, unable—or perhaps unwilling—to utter the next words, knowing the falsehood would seal his fate.

"She is what?" Terrence's florid face lit with expectancy.

"She is . . . that is, we are . . ."

"Engaged to be married."

Matthew froze at Deirdre's voice behind him. He turned his head as she floated into the room, a welcoming smile creasing her cheeks. Matthew stared. In a lemon-yellow dress, her auburn hair pulled away from her face to fall in perfect curls over her shoulders, Deirdre had never looked more beautiful.

She came forward to loop her hand through his arm. "You must be Mr. and Mrs. Pentergast. It's lovely to meet you."

Terrence had risen from his chair, but Helen stayed seated, her eyes wide with shock. "Did you say you were *engaged*?" she shrilled.

Matthew willed his mouth to open, but it remained firmly shut.

Deirdre gave a light laugh. "Matthew, darling. You didn't tell them?" She stepped forward and extended a hand to Terrence. "I'm Deirdre O'Leary, Matthew's fiancée."

Terrence shook her hand, seemingly stunned into silence.

Unfazed by the tension thickening the air, Deirdre went to sit beside Helen. "You must be Phoebe's grandmother. She's told me so much about you."

Helen stiffened, shifting away as though Deirdre might contaminate her, and turned furious eyes on Matthew. "I don't believe it. How long have you even known each other?"

Deirdre's smile seemed strained, little grooves etched beside her mouth. "It was rather sudden, but when Matthew and Phoebe were about to leave, we realized we couldn't bear to be apart." She shot Matthew a coy look from under her lashes. "Isn't that right, darling?"

Still at a loss for words, Matthew gave a hapless shrug. Perhaps Deirdre had missed her true calling as a stage actress. He licked his dry lips in a desperate attempt to regain his ability to speak.

"I don't see any ring." Helen sniffed as she eyed Deirdre's left hand.

"It's at the jeweler's, adjusting the size." Deirdre leaned toward Helen. "We're waiting to tell Phoebe until we get it back and make it official. So I guess you two are the first to know." Her smile now looked ready to crack.

Matthew's stomach sank to his shoes, preparing for the explosion to come. If Deirdre had hoped her friendliness would dissuade his in-laws from reacting badly, she'd wasted her acting talents.

Helen's features hardened, her eyes narrow. "If you think you can take our daughter's place in Phoebe's life, you couldn't be more mistaken, *Miss* O'Leary." Helen jerked to her feet, clutching her handbag, and yanked her husband from his seat. "Come, Terrence. We have an appointment with our lawyer."

"But Helen—"

She ignored her husband's pleading look and marched across the room.

As she reached the door, Phoebe entered, holding a platter of cookies. "Where are you going, Grandma? You haven't tried the cookies."

Helen bent to pat Phoebe's head. "I'm afraid we have to leave, sweetheart. Perhaps you can come and visit at our house next time."

Phoebe's bottom lip trembled.

Terrence offered Matthew an apologetic shrug as he moved

by. When he reached Phoebe, he bent to her level and picked up a cookie. "I'll bet these are delicious. See you soon, princess." He whispered something that made Phoebe smile.

Then he bit into the cookie, winked at Phoebe, and followed his wife out the door.

⁂

Deirdre sagged back against the sofa. So much for winning over the Pentergasts. All she'd done was escalate the already tense situation.

"Why did Grandpa and Grandma leave so soon?" Phoebe frowned as Matthew took the tray from her and set it on a side table.

Matthew's face had turned a sickly gray. "They remembered they had an appointment to keep. But you'll see them again soon."

"Can I go to their house tomorrow?" Phoebe plucked a cookie from the plate and bit into it.

"We'll see." Matthew gripped the back of a wing chair, his knuckles whitening.

Deirdre rose and crossed to his side. "I'm sorry. I didn't mean to make things worse," she said in a low voice. She'd sensed the friction in the room when she'd entered and had assumed things weren't going as Matthew had hoped.

"You didn't." His tight tone did little to reassure her.

She laid a hand over his on the chair.

Immediately he stiffened, stepping away from her. "If you'll stay with Phoebe, I have to check in at the hospital." He avoided her gaze, looking past her shoulder.

Deirdre's stomach plummeted. Was it only the Pentergasts, or had she done something to upset him? She longed for him to confide his worries to her. However, with Phoebe hanging on their every word, it would have to wait.

She forced a smile. "Of course. Uncle Victor's driver will pick me up whenever I wish to leave."

He raised troubled eyes to hers. "You're free to leave anytime, you know."

Her heart knocked out an unsteady rhythm. Was he testing her commitment? She met his gaze without blinking. "I'm here for as long as you need me."

The muscles in his throat bobbed. "Thank you."

If anyone needed a hug, it was Matthew. Yet everything about his demeanor screamed *stay away*.

"Don't worry," she said. "We'll get through this—together."

He held her gaze for a second or two, then with a brief nod, he left the room.

In the basement of the military hospital, Matthew opened the door to his office, flicked on the overhead light, and stood to survey his domain. Nothing had changed since he'd left more than six weeks ago, except the dust had gotten thicker.

That was what happened when you gave the cleaning staff strict orders not to move anything.

He took off his hat and gloves and laid them on his desk. The ledger where he recorded his patients' progress sat precisely where he'd left it. Had Dr. Marlboro not used it?

Matthew took a seat and opened the book, relieved to find notations in a different handwriting. He scanned the meticulously penned reports on each patient. As the words penetrated, Matthew scowled and read faster. Almost every soldier had been dismissed from care.

What had Dr. Marlboro done?

Matthew jerked up from his seat, sending the chair scuttling backward. A sharp pain shot through his bad leg. He grimaced and braced himself on the desk until the pain subsided to a dull

257

ache. His leg had hardly bothered him at all the past few weeks while at Irish Meadows. So why had it flared up now?

Clamping his lips into a tight line, he limped from the office and down the corridor to the therapy room. He switched on the lights and stared at the almost-empty space. The only remaining evidence of Matthew's work here was his equipment tucked into the far corner and the cabinet of weights beside it.

Matthew's insides churned, sweat streaked down his back, and his leg throbbed. How could his whole practice disappear within a matter of weeks? Did his patients believe he'd abandoned them and in turn had found another doctor? He would have to call all of them and find out—

"Hello, Dr. Clayborne. I heard you were back and took a chance you might be here."

Fred Knox.

Relief spilled through Matthew's torso. At least one of his patients hadn't left.

"Fred. It's good to see you." Matthew turned. Shock slammed through him.

The man was walking with only a cane for assistance. Where was his wheelchair?

Fred's brown eyes danced as he came forward. "Surprise! I had to come and show you this." He swept an arm out.

Matthew gaped, struggling for words. "When . . . how?"

Had Dr. Marlboro proved a better therapist than he? Had he been able to help Fred achieve what Matthew hadn't?

"My wife and I wanted you to be proud of my progress when you got back. She bought me this cane, and I practiced at home every night. It took about four weeks, but I finally did it."

"I . . . I don't know what to say."

Fred shook his head, a slow smile spreading. "That's not the best part. I got my old job back, and . . ." He chuckled. "Marjorie and I are expecting another baby."

The air whooshed from Matthew's lungs as though he'd

been sucker-punched. Fred had his entire life back. His marriage, his job, and a new addition to the family. He no longer needed Matthew.

Matthew fought to suppress his negative reaction. He should be happy for Fred. After all, hadn't this been the ultimate goal of his physical therapy? Then why did Matthew want to pound his fist into the wall?

"You okay, Doc?" Lines creased Fred's brow. "You've gone white."

"I'm fine. Just surprised." Matthew tried to smile. "And pleased, of course."

"Not as much as we are." He winked. "Marjorie wants you to come to dinner one night, as a small token of our appreciation." Fred's expression sobered. "I couldn't have come out of those dark days without your help. I'll never be able to repay you for that."

He leaned in and gave Matthew a one-armed hug.

Matthew stiffened. Why couldn't he simply accept the man's gratitude?

Fred straightened and repositioned his cane. "Well, I'd best be on my way. We'll call and make a date for that dinner." He flashed another grin, then turned and walked out the door.

Matthew sagged back against the wall, his legs shaking. Had all his patients made such drastic recoveries in his absence? If so, what did that say about him?

Once his breathing evened out, Matthew pushed himself upright and crossed to the door. He let his gaze roam the room, barbs of bitterness piercing his chest.

Then he turned off the lights and closed the door on his life for the past four years.

Minutes later, Matthew limped into Victor's office. "Why didn't you tell me all my patients have left?" he snapped.

Victor stared across the desk at him. "Sit down, Matthew."

The quiet authority of Victor's voice seemed to drain the anger from Matthew. He crossed the room and sank onto one of the chairs, feeling like a sullen schoolboy about to be chastised by the principal.

"I only learned about the state of your practice this morning." Victor pushed a paper across the desk. "Dr. Marlboro came by and gave me his final report. I understand most of your patients have decided to discontinue therapy."

"But why? Was Marlboro behind it?"

"I believe many of the soldiers felt they were ready to move on, but they hadn't known how to break it to you. Your absence gave them the opportunity to leave." He sighed. "I'm sorry, Matthew, but you did know this day was coming."

Matthew couldn't remain seated. He got up to pace the tiled floor, wincing at the discomfort in his thigh. "What am I going to do now?" He stopped pacing as a horrific realization dawned. "The Pentergasts are looking for something to use against me in court. An unemployed father who can't support his child—"

"Hold on. You're hardly unemployed."

A vise grip cinched the muscles in Matthew's chest as he dropped back onto the chair. He bent his head over his knees, attempting to breathe normally.

"You told me you had a plan for when the soldiers no longer needed you," Victor said. "Why don't you tell me about it?"

Matthew fought to pull his thoughts together. "I'd hoped to recruit new patients, or possibly open my own clinic. But that will take time and money, and right now I don't have that luxury."

"There's another option." Victor regarded him soberly. "The new Toronto Therapy Clinic has recently opened. I'm almost certain they'd jump at the chance to have you onboard."

Matthew straightened. "I've heard about this clinic."

"It could serve as a temporary measure until things settle

down with the Pentergasts. In the meantime, it would provide a stable position with a good salary. Or there's always the option of rebuilding your patient base here."

Matthew's temples throbbed. "I'll have to think about it."

Victor nodded. "I understand."

Matthew rose, his head spinning. The thought of not being in the same building as Victor saddened him. Victor had been like a second father to him. "Thank you for being the voice of reason in the midst of chaos." He lifted one corner of his mouth, the closest he could come to a smile.

"My pleasure." Victor rose behind his desk. "By the way, Phoebe and Deirdre are at my house right now. Maimie has invited you all for dinner."

Matthew couldn't imagine swallowing one bite of food, not with the unsettling events of the day closing in on him. But for Phoebe's sake, he'd pretend to enjoy the meal.

And pretend that his life wasn't unraveling around him.

27

T HE NEXT MORNING, Deirdre removed her hat and coat in the foyer of Matthew's house and handed them to the housekeeper. "Thank you, Mrs. Potts. Has Phoebe had breakfast yet?"

"The lamb is still sleeping." Mrs. Potts chuckled. "Seems she wore herself out yesterday."

A trickle of alarm surfaced. "Perhaps I should check on her."

"No need, dear. I left her room moments before you arrived. She's fine." Mrs. Potts's sunny disposition helped put Deirdre at ease. "Dr. Clayborne wishes to speak with you in his study." She pointed down a hallway. "Second door on the left."

Deirdre hesitated. What mood would Matthew be in today? Last night, Deirdre's initial elation at having Matthew join them at the Fullmans' had faded the moment she saw his face. Instead of being happy to be back at his practice, Matthew had seemed even more somber. Perhaps he'd had unpleasant news about a patient.

She'd hoped to have a chance to talk to him before he and

Phoebe left, but Matthew had taken Phoebe home right after the meal. Maybe now she'd find out what was bothering him.

She knocked on the door.

"Come in."

Deirdre entered a very masculine room. Matthew sat behind a large oak desk adorned with piles of books and papers, his reading glasses perched near the tip of his nose. *Haggard* was the only word to describe his appearance. Dark circles shadowed his eyes, adding to the hollowness of his cheeks.

"Good morning, Matthew. Mrs. Potts said you wished to speak with me."

"Yes. Please sit down."

Deirdre moved a stack of books from one chair. She threw an amused glance at Matthew, recalling their first meeting in his basement office.

A spark of recognition flickered in his eyes before the serious demeanor returned. "It appears the Pentergasts are moving forward with their bid for custody," he said without preamble.

Deirdre sank onto the wing chair. "That's unfortunate, but not unexpected."

"Are you still prepared to go through with this charade?" His blue eyes bored into hers.

Was he testing her again? Or giving her a chance to back out? "Of course I am."

"You're willing to lie under oath?"

She leaned forward, determination stiffening her spine. "I won't have to lie, Matthew, because we *will* be engaged. Whether it's for a few days or a few months, it doesn't matter."

For a brief second, the despair left his features.

"The question I need you to answer," she said with a pointed stare, "is—can you act like a fiancé?"

He bristled as he stacked a pile of papers on the desk. "If you expect me to parade around like a lovesick fool, you're doomed to disappointment."

Deirdre couldn't help but laugh. "Lovesick, no. But you could at least act as though you want me around."

Color bled into his cheeks. "I wasn't aware I behaved in such a boorish manner."

She softened her voice. "Ever since we left Irish Meadows, you've been keeping me at arm's length. If we want the Pentergasts to believe we're a couple, a smile would go a long way."

Matthew rose from his leather chair and walked to the window behind him. "I don't seem to have much cause to smile lately." He moved the lace curtain aside to stare out.

Deirdre wished she could do something to bring the light back to his eyes. "I thought you'd be happy to be home," she said. "Back to your patients."

His shoulders tensed, and when he turned around, dejection shadowed his features. "Turns out I don't have much of a practice left."

She got to her feet. "What do you mean?"

"It seems in my absence, the majority of my patients have chosen to discontinue therapy."

Outrage on his behalf flooded her system. She moved toward him, past the desk. "That's unbelievable. Can't Uncle Victor do something?"

"It's out of his control." He shrugged. "I can either try to rebuild my practice somehow . . . or find work elsewhere."

She knew how much the soldiers meant to him. And now, because he'd left to help her mother, Matthew had lost everything. "I'm so sorry." She laid a hand on his arm, but even the light touch on his sleeve caused him to tense. "What about opening your own clinic?"

"That would still mean finding a new patient base." He gripped the back of his chair and released a harsh breath. "The timing just isn't right. Especially with this impending court date. The hearing is next week."

She gasped. "How could they get a judge so fast?"

"Money and power go a long way." His lips twisted. "Terrence likely pulled some strings to speed up the process."

No wonder Matthew looked so depressed. It must appear to him that every aspect of his life was spinning out of his control.

She tilted her chin. "We can't give up yet, Matthew. We have God on our side. He'll help us find a way."

He shook his head and gave a defeated sigh. "I wish I had your faith. At this point, it will take a miracle for me to keep my daughter."

"Then that's exactly what we'll expect." She squeezed his hand as though by sheer will she could infuse him with her strength.

He stared at her for a long moment, but at last he squeezed her hand in return, with the barest lessening of the pinch between his brows. "I'm afraid you'll have to have faith enough for the both of us."

***

"I think Papa needs to go back to Irish Meadows," Phoebe announced at the breakfast table.

Deirdre looked up from the newspaper she was reading while the girl ate her oatmeal. "Why do you say that?"

"Because he's sad all the time. And he wasn't sad at Irish Meadows."

Deirdre's chest constricted. If only things were that simple. "Your father has a problem to take care of right now. Once that's over, he'll feel better."

Phoebe plopped her spoon into the bowl of oatmeal. "After that, can we go back to New York?"

"I don't know, honey." Deirdre smiled. "In the meantime, maybe we can think of a way to cheer your father up."

Phoebe's face brightened. "We could make him a birthday cake."

"Is it his birthday?"

SUSAN ANNE MASON

"Mrs. Potts said it's tomorrow." She beamed at Deirdre. "We could decorate the cake with marshmallows. Papa likes marshmallows."

"That's a fine idea." Deirdre tapped a finger to her lips. "In fact, why don't we have a birthday dinner tonight when he really wouldn't be expecting anything?"

Phoebe hopped up from her seat, the oatmeal forgotten. "I'll go tell Mrs. Potts."

"And I'll invite Uncle Victor and Aunt Maimie."

Deirdre's spirits lifted for the first time in days. She had a concrete task to focus on. A surprise to show a man in desperate need of reassurance that he truly mattered to the people who cared about him.

By the time Matthew arrived home later that day, the sky was shrouded in darkness. Winter was truly upon them when it got dark before dinner.

Wearily, he set his case on the floor, removed his overshoes and coat, and hung his hat on a hook by the door.

He'd spent the greater part of the day organizing his office, sorting through files and journals. The rest of the time, he'd conferred with Victor about possible job opportunities, as well as ways to increase his patient load.

One thing Victor said had stayed with him. "We don't have to let anyone know about the state of your practice. It's a private matter."

That had gone a long way to relieve Matthew's fears. Victor was right. Nothing had been announced, so the Pentergasts would have no way of knowing he might be out of a job.

Mrs. Potts appeared in the hallway. "Good evening, Doctor. They're about to start the meal, if you'd care to join them."

"I would indeed, Mrs. Potts. Thank you." He straightened his tie and headed into the dining room.

"Happy birthday!" a chorus of voices shouted as he entered.

Matthew stopped and stared. Phoebe and Deirdre stood smiling at the side of the room, and Victor and Maimie were seated at the table.

"What is this?"

Deirdre stepped forward. "It's an early birthday celebration."

Matthew stared at her, taking in the lavender dress that hugged her figure, her hair swept up in a fancy style with several loose wisps teasing the nape of her neck. Phoebe, too, was dressed in her best attire.

His gaze traveled to a two-tiered frosted cake in the center of the table. Far from the professional-looking cake the O'Learys' cook had made for Phoebe, this one tilted to one side as though the amount of chocolate shavings and marshmallows had knocked it over.

"Miss Deirdre and I made you a cake," Phoebe announced. "It's chocolate just like mine."

Matthew narrowed his eyes at Victor. "You knew about this?"

Victor chuckled. "I was sworn to secrecy by a very persuasive young woman." He winked at Deirdre.

Matthew's attention swung to her flushed face. "You did all this?"

She shook her head. "It was Phoebe's idea. I only helped with the details."

Phoebe rushed over to tug at Matthew's hand. "Come and sit down so we can eat. There's presents, too."

Somewhat dazed, Matthew allowed Phoebe to lead him to his seat at the end of the table.

A small pile of oddly wrapped gifts sat stacked beside the cake. Matthew couldn't remember the last time anyone had made a fuss over his birthday. He usually ignored the date altogether. His throat tightened and itched. "Thank you. This is most unexpected."

Phoebe hopped onto her seat. "Miss Deirdre said we have to

eat our brussels sprouts before we can have cake." She grimaced but picked up a fork, prepared to dive in.

Maimie cleared her throat. "First let's give thanks for the Lord's blessings. Including the brussels sprouts."

Matthew hid a smile and bowed his head over his hands while Maimie blessed the meal.

Half an hour later, his belly filled with good food, his soul nourished with pleasant conversation, Matthew leaned back in his chair. This was exactly what he'd needed to put things into perspective. Family and friends. The important things in life. All other problems could wait.

Deirdre lifted the cake and set it in front of him, and everyone began to sing. An odd tightness invaded his chest.

"Make a wish, Papa."

He raised his head and met Deirdre's gaze, which was tinged with sympathy. She knew exactly what he would wish for. That all threats from the Pentergasts would disappear and Phoebe would remain with him.

"Why don't you help me with the candles?" he asked Phoebe, forcing a cheerfulness to his tone.

Phoebe eagerly climbed on his lap and blew out the candles with an exaggerated huff.

"Who wants the honor of cutting the cake?" Matthew looked hopefully around the table.

Maimie rose from her chair. "I will. Phoebe can pass the plates."

"And I'll get the presents." Deirdre gathered the strange assortment of packages and moved them to Matthew's spot.

Matthew picked up a colored piece of paper with large words printed on it—*Happy Birthday, Papa*. Some of the *P*'s were backward, and below the writing Phoebe had drawn a picture of a man and a girl standing beside a very large cake.

"Thank you, Phoebe. This is a beautiful picture."

She beamed at him. "I hope you like your presents. We didn't have time to go shopping."

"I'm sure I'll love them." He picked one, unwrapped the homemade paper, and found one of his fountain pens inside.

The next contained a rock Matthew recognized from Phoebe's collection, and the rest followed suit. She'd taken items from around the house and wrapped them.

"This was so thoughtful, sweetheart. Thank you."

"You're welcome, Papa. We wanted to make you happy again."

Her serious declaration brought about a wave of shame. He held out his arms to her, and she hopped onto his lap. "You make me very happy, Phoebe. Nothing else in the world matters more than you."

He hugged her tight until she wriggled out of his grasp. "Can we eat the cake now?"

He chuckled. "Yes, we can."

After they had finished eating, Deirdre slid one more package in front of him. "It's not much, but I hope you like it." A becoming blush stained her cheeks.

Matthew opened it and found a book of poetry by Robert Frost. She'd remembered an offhand comment he'd made that he enjoyed poetry when not studying medical journals. A warmth spread through his chest as he ran his fingers over the leather binding and flipped open the cover. Inside he found an inscription. *To my darling Deirdre, may these poems bring you pleasure. Your loving mama.*

Matthew looked up. "I can't accept this. It was a gift from your mother and obviously means a lot to you."

She leaned toward him, green eyes earnest. "But I want you to have it."

At her disheartened demeanor, Matthew relented. "I will consider it a loan and will return it once I'm finished."

The lines creasing her forehead eased. "All right. In the meantime, I'll search for a new copy to give you. If you enjoy the poetry, that is."

"I'm sure I will. Thank you."

"You're welcome." The warmth in her gaze held him captive.

Reluctantly, he pulled his attention back to the rest of his guests. "And thank you all for making my birthday most special indeed."

"Our pleasure." Victor patted a napkin to his mustache and pushed his chair back. "But I fear we must be leaving, as I have an early start in the morning. Is that suitable for you, Deirdre? If not, I can send Davis back for you."

"No need. I'll go with you now. If Matthew doesn't mind tucking Phoebe in."

Matthew swallowed a rise of disappointment at her early departure. "Not at all."

They all rose, except Phoebe, who continued to scrape frosting from her plate.

Matthew helped Maimie and Deirdre with their coats, and as he bid the Fullmans good night, he suddenly remembered the item in his pocket. "Deirdre, may I speak to you for a minute before you go?"

"Take your time, my dear." Victor tipped his hat. "We'll be in the car."

As the door closed behind them, Matthew turned to face her. In the glow of the hall light, she seemed ethereal.

"Thank you again for tonight. It was just what I needed to lift my spirits." He smiled, and though the temptation to touch her burned hot in his chest, he dared not. He stuffed his hand in his pocket and cool metal met his fingers. "I have something for you as well."

"For me?" A becoming wrinkle marred the area between her brows.

He took out the small emerald ring and held it up. For a moment he hesitated, thinking the situation too intimate. He'd planned to give her the ring in a businesslike fashion, but in light of all she'd done for him, it didn't seem right. Instead, he lifted her left hand and slowly slid the ring onto her finger. It fit perfectly. "It was my mother's birthstone."

She looked up at him with luminous eyes. "I'll take good care of it, I promise."

Unable to get a word out, Matthew nodded. Suddenly he wished he was giving her a real engagement ring, one he'd chosen specifically for her.

She placed a soft kiss on his cheek. "Happy birthday, Matthew. I hope all your wishes come true."

Then, leaving him with the lingering scent of her perfume, she walked out the door.

28

THREE DAYS AFTER Mr. Miller's death, Connor rode over the cold-hardened ground toward the foreman's cabin on the Sullivans' property. Despite the frigid temperature, Connor's palms slicked with sweat beneath his gloves. His heart pumped as fast as when he'd ridden Excalibur for the first time, and the same emotions swirled inside him. Half fear, half thrill—not knowing exactly how the horse would react.

Just as he wasn't sure how Jo would react to this visit.

Connor had thought long and hard over the last few days, trying to figure out a solution to her problem. One where she wouldn't need to leave the area to look for work. The best idea he'd come up with seemed a little drastic at first, but the more he prayed about it, the more it seemed like God was on board with Connor's plan.

Now if only he could convince Jo.

Connor approached the lean-to, relieved to see Jo's sorry old mare inside, which meant she was around, unless she'd wandered off on foot.

He slid off Dagger's back and tied the reins to a post.

He paused to utter one last earnest prayer that the Lord might see fit to bend Jo to Connor's way of thinking, or that she'd at least be open to the solution he was about to propose. Then, squaring his shoulders, he walked up to the front door of the cabin and knocked loudly three times.

Several seconds later, the door opened. Surprise registered in Jo's pretty eyes, the bright color highlighted by her blue dress. Her long hair flowed freely over her shoulders in golden waves.

Realizing he was staring, Connor swallowed and pulled off his cap. "Good morning, Jo. May I come in?"

She frowned. "Why are you here?"

"I have an idea I'd like to . . . discuss with you." He stuffed his cap in his pocket.

She eyed him doubtfully, then shrugged. "As long as it doesn't take too long. I have to finish cleaning." She moved inside, and he entered behind her, pulling the door shut.

The interior smelled like lye and vinegar. A bucket of water sat on the floor near the sink.

He looked around and whistled. "This place has probably never been so clean."

Jo wiped her hands on her apron. "I want to leave it in good condition for the next people."

He stiffened. "Has Caleb hired a new foreman already?"

She moved to the sink. "Yes. A man with a wife and three young children. He needs the cabin by tomorrow."

Connor kept his expression neutral, all the while thinking this might work to his advantage. Seth had accepted a job as a stable hand, so he had quarters in the bunkhouse. But where was Jo planning to go?

"What did you want to discuss?" she asked over her shoulder.

Connor took a deep breath and walked toward her. "I think I've come up with a solution to your . . . situation, and I hope you'll hear me out." He took her by the hand and led her across the room to the battered sofa in the living area.

They sat down, and though she tried to pull her hand free, he kept it tucked in his, feeling somehow more confident with that tangible connection.

He cleared his throat. "Jo, I hope you know how much I admire and respect you. Your talent with the horses, your hard work, and your loyalty to your family are a few of the wonderful qualities you possess."

Wariness crept into her eyes.

"Even when I thought you were a boy, those qualities grabbed my attention. Then when I discovered you were a girl . . . well, everything made sense."

She pulled her hand free. "What do you mean by that?"

He ignored her question, intent on saying the speech he'd prepared. "I think I've come up with a way you can stay at Irish Meadows and continue to train the horses."

Hope lit a flame in her eyes, and she leaned toward him. "Really? How?"

He licked his bone-dry lips and swallowed. "You can marry me."

Her mouth fell open. "You can't be serious."

Connor shifted on the lumpy sofa, battling his ego at her look of incredulity. "Think about it, Jo. As my wife, you could train the horses without having to pose as a man. You wouldn't have to worry about where to live or having enough food to eat. And you'd still be near your brother."

He held his breath, waiting for her reaction. Once the ramifications of the idea set in, surely she'd see the logic in his plan.

However, instead of seeming relieved, Jo jumped up and strode to the hearth. She stood with her back to him, her toe tapping on the wooden floor.

Connor swallowed and got to his feet, banking his impatience until she turned to face him.

She planted her hands on her hips. "I think you're overlooking a few minor details."

Annoyance flared. She didn't seem the least bit grateful for his solution. "What details?"

"Even if your father agreed to the idea—"

"I can handle my father. What else?" He crossed his arms.

Her nostrils flared, reminding him of an annoyed filly. "Did it ever occur to you I might not have the slightest interest in marrying you?"

⁂

Jo fought the urge to smack the baffled look from Connor's face. Were all men clueless as to what motivated a female?

And what didn't?

"I'm sure you thought I'd swoon at the idea of becoming Mrs. Connor O'Leary, but on the contrary, I value my independence and the ability to make decisions for myself."

Connor scowled, looking as prickly as a porcupine ready to attack. "Really? And how is that going?" Sarcasm dripped from his words. "You're currently jobless with nowhere to live. Your brother is doing nothing to help you. I thought you might appreciate someone who actually cares what happens to you."

Each of his words hit her nerves like the blow of a hammer. As quickly as her dander had been raised, the fight drained out of her. Her bottom lip began to quiver, and she whirled toward the bedroom so he wouldn't see her cry.

He caught her by the arm before she could disappear into the other room.

"Jo, wait." He released a weary breath. "This is not how I intended our conversation to go."

She yanked her arm free. "No, you expected me to fall at your feet in gratitude for the great sacrifice you're willing to make. Well, I don't need that kind of charity."

"Who said anything about charity?"

She wrapped her arms around her middle, the wood of the door solid against her back. "Then what's in it for you other than free help around the farm? You'd be stuck with a wife you didn't want. What if you met a girl and"—her voice quavered—"fell in love? You'd be trapped in a marriage to me." She shook her head. "I won't let you throw away your life."

"You've got the wrong idea."

She pushed away from the wall. "You should leave now. I have to be out of here by this afternoon."

"Jo—"

"Please, Connor. Just go."

He let out a low growl that raised the hairs on the nape of her neck. His arm whipped out to haul her against his broad chest. Then he very deliberately lowered his mouth to hers.

Her heart gave a primal leap into her throat, thudding so loudly she couldn't hear anything else. Though she wanted nothing more than to kiss him back, the rational part of her brain knew she had to stop him.

Mustering every ounce of internal fortitude, she splayed her hands against his chest and pushed him back—hard.

"So that's what you want out of the deal," she said, breath heaving in her lungs. "A willing body to warm your bed. Well, it won't be me. I'm sure I can find a way to make a living and keep my self-respect."

Hurt flashed across his face, causing a stab of guilt to rip through her.

He stiffened, his features hardening to granite. "Have it your way," he bit out. "I'll leave your last pay with Mac. You can pick it up on your way out of town."

He stared at her for a second longer, then marched out the front door, slamming it behind him.

Two days later, Connor strode through the barn, irritation cinching his spine. He pulled off his gloves and slammed them to the ground. "Why are these stalls not clean?" he hollered to anyone within hearing distance. "I can't bring the horses back to this filth."

"Sorry." Mac brushed by him. "This used to be Joe's job, so—"

"Get someone on this. Now." Connor retrieved his gloves and stalked off, fighting the urge to put his fist through a wall. He may not be their boss anymore, but he was still the lead stable hand.

He stormed out of the barn and across the frost-packed earth. Nothing seemed to appease the anger that constantly bubbled to the surface ever since Jo had rejected him.

At the fence, he blew out a breath. The ugly truth sifted through his foul mood, bringing more shame than anger. He owed Jo an apology for his boorish behavior. She'd been right. He'd expected that, after only a couple of kisses, she'd accept his marriage proposal and fall into his arms in gratitude—without even considering what she truly wanted.

Now, not knowing how she was doing was eating at his insides. Where was she living? Did she have a job? What if she were forced to sleep out in the cold?

Connor abruptly turned. For his peace of mind, he needed to find out—and the only person who might know was her brother.

Two hours later, after a brief conversation with Seth Miller, Connor pulled his father's car to a halt outside Mrs. Bingham's estate. According to Seth, Reverend Filmore had helped Jo get a position cleaning the Bingham mansion. Though Connor should have been happy to know she was okay, he had to see for himself and offer an apology. He couldn't leave things the way they'd ended between them.

Not wanting to disturb the residents, Connor walked to the rear of the house and rapped loudly on the back door.

A plump, middle-aged woman answered the door. "Yes?" She sized him up, taking in his sheepskin jacket and denim pants.

Perhaps he should have taken time to change into something more suitable.

"Is there a Miss Miller working here?" he asked.

"The new girl?"

"Yes. I need to speak with her. It won't take long."

The woman shrugged. "You can find her in the cellar." She pointed to a set of cement stairs just inside the back door.

"Thank you, ma'am."

Connor made his way down the narrow staircase and into the damp cellar below. A musty smell permeated the air in the dimly lit area. He followed the sound of a scrub brush until he came upon Jo, kneeling on the cold stone floor, scouring a metal washtub.

With the intensity of her work, she obviously hadn't heard him arrive, and he took a second to drink her in, from the brown work dress and striped apron, to her hair, mostly hidden under a white, frilled cap.

His pulse sprinted to life, simply from being in the same room with her. He cleared his throat. "Hello, Jo."

She let out a squeak. Her arm jerked, sending the brush sailing across the floor.

"What on earth are you doing here?" She rose and ran her wet hands down the front of her apron. A rosy hue infused her cheeks.

He bent to retrieve the brush and handed it back to her. "Seth told me where you were. I came because I owe you an apology." He hesitated, shoving his pride aside to do what was right. "I was wrong to assume you'd want to marry me. It was arrogant and insensitive, and I should have considered your feelings."

She sighed. "It's all right, Connor. You were only trying to help." She pushed at a strand of hair that had escaped her cap.

"It doesn't excuse the fact that I acted like an oaf." He gave a sheepish grin. "Trying to solve everyone's problems is one of my biggest failings. That and thinking I know all the answers."

She stepped toward him, her chin lifted. "It's not a failing. I think it's a noble trait to want to help people."

He leaned one shoulder against the stone wall and crossed his arms. "I'm glad you feel that way, because I have another proposition for you."

A wary light crept into her eyes. "What kind of proposition?"

"I spoke to my brother-in-law, who's the director of an orphanage in Manhattan, about a possible job for you." He paused. "Rylan said he'd be glad to meet you and see if you might fill in for my sister, Colleen, when she has her baby. You'd have a room and your meals provided." Connor watched her closely to ascertain a response.

A wrinkle formed above her pert nose. "But I just started here . . ."

He scanned the dingy room and the stacks of bins to be cleaned. "Do you enjoy the work?"

Her gaze slid to the bucket at her feet. "Not really," she whispered.

Connor withdrew a piece of paper from his jacket pocket and handed it to her. "Here's Rylan's information. Do with it what you will. No pressure." He dropped his hand to his side, wishing he could prolong the visit. "Well, I'd best let you get back to work." Reluctantly, he tore his gaze from her and started up the stairs.

"Connor?"

He held his breath, hoping that she'd changed her mind about marrying him. "Yes?"

"Thank you. For the apology . . . and the information."

He swallowed and nodded. "You're welcome. I hope everything works out for you."

Then, before the blueness of her eyes distracted him any further, he jogged up the stairs and back outside to the harsh light of day.

29

THE MORNING of the custody hearing dawned gray and cold with the distinct threat of snow in the air. Despite her warm coat with the fur collar, Deirdre shivered as she followed Matthew up the stairs into the limestone building that served as both the Toronto City Hall and the county courthouse.

Nerves swirled in her stomach as they walked down the tiled corridor, the taps of their heels echoing in the cavernous hall. She removed her gloves as they walked, careful to make sure Matthew's ring was still in its proper place. She shoved her gloves in the deep pockets of her overcoat and scanned the rows of ominous-looking doors. Mr. Bancroft had said he'd meet them here an hour earlier than their expected time before the judge.

She glanced at Matthew, whose tense jaw gave evidence of his anxiety. They had rehearsed what they would say to the judge if questioned, but it didn't eliminate the fear of the unknown. All morning, Deirdre had prayed God would allow her to say the right thing to help Matthew keep his daughter.

"There's Mr. Bancroft now." Matthew pointed down the corridor.

The lawyer waved his free hand and headed toward them. "Good morning, Dr. Clayborne, Miss O'Leary." He beamed at them, not a trace of nerves showing.

Deirdre decided all lawyers must have extraordinary amounts of self-confidence—or at least a good sense of bravado.

The lawyer motioned them to a bench along the corridor wall. Deirdre swept her skirt beneath her as she sat and undid the buttons of her coat. She mustn't let her good suit wrinkle before the hearing.

"Try not to be nervous," Mr. Bancroft began. "And act as naturally as possible."

Deirdre twisted the ring around her finger, still not used to its weight.

Matthew leaned forward on the bench. "How long will this take?"

Mr. Bancroft pursed his lips. "Probably less than an hour." He studied Matthew, then Deirdre. "I know you two aren't well-versed in the art of acting, but could you both try to look a little less like the end of the world has arrived? And maybe sit closer, show some affection like a real couple would?"

Heat flared in Deirdre's cheeks. Her attempt to play the loving fiancée with the Pentergasts hadn't gone over very well—with them, or with Matthew. But now when everything might depend on her acting skills, she would try again.

She scooted closer to Matthew, held out a hand, and waited. With a long exhale, he placed his hand in hers. She entwined her cold fingers with his, finding comfort in the simple joining of hands.

"It's going to be okay," she said.

His Adam's apple bobbed. "I hope you're right."

Just then, the Pentergasts appeared in the corridor before them. They halted on their way, acknowledging them with a slight inclination of their heads, then continued on.

Deirdre leaned in and whispered, "Don't let them get to you. Remember, in their own way, they want what's best for Phoebe."

Mr. Bancroft rose. "Sorry to interrupt, but we should make our way to the courtroom. Judge Blackthorn hates to be kept waiting."

Matthew focused on the amazing architecture of the building as Mr. Bancroft led them down the corridor and through a set of double doors. Anything to keep his mind off the events about to transpire in this room, where the fate of his daughter would be decided.

Would Judge Blackthorn be a compassionate man, sympathetic to a father's right to raise his child? Or would he be a biased friend of the Pentergasts, eager to see the couple rewarded for their extravagant donations to various causes in the city?

Matthew walked up a short aisle behind his lawyer and through a set of swinging doors.

Mr. Bancroft deposited his attaché case on the tabletop and motioned for Matthew to sit down. "Miss O'Leary, you may sit behind us."

Instead of complying, Deirdre walked toward Matthew and took his hand in hers.

"I'll be right behind you, and I'll be praying." She squeezed his hands. "Try not to worry. God is on our side." With that, she rose on her tiptoes and kissed his cheek.

Matthew flushed, his gaze shifting to the aisle where the Pentergasts had stopped to stare at him. Heat flared in his face, but he returned their stare without flinching.

"Thank you, Deirdre," he said with a poor attempt at a smile.

She dipped her head and made her way to the row of seats behind the low wall.

Matthew sat down next to Mr. Bancroft. He looked ahead at the imposing desk where the judge would hear both parties' testimonies. From the corner of his eye, he was aware of the Pentergasts and their lawyer taking their places across the aisle. Matthew pressed a hand to his stomach, willing the nerves to subside, then twisted in his chair to look behind him. A few spectators sat on the Pentergasts' side of the room, likely friends or colleagues. His side was empty except for Deirdre. Victor had an appointment this morning but hoped to make it later. For a moment, Matthew watched Deirdre, who sat with her hands folded on her lap, eyes closed, lips moving in silent prayer. Warmth curled in his chest. Having this amazing woman here to support him seemed too good to be true.

You are not alone.

The words drifted through his consciousness. Matthew turned to face the front of the courtroom, not sure whether he had thought those words or if they had come from a higher power.

Either way, a sense of peace invaded his soul. Deirdre was right. He had to believe God was on his side, that He wouldn't take away the last person Matthew had left in the world.

A door on the side of the room opened, and a uniformed man entered the room.

"All rise. Judge Aloysius Blackthorn presiding."

Chairs scraped the floor as everyone stood. A large man with white hair and a flowing black robe entered the room and climbed up to the judge's bench.

He glanced out over the room. "Be seated."

The judge peered over some papers on his desk, then raised his head. "I understand this is a case to decide custody of a minor by the name of . . ." He glanced down at the papers. "Phoebe Helen Clayborne."

"That is correct, Your Honor." The Pentergasts' lawyer, a Mr. Whitmore, rose from his chair.

"And the parties in question are the father, Dr. Matthew Edward Clayborne, and the maternal grandparents, Mr. and Mrs. Terrence Wilson Pentergast."

"Yes."

Judge Blackthorn skimmed the pages in front of him. "Mr. Whitmore, please proceed."

Mr. Whitmore hooked his thumbs in his pants pockets and strutted to the area in front of the bench. "To open, Your Honor, I would like to give a bit of the history behind this suit."

The judge held up one hand. "I think I would like to hear directly from your client, if you don't mind, Mr. Whitmore."

"Of course, Your Honor. I call Dr. Terrence Pentergast to the stand."

Terrence rose with his customary dignity, tugged his suit jacket into place, and proceeded to the witness stand. Once he was situated, the bailiff swore him in and he sat down.

"Dr. Pentergast, would you please tell us a little of your relationship with Dr. Clayborne?" Mr. Whitmore began.

"Certainly." Terrence glanced at Matthew before focusing back on his lawyer. "I met Matthew when he did an internship at the Toronto General Hospital. I found him to be a most promising young man and introduced him to my daughter, Priscilla."

Mr. Whitmore leaned on the wooden railing surrounding the witness stand. "I take it your daughter found Dr. Clayborne equally compelling?"

A slight smile hovered on Terrence's mouth. "Yes, they were married the year before Matthew graduated from medical school, with the understanding that he would join my practice."

"But this didn't happen, did it?"

"No." Terrence's mouth thinned. "By then the war had been going on for several years, and Matthew became determined to join as a medic. Priscilla adamantly opposed his leaving, especially since she suspected she was with child."

"And did this make Dr. Clayborne stay?"

"No." Terrence's posture slumped. "He didn't even come home for his child's birth."

A murmur sounded from the people seated behind the Pentergasts. Matthew's ears burned at what they must be thinking.

"But Dr. Clayborne did come home at some point?" Mr. Whitmore continued.

"On a Christmas leave." Terrence looked over to where Helen was sitting. His nostrils flared, and he turned his attention back to his lawyer. "Phoebe was about six weeks old by then and Priscilla was struggling with being a new mother—alone." The final word hovered in the quiet room.

Matthew quivered with repressed anger. He had known the Pentergasts would try to make him look bad, but Terrence was making it sound like he'd abandoned his wife and child. He wasn't the only man who'd had to leave a family behind to serve his country.

"So Dr. Clayborne returned to the war?"

"Yes. Priscilla found it increasingly difficult to cope with a fretful baby so she moved back home with us."

"I see. And when did you receive news of Dr. Clayborne's fate?"

"I believe it was in March of 1918. We learned he'd been injured and flown to England for treatment."

"And when he finally returned home, did he take up his rightful role as a husband and father?"

Terrence shifted on his seat and once again glanced in his wife's direction. "Matthew tried. I will give him that. He came to work with me for a brief period of time until the military hospital wooed him away."

"I assume your daughter moved back in with her husband when he came home?"

"She did. But things were tense between them. A lot of resentment had built up on both sides."

"What happened next?"

Terrence's features crumpled. He took a moment to collect himself. "Priscilla contracted tuberculosis."

Mr. Whitmore tsked. "And how did Dr. Clayborne handle it?"

"He insisted on treating Priscilla himself."

"I take it you didn't agree with this."

"No, I wanted her sent to a sanatorium."

"Ultimately, your granddaughter came down with the disease as well. Did Dr. Clayborne finally relent and send them to the sanatorium?"

"Yes, but it was much too late. Priscilla died a week later." He swallowed and blinked.

"Tell me, Doctor, do you hold your son-in-law responsible for your daughter's death?"

An expectant hush fell over the room.

Terrence let out a weary sigh. "If Priscilla had gone into the sanatorium sooner, she likely would have survived."

Matthew closed his eyes, each word hammering him with the ever-present guilt that had plagued him since his wife's death.

"What did Dr. Clayborne do about his daughter?" Mr. Whitmore's confident tone indicated he knew what the answer would be.

"Phoebe remained in the sanatorium for the better part of a year. Matthew visited her on occasion, but his focus remained on his work."

"And what transpired when Phoebe had recovered enough to be released?"

"My wife and I wanted to bring her home with us. But Matthew wouldn't hear of it. Instead, he hired a nurse and a nanny and left Phoebe in the care of strangers."

The anger drained from Matthew, replaced by waves of shame as the truth of Terrence's words hit home. Had he truly been that blind? That unfeeling to his daughter's needs? No wonder the Pentergasts despised him. He bowed his head, unable to look at anyone.

When the judge dismissed Terrence from the stand, Matthew

tried to get control of his emotions, steeling himself for his upcoming testimony.

"One last thing, Your Honor." Mr. Whitmore stood before the judge.

"Go ahead."

"It appears Dr. Clayborne has recently acquired a fiancée. A woman he met only weeks ago. The Pentergasts doubt this is a legitimate union, and fear it merely a ruse to sway the court in Dr. Clayborne's favor."

The air clogged in Matthew's lungs. Chills swept over his body.

The judge scowled at Mr. Whitmore. "What proof do you have of this?"

"None, Your Honor. But we thought we should bring it to your attention, including the fact that this engagement happened just as the Pentergasts threatened legal action."

"Indeed the timing does seem circumspect." Judge Black-thorn turned to Mr. Bancroft. "I'd like your client to address the issue now."

Matthew's heart pounded in his ears. Mr. Bancroft rose from his chair, giving Matthew a look as if to say, *Are you ready?*

But before he could utter a syllable, a chair scraped behind them.

"Your Honor, I'd like to explain." Deirdre's tremulous voice floated over his shoulder.

What on earth was she doing?

Deirdre held her breath, awaiting the judge's response as to whether or not she could speak. She had no real idea what she was going to say. But she doubted Matthew could handle the spontaneity of such direct questioning without making a mess of their carefully constructed plan. Of the two, she was the better actor.

The judge frowned over his glasses. "And who are you?"

"Deirdre O'Leary, Dr. Clayborne's fiancée."

A bead of perspiration trickled down her spine, but she held herself rigid under the man's stare, all the while avoiding Mr. Bancroft's glower.

"Very well, Miss O'Leary. Please come forward."

Willing her legs not to shake, Deirdre walked through the small swinging door and took her place on the witness stand. The uniformed bailiff approached her with a Bible. Quickly she swore to tell the truth and took her seat, praying for God's wisdom to guide her words.

The judge twisted in his seat to face her. "Tell me a bit about yourself, Miss O'Leary."

She ran her tongue over her dry lips. "I'm from Long Island, New York. I recently graduated from the nursing program at Bellevue Hospital in Manhattan." She almost added that she was attending medical school but held back that information, certain it wouldn't aid their cause.

"So you're working as a nurse?"

"Not at present. My mother recently suffered a stroke, and I came home to care for her."

His eyebrows rose. "And how did you meet Dr. Clayborne?"

"My father hired him to treat my mother's paralysis. Dr. Clayborne and I worked quite closely together and developed a . . . good rapport."

"I see. And when did this rapport become a romance?"

Deirdre forced herself not to look at Matthew. She swallowed hard. "When Matthew told us he had to return to Toronto, we realized that we"—she exhaled softly—"didn't wish to be separated."

"So he proposed?"

She hesitated, searching for the best words without lying. "It was a mutual decision, arrived at after much prayer and discussion."

An uncomfortable silence descended over the room. Deirdre's heart sank. Would her story convince the judge?

"Tell me, Miss O'Leary, do you love Dr. Clayborne?"

She stiffened on her chair and gave the answer she had rehearsed. "Yes, of course."

Simple enough. If questioned, she could tell Matthew she hadn't lied, that of course she loved him, just as she loved Phoebe and all her close friends.

"I see." He studied her with a shrewd look. "But are you *in love* with him?"

All the air rushed from her lungs. Her tongue seemed glued to the roof of her mouth. Twisting her fingers together, she prayed for something to save her from answering. A fire or an earthquake perhaps?

"May I remind you, Miss O'Leary, that you are under oath?" The judge's tone softened.

Her heart pumped at a furious rate. What choice did she have but to answer truthfully?

"Please answer the question. Are you in love with Dr. Clayborne?"

Deirdre expelled a long breath, then raised her head to look the judge in the eye. "Yes, Your Honor." She held his gaze, unwavering in her response.

At last, he nodded. "Thank you, Miss O'Leary. You may step down. We will take a short recess and reconvene in fifteen minutes."

Not daring to look at Matthew, Deirdre made her way on trembling legs past the tables, through the swinging doors, and straight out of the courtroom. She rushed blindly into the women's lavatory, where she leaned against the wall and closed her eyes, attempting to slow her erratic pulse.

Her whole body shook with suppressed emotion.

How would she ever face Matthew after this?

30

MATTHEW BARELY HEARD Mr. Bancroft excuse himself from the room. Still seated at the courtroom table, he stared blankly ahead at the witness stand where Deirdre had just admitted to being in love with him.

His heart thudded as emotions waged a battle in his system. Was she telling the truth, or had she perjured herself to save him from doing the same?

Either answer proved as dire as the next. The idea that she could truly be in love with him caused elated chills to rush through him one moment and his muscles to seize in a form of paralysis the next.

What was he supposed to do with this terrible knowledge? Knowledge that he had the power to ruin Deirdre's life—since nothing but certain heartbreak could come from loving him.

A fact Priscilla could attest to if she were still alive.

He took in a deep breath and looked around. The room had emptied save for two women at the back. He needed some fresh air, even if only for a few minutes, to gather his emotions and mentally prepare for his upcoming testimony.

His injured leg throbbed as he limped out the door and down the main corridor. The people in the hall became nothing but muted background noise to the battle raging in his head.

He had turned a corner when the sound of Mr. Bancroft's voice stopped him.

"Congratulations, Miss O'Leary. Your testimony may have single-handedly saved our case."

Matthew peered around the corner to see the pair huddled in an alcove, obviously unaware they could be overheard. He stepped back so they wouldn't see him, unwilling to face them before he'd regained his composure.

"I'm glad," he heard Deirdre say. Yet something about the shakiness of her voice belied that statement.

"I must say, you're quite the actress to pull that one off." Mr. Bancroft chuckled.

His words sent a barb straight to Matthew's heart. Had his lawyer coached her on what to say in the event the judge asked that particular question? It certainly seemed like he had.

Which meant that Deirdre had lied after swearing on a Bible. Why would she do such a thing?

Because Deirdre loved Phoebe more than anything.

Enough to risk lying on the stand.

He leaned back against the wall, his breathing shallow. Everything about this farce had felt wrong from the beginning. He couldn't let it go on any longer. He had to release Deirdre from this charade and rely on God's mercy to help him win his case.

By the time the judge called the court back into session, Matthew had carefully strapped down his emotions so that when he took the stand, nothing but an icy calm remained. Staring out over the room, Matthew felt Deirdre's gaze on him, but he refused to look at her.

The court official swore Matthew in, and Mr. Bancroft came forward to lean an elbow on the wooden railing.

"Dr. Clayborne, we've heard one account of your story. I'd like to hear your version of the events." He straightened. "What was the state of your relationship with your late wife?"

Matthew unclenched his hands in an effort to relax. "It's no secret my marriage was not a love match. Priscilla and I were fond of each other and quite compatible, or so I thought. We viewed our marriage as a partnership, one that would benefit us both."

"When did things begin to deteriorate?"

Matthew stiffened on the chair. "Rather quickly, I'm afraid. Priscilla was resentful of the many hours I was required to be at the hospital during my final year of medical school. When I graduated, and the war was still on, I wanted to use my skills to help the injured soldiers, so I signed on as a medic with the Canadian Army Medical Corps."

"Against your wife's wishes?"

"Yes. I felt it was my duty to my country."

"And when you learned that your wife was indeed expecting, what did you do then?"

"I attempted to get a leave so I could be home for the birth." He risked a glance at the Pentergasts. "Unfortunately, the leave was postponed until mid-December. I thought the timing would be better since I would be home for Christmas with my wife and child."

"How did you feel when you first met your daughter?"

The memory of looking into baby Phoebe's eyes for the first time rose in Matthew's mind, gripping him with the force of that love. "It was the best moment of my life," he said hoarsely.

"So why did you return to the war?"

Matthew bristled. "I had an obligation to fulfill. Every man fighting had left someone behind. Why should I have been any different?" Visions of dying soldiers clutching faded photos of loved ones, begging to write one last letter home, still haunted Matthew.

"And when you returned after being injured, why didn't you join Dr. Pentergast's practice?"

"I had benefited from physical therapy that allowed me to regain the use of my leg. I hoped to do the same for the injured soldiers at home."

"I see that as an admirable choice. Your wife, however, did not."

"No."

Mr. Bancroft continued to rehash the events of Priscilla's illness and death. Matthew answered all the questions as succinctly as he could.

"Let's jump ahead now to when your boss asked you to treat the wife of a friend. Why did you agree to take the position with the O'Learys in New York?"

Matthew drew in a deep breath. "My daughter had suffered a setback in her health. Her physician suggested that country air would help. When I learned the O'Learys lived on a horse farm, I thought I could benefit both my daughter and Mrs. O'Leary."

"I see. And did it help?"

Matthew smiled for the first time. "Indeed. Phoebe was like a different child—both physically and emotionally."

"So it was a good decision, then?"

"Very much so."

"And now to the subject of your recent engagement. Could you tell us how this happy event came about?"

A band of tension seized Matthew's shoulders. The decision that had been so firm in his mind now wavered. He risked a glance across the room at Deirdre. Her forehead was wreathed in lines, her eyes a mirror of anxiety. His gut twisted, firming his resolve. He couldn't keep her trapped in the snare of this deception. He had to set her free.

Matthew lifted his chin. "I'm afraid our engagement has been a mistake."

A loud gasp sounded. Mr. Bancroft stared at him as though he'd lost his mind.

"Miss O'Leary and I share a friendship, as well as a great love for Phoebe, but we entered into a betrothal for the wrong reasons." Unable to look at Deirdre or his lawyer, he turned to the judge. "Please understand I meant no disrespect, Your Honor. We both feel strongly that my daughter's well-being depends on her staying with me. And when it was suggested that marriage could help me win this case, I acted perhaps too quickly." He paused. "While I care deeply for Miss O'Leary, I don't think either of us is ready for such a commitment."

The judge frowned. "What are you saying, Doctor?"

He let out a slow breath. "I am releasing Miss O'Leary from the engagement." Against his will, his gaze swiveled to Deirdre.

Instead of seeming relieved, she appeared horrified, her hand covering her mouth.

Tension swirled through his system. Had he done the right thing? He turned back to the judge, who studied him with a look of disappointment.

"This is a most unusual turn of events, Dr. Clayborne. And I must say, it gives me pause to think you purposely entered into an engagement solely to sway the courts."

Matthew's pulse pounded in his ears.

"However, the fact that you would go to such lengths to keep your daughter does speak to your commitment."

"Phoebe is the most important thing in the world to me." His voice cracked. "I'll do whatever it takes to keep her safe and happy."

Mr. Whitmore popped up from his seat as though he could no longer contain himself. "I must object, Your Honor. This man has lied, and that woman"—he gestured toward Deirdre—"has perjured herself. The child has two upstanding grandparents ready to take her in."

The judge shook his head. "I need some time to consider all aspects of this case before I render my decision." He turned to Matthew. "You may step down, sir."

Matthew willed his legs to support him as he rose from the chair. Mr. Bancroft had resumed his seat, his scowling countenance proving he was less than pleased at this unexpected development. As Matthew moved to take his place, he risked a glance at Deirdre. His heart clutched at the hurt and bewilderment on her face.

He forced his gaze away and sat down.

The judge gathered his papers and addressed the room. "This court is in recess. Miss O'Leary, I'll see you in my chambers—immediately." He banged the gavel and rose.

Matthew shot to his feet. What did the judge want with Deirdre? Surely he wouldn't arrest her?

Staring straight ahead, Deirdre walked to the front of the courtroom, where the court official led her out a side door.

Helpless despair raced through Matthew's body, turning him hot then cold. He raked a hand through his hair, wishing he could charge out the door after her. Protect her. Tell the judge it was all his fault.

He sank onto the chair and let his head fall into his hands, using the only tool at his disposal to help her.

Lord, don't let Deirdre suffer for my mistakes.

Nerves threatened to swamp her stomach as Deirdre followed the judge into a spacious back room. What had Matthew been thinking? He'd destroyed their carefully constructed plan with one sentence.

"Please have a seat." Judge Blackthorn removed his robe and

hung it on a hook. He adjusted the sleeves of his suit jacket and then took his seat behind a massive desk.

Deirdre sat on the edge of the guest chair, clutching her purse on her lap. She inhaled deeply to calm herself, drinking in the aroma of pipe tobacco and lemon oil—scents that evoked memories of her father's study back home.

The man took his time before speaking, shuffling a few papers and books on the desk before pinning her with a narrow-eyed gaze. "Now, young lady, tell me why I shouldn't arrest you for perjury."

Her heart hammered hard against her ribs, but she held firm. "Because I didn't lie."

He peered at her. "You lied about your engagement."

"I respectfully disagree, Your Honor." She held up her left hand, still containing Matthew's ring. "There was an engagement, albeit a rather unconventional one."

The judge inclined his head. "You have a point. However, you expect me to believe that all your answers were truthful?"

"Yes, sir." Deirdre bore his regard with quiet dignity. "If you review the answers I gave, you will find I did not utter one falsehood."

His features appeared to soften. "So you *are* in love with Dr. Clayborne?"

Deirdre winced at the uncomfortable truth. She lowered her gaze to her lap. "Unfortunately, yes."

"Why? Does he not return your feelings?"

She recalled their one amazing kiss and Matthew's subsequent rejection, and gave a quiet sigh. "I . . . expressed my interest, but Dr. Clayborne did not seem to reciprocate." Sudden worry for Matthew overshadowed everything else, and she leaned forward. "Please, Your Honor, don't hold this against Matthew. He wasn't in favor of the engagement idea in the first place."

The judge studied her again. "Tell me, Miss O'Leary, if I

were to decree that Phoebe must live with her grandparents, how do you think it would affect the child?"

Deirdre's heart squeezed so hard she could scarcely catch her breath. Was he leaning toward granting the Pentergasts custody? She longed to be able to tell him they were terrible people and he shouldn't allow them anywhere near Phoebe. But that simply wasn't the case.

She closed her eyes, trying not to feel like she was betraying Matthew. "I think," she said slowly, "once Phoebe adjusted, she would eventually be fine with her grandparents. They love her dearly and are acting in what they consider to be her best interest." She drew herself upright. "But I do fear the Pentergasts may try and turn Phoebe against her father, since it's clear they bear him a huge grudge." She leaned forward again, determined to plead Matthew's case. "I beg you, Your Honor, don't take Phoebe away from her father. She's already lost one parent. Don't make her lose another."

Despite her best efforts to remain in control, the backs of her eyes burned with the threat of tears. She swallowed hard and sat back on her chair. "I hope I haven't overstepped."

The judge's features bore no anger. "No, Miss O'Leary. It's clear you love the child, which is commendable. I will give your words their due consideration."

She squared her shoulders. "Does that mean I'm free to go?"

A smile broke out over his weathered features. "Since I can find no evidence of perjury, I won't be arresting you today."

"Thank you, Your Honor." A relieved sigh escaped as she rose.

"Miss O'Leary?"

"Yes?"

"If I were Dr. Clayborne, I wouldn't be in such a hurry to terminate your engagement." He sent her a wink that heated her cheeks.

"Thank you, sir."

She wished she could say something else that might influence his decision in Matthew's favor. But since there was nothing left to do, she walked out of the chambers and closed the heavy door behind her.

❦

"There you are." Matthew surged forward as Deirdre exited the judge's chambers. He'd spent the last twenty minutes pacing the corridors, praying the bailiff hadn't arrested Deirdre and whisked her off to jail.

Deirdre stopped. Her eyes widened as though she was surprised to see him.

He came closer. "Are you all right?"

"I'm fine." A blush spread across her cheeks.

She hurried past him, and Matthew fell in line beside her. "Well, what did the judge want?"

"To discuss my testimony." She kept her chin high as she walked.

He gripped her elbow and pulled her to a halt. "Please tell me he didn't order your arrest."

"You mean after you purposely derailed our plan?" Her sarcastic tone matched the fury snapping in her eyes. "No, Matthew. I showed him the ring and assured him we didn't actually lie about being engaged, although the nature of the engagement might not have been as it appeared."

"What else did he say?"

She shrugged. "He asked me some questions and sent me on my way."

"What type of questions?"

Her gaze slid past his shoulder. "About you and the Pentergasts." When she finally looked at him, the anger in her eyes had turned to misery. "I'm sorry, Matthew. I couldn't lie. I told the judge the Pentergasts only want what's best for Phoebe."

He sucked in a long breath. She'd advocated for his in-laws against him? The thought seared pain through his midsection.

"But I also told him Phoebe belonged with you. I hope he'll take my opinion into consideration when he makes his ruling."

He should have known better. It was against her nature to lie, which was why her earlier testimony confounded him. "What about . . . the other things you said under oath? Did he ask you about that?"

She stilled, her gaze sliding to the patterned floor. "The judge knows everything I said was the truth."

"Everything?" he rasped out.

She raised her head. "Yes."

Matthew's mouth went dry as a flood of fear rushed through him.

Defiance flashed in her eyes. "No need to panic, Matthew. My feelings are my responsibility. I will handle them." With that, she took off at a fast clip down the tiled hallway.

Matthew raked a hand through his hair. He should go after her and tell her . . .

Tell her what?

That he loved her, too, but didn't deserve her? That he wasn't sure he could ever be a good husband? That he didn't think he could make her happy?

And what about her career? How could he dismiss her goals over such uncertainty?

Slowly he made his way back to the main corridor, where Mr. Bancroft waved at him. "Dr. Clayborne. The judge just sent word that he wishes to speak to your daughter in his chambers before he issues his ruling."

Matthew stood silent for a minute, attempting to absorb the ever-changing events. Like a boat being tossed on the waves of a storm, he was powerless to stop the momentum and terrified of the outcome.

"Very well," he said with a weary breath. "I'll go and get her."

31

D EIRDRE STOOD in the main corridor of the courthouse and waited with Phoebe. All around her, bar-
risters and laymen hurried to their appointments, but
amid the bustle, there was no sign of Matthew or Mr. Bancroft.

Matthew had disappeared to confer with the lawyer and
Judge Blackthorn before Phoebe went in to see him. He meant
to ensure the judge would respect Phoebe's boundaries and also
to make certain there would be no mention of an engagement,
false or otherwise.

"Miss Deirdre?" Phoebe's small voice drifted up to her.

"Yes, honey?"

"What do I have to say?"

Deirdre bent to her level. "The judge will ask you about
your father and about your grandparents. Answer as honestly
as you can."

Her bottom lip trembled. "Will you come with me?"

Deirdre's heart swelled. She would love nothing more, but

she doubted the judge would allow it. "I wish I could, sweetie. But your daddy and I will be right outside the door, and if you feel uncomfortable, just tell the judge, and he'll let us in."

Deirdre looked up to see Matthew coming toward them, his face pinched with worry. "It's time."

Phoebe turned her face into Deirdre's shoulder.

"It's all right," she soothed the child. "Judge Blackthorn is a very nice man. I promise."

Phoebe lifted her head. "Okay." The trust in her eyes nearly undid Deirdre's control.

She gave Phoebe a squeeze, then rose with the girl's hand firmly in hers. Matthew threw her a worried glance over Phoebe's head as he took his daughter's other hand.

Standing in front of the judge's chambers, nerves fluttered in Deirdre's stomach. So much was riding on Phoebe's interview. She prayed the girl wouldn't do anything to harm Matthew's case.

Matthew knocked twice, and the judge answered, "Come in."

They entered the chambers and found the judge sitting in one of the guest chairs. He rose to smile at Phoebe. "Hello, young lady. You must be Phoebe."

She nodded.

"Come and sit down, and we'll have a little chat."

Deirdre helped her onto the chair. "Remember, after this, we'll go for some ice cream." Deirdre kissed her good-bye, praying the girl wouldn't pick this time to go mute again.

Matthew also bent to whisper something in her ear and kissed the top of her head. "We'll be right outside the door," he said, staring at the judge.

"Understood. We won't be long."

Minutes passed like hours as they waited. Deirdre couldn't remain seated on the hard wooden benches that lined the corridor. She had to pace to expend her nervous energy.

At last, the door opened and Phoebe skipped out with a happy smile, a green lollipop clutched in her hand. "The judge said I did really good and gave me a lollipop, just like the doctors in the hospital."

Dizzy with relief, Deirdre laughed. "That's wonderful." She looked at Judge Blackthorn and mouthed the words, "Thank you."

He gave her a wink, then turned to Matthew. "That's a bright young lady you have there, Doctor."

Matthew seemed to sag with relief. "Thank you, sir. What happens now?"

Judge Blackthorn folded his arms over his broad chest. "Why don't you get Phoebe her ice cream? Once I review my notes and spend some time in prayer, I will make my decision." He smiled and disappeared back into his chambers.

Deirdre released a long breath. *Lord, infuse Judge Blackthorn with your wisdom and help him make the best decision for Matthew and Phoebe.*

After Matthew conferred briefly with Mr. Bancroft, the three of them collected their coats and made their way outside onto the sidewalk. A cold gust of wind blew Deirdre's coat around her legs. She reached up to secure her hat.

Matthew stepped in front of her and leaned in close. "After this, I need you to take Phoebe home." His intense blue gaze bore into hers.

"But the verdict . . ." She trailed off at the stubborn set to his jaw.

"I don't want her there, just in case . . ." A muscle worked in his throat.

In case the judge grants custody to the Pentergasts.

"Please, Deirdre, can you do this for me?"

She swallowed her grief and nodded. "All right."

The pain in Matthew's eyes caused her throat to seize. If only she could give him a hug, offer him comfort.

With a forced smile, he held out his hand to Phoebe. "Come on, sweetheart. Let's get that ice cream."

Matthew breathed into his hands and rubbed them together, pacing the halls of the courthouse. He could not get warm no matter what he did, and it wasn't due to the cold weather. Desperate pleas arose in his mind, pleas he couldn't quite form into a prayer. He couldn't bear to think about losing Phoebe. Or what his life might look like then.

He stood at the bottom of the great split staircase and stared up at the immense stained-glass window that graced the wall above. A lady holding a flag shook hands with a laborer. What did she represent? Justice? Liberty? Would justice be served today with the judge's decision? And if so, whose version of justice?

If only Matthew knew whether the judge was sympathetic to his cause. He'd tried to gently question Phoebe as to what she had told the man, but other than talking about her puppy, he got nothing out of her. Yet Matthew felt his daughter's words would be the key to the judge's decision.

Matthew scrubbed a hand over his face, thankful that Deirdre had taken Phoebe home. At least he didn't have to put on a brave face for them, or attempt to keep them calm. He could wallow in his nerves and face his fate alone.

Lord, I need your strength. I don't think I can do this without you.

Footsteps echoed across the tiles. "Dr. Clayborne. The judge is ready." Mr. Bancroft's solemn demeanor did nothing to ease Matthew's anxiety.

He nodded and followed his lawyer back to the courtroom. As he walked up the aisle to the front of the room, he couldn't help but glance at the empty seat Deirdre had occupied earlier. A twinge of regret pinched his heart, but he forced himself to take his place.

Matthew glanced across the room to where Terrence Pentergast stood with his arm around his wife. Were they as nervous as he, or were they confident of their victory?

Matthew lowered his head over his entwined hands, searching for a prayer, anything to ease the worry that choked the breath from his lungs.

From behind him, a warm hand squeezed his shoulder. The tension radiating through him eased slightly. Victor had managed to get away from the hospital after all. He twisted in his chair to look behind him, and his mouth gaped open.

Deirdre stood beside Victor, a tremulous smile on her lips.

"Victor." Matthew shook his hand. "Thank you for coming. But . . ." He frowned at Deirdre. "Where is Phoebe?"

"I asked Aunt Maimie to watch her. I hope you don't mind."

A host of emotions sifted through Matthew—relief, regret, fear. But then she reached across the small wall separating them and took his hand with a smile that warmed him through to his core.

"I couldn't let you go through this alone," she whispered. "Whatever happens, we'll face it together." A sheen of moisture rimmed her luminous green eyes.

The immenseness of his gratitude swept every word from his mind. All he could manage was a single nod and a squeeze of her fingers in return.

A door at the front of the courtroom opened, and the official entered.

"All rise. His Honor Judge Aloysius Blackthorn presiding." Everyone stood as the judge took his place.

"Be seated. This court is once again in session."

Matthew sat, fearing the thudding of his heart could be heard across the room. With supreme effort, he focused on the words the judge was saying.

"I thank you all for your patience in this matter. Though it pains me to take sides in this case, I have reached a decision." He looked at the Pentergasts and then at Matthew.

From his inscrutable expression, Matthew could not glean any clue as to which way he had ruled.

"Cases such as this are some of the hardest ones to hear. Both sides are caring, upright members of society. Both men are physicians, dedicated to serving others, with sterling reputations. And both parties obviously share a deep love for the little girl in question."

Matthew's tongue seemed pasted to the roof of his mouth. He dared not blink lest he miss one word uttered.

"Because of such evenly matched sides, I chose to interview Phoebe herself in order to ascertain from the child's perspective who would be best suited to meet her needs, both physical and emotional." A smile tugged the judge's lips. "And indeed she helped clarify the matter immensely."

Matthew's stomach clenched. Phoebe adored her grandparents. What if she'd told the judge how wonderful they were? What if she'd said something damaging about Matthew? About his working all the time, or the strict nanny he'd left her with for most of her childhood?

Beads of sweat gathered under his shirt collar as he viewed the situation from a judge's perspective. Of course Terrence and Helen would be the obvious choice. Terrence was retired and, other than sitting on several hospital boards, had plenty of time to devote to his granddaughter. And Helen, despite her haughty ways, could give Phoebe a woman's love and guidance, something she would lack under his roof.

Tremors rushed through him. The blood pounded in his ears so that he couldn't hear a thing. The judge's lips moved, but Matthew couldn't seem to understand what he was saying.

". . . so while I'm assured that both parties have their strengths and their weaknesses, I have followed my conscience, as well as a wise piece of advice I received in my chambers, and . . ." He paused to direct his gaze to Matthew. "For the present time, I have chosen to leave Phoebe in the care of her father."

An explosive gasp came from the Pentergasts' table.

Matthew sat frozen in place, not daring to believe his ears.

Judge Blackthorn glared at Mr. Whitmore, then turned his attention back to Matthew. "You may have noticed I stipulated *for the present time*. I have scheduled a follow-up meeting in six months' time to make sure certain conditions are being met. One of which is adequate visitation for Dr. and Mrs. Pentergast. I feel they have a right to play an active role in Phoebe's life. And I also believe it to be in Phoebe's best interest to have frequent contact with her grandparents." He paused to stare at Matthew. "I hope I don't hear any objections to this, Dr. Clayborne?"

Matthew cleared his throat. "No, Your Honor."

"Good." The judge turned to the Pentergasts. "And in return, I expect you to dispense with any animosity you might still harbor toward your former son-in-law. I'd like you to consider yourself a team working toward a common goal—the happiness of your granddaughter. Is this clear?"

Terrence turned to give his wife a pointed look. "Yes, sir," he said gravely.

"Then if everyone is in accordance, I pronounce this case closed. Mr. Bancroft, you may pick up the paperwork in my chambers." He banged the gavel.

Once the judge left the room, Mr. Bancroft extended his hand. "Congratulations, Matthew."

Matthew grasped it in sincere gratitude. "Thank you, Mr. Bancroft. I can't tell you how much I appreciate your help."

"Glad to be of service. I'll get those papers to you."

Matthew turned, seeking the one person he needed. Deirdre's face was pressed against Victor's suit jacket. She lifted her head, and the tears streaming down her cheeks tore a strip off Matthew's already raw heart. She pushed past the few spectators and came through the swinging doors. He moved toward her, unprepared for her to throw her arms around him and bury her face in his neck.

307

"Oh, Matthew. God heard our prayers."

He enveloped her trembling frame in his arms and closed his eyes to pinch back the sting of tears. Tears of gratitude that God had seen fit to give him another chance with his daughter. Tears of gratitude for the woman in his arms. He didn't care who saw him hugging Deirdre. He craved her comfort, knowing she shared his joy and relief.

Deirdre pulled away and drew a handkerchief up to her nose.

Victor clapped Matthew on the back. "Congratulations, Matthew. Maimie and I are very happy for you."

"Thank you, Victor." Matthew's voice turned to gravel.

Victor nodded. "I'll wait for you in the hall."

As he walked away, Terrence Pentergast approached the table, a somber expression on his face.

Deirdre took a step back. "I'll wait with Uncle Victor."

Matthew didn't want her to go but conceded it might be for the best.

Terrence made no move to shake Matthew's hand. Lines ravaged his face. Behind him, Matthew caught a glimpse of Helen's stony countenance.

Warring emotions filtered through Matthew's system, temporarily overriding the joy of his victory. He couldn't forget the angst these people had put him through. Still, he knew the Pentergasts must be suffering a great loss. He could be magnanimous and hold out the proverbial olive branch. "I hope we can put our differences aside once and for all. For Phoebe's sake."

Terrence studied him for several seconds. "You're willing to do that?"

"Of course. You're Phoebe's grandparents. She loves you both very much. I would never interfere with that."

Terrence's brow wrinkled. "And what of Miss O'Leary?"

"What about her?"

"It's clear you share a strong connection. What if you do decide to marry? Will you move to New York?"

Matthew's shoulders stiffened. "No one is getting married. And no one is moving anywhere." Especially now with the judge's ruling.

The man's brow relaxed, and he heaved a loud exhale. "Could we perhaps work out a visitation schedule?" The hope in his eyes drew out Matthew's compassion.

"That sounds like a good idea." He held out his hand in a true gesture of reconciliation. "I hope we can put the past behind us and move forward. We need to work together, for Phoebe's sake."

Terrence's lips twisted. "Helen might be harder to convince, but I'm willing if you are." He shook Matthew's hand. "I'll be in touch."

With that, he returned to his wife's side.

Matthew let out a long breath. Perhaps another prayer had been answered and the Pentergasts would at last forgive him for not being able to save their daughter's life.

Perhaps now he could learn to forgive himself.

32

EARLY THE NEXT MORNING, Deirdre entered the Fullmans' dining room to the enticing aroma of eggs and sausage. She poured herself a cup of coffee from the silver service on the side table. As she took the first sip, her thoughts circled back to Matthew and the wonderful moment where they had shared a hug of congratulations after the verdict, recalling the joy and relief that had quivered through every cell in his body as he'd embraced her. She'd never felt more in tune with another human being.

Unfortunately, the connection didn't last, and when they left the court to pick up Phoebe, it seemed Matthew had stored his emotions safely behind his wall of reserve once again. After a celebratory dinner in this very dining room, Matthew had bid her a polite good night and asked what time to expect her in the morning.

Now that this crisis was over, where did it leave them?

She'd spent sleepless hours last night going over Matthew's

every word, every gesture, every facial expression in an attempt to determine where their relationship stood, but she hadn't been able to draw any conclusion. If he'd given her any indication that he returned her feelings, she might not feel so awkward to remain in his employ. But the thought of caring for Phoebe every day in Matthew's home, only to leave each evening when he arrived, seemed the worst sort of torture.

One she wasn't sure she could bear.

"Good morning, Deirdre. You're up early this morning." Uncle Victor's cheery voice preceded him into the room.

As soon as he took his seat, a maid bustled in to serve him a plate, while another poured his coffee and set it beside him.

Uncle Victor thanked them, then peered at Deirdre as she sipped her coffee. "Are you not eating?"

"Not hungry, I'm afraid."

"I thought you'd be ecstatic after yesterday's good news." His brow furrowed. "But I can see something is troubling you."

She nodded, her fingers tightening around her cup.

"Is it Matthew?"

She nodded again and set her cup down with a noisy *clink*. "I don't know what to do."

"About what?" He dug into his eggs.

She plucked the linen napkin from the table and ran her fingers over the embroidered flowers. "I promised to help Matthew care for Phoebe until he could hire a new nanny. It seemed the right thing to do at the time, especially since I'd lost my spot in medical school." She exhaled a tense breath. "But I don't think I can continue any longer."

He chewed, eyeing her thoughtfully. "Is it because you're in love with him?" he asked gently.

The words ripped through her. She squeezed the napkin into a tight ball in her fist. "Yes. But I'm afraid he doesn't feel the same."

Uncle Victor shook his head. "He cares for you, Deirdre,

mark my words. I've never seen Matthew react to any woman as he does to you."

"Yet he's determined to remain alone." She sighed. "And even if he were to declare his feelings, I don't know what to do about my career. Marrying would mean forfeiting any chance at medical school, yet if I continue with my studies, I'll have at least five more years to go. It wouldn't be fair to ask Matthew and Phoebe to wait that long."

Uncle Victor set down his fork and reached over to engulf her hand with his. "I think some serious soul-searching is in order, my dear." He gave her hand a light squeeze. "God put Matthew in your path for a reason. Maybe it's time to figure out why."

Her throat convulsed with a rush of emotion. She did her best to hold back the threat of tears. "Thank you, Uncle Victor. You may be right." She pushed away from the table. "And I think some distance is required to do that kind of soul-searching."

"If you do decide to continue with your career," he said, "I'd be happy to use my limited influence to find you another medical school."

She looked into his kindly eyes and walked over to kiss his cheek. "You are a treasure, Uncle Victor. Aunt Maimie is a lucky woman."

He chuckled. "And doesn't she know it."

<hr />

Later that morning, Deirdre's stomach churned as she entered Matthew's house. She'd made her decision, and now she just needed the courage to see it through.

Mrs. Potts greeted her in the foyer and took her coat. She informed Deirdre that Phoebe had already eaten and was playing in her room and that Dr. Clayborne was in the study.

"Thank you, Mrs. Potts. I'll join him there for a minute before I go up."

Deirdre paused to steady herself, then headed down the hall.

Seated at his desk, Matthew smiled as she entered the open doorway. "Good morning, Deirdre. You're here early." For the first time since Phoebe's birthday, he looked relaxed, the lines of tension gone from his face.

His happiness normally would have filled her with delight; however, knowing she was about to ruin his good mood made her want to cry.

She took a tentative step inside. "I need to speak with you."

His smile faded, and he lowered his cup, his brows cinching. "Something is wrong."

Standing before his desk, she kept her features passive. "Nothing's wrong. But I've come to a decision—one I hope you can respect."

His frown deepened, and he leaned back in his chair. "What sort of decision?"

With the air thinning in her lungs, she squared her shoulders. "Now that the custody issue is no longer a threat"—she hesitated, then forged ahead—"I've decided to return home and see about applying to another medical school."

Matthew's eyes glittered like blue ice. "I see."

"I'm sorry to give you such short notice, but Aunt Maimie has offered to mind Phoebe until you can hire someone. From what Mrs. Potts told me, she had several candidates lined up before I arrived, so I shouldn't be too hard to replace." She knew she was prattling on too fast, her nerves getting the best of her.

Without a word, Matthew rose and came around the desk toward her.

Unable to bear the accusing look on his face, Deirdre dropped her gaze to the floor. Her heart pumped painfully in her chest at his nearness. He stood so close she could smell the familiar scent of his sandalwood soap.

"Why?" The tortured tone of that one word shook Deirdre to the core.

"I think you know why," she whispered. "It will be better for both of us this way."

"Better for you, but not for Phoebe." Hurt and anger etched in the lines around his mouth, fueling her guilt.

She took a shallow breath. The pain of abandoning Phoebe cut just as deeply, if not more, than the pain of leaving Matthew. "I'm sorry" was all she could manage.

"What can I do to make you stay?"

For one crazy moment, Deirdre imagined Matthew taking her in his arms, declaring his love for her, and begging her to become his wife.

What would she do?

Her heart jolted with the truth of her answer. She would forfeit all her dreams, all her goals, to become Matthew's wife.

If only he loved her enough to ask.

She reached into her pocket and withdrew the ring Matthew had given her for their pretend engagement, running her fingers over the gold with a last caress.

"There's nothing you can do." She held out the ring to him, finally meeting his gaze when he didn't move.

The unmasked agony in his eyes nearly buckled her knees.

"Please, just take it," she said.

His fingers surrounded her hand. "Deirdre, I wish . . ."

She slipped her hand free, leaving the ring in his palm, and stepped back.

"I know. I wish things could be different too." A lump of raw emotion lodged in her throat. She forced herself to look into his face, if only to memorize his features—the fall of his hair across his brow, the strong jaw, those ever-changing eyes. "I hope you find happiness, Matthew. You and Phoebe will be in my prayers—always."

He stared at her with a hollowed-out expression. "You will say good-bye to Phoebe before you go." It was a statement more than a question.

"Of course I will."

She turned away from the pain in his eyes and exited the room, heading down the hall.

"Miss Deirdre, what are you doing?" Phoebe stood at the foot of the stairs with the doll Deirdre had given her clutched under one arm.

Deirdre pressed her lips together, desperate to keep her emotions at bay for a few more minutes. On legs that shook, she walked toward the tree stand in the hall. "I'm afraid I have to go home, sweetie. Aunt Maimie is going to mind you today."

Matthew came up beside Phoebe and laid a hand on her shoulders as if to protect her.

From the hurt Deirdre was about to inflict.

Phoebe frowned. "When will you be back?"

"I'm not sure." She forced a fake smile to her lips as she pulled on her coat. "But you'll have to come to Irish Meadows soon for another visit."

The girl's lip trembled. "I don't want you to go. Can't I come with you?"

"No, honey. You have to stay with your daddy and your grand-parents."

"But I want you to stay, too." With a strangled cry, she pulled away from her father and dashed over to clutch Deirdre by the waist.

Deirdre bent and pulled her into a tight hug. The little-girl scent of talcum powder swirled around her. Hot tears dampened Deirdre's neck, shattering Deirdre's heart into tiny pieces. She wished she could stay here with this precious child who needed her. But one glance at Matthew's rigid frame reminded her why she couldn't.

"You're very special to me, honey, and I will always love you. But I have to go back home where I belong." Tears blurred her vision until she couldn't hold them back. They rolled down her cheeks and onto Phoebe's wispy blond curls. Deirdre kissed the top of her head and rose.

With one last tortured look at Matthew, she whirled and ran out the front door.

Not bothering to wait for the chauffeur, Deirdre climbed into the backseat beside her luggage and slammed the door shut. "Take me to Union Station, please."

"Very good, Miss."

As the car pulled away, Deirdre twisted on the seat to peer out the rear window.

Only Phoebe stood on the front step, waving as the car drove away.

33

SEATED IN RYLAN MONTGOMERY'S OFFICE, Jo admired the intricate woodwork of the bookshelves and the large mahogany desk. Even after a week of working at the orphanage, she was still in awe of the building's elegant décor. Before she'd arrived, she'd pictured a stark, hospital-like setting. Nothing like this stylish establishment fit for royalty.

In fact, Jo loved everything about St. Rita's—the couple who ran it, the adorable children, even the austere nuns who lived on the third floor.

It hadn't taken her long to use the information Connor had given her and set up an appointment with Rylan Montgomery to discuss potential employment. Anything had to be better than the fourteen-hour days of grueling labor at the Bingham estate.

Though nervous at her first meeting with Rylan, she'd soon felt at ease with the handsome Irishman. After a recommendation from Connor, he'd hired her on the spot, even offering to drive her back to Long Island to pick up her things.

Jo shook off her musings at the sound of muffled footfalls on the carpeted floor.

"Sorry to keep you waiting, Miss Miller." Rylan entered the room, a wide grin on his face. "One thing you'll learn quickly around here is you never know what each day will bring."

She smiled. "Please call me Jo."

"Jo it is. Though somehow Josephine seems more fitting for the lovely young lady in front of me." He winked at her, sending a blast of heat to her cheeks.

"Flirting with the staff again, Mr. Montgomery?" Colleen swished through the door, brows arched.

Rylan only grinned wider. "Aye, but you know I only have eyes for you, darlin'." He kissed Colleen's cheek and helped his very pregnant wife onto a chair.

The obvious adoration in Rylan's gaze matched his wife's. What would it be like to have such a wonderful husband?

Jo's thoughts swung to Connor with a tug of regret. Though she loved working with Colleen, her resemblance to Connor was a constant reminder of how much Jo missed seeing him every day.

Rylan took his seat behind the desk. "Jo, we wanted to have a chat and make sure you were enjoying your job here. Is there anything else you need?"

"Goodness, no. You've both been so kind already. I love working with the children. And my room is"—she paused to contain her emotions—"well, it's the nicest room I've ever had. I truly can't believe my good fortune."

All thanks to Connor.

"And you're a godsend to us, since my beautiful wife can now slow down a bit. With the holidays coming, there's much work to be done."

Colleen shifted on her seat and grimaced. "Which brings us to another reason we wished to speak with you. Our tradition here on Christmas Day is to take the children to church, come back for brunch, and then open presents. Once the excitement dies down, the nuns take over while Rylan and I and our children spend the rest of the day at Irish Meadows."

"Sounds lovely." Jo fought to keep the wistfulness from her voice.

"We'd like you to join us—if you have no other plans." Colleen's kind gaze filled Jo with inexplicable emotion.

Christmas at Irish Meadows? Though the thought of seeing Connor was definitely appealing, she couldn't imagine enduring Mr. O'Leary's disapproval. "Thank you, but I've promised to spend the day with my brother. The Sullivans put on a Christmas meal for their employees and families." She'd only talked to Seth once since he'd taken a position as a stable hand, so she was more than glad to receive his invitation.

"Well, you could still drop by my parents' afterward. We usually have singing and games going on all evening."

Jo forced a smile. "Thank you. I'll keep that in mind."

A private look passed between Colleen and her husband. Rylan stood. "If you ladies will excuse me, I have a matter to see to." He dropped another kiss on his wife's cheek before bounding from the room.

Jo's stomach swirled with instant tension. It was obvious Colleen wanted to be alone with her, though Jo couldn't fathom why.

Colleen gave Jo a blinding smile. "I'm glad you're enjoying your position here. It was thoughtful of my brother to recommend you for it."

She seemed to expect Jo to answer. "Very thoughtful," she said carefully, feeling like she was walking on ice about to crack.

Colleen arched a brow. "Do you know Connor calls almost daily to ask about you? To make sure you're happy in your job."

Jo's heart turned a slow somersault in her chest. "He does?" Her eyes stung with sudden tears that she blinked away. Connor cared enough to find her this job and even inquire after her. Every day.

"Indeed, he does." Colleen pursed her lips, studying Jo. "It's pretty evident that Connor has strong feelings for you. What I'd like to know is . . . how do you feel about him?"

A streak of heat followed by a chill raced up Jo's spine at Colleen's question. "I . . . I don't understand why you're asking this."

Colleen grinned. "Because I'm an incurable matchmaker and I believe my brother may be in love with you."

"Oh." The air whooshed from Jo's lungs, replaced by a rush of panic. She fought to clear her head. "It doesn't matter how I feel because your father would never allow Connor to be involved with someone like me. He made his views very clear when he caught us kiss—" Jo bit back a groan at her slip.

Colleen's eyes gleamed. "Daddy caught you and Connor kissing?" She laughed out loud. "This just keeps getting better. I think you definitely need to come to Irish Meadows on Christmas, Jo."

A bead of perspiration slid down Jo's back. "But what about your father?"

"Don't worry about Daddy. He's never approved of any of his children's partners initially. It just takes him a while to warm up to the idea." She laughed again. "Now we just need to find you the perfect dress."

❧❧❧

Three days after leaving Toronto, Deirdre stretched under the eiderdown quilt on the large brass bed in her nieces' cozy attic room. This was exactly what she needed. A brief respite, surrounded by the unconditional love of Colleen and her family, while she allowed her bruised heart to heal.

Deirdre had come straight to her sister's house from the train station, unwilling to face her parents until she'd had time to lick her wounds. She'd spent two whole days sleeping, barely coming down to eat. Colleen must have sensed Deirdre's need to nurse her pain in private, for she hadn't pushed her to tell her tale. But last night, after Colleen had put the two youngest Montgomerys to bed, Deirdre had finally spilled the details of her unexpected feelings for Matthew. To her great relief, Colleen had listened and expressed copious amounts of sympathy without suggesting some crazy plan to win Matthew's heart. Perhaps pregnancy had mellowed her sister.

Now, on her third day of sanctuary at Colleen and Rylan's brownstone, Deirdre repacked her suitcase and took a fortifying breath. It was time to go home. Time to get back to Mama's therapy and help her regain her independence—so Deirdre could regain hers.

Perhaps by now Uncle Victor would have news about a possible medical placement. If not, Deirdre planned to contact Aunt Fiona, Daddy's sister, who worked for Barnard College. As a distinguished university professor, her aunt might be able to use her influence to secure a place for Deirdre in one of the local universities. That way she could still be close enough to assist Mama if needed.

Voices in the kitchen drifted up the staircase as Deirdre descended. The distinct Irish lilt made Deirdre smile. Her sister-in-law, Maggie, must be visiting. With her cheerful personality and unquenchable optimism, Maggie was one of Deirdre's favorite people.

Sure enough, Maggie and Colleen sat at the kitchen table, a pot of tea gracing the middle.

"Deirdre!" Maggie popped up to envelop Deirdre in a warm embrace. "I'm so sorry to hear of your troubles, love." Her gray eyes swam with sympathy.

Colleen struggled to her feet as well. "I hope you don't mind. I told Maggie about your . . . situation."

Deirdre gave a quick smile, thankful her supply of tears

seemed to be dried up. "Of course not. We're family after all." She frowned. "But why aren't you at the orphanage today?"

Colleen pulled a mug from the cupboard. "Rylan insisted I stay home. He even invited Maggie over to baby-sit me." She rolled her eyes in an exaggerated display as they all took a seat at the table.

Maggie laughed. "It's no hardship, trust me. Especially since the older children are in school. And wee Molly likes to sit with the nuns."

"Take advantage while you can." Colleen winked at her.

Deirdre's eyes widened. "Not you, too?"

A blush colored Maggie's cheeks. "I'm afraid so. Three O'Leary babies are on the way, though Brianna and I aren't due until spring."

Deirdre smiled. "Congratulations. Adam must be thrilled."

"Aye. I'm surprised he can fit his big head through the door," she said with affection.

From across the hall, the telephone rang. Colleen sighed. "Maggie, could you answer that? I can't rush in this condition."

"Certainly." Maggie rose and darted across the hall to the parlor.

Moments later, she returned, her eyes filled with tears. "That was your father. I'm afraid your mother's had a bad fall. He wants Deirdre to come home right away."

Matthew stared out the window of his study at the gray view in front of him. Melancholy hovered around him like a black cloud. Not even the news that Victor had found two potential backers for his therapy clinic could cheer Matthew.

He let the curtain fall back into place and turned to his desk, staring at the unruly mound of books and papers. He had no interest in anything as mundane as paperwork. Not since Deirdre had left him.

Like everyone seemed to.

Matthew glanced at the calendar on his desk. Mid-December already. Soon the city would begin its preparations for Christmas. The crèche would go up in his church, awaiting the Baby Jesus on Christmas Eve. Likely Victor and Maimie would invite him for dinner, or perhaps this year the Pentergasts would include him in their festivities. For Phoebe's sake, Matthew would have to dredge up some sort of Christmas spirit.

Yet his heart remained encased in a cement-like wall. Nothing, it seemed, could penetrate it. He hadn't even mustered the energy to interview the candidates for a new nanny, imposing instead on Maimie's good nature to care for Phoebe. Sooner or later, however, he'd have to hire someone to take Deirdre's place.

He sank onto his chair and bowed his head over his hands, attempting to corral his thoughts into some semblance of prayer. Only with the Almighty's help would he be able to get over the pain of Deirdre's departure. He'd known she'd leave them eventually but had thought he'd have time to prepare, time to ease Phoebe into the idea. Maybe plan a little good-bye party. Deirdre's abrupt parting had left him reeling, stirring up the pain of all his past wounds.

Matthew blasted out a loud sigh. He'd thought he'd returned to his faith, but at the first sign of adversity, his trust in God became buried in self-pity. Some Christian he'd turned out to be.

A knock pulled his attention to the door.

Victor entered the room. "Good morning, Matthew. I hope you don't mind the intrusion. Mrs. Potts has gone to get Phoebe ready."

Matthew rose. "Did I miss something? I wasn't aware you were picking Phoebe up."

"I wanted to speak with you about a personal matter, so I decided to come here and save you the trip." He gestured to the chairs. "May I?"

Matthew gave himself a mental shake. "Of course." Whatever Victor wanted to talk about must be serious. "I hope nothing is wrong with Maimie."

"Maimie's fine. I wanted to talk to you about . . . Deirdre."

Alarm twisted Matthew's midsection. "Is she all right?"

"I wouldn't know since I haven't spoken to her since she left. We did, however, have quite an interesting conversation the morning of her departure."

Matthew took a moment to let his system settle. "I understand you offered to find her a place in another medical school. That was nice of you." He tidied some papers on his desk, uncomfortable under Victor's direct gaze.

"Do you know the real reason Deirdre left so abruptly?" Victor asked.

"I believe so."

"Then you know it's because she's in love with you. That it would be too hard to stay here knowing you didn't return her feelings."

Heat flashed up Matthew's neck. He pressed his lips into a hard line to keep from blurting out something he'd regret.

Victor's gaze narrowed. "But you and I both know that isn't true. You do have feelings for Deirdre, very strong feelings, I'd venture to say. But for some unknown reason, you're unwilling to do anything about it."

"That is my business." Matthew shoved away from the desk and walked to the window. He stared out blindly, as though the scenery could soothe his angst.

"Matthew, I realize your marriage to Priscilla was less than ideal, but you can't judge your relationship with Deirdre by that flawed yardstick. I mean no disrespect to your late wife, but Deirdre is nothing like her. She's strong, loving, and kind. And she shares your passion for healing. She wouldn't resent your career like Priscilla did. Don't you think you owe Deirdre the truth about your feelings?"

Matthew whirled to face him. "To what end, Victor? If she gives up her dream of becoming a doctor to marry me, she would eventually resent me for a whole different reason." He raked his fingers through his hair. "Don't you see? I only make the women in my life unhappy."

Victor frowned as he pushed to his feet. "You mustn't compare Deirdre to Priscilla—"

"It's not only Priscilla. I couldn't make my mother happy either." A sigh of exasperation leaked from his lungs. "After my brother died, I tried everything in my power to please her, to make her smile again, yet my presence only seemed to irritate her. The more I tried to be near her, the more she pushed me away. Until one day, she decided she had nothing to live for. Certainly *I* was not worth living for." Matthew closed his eyes and clenched his hands into fists to stop the tremors that coursed through him. Why had he said anything?

Victor came up behind him and laid a hand on his shoulder. "My dear boy, you must realize that when someone is in enough pain to end their life, there is little anyone can do. Certainly not a child. If anything, your father should have gotten her psychiatric help."

Matthew shook his head. His father had been mired in his own grief, barely able to cope himself, never mind help his wife.

Victor squeezed his shoulder. "I'm afraid," he said in a quiet voice, "that if you're not careful, the cycle will continue with Phoebe. She will believe that after her mother died, she wasn't enough for you. Because you went through life miserable."

The air clogged Matthew's lungs.

"You need to understand that your mother's death did not negate her love for you. She simply wasn't strong enough to overcome the pain. Don't let that tragedy define your life, your relationships. Put the past behind you once and for all—for Phoebe's sake."

Matthew's eyes burned as he turned to look at his friend. "I don't know, Victor. What if I open myself up and it doesn't work? What will happen to Phoebe then?"

Victor's kind face was wreathed in sadness. "No one has the answer to that, I'm afraid. Not even the Almighty himself. Sometimes all you can do is reach out in faith and let God do the rest."

"Excuse me, sir." Mrs. Potts appeared in the open doorway. "Miss Phoebe is ready to go."

Matthew attempted to pull himself together. "Thank you, Mrs. Potts. We'll be right out."

"I hope you'll forgive my interference, my boy. You are like the son I never had, and I only want you to be happy." He clapped Matthew on the back. "Give it some thought and prayer. I'll see you later at the hospital."

Once Victor and Phoebe had gone, Matthew sat in front of the fire and tried to clear his head. Victor's words played over and over like a gramophone stuck in a groove. No matter how he tried, Matthew could not dispute the truth of his statements.

They left the metallic taste of fear on his tongue. Could he let go of his long-held beliefs about Priscilla and his mother and risk opening his heart?

He thought back to the cherished moments spent with Deirdre. The bond they'd forged at the cabin, their first kiss, holding her when she'd lost her position in medical school, their shared elation at winning custody . . .

His whole being ached from missing her vivacious presence, her bright eyes, her infectious smile. Yet he understood why she'd left. That she was not only protecting herself, but she was saving Phoebe from getting even more attached to her.

The sharp ring of the telephone on his desk jarred Matthew from his thoughts.

While he really didn't want to speak to anyone, he couldn't

afford to miss a call from the potential investors Victor had said might call today.

With a reluctant sigh, he crossed to the desk and picked up the phone.

"Matthew? It's James O'Leary."

Matthew stiffened, the mere mention of the name O'Leary bringing with it a jolt of pain. "James. What can I do for you?"

"It's Kathleen. She's had a bad fall and suffered a major relapse." His voice cracked. "She's asking for you. I hate to impose a second time, but could you come back and assess the situation? Tell us where to go from here?"

Matthew's fingers froze around the receiver. Go back to Irish Meadows where he'd have to face Deirdre again? Impossible.

"I'm sure Deirdre can handle any—"

"You don't understand. Deirdre can't get through to her. Kathleen won't even lift her arm to eat. All she does is beg for you."

Matthew gouged his hand through his hair. Had this been his fault? Did he leave too soon, abandoning a patient before treatment was complete?

"I'm only asking for a week or so," James said. "Then maybe you can help me find someone locally to take on her continued care."

Guilt swamped him. He owed Kathleen that much at least. Besides, he still had to go back and get Phoebe's puppy. "Very well. I'll try to get a train out tomorrow."

"Thank you, Matthew." James's relief was palpable. "You don't know how much I appreciate it."

Matthew hung up the receiver, his hands unsteady, his mind spinning. What would he do about Phoebe? As much as he hated the idea of leaving her, he couldn't bring her with him. Couldn't subject her to seeing Deirdre and the O'Learys once more only to rip her away again.

As a show of good faith, he would ask the Pentergasts to look after her until he returned. The thought of being separated for even a week made his stomach cramp. He took a deep breath and attempted to will away his fear. Terrence was a doctor. Phoebe would be in excellent hands.

Matthew would use this as a first step in loosening his grip on his daughter.

And a test of his own strength at seeing Deirdre again.

34

"MAMA, YOU HAVE TO EAT. Won't you take one bite?" Deirdre held out a spoonful of Mrs. Harrison's beef stew, Mama's favorite, but she only shook her head and turned her face into the pillow.

With a weary sigh, Deirdre set the spoon back in the bowl. It had been three days since Mama's fall. Dr. Shepherd had examined her and proclaimed her injuries minor in nature, yet an uneasy thread of worry invaded Deirdre's heart. She'd never seen Mama this despondent, not even after her stroke. She seemed to have lost the will to live, refusing to eat and only sipping at her beloved tea and honey.

Could she have hit her head harder than they imagined? A severe head injury could cause depression and listlessness. Maybe she should persuade Daddy to take Mama to the hospital for more tests. If they didn't get to the bottom of her melancholy soon, Deirdre shuddered to think of the consequences.

She picked up the tray of untouched food. "I'll take this back to the kitchen and let you rest."

At Mama's weak nod, Deirdre fought the lump that rose in her throat. She should never have left her to go with Matthew and Phoebe. If she'd been here, Mama wouldn't have tried to get out of her wheelchair unassisted, wouldn't have fallen and hit her head against the table.

Mama, can you ever forgive me?

She took a last look at her mother's pale face, eyelids fluttering as she lay unmoving.

Lord, please show me the way to help my mother. There must be something I can do.

She left the door ajar as she carried the tray back to the kitchen.

Mrs. Harrison shook her head. "No luck?"

"I'm afraid not."

Mrs. Harrison took the tray and set it on the counter. "We can try again later. Perhaps she'll be hungry then." Her skeptical look told Deirdre she didn't expect that to be the case.

"Let's keep tempting her with the foods she loves," Deirdre said. "Eventually she'll have to eat."

"From your lips to God's ears."

Deirdre wandered out into the main hallway. She'd told Colleen she would call with an update, but she hated to report nothing but bad news. Especially in Colleen's delicate condition, when emotional upset could trigger labor. Maybe she'd wait until later to call. Maybe then Mama—

"Hello, Deirdre."

Deirdre's head flew up, and she gasped. She blinked to make sure she wasn't dreaming, but there he stood, as tall and handsome and solid as she remembered. "Matthew. What are you doing here?"

"Your father called and asked me to come."

She stared into those familiar blue eyes, which lacked their usual warmth, shadowed by the deep circles beneath them. "And just like that you came?"

"Kathleen's my patient."

Of course. Ever the dedicated healer, loyal and true, faithful to his promise.

Unlike her.

Despite her discomfort at his presence, a small bud of hope unfurled. "If you can do anything to get through to her, to even take a bite of food, I'd be most grateful."

His eyes narrowed. "She won't eat?"

Deirdre gave an exasperated sigh. "She won't lift her head from the pillow. Yet Dr. Shepherd can't find any evidence of further injury. It's as if the life has gone out of her." She swallowed hard, unwilling to become an emotional mess in his presence.

"Let me see what I can determine."

"Thank you." She looked behind him. "Is Phoebe here?"

He stilled. "No. She's staying with her grandparents."

Deirdre's stomach sank. For Matthew to leave Phoebe behind, he had to have deemed it better for her than coming here. Deirdre hoped her leaving hadn't undone all the progress Phoebe had made. She'd thought she was doing the right thing, letting everyone get on with their lives, since staying would only have prolonged the inevitable.

"If you'll excuse me, I need to see your mother." Matthew moved away from her as though he couldn't bear to be near her.

She watched him walk away, sadness encompassing her at the chasm that now existed between them. Somehow she'd have to endure the pain of Matthew's presence, for Mama's sake.

❧❦❧

"Truly, Colleen. Matthew has worked a miracle. Ever since he arrived a week ago, Mama's will to live has returned."

Colleen's relieved sigh sounded over the line. "I can't believe it. I thought this time she might not recover."

Deirdre leaned back in Daddy's desk chair. "You and me both. She's sitting up and eating. Even starting light therapy exercises again. I don't know what Matthew did, but it worked."

A slight pause ensued before Colleen asked, "How are things going between you and Matthew?"

Deirdre's heart pinched with regret. "Matthew's giving me the cold shoulder. Not that I don't deserve it after the way I left them."

"Nonsense. You weren't trying to hurt anyone. You were just protecting your heart."

"And breaking it in the process." Deirdre wisped out a breath. "I just wish I hadn't hurt Phoebe."

"I'm sure she'll be fine. One of the beautiful things about children is their resilience. Speaking of children, I'd better check on the boys. They're much too quiet. Give Mama my love."

"I will. Take care of yourself."

Deirdre pushed a lock of hair off her forehead and glanced at the calendar on Daddy's wall. December 23. Christmas was almost upon them. Would Matthew return to spend the holidays in Toronto?

A pang hit at the thought of saying good-bye to him—again. She couldn't deny the hiccup to her heart each time she ran into him in the house.

With a deep sigh, she rose from the chair. Instead of wallowing in negative thoughts, she would help Mrs. Johnston with the decorations in the parlor, in preparation for the fir tree Connor would bring home tonight. He and Gil were out cutting down trees for both houses.

The telephone shrilled before she could leave the room.

"Deirdre? It's Aunt Fiona. How are you, dear?"

Deirdre's heart jolted to life. Would she have news about medical school? "Fine, Auntie. And you?"

"My arthritis is flaring up these days, but otherwise I'm fine. How is your mother coming along?"

"Much improved, thank you."

"Ah, the good Lord has answered our prayers, I see. And now

I'm about to answer one of yours." Her aunt's birds twittered in the background.

"You have news?"

"I do indeed. I've managed to secure a place for you in Columbia's medical program beginning in January."

Deirdre's knees buckled, and she sank onto the chair. "January?"

"Isn't it marvelous? And from the sounds of it, your mother is on the road to good health, so you'll be free to get on with your career."

"That is wonderful news. Thank you, Auntie."

"I couldn't wait to tell you. Happy Christmas, Deirdre."

"Happy Christmas."

Deirdre hung up the receiver and closed her eyes. In a matter of weeks, she would be enrolled in a new medical school. Starting over fresh with a new lease on her future.

Then why didn't she feel . . . anything?

The door creaked inward.

Deirdre's eyes flew open to find Matthew standing before the desk, his brow furrowed.

"I'm sorry. I came to use the phone. I didn't realize anyone was in here."

"It's all right. I was just leaving." She went to get up, but a wave of dizziness hit. Bracing her hands on the desktop, she sucked in a breath.

"Are you all right?" Matthew's concerned voice sounded by her ear.

"I guess I forgot to eat today."

"You're as bad as your mother. At least she had an excuse." He regarded her without aloofness for the first time, gentling with subtle concern. "You've lost weight since you left Toronto."

"Have I?" She really hadn't paid much attention to her health, first consumed by grief, then with worry about Mama.

"Yes." His eyes scanned her in a way that brought the heat to her cheeks.

"Well, Christmas dinner will fatten me up, no doubt. What with Mrs. Harrison's roast duck, stuffing, and plum pudding."

A hint of a smile hovered on his mouth. "Sounds delicious. I suspect the Pentergasts' fare won't be quite as homey."

She drew in a shaky breath. "So you're planning on spending Christmas there?"

An unreadable expression came over Matthew's face, and he nodded. "I leave tomorrow."

If Deirdre hadn't been dizzy before, this news would certainly have done the trick. That and Matthew's nearness as the hint of his sandalwood soap teased her senses. She raised her gaze to his, and time seemed to grind to a standstill. A thousand regrets weighed heavy on her heart.

She loved him with an intensity that stole her breath.

Why, Lord? Why make me love a man who doesn't return my feelings? A man I can never have?

"I heard you say something about good news. Is there a reason to celebrate? Another O'Leary birth perhaps?" His teasing tone brought back a flood of happy memories of their former friendship.

"Not for another few weeks." She forced a smile. "The good news is that my aunt has secured me a place in Columbia's medical program beginning in January."

His eyes flickered with a hint of despair before he masked his expression. "Congratulations, Deirdre. I know this is what you've been hoping for."

"Thank you, Matthew. And thank you for helping Mama. Because of her recovery, I'll be able to accept the position."

Why, then, am I not happier?

He straightened, his reserve back in place. "Glad I could help."

She rose, this time forcing her legs to move properly. "I'll let you make that phone call. Wouldn't want you to miss getting home for Christmas."

⁂

The next morning, Matthew stared out the parlor window at the ice-encrusted scenery and suppressed the urge to bang his head on the glass.

"An ice storm? Could it not have waited one more day until I was safely home?"

According to the stationmaster, the tracks were so coated with ice that none of the trains could run for at least twenty-four hours.

"Some say talking out loud is a sign of insanity." James's laugh boomed out, not helping Matthew's foul mood.

He dragged a hand over his jaw. "You don't understand. I promised Phoebe I'd be home for Christmas. She's going to be devastated."

"Unfortunately, you can't control the weather. Give the Pentergasts a call and tell them you'll be home on Tuesday."

Matthew blasted out a breath. "I guess I have no choice."

James clapped him on the back. "Seems it's been ordained by the heavens that you spend Christmas with us. You might as well enjoy it."

⁂

And, other than missing Phoebe, enjoy it he did.

In fact, Matthew couldn't remember a time since his childhood when he'd enjoyed Christmas more. Starting with the service at St. Rita's church and ending with the amazing meal Mrs. Harrison had prepared for them.

Matthew sat back on the sofa in the O'Leary parlor and allowed the one glass of wine he'd indulged in from James's private stock to totally relax his muscles.

Under the six-foot pine tree, decorated with every manner of twinkling ornament, as well as several long strings of popcorn, the children sat playing with their gifts. Sean had chosen the company of his father and Uncle Connor, who were teaching him the finer points of chess.

Matthew patted his full stomach, sleep tugging at his eyelids. Perhaps he should have followed Colleen's example and indulged in an after-dinner nap.

Giggles preceded the women's entry into the room. Matthew's eyes automatically sought Deirdre. She looked breathtaking in a green velvet dress that sat just off her shoulders, enhancing her elegant neck. A fall of auburn curls teased her shoulders. She laughed at something Brianna said, and her dimples peeked out from each cheek.

Matthew's pulse stuttered to life like a dry car motor receiving an infusion of gasoline.

She turned, caught him staring, and smiled. Heat crept into Matthew's cheeks.

What would it be like to see her every day? Laugh with her? Kiss her again?

He stiffened against the back of the sofa. The wine must be playing havoc with his senses. He needed to nip these unwelcome thoughts in the bud.

"Let's have some music," Kathleen suggested. "It's an O'Leary tradition to dance on Christmas. Maggie, would you do the honors?"

"I'd love to." Maggie took a seat at the piano and began to play.

Matthew had never heard anything so exquisite. No wonder she'd been promoted to head organist at the cathedral.

Gil rose from his chair and held out his hand to Brianna, who snuggled into his arms for a waltz.

"Matthew, why don't you ask Deirdre to dance?" Kathleen suggested.

Her all-too-innocent request had warning bells ringing in his head. "I'm sure she'd prefer to dance with her father or brother."

James shot him a strange look and took a seat in the wing-back chair beside Kathleen. "If I can't dance with my best girl, I won't dance at all."

Kathleen smiled adoringly at her husband.

Connor quirked a brow. "I'm involved in a riveting game of chess here. Can't afford to break my concentration." Connor winked at Sean, who giggled. "And Adam's disappeared with Rylan."

Matthew glanced over at Deirdre, who seemed as uncomfortable as he.

"Oh, come on, you two," Gil scoffed. "It's a dance, not a marriage proposal."

Matthew swallowed and loosened the top button of his shirt. Deirdre's cheeks blazed as red as the Christmas bows.

With a reluctant sigh, he rose and held out his hand. "May I have this dance?"

She shook her head, sending those mesmerizing curls into a spin. "You don't have to do this."

"I want to." *More than I should.*

"Very well." She lowered her lashes and placed her hand in his.

He drew her closer so his arm could encircle her. Conscious of the people watching them, he held her at a respectable distance, yet his treacherous pulse sprinted faster than the music. They moved in time to the melody as if they'd been made to dance together.

The scent of some new perfume blended with a trace of cinnamon from her dessert. A few inches more and his nose would be in her hair, right by her ear. A wave of heat pulsed through his body and he ground his teeth together, fighting for control.

Her fingers trembled in his. The shallow puff of her breath heated his neck. Was she as affected as he?

Finally, the last note hung in the air with a flourish. Matthew stepped back with a half bow. "Thank you, Miss O'Leary."

When she met his gaze, moisture welled in her luminous eyes. His chest clutched with a wave of such longing he could barely bring air into his lungs.

I'm in love with her.

The thought roared through his mind with clarity no amount of wine could hide. God help him, he loved her more than the next breath he would take.

Would it make a difference if he dared confess his feelings for her? She'd already admitted she loved him, but was it enough to sacrifice her dreams for the future? Or would she only grow to resent him after a while?

As Priscilla had.

Matthew slowly released her hand and moved away. No, he couldn't take that chance. He needed to put all foolish notions aside and let her move ahead on the path she'd chosen.

❧

Standing on the top step of the veranda, Deirdre buffed her arms to ward off a chill. No matter how crazy it was to be outdoors, she needed the blast of cold air to temper the inferno her waltz with Matthew had incited within her. Being held within the circle of his arms, swaying in time to the most romantic of music, his eyes smoldering with a passion she doubted he was even aware of, all combined to engulf her body in a flood of heat—a longing so sweet she dared not indulge it.

She needed to put the dashing doctor far out of her mind, for tomorrow he would return to his life in Toronto.

Deirdre turned to head back inside, but the sight of three figures walking toward the house caught her attention. In the evening light, she recognized Jo Miller and her brother accompanied by Caleb Sullivan. Their cheery waves lifted her spirits. Just the distraction she needed from her brooding.

"Happy Christmas to you," she called out.

"Merry Christmas, Miss O'Leary." Jo smiled as she reached the top of the stairs.

"Please call me Deirdre. I hope you've had a pleasant day so far."

"Very. Mr. Sullivan put on a lovely meal for all his staff."

"It's tradition to provide a celebration for our employees and their families to show our appreciation." Caleb stepped forward to kiss Deirdre's cheek. "Happy Christmas, Dee."

"Same to you, Caleb. Please come in and join the festivities." They entered the foyer, stamping the snow from their overshoes. Mrs. Johnston appeared to help with the coats.

"Most of us are in the parlor." Deirdre laid a hand on Jo's arm and leaned in to whisper, "Connor is playing chess with Sean. You might be just the distraction Sean needs to win."

A pretty blush spread through Jo's cheeks. "Thanks to Colleen's loan of this gown, I feel like a princess." She smoothed a hand over the bodice.

In the striking blue taffeta dress, with her hair curled and styled, the girl did indeed look like royalty. Quite a transformation from the baggy overalls and ugly hat.

Deirdre smiled. "I'm glad Colleen could help. Now go in and watch Connor's eyes fall out of his head."

Caleb tapped Deirdre's shoulder. "May I speak to you in private for a minute?"

At his serious tone, a thread of trepidation ran through her, but she managed a bright smile. "Of course. We can use Daddy's study."

⁂

Matthew used the excuse of needing to telephone the Pentergasts to leave the parlor in search of Deirdre. After their dance, she'd disappeared and hadn't returned. He hoped he hadn't offended her in some way, or that she hadn't suddenly felt unwell. Her dizzy spell in the study the other day had worried him, even with her reasonable explanation. Still, he'd feel better when he made sure she was all right.

In the entranceway, he encountered Jo and Seth Miller and offered his greetings before heading to find Deirdre.

Farther down the hall, Caleb Sullivan exited James's study. He barreled past Matthew without a word, and seconds later, the front door slammed.

Matthew turned to see Deirdre emerge from the study, her face wreathed in sadness.

His heart hiccupped in his chest. What had gone on in there? "Deirdre, did Caleb say something to upset you?"

She came to stand at the base of the staircase, staring toward the entranceway. "Yes." Her answer was so low, he almost missed it. "He proposed."

Matthew's gut clenched as a stab of pure jealousy knifed through him. Surely she hadn't accepted, or Caleb wouldn't be so angry.

She gave a soft sigh and turned her gaze to him. "I turned him down, and he didn't take it too well."

He shoved his fists into his pockets. "I'm sorry he put a damper on your day."

She seemed to pull herself together and managed a smile. "Not to worry. I just wish I hadn't had to ruin his Christmas."

The urge to comfort her rose strong inside him. Instead, Matthew cleared his throat. "Well, I was about to place a call to—"

Above them, the pounding of frantic footsteps sounded on the staircase.

Rylan appeared, hair disheveled, eyes wild. "Matthew, Deirdre," he said when he spotted them, "I think Colleen's gone into labor."

"Are you sure?" Deirdre started up the stairs at a swift pace. "It could be discomfort from eating a big dinner."

Rylan shook his head. "I know what labor looks like, and this is it."

Matthew gripped the newel post of the staircase, feeling the blood drain from his face. He'd only assisted at one birth during his residency training, and he'd really only been an observer, not the one responsible for bringing a new life into the world. He remembered the anxious moments when the mother had started to hemorrhage. They'd managed to stop the bleeding and she'd survived, but they'd been in a hospital with equipment at their disposal—

"Matthew, are you coming?" Deirdre had stopped halfway up the stairs to peer over her shoulder.

He tried to swallow, but his throat was as dry as dust. Instead, he forced his feet to move.

And prayed with every step that it was a false alarm.

35

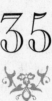

D EIRDRE PUSHED OPEN THE DOOR to her sister's childhood bedroom. Colleen lay on her side in the middle of the bed, clutching her belly and moaning.

Immediately, Deirdre's nursing instincts took over. With brisk efficiency, she moved to Colleen's side and laid a calming hand on her shoulder. "I'm here, Colleen. Everything's going to be fine."

Colleen opened her eyes on a grimace. "Dee. Thank goodness. My water broke when I tried to get up, and the pains are coming fast."

"Looks like the newest Montgomery is about to make his entrance. But don't worry. Matthew and I are here."

Colleen grabbed Deirdre's hand. "Rylan," she huffed out. "He doesn't do well in the birthing room. Keep him busy elsewhere."

Deirdre grinned at her. "I'll have him boil pots of water in the kitchen."

Colleen's laugh turned to a groan. Deirdre took the clock

from the nightstand and counted how long the contraction lasted.

From the corner of her eye, she noticed Matthew in the doorway. His face was drawn, lines of tension etching his features. Perhaps he'd never had the opportunity to assist in a birth, since his career had been spent with dying and wounded soldiers.

She walked over to him. "Are you okay?" she whispered.

Anxious blue eyes met hers. "I've only done this once before," he said in a low voice. "Colleen should be in a hospital."

Once again Deirdre sensed his fear of making a wrong step. She needed to help him overcome his apprehension. "I'm pretty sure it's too late to move her. But she's delivered two healthy boys. I'm sure she'll be fine." She gave him an encouraging smile. "We can do this, Matthew. I'll be right here beside you." She pointed to her dress. "As soon as I change out of this. And give Rylan something to keep him busy."

Matthew nodded, the lines on his brow easing a fraction.

Another moan sounded from the bed.

Deirdre glanced at the clock. "The pains are about two minutes apart. I'd better hurry."

Matthew removed his jacket and rolled up his shirt sleeves as he crossed to the bed. "Hello, Colleen. As soon as this contraction ends, I'll need to examine you and see how soon this baby will be born. Try not to worry. You're in good hands."

Deirdre nodded at him before stepping out into the hallway, where Rylan paced the carpet like a crazed man.

He rushed over as soon as he saw her. "How is she?" he asked.

"Definitely in labor. I think we might get a Christmas baby after all."

Rylan grasped her arm. "Sweet saints above."

"Come on." Deirdre led him toward the stairs. "I need you to start boiling water, and ask Mrs. Johnston for some clean towels. Oh, and you might want to get Mama and the others praying. It never hurts to cover all our bases." She pressed a kiss to his befuddled face and rushed into her bedroom to change.

Jo pressed a hand to her stomach and hesitated in front of the O'Leary parlor door. She hoped Mr. and Mrs. O'Leary wouldn't think her too forward dropping by like this. But Colleen had invited her and had offered her a ride back to the orphanage tonight. That—and getting to see Connor—would be worth one uncomfortable glass of Christmas cheer with Mr. O'Leary.

"Everything okay, kid?" Seth's voice sounded by her ear.

"Of course. Why wouldn't it be?"

"Because you're as nervous as a polecat in a kennel of coyotes. So what gives?"

She glanced at her brother, for once very glad of his presence. "I've never . . . that is . . . I feel like I'm masquerading as a girl this time—instead of the other way around." She smoothed a hand down the blue taffeta material. Thankfully the neckline of the dress was high enough that she didn't feel too exposed. Though with the way Colleen had done her hair, swept up at the back with only a few curls around her face, her neck felt distinctly bare.

"Well, you look wonderful." He winked. "I'm sure Connor will think so too."

Jo gulped. Were her feelings that obvious?

Seth gestured to the door. "After you."

They entered a room of complete chaos, making the orphanage seem as sedate as a library. Jo recognized Colleen and Rylan's kids playing with a number of other children, likely the cousins Colleen had mentioned.

Her gaze skimmed over the room and collided with a familiar hazel stare. Connor rose from his chair by the hearth, his mouth agape. Nerves danced down her arms at the heat in his eyes.

In a dark suit, linen shirt, and striped tie, Connor looked very dapper himself. His hair had been tamed back in a manner that made his chestnut locks shine.

He came toward them. "Jo. This is a surprise. Happy Christmas." He bent to kiss her cheek, sending shivers down her spine.

"Merry Christmas, Connor."

"You look beautiful." The awe in his voice bolstered her confidence.

"Thank you." Jo labored to breathe. "Seth and I had dinner at the Sullivan place, so I thought we'd stop over to wish your family a merry Christmas."

"I'm glad you did. Come in and have some eggnog. And say hello to my parents."

They made their way around the room, greeting many members of Connor's family. Mrs. O'Leary was more than gracious with her welcome, though Mr. O'Leary's reserved greeting reminded Jo of his disapproval.

Seth joined a conversation with Connor's older brother, Adam, and somehow she and Connor ended up in a corner by themselves.

"How are things working out at the orphanage?" he asked as he handed her a glass of eggnog.

"I'm enjoying it. Thank you again for your recommendation."

"So you're happy there?" He studied her face as if reading every thought that flitted through her mind.

"Very happy. Though I do miss working with the horses. How is Excalibur?" She'd worried the animal would refuse to cooperate with Connor without her calming presence.

Connor's jaw tensed. "He's doing fine . . . from what his new trainer tells me."

"New trainer? Why aren't you working with him?"

Connor's glance shot to Mr. O'Leary at the fireplace. "My father decided to switch trainers."

She set her cup on a table. "It's because of me, isn't it? He's punishing you because you let me work with Excalibur."

Connor said nothing, but the nerve ticking in his jaw gave her the answer.

"I'm so sorry, Connor."

"It's nothing for you to worry about."

But she was worried. Worried that his kindness to her had damaged his relationship with his father. She laid a hand on his arm, wishing she could ease the lines of tension around his mouth.

The sudden pounding of footsteps on the main staircase brought the activity in the room to a stop.

Connor immediately strode into the hall. Jo peered out to see a distraught Rylan grip Connor's arm and then rush down the corridor.

"Is everything all right?" she asked.

Connor turned to her. "Rylan wants everyone to pray. Sounds like Colleen is about to have her baby."

An hour later, Jo sat on the sofa in the O'Learys' parlor with eight-year-old Ivy Montgomery asleep on her lap. Ever since Jo had started working at St. Rita's, Colleen's daughter had taken an instant liking to her, and the feeling was mutual.

Maggie O'Leary came to stand before her. "Adam will take Ivy upstairs to bed. We've decided there's no sense in any of us heading back to the city at this time of night."

Jo blinked, worry creeping through her. With Colleen in labor, she'd wondered how she would get back to the orphanage, but Connor had assured her that Maggie and Adam would take her.

"You're welcome to stay as well," Maggie said as Adam lifted Ivy from Jo's lap. "There's plenty of room."

Jo hesitated, feeling more than a little out of her element. She was nothing more than an acquaintance of the family, an employee. She didn't belong here. Her mind swirled with thoughts of the orphans doing without their director and his wife. It was one thing to leave the nuns in charge for an evening, but Jo wanted to be there in the morning to help.

Maggie's warm hand covered Jo's. "If you're uncomfortable staying, I'm sure Connor will take you home."

"I . . . I don't want to bother him."

Connor had gone upstairs to help put some of the children to bed and hadn't returned yet.

"He won't mind, but whatever you decide is fine." Maggie followed Adam out the door.

Jo looked around the once-chaotic room, now almost empty save for Brianna and her parents. Brianna had refused to leave until the baby arrived safely. Mr. O'Leary sat in an armchair near the fire. His gaze met hers, and her heart gave an uncomfortable thump.

Jo got to her feet and brushed the creases from her dress. She couldn't pass up the opportunity to speak to Mr. O'Leary on Connor's behalf. After all he'd done for her, the least she could do was try to make amends with his father.

Mr. O'Leary rose as she crossed the room.

"May I speak with you a moment?" she asked, attempting to ignore the nerves rolling in her stomach.

Mr. O'Leary gave a stiff nod and led her to the opposite side of the room. "What can I do for you, Miss Miller?"

The way he said her name didn't inspire much optimism. She swallowed. "First of all, I want to apologize for my . . ."

"Deception?" He quirked a brow.

"Yes." Jo took a breath. "And I wanted to assure you that Connor had no idea I was a girl. When he discovered my identity, I begged him to let me continue working until my father recovered." A fresh wave of grief hit hard. She paused to rein in her emotions before they got the best of her.

Mr. O'Leary's features softened. "My condolences for your loss. Connor informed me your father has since passed away."

"That's right," she said quietly.

"I also understand my daughter and Rylan hired you at the orphanage."

"They did, and I'm most grateful."

Mr. O'Leary crossed his arms, studying her. "Then what is it you wish from me?"

Heat blazed into her cheeks, but she didn't lower her gaze. "Nothing for myself." She lifted her chin. "I want to make sure you don't hold Connor responsible for my actions. Please don't punish him for showing compassion to someone in need."

"What makes you think I'm punishing my son?"

Jo's heart pounded against her ribs. "You've taken him off Excalibur's training, which, I must point out, isn't in Excalibur's best interest. Switching trainers now will probably cause a setback in his progress."

The man pursed his lips. "The stallion has become difficult again. The new trainer isn't having much luck with him."

Jo twisted her hands together. She hated thinking of Excalibur reverting back to being skittish and terrified. "I know he'd do better with Connor. Excalibur's used to him. And to me." She hesitated, moistening her dry lips. "If you wanted, I could come back on my days off and continue working with him, too."

Mr. O'Leary frowned. "Why would you do that?"

"To help an animal I became fond of and to work with the horses, which I miss."

He moved closer, looming over her. "And as an added bonus, you'd be near my son."

She stiffened. What was he trying to insinuate?

Mr. O'Leary continued to regard her coolly. "That's it, isn't it? That's what you really want." He shook his head, his lips twisting into a cynical smile. "Connor is far too soft-hearted.

He would never think a destitute young woman might be out to snare the son of a wealthy family."

Jo's mouth fell open. Her hands shook as outrage slammed through her "If that were the case, I would have accepted his marriage proposal instead of going to work as a maid."

The leap of surprise in Mr. O'Leary's eyes gave her a surge of satisfaction.

"That's right. Connor offered to marry me, but I turned him down. Unlike you, I have the utmost respect for your son. Maybe you should try showing some faith in his abilities instead of expecting the worst."

She whirled around, vaguely conscious of Mrs. O'Leary and Brianna's stares, and stormed out into the hallway. Blindly, she headed toward the foyer, hoping someone would help her find her coat.

A maid appeared and quickly retrieved Jo's wrap. She thanked her and stuffed her arms into the sleeves.

Though she had no idea how she would get home, she couldn't stay in that room with Mr. O'Leary a moment longer. Nor could she sleep under his roof, knowing how little he thought of her. He'd only assume it was another manipulation on her part to get Connor.

The beginnings of tears burned beneath her eyelids. The maid opened the front door for her.

"Jo, wait." Brianna rushed into the foyer. "I'm so sorry if my father offended you. He's overly protective of his family, I'm afraid."

Jo forced a shaky smile. "I understand." She tugged on her gloves. "Please tell Connor good night for me."

"Won't you wait and tell him yourself?" Brianna asked softly.

The temptation to do so climbed through her, but she shook her head. "I have to go. Good night."

Before Brianna could attempt to detain her, Jo rushed out the door.

Connor's pulse rate sprinted as he headed downstairs at last. After three bedtime stories, his nieces and nephews had finally settled down to sleep, and he now looked forward to getting back to Jo. Maggie told him she'd invited Jo to spend the night at Irish Meadows. The idea of waking up to her beneath his roof made Connor ridiculously happy.

When he neared the main level, he saw Bree heading up.

She stopped, hand on the rail. "I was just coming to find you."

He took in her pinched features. "Is something wrong?"

"It's Jo. Daddy and she argued, and she left."

Anger and alarm slammed through him. "You let her leave alone at this hour?"

"I tried to get her to wait, but she wouldn't listen."

He continued down the stairs at a faster clip, with Bree keeping pace. In the foyer, Connor grabbed his overcoat from the hook. "How long ago?"

"Not long."

He shoved on his cap. "Daddy had better pray I find her."

Connor slammed out the front door and jogged over to the car. Raw anger at his father burned in his chest, warring with a deep concern for Jo's safety. A woman shouldn't be out alone at this time of night.

He started the car, threw it in gear, and roared down the drive to the main road. Where would she be headed? To the Sullivans to find Seth?

Around the next bend, a whoosh of relief hit him. Up ahead, a slim figure picked her way over the icy terrain. He slowed and pulled to the side of the road in front of her, then yanked up the brake and jumped out, not entirely sure what he was going to say.

She stopped as soon as she recognized him. The glimmer of moisture on her cheeks relit the fire of his anger.

"Jo," he said as he approached. "I'm so sorry for whatever my father said to hurt you. Please let me drive you somewhere."

"That's not necessary." She made to go around him, but not before he noticed her shivering.

He wanted to grab her and stuff her in the automobile, but he reined in his impatience and fell in step beside her. "Fine. Then I'll walk with you."

She stopped abruptly. "I'd rather be alone."

"Not until I know you're safe. So we can walk, or you can let me drive you. Where are you headed?"

Light snowflakes began to drift from the sky. Connor hoped the threat of bad weather might sway her decision in his favor.

She bit her lip, indecision flashing over her features. "I g-guess the train station to wait until the first train." Her teeth chattered, and the defeat in her voice raised his protective instincts.

Connor bit back a growl of frustration. "That's not until morning. Let me take you back to my house."

"No. Not after the things your father accused me of."

"Then I'll drive you to the orphanage." He took her gently by the arm and steered her back toward the car. "Either that or I'll sit with you in the train station. Your choice." He waited for her to make the decision, walking in silence until they reached the car. He opened the door for her, helped her in, and went around to the driver's side.

"So what will it be?" he asked quietly.

"I guess . . . if you don't mind, I'd like to go back to the orphanage."

He nodded. "The orphanage it is."

As he turned the car around on the deserted stretch of road, he thanked God for keeping Jo safe until he found her, and for giving him the chance to hopefully make amends for the damage his father had done.

They drove in silence, making good time without any traffic.

When they reached the Queensboro Bridge, the quiet became too much to bear.

"I'd like to know what happened, so I have my facts straight before I tear a strip off my father."

She turned to him, eyes widened in horror. "No, please. I don't want to cause any more problems. I was trying to fix things—"

"So you started the conversation?"

"Yes. But it all backfired and I ended up making matters worse."

Connor let the statement settle for a few seconds. "What did you say?"

She shook her head and bit her lip.

"I need the truth, Jo."

She released a sigh. "I asked him not to punish you for my mistakes."

The air stilled in Connor's lungs. She'd gone to his father, an extremely intimidating man, on his behalf. That took courage. He steered the car along Fifty-Ninth Street, blessedly quiet at this hour. "What did my father say?"

She remained silent.

"You might as well tell me. I'll find out anyhow."

She straightened in the seat. "He accused me of trying to . . ."

"Trying to what?"

"I believe his words were 'to snare the son of a wealthy family.'"

Connor groaned. "I can't believe he said that."

"I told him if that were the case, I wouldn't have turned down your marriage proposal."

Wonderful. Now Daddy knew that he'd proposed once and been shot down. Not exactly proof of stellar judgment.

Jo laid a hand on his arm. "Please don't fight with your father over me. I don't want to cause problems in your family."

Connor glanced at her anxious face. "I can't let him get away with disrespecting you. I will have it out with him."

The streetlamps cast a glow over her features. The misery in her blue eyes nearly undid him.

"I'm sorry if I ruined Christmas for you," she said softly.

"You didn't, believe me. Having you there made my day. I'm only sorry it ended on a sour note."

Connor turned onto Lexington Avenue toward the orphanage, and soon he stopped the car at the curb in front of the building. He frowned, scanning the front entrance. "Everything will be locked up. Any chance you have a key?"

"I do." She drew a key out of her purse, then turned to look at him. "Thank you again, Connor. You seem to have a habit of coming to my rescue."

He smiled. "So it appears."

He walked her up the stairs to the entrance. She unlocked the door with hands that shook. He wished he could accompany her inside, but it wouldn't be proper.

"Sweet dreams, Jo," he said, his voice husky.

"Good night, Connor." She reached up to kiss his cheek.

Unable to help himself, he pulled her to him in a light hug, then stepped back. "Take care of yourself."

She nodded and held his gaze for a minute, her eyes saying things she hadn't verbalized. Then she disappeared into the building, leaving Connor alone on the doorstep.

36

MATTHEW TOOK A MINUTE to roll his shoulders and attempt to ease the tension in his muscles. After almost three hours of labor, the first wisps of downy hair had become visible. It wouldn't be much longer now. On the next contraction, he'd prepare Colleen to push. Luckily for him, this wasn't her first child, and though the labor was intense, Colleen's body instinctively remembered what to do.

Deirdre stood near the headboard and bathed Colleen's face with a cool cloth, murmuring words of encouragement and praise, helping her sister through each contraction, making sure she rested in between.

Deirdre had been a rock this whole time, steadying both Colleen and him with her calm demeanor, her soothing tone and touch. Matthew smiled, recalling the moment she'd come back into the room, nursing uniform in place, and requested that the three of them start with a prayer. She'd taken his hand and Colleen's and offered the most simple, yet heartfelt, words of gratitude for Matthew's presence, as well as a plea for God's assistance in delivering a healthy child.

The humble prayer had brought a rare measure of peace to Matthew, giving him the confidence to cast aside his fear and let his doctoring skills take over.

Somehow, taking his ego out of the equation and leaving the matter in God's hands eased the pressure he always put on himself.

"*God has given you the talent to heal, Matthew,*" Deirdre had once told him. "*You just need to stay out of His way and let Him use you.*"

Now, as they worked together to help usher this new life into the world, Matthew realized his past mistakes. Medicine wasn't a solo effort. It took a dedicated team of doctors and nurses to heal a patient, in addition to God's grace and mercy. A doctor was merely the instrument of God's healing power.

Colleen's body tensed, and a groan ripped from her throat.

"Time to push, Colleen." Matthew nodded to Deirdre, who gripped Colleen's hand.

Once the contraction faded, Colleen slumped back. Perspiration bathed her face, her hair clinging in wet strands to her cheeks. Immediately, Deirdre used the cloth to freshen her face.

"Another few pushes should do it," he said. "You're doing well."

Her ragged breath panted out.

"Try to take deep, even breaths if you can."

Colleen tensed as another contraction started.

"Here we go again." Matthew ignored her cry of pain and kept his focus where it was needed. "Keep pushing. That's it."

Colleen labored until her cheeks were crimson. Then she whooshed out a great breath and flopped back.

The baby slid out into his waiting hands. He stilled, immediately aware something was wrong. The child's face was a faint shade of blue, due to the cord that was wound tightly around its neck.

Matthew's pulse sprinted with a hard surge of adrenaline. "Scissors," he barked.

Deirdre jumped to hand him the sterilized instrument, and he cut the umbilical cord. Then he quickly and carefully unwrapped the cord from the baby's throat.

The little chest didn't stir.

"Why isn't the baby crying?" Colleen's frantic voice made the hairs on Matthew's neck rise.

He glanced at Deirdre's anxious face and gave his head a slight shake. Deirdre turned her attention to Colleen, murmuring soothing words to keep her calm.

Matthew laid the infant on the bed and ran a finger around its mouth to ensure there was no obstruction. Then he lifted the baby, turned it over, and patted its back.

Please, Lord, help this child breathe.

Sweat poured from his brow. He patted again—harder. Waited another second, then tried again. No response. He flipped the child over and, going on sheer instinct, blew a breath into its mouth. He waited, watching for any movement, then blew again.

At last, the baby's chest rose, and a mewling noise erupted, followed by a loud wail. The blueness receded from the baby's face, quickly turning to a mottled shade of red.

Matthew's shoulders sagged in relief. Deirdre's face streamed with tears as she passed him a towel to swaddle the squalling infant.

Tenderly, he wrapped the baby and then handed the tiny bundle to Colleen. "Congratulations, Mrs. Montgomery. You have a daughter. A very feisty one by the looks of things."

Colleen smiled through her tears as she gazed down at the new life in her arms.

"Thank you, Lord," Deirdre whispered. She leaned down to kiss the top of Colleen's head.

Then she walked over and threw her arms around Matthew. "And thank *you*," she said. "You saved the baby's life."

A tidal wave of euphoria and relief flooded his system as he clasped Deirdre to him. They clung together, overwhelmed by the enormity of the moment. He breathed in her familiar scent as their hearts beat in tandem. Then, reluctantly, he released her. "We'd better let the father know."

Matthew found Rylan still pacing the hall. "Come and meet your new daughter."

Instant tears rolled down the man's cheeks. "Is everyone all right?"

Matthew smiled. "Everyone's just fine."

"Thank you, Doctor. Thank you." Rylan pumped Matthew's hand and rushed into the room.

Matthew inhaled and then blew out a long breath. With it, he offered prayers of gratitude to a most benevolent God who had guided his hand and his breath to save the infant's life.

Truly doctoring was a partnership of the best kind.

Deirdre's slippers made no sound as she descended the back staircase and entered the empty kitchen. After all the excitement of the day, her mind was too keyed up for sleep, and she hoped some warm milk might soothe her.

Grateful for the light Mrs. Harrison kept burning, Deirdre moved to the icebox and took out a bottle of milk. She poured some into a saucepan and set it on a low flame on the stove.

Pulling her robe tighter, she leaned back against the counter and smiled, reveling in the miracle she'd witnessed tonight. The joy on her sister and Rylan's faces as they gazed at their precious daughter was more than words could express.

Her eyes burned at the memory. Would she ever experience such joy, such fulfillment? With a husband so besotted and filled with pride that he could scarcely contain himself?

Unbidden images of Matthew came to mind, and a soft sigh escaped her lips. He'd been wonderful tonight. Despite his initial trepidation, he'd risen to the occasion and guided them through the birth with a confidence that inspired complete trust. And he'd saved her niece's life, calmly dealing with the wrapped cord and helping the child draw her first breath.

And yet she sensed no arrogance in the man. He wore a simple humility Deirdre found immensely appealing. Strong yet gentle, knowing yet kind. Matthew embodied every positive trait a good doctor should possess.

As well as a good husband.

Deirdre stirred the milk, trying to ignore the fact that in a few short hours, Matthew would leave for the train station, and she would have to say good-bye once again—this time for good.

Lord, I'll need your strength to get through this next challenge.

The milk sputtered in the pan. Deirdre turned off the flame and poured the liquid into a large cup. Reaching for the cinnamon shaker, she sprinkled a generous amount over the frothy milk.

She lifted the cup to breathe in the pleasant aroma.

A shadow fell across the kitchen floor, and Matthew entered the room with a sheepish shrug. "Looks like we both had the same idea."

Deirdre's heart skipped in her chest. His golden-brown hair sat in unruly tufts over his forehead, his plaid robe belted tight around his waist. The glow from the lamp highlighted the planes of his handsome face.

He rubbed a hand over the back of his neck. "I kept reliving tonight like a newsreel going around in my head. I thought some milk might help."

She smiled. "You can share mine. I made too much for one."

She reached for another cup and poured half the contents

into it for him. As she passed it to him, she hesitated. "Oh, I should have asked if you like cinnamon."

He wrapped his hands around her fingers still holding the cup. "I adore cinnamon," he said, his eyes never leaving hers. "It reminds me of you." With his thumb, he brushed circles over the back of her hand, sending a cascade of tingles through her arms.

In the dim light, his eyes appeared as dark as cobalt. She couldn't seem to gather her thoughts to get a word out.

He took the cup from her and sipped the concoction. "Hmm. Very good."

"Thank you." She took a quick sip from her own cup.

Matthew set his mug on the counter and moved closer. "I'm glad I have the chance to talk to you before . . . tomorrow."

Before you leave.

"I wanted to thank you," he continued. "I couldn't have delivered that baby without you."

"Of course you could've. You were brilliant in there. A true example of grace under pressure."

"If anyone displayed grace under pressure, it was you. But overall, I'd say it was God's grace that carried us through."

She smiled, her heart full. "That's one thing they don't teach you in school. That all healing should begin with prayer."

He took one of her hands in his. "Thank you, Deirdre, for believing in me. Your faith in my skills has given me back my confidence."

Her lips trembled into a smile, so thankful was she to have gifted him something during their time together. "I guess we made a good team."

"We certainly did."

A charge of electricity zapped between them. She could almost feel the racing of his heart beneath his robe. She gave a soft sigh. "I thank God for bringing you into my life, Matthew. And I wish you and Phoebe nothing but happiness in the future."

He hesitated, a thousand unspoken words swirling in the

depths of his eyes. "And I you, Deirdre. I hope you find fulfillment in your career." He reached out to brush a finger down the length of her braid.

Her heart fluttered in her chest. She needed one last kiss to remember for the rest of her days.

On a sigh, she clutched the lapel of his robe and raised herself up on tiptoes until their mouths were even. She waited a beat, waited for him to push her away, searching his face for permission. He pulled her to him with a groan and kissed her. Her arms wound their way around his neck, her fingers pushing into his hair. One of his hands cupped her jaw, and he pressed kisses to her temple and her eyes and then back to feast on her mouth.

I love you. The unspoken words reverberated through her soul, begging to be uttered, but she dared not, knowing they wouldn't be welcome. Instead, she memorized the planes of his face, the taste of his lips, the thunder of his heart against hers.

At last, when she thought her legs might not hold her, he released her. Cool air rushed in between them as he stepped away. Her whole being cried out in protest.

Don't go, she wanted to beg.

But her path lay in a different direction—while his was anchored back in Toronto.

This had been a lovely sojourn, a respite from the world.

But it ended here.

"Good night, Deirdre," he said, his voice rich with regret. "I wish you good dreams—tonight and always."

"And you as well, Matthew."

He stood in the doorway, a halo of light surrounding him. Then, with a last smile, he was gone.

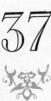

37

PLAGUED ALL NIGHT BY DREAMS of Mr. O'Leary throwing her out of Irish Meadows, Jo gave up trying to sleep and rose early the next morning, before any of the children had stirred. It seemed the festivities of Christmas had worn them out, which was a good thing since it afforded her a peaceful start to the day.

She quickly braided her hair, thinking back to Connor driving her all the way out here. Had he made it back home without incident? Would he have confronted his father when he got back or waited until today?

With a sigh, she descended the back staircase, intent on starting breakfast for everyone.

She walked into the kitchen and gasped.

Connor stood at the stove, his sleeves rolled up past his elbows, wielding a spatula over the cast-iron frying pan.

"Connor! What are you doing here?"

He turned with a grin. "Good morning, Jo. I hope you slept well." He flipped a few eggs in the pan and then set the spatula down. "I realized after I left you last night that Colleen's house was empty and that their poor old dog, Chester, would need tending to. Luckily I know where they keep their spare keys."

Jo moved into the large room, her stomach growling at the delicious aroma of fried ham and eggs. A pot of coffee simmered on the back of the stove.

"I also remembered," he continued as he took out a cup, "that Colleen always gives Mrs. Norton a few days off at Christmas, and with Colleen out at Irish Meadows, someone would need to cook breakfast. I got here right in the nick of time to save the nuns from having to do it. They were quite happy to let me take over and have some extra time for morning prayers."

Connor pulled out a chair for her. She sat facing the stove, and he poured her a cup of coffee.

"It occurred to me, too, during the wee hours of the morning that I needed to make a few things clear between us. To avoid any future misunderstandings."

She frowned. "What kind of misunderstanding?"

He stepped back to the stove, flipped the pieces of meat, and lowered the flame. With deft movements, he slid the eggs and ham onto two plates and set them on the table.

Then he sat down on the chair beside her. "Unless you have any major objections," he said with a smile, "I'm going to tell my father that I intend to marry you. And starting today, I will begin courting you in the fashion you deserve."

Her pulse beat a frantic rhythm. She wanted to pinch herself to see if this was a continuation of her crazy dreams last night. "This is silly, Connor. You can't marry me."

"Why not?"

"Because . . ." Her mind went blank. "Because your family doesn't approve."

"Only my father objects, a fact that will resolve itself during our courtship." He took a large forkful of eggs and chewed, watching her, his hazel eyes twinkling.

"What if he doesn't change his opinion?"

"He'll have no choice." Connor took a swig of coffee. "Because once he gets to know you, he'll understand why I'm hopelessly in love with you."

She covered her mouth with her hand, instant tears brimming on her lower lashes. "You can't be serious."

His grin faded, and a blaze of intensity flared in his eyes. "I've never been more serious in my life. I love you, Jo, and I know I made a huge mess of things, but I will make it up to you one way or another." He paused, his gaze searching hers. "Unless, of course, I'm wrong and you don't care for me that way." A furrow appeared between his brows. "Am I wrong?" he asked in a husky voice.

More tears trailed down her cheeks as she shook her head. "You're not wrong."

"Thank heavens." He got up and pulled her to her feet. Gazing down at her, he brushed at the moisture on her cheeks, then slowly lowered his mouth to hers.

He kissed her with a tenderness that erased every objection, every thought.

Jo's breathing was ragged as she pulled away. "Are you sure about this? Because I won't have my heart broken if you decide you were wrong, or your family won't accept us."

He brushed a finger over her cheek. "If I ever have to choose between my family and you, I will choose you, Jo. For better or worse, my heart is yours for the taking. If you'll have it, that is."

"Oh, Connor." More tears bloomed. "I love you, too."

She kissed him again, and when they drew apart at last, he grinned at her.

"Promise me one thing," he said.

"Anything."

"You'll keep that big, ugly hat you always used to wear. I have fond memories of that thing."

She giggled and swatted his arm. "I was going to give it to

Seth, but I couldn't part with it. Because it reminded me of my time with you."

He grabbed her to him for another resounding kiss. Then he broke it off with a sigh. "As much as I'd love to do this all day, I have to get home. Dr. Clayborne needs a ride to the train station this morning." He gestured to the stove. "There's a platter of ham and scrambled eggs warming in the oven for the rest of the brood."

He kissed her again and, by unspoken agreement, they walked to the back door. It wouldn't look seemly to have a man leaving at this hour out the front.

"Thank you for breakfast," she said, suddenly shy.

He shrugged into his coat and laughed. "It's only the beginning. I plan to turn your head with all my many talents."

She smiled up into his eyes. "You already have, Mr. O'Leary. You already have."

38

MATTHEW STOOD at the French doors in the O'Learys' parlor and gazed out over the expanse of snow, attempting to sort through his thoughts.

The events of the previous night lingered in his mind. The elation of witnessing a new life come into the world, the joy of sharing that precious moment with Deirdre, their amazing kiss in the kitchen. He'd never felt closer to another human being—so much so that he'd almost thrown caution to the wind and blurted out his feelings for her. Yet he knew enough not to let his heightened emotions override his common sense. Instead, he'd spent the rest of the night reading his Bible and praying, attempting to discern God's will for him—and for Deirdre.

As he prayed, he couldn't seem to get Victor's words out of his head, urging him to tell Deirdre the truth and let her make her own decision about her future. After the kiss they'd shared, he realized the validity of Victor's advice. Deirdre deserved to know how he felt about her. If she rejected him, it would hurt, but at least they'd both have no regrets. No reason to wonder what might have been if only he'd spoken up.

Still, gathering the courage to reveal his heart was proving more daunting than he'd imagined.

Old fears and uncertainties rose up to taunt him. Would he ever be enough for her? Could she accept his faults? Tolerate his mistakes when he disappointed her?

Because of Deirdre, Matthew was a different man. One who put his daughter first, before his work, before his own needs. And never again would he jeopardize that relationship.

Could he extend that same commitment to Deirdre and, if so, would their love be enough to see them through the trials of life?

My love will sustain you.

His throat cinched as a new realization formed. God had played no part in his first marriage. But Deirdre's deep spiritual conviction had bolstered his own fledgling faith—faith in a God who would strengthen and sustain them over the course of their marriage, no matter what the future held.

"Matthew?"

He turned to see Deirdre enter the room, the morning sun dancing off her auburn curls, and his breath caught. In a simple skirt and blouse, she had never looked more beautiful.

Matthew lifted one last fervent prayer, then moved to greet her. "Good morning. I hope you managed to get some sleep after all."

"I did. Are you all ready to go?" She smiled, yet her eyes remained shrouded in sadness.

She looked so forlorn that every fiber in him wanted to kiss her. To take her in his arms and never release her. But he wouldn't rush things.

"Not quite," he said. "There are a few things I need to say before I go."

Her brow crinkled. "What is it? You look serious."

He moved closer. "I can't leave without telling you the truth."

Confusion flashed over her features. "I don't understand."

Matthew reached for her hand and led her to the sofa. "Please hear me out before you say anything,"

He sat beside her and drew in a breath, willing the right words to come. "Since I've met you, Deirdre O'Leary, nothing in my life has been the same. You've changed me in more ways than I can count. You've rekindled my faith, given me back my confidence, helped Phoebe thrive, and . . ." He inhaled and slowly released his breath. "You've taught me how to love."

Deirdre's hand flew to her trembling lips.

"As much as I fought it"—he swallowed, his voice a whisper—"I'm afraid I've fallen in love with you. I thought you had the right to know." He held his breath, hardly daring to hope what she might say next.

Tears stood out in the green of her eyes. "Oh, Matthew," she whispered. "I love you, too. So very much."

He gazed down into her beautiful face, wanting to memorize every detail, every lash, every pore of her delicate skin. Get lost in the depths of her eyes. Eyes that shone with love for him.

Her lips parted, drawing him in, and he kissed her. Her mouth melded to his with an intensity that left him weak. She tasted of sweetness and strength. Her familiar scent of cinnamon and vanilla engulfed him. Tendrils of her hair caressed his jaw. He was lost, at sea in a storm of emotion such as he'd never experienced before.

This was true love, true passion. A soul mate to share his good days and his bad. Together, he knew they could weather any storm.

Deirdre's heart filled with such joy she thought she would burst. She could scarcely believe what Matthew had just told her, yet his kiss bore evidence of his sincerity.

Moments ago, she'd entered the room to bid him a final

farewell. The weight of it had pressed on her soul to such a degree that she'd almost taken the cowardly way out and stayed in her room until he'd gone. But she couldn't resist the profound yearning to see him one last time.

Now he released her with a gentle sigh and looked deeply into her eyes. "I know how much becoming a doctor means to you, and I would never deprive you of that. I'm willing to wait, if that's what you wish."

Gazing at his handsome face, her addled mind struggled to make sense of his words. "Are you . . . are you asking me to marry you?"

He smiled. "That would be the ultimate goal—after you finish your schooling."

"But that could take years." She got up from the sofa and crossed to the fireplace, her spirit shuddering at the thought. Years of precious time lost. Years of Phoebe's childhood missed.

Yet, the fact that he cared enough to consider her dreams only made her love him more.

Matthew rose and came to stand beside her. "Would you consider switching to the University of Toronto?" he asked softly. "That way you could still be an important part of our lives."

"No, Matthew. That's not good enough." She lifted her chin, leveling him with a determined look that matched her resolve. "Phoebe needs me now. My career can wait."

He frowned. "But if we marry, you'll forfeit your chance at medical school. You know they don't accept married women."

Deirdre smoothed her hand over the front of his jacket, where the rapid beating of his heart belied his outward calm. "Lately, I've come to realize that becoming a doctor isn't as important as it once was. When Aunt Fiona told me she'd found a place for me, I didn't feel . . . anything. Certainly not the happiness I expected." She took one of his hands and pressed it to her cheek. "Right now being with you and Phoebe is what brings me joy. And who knows, the rules regarding women doctors might change over time."

His anxious eyes searched hers. "You're sure? I don't want you to resent me down the road for ruining your dreams."

She smiled, filled with tenderness at his concern. "Dreams change, Matthew. I've simply exchanged one dream for another." She kissed him then, pouring all her love into the joining of their lips.

When they parted, he shook his head. "I'm bound to disappoint you, you know. To inadvertently cause you pain. Neglect your needs."

"And I will likely do the same. No marriage is perfect. That's where God comes in. He will strengthen our love. Help us to forgive our mistakes and remember what true love is really about."

His face seemed to light with hope, as though he'd finally started to believe they could be together. "If you're certain about forgoing medical school, I have another idea." His fingers twined with hers. "Some of the patients in my new clinic are bound to be children and I know you wanted to work in pediatrics. Would you be willing to help out—even on a part-time basis?"

She blinked. "You want to work with me?" A thrill went through her at the idea that Matthew valued her not only as a woman but as a peer, and that he'd welcome her working alongside him.

"Absolutely. It would be a sin to waste your nursing degree and your gift for healing. I think we've already proven that we make a remarkable team." He gave her a bold wink. "In more ways than one."

She held back a laugh. "Why, Dr. Clayborne, are you making inappropriate overtures to a colleague?"

Smiling, he tugged her back against his chest. "Yes, and I plan to continue doing so for a very long time. If you accept my proposal, that is." He raised his brow, a touch of humor dancing in his eyes.

Sudden tears welled and she swallowed a rush of emotion. God had answered her prayers and given her the truest desire of her heart. "I would be honored to marry you, Matthew. I love you and Phoebe more than words can express."

Relief spread over his features, and he grinned. "Well, since you claim to be at a loss for words, I believe kisses will have to suffice."

Love radiated from his eyes as he touched his lips to hers and made good on his promise.

Buoyed with happiness, Connor entered the house, still hushed due to the early hour, and steeled himself for a confrontation with his father. Best to say his piece and get it over with.

Connor poked his head into the parlor, thinking Daddy might be reading the morning paper there, but only Deirdre and Dr. Clayborne occupied the room. The two seemed engrossed in a very intense conversation, so he slipped down the hall to the dining room. Daddy sat with his morning coffee, alone at the table. Just as well. Connor did not want Mama to be part of this conversation.

"Good morning, Connor," Daddy said when he spied him. He studied his attire and frowned. "Have you been out all night?"

Connor ignored the question and pulled out a chair. "We need to talk."

Daddy folded his paper and set it aside. "Very well. What's on your mind?"

For once, Connor felt calm and assured, not letting his temper get the upper hand. "First of all, I want you to know that I'm in love with Josephine Miller and I intend to marry her. Secondly, you owe Jo an apology for the way you treated her last night. I will not allow you to disrespect the woman I love." He leaned back and crossed his arms. "If any of this is unacceptable, I'm prepared to tender my resignation right here and look for somewhere else to live." Connor congratulated himself on keeping an even tone.

Daddy studied him. "Are you finished?"

"I think that about covers it, yes."

"Good. Then I will apologize to Josephine the next time I see her."

Connor's eyebrows shot skyward. "Just like that?"

"I have no qualms about apologizing. There was a reason I said what I did, and since your young lady passed my test with flying colors, I will make things right between us."

"What test?"

"I wanted to ascertain her true motives—to see if she truly cared about you or was merely trying to snag a rich husband. Her fiery defense of you told me all I needed to know. That and the fact that she refused to marry you when you proposed." A smile spread across Daddy's face. "I do admire a woman with gumption. I believe Miss Miller will be a fine asset to this family."

Connor's mouth gaped open. This certainly wasn't the reaction he'd expected. He frowned, still not quite ready to let his father off the hook. "How could you let Jo leave alone like that? She could have been in real danger if I hadn't found her."

Daddy chuckled. "Relax. I was ready to go after her, but Brianna told me you'd already charged to her rescue. Didn't want to ruin your moment."

"I can't believe this." Connor scratched his head. "You sure you're all right with me marrying Jo?"

"I am. In fact, now that you've proved you're ready, I believe a promotion is in order. How would you like the position of head trainer?

Connor blinked. "But that's Sam's job."

"It seems Sam has decided to stay on with his brother and help run his ranch. He'll be back in a few weeks to wrap things up here before he moves out West for good."

Still bewildered, Connor stood and held out his hand. "Then I accept the job, sir. With pleasure."

Daddy rose and shook his hand. "I'm sorry if you felt I rode you a bit too hard. Sometimes being the boss's son means you have to work a little harder to prove yourself. But I always knew you'd rise to the challenge." He pulled Connor into a tight embrace. "I'm proud of you, son. Not only for being a good trainer, but for being an honorable man."

Connor's throat tightened. "Thank you, Daddy. That means a lot."

He slapped Connor on the back. "Well, with you and Gil running Irish Meadows, maybe now I can spend a lot more time fishing—and kissing your mama on the porch swing."

Connor laughed out loud, imagining his mother's reaction to that.

After yet another kiss, Matthew reluctantly pulled away from Deirdre's intoxicating nearness. "If you'll excuse me, my love, I need to have a word with your father."

Her eyes glowed with mischief. "Are you going to ask him for my hand?"

With a grin, he raised her knuckles to his lips. "It's the proper thing to do."

She pressed closer. "We could do the impulsive thing and elope."

"Is this when you expect me to curtail your rash ways with my common sense? Because I warn you, I'm not feeling very sensible right now."

She laughed out loud. "I think I like you this way."

He dropped a light kiss on her lips.

"What if Daddy says no?" she teased.

His lips twisted upward. "Then prepare to grab your bags and be off."

Before he gave in to the temptation to kiss her again, he left the parlor in search of James. He found the man in his study, staring out the window.

James turned with a nod. "Matthew. All set to go?"

Matthew clasped his suddenly unsteady hands behind his back. "Not exactly." He squirmed under the man's gaze. "Actually, sir, I've come to ask for your blessing . . . on my marriage to your daughter."

James's mouth slacked open. "Sweet saints above, Katie was right." He moved across the room toward Matthew. "Kathleen kept insisting Deirdre was in love with you, and you with her, but I didn't believe a word of it. Not that I'm sure it justifies her faking that fall."

Matthew stiffened. "She what?"

James shook his head. "I'm afraid I only discovered the truth after you'd arrived. Colleen convinced my wife to go along with this scheme to get you back here. They even had Mrs. Johnston sneaking Katie food at night. But don't tell Deirdre. She'd be furious with them."

Matthew released a breath. It was pointless to be upset over it now, especially when things had turned out so well. "Kathleen was right about one thing. I love Deirdre very much. It just took me a while to get the courage to do something about it."

James leaned back against his desk. "What about her career? Is she giving it up?"

"Not altogether. I've asked her to work in my clinic when it opens." He gave a hopeful smile. "I find I'm a much better doctor with Deirdre by my side. I'm confident our partnership will work well in all areas of our life together."

James's chest heaved beneath his vest. "Lord knows I have nothing but respect for you, Matthew. And if this is what Deirdre wants, well . . . I won't stand in her way." A muscle in his jaw ticked. "Her happiness is all I've ever wanted."

"On that we definitely agree."

James held out his hand. "Then I guess you have my blessing. Welcome to the family, son."

Matthew swallowed hard and shook his hand. "Thank you, sir. I can't tell you how much I appreciate that."

"There's one more thing before you go." James returned to his desk and picked up an envelope. "We seem to have overlooked the small matter of your fee."

Matthew stilled. He'd forgotten all about payment, so entrenched had he become in the O'Learys' lives. He waved James off. "I couldn't, sir. You're family now."

"Nonsense. I promised you hefty compensation for abandoning your practice and devoting your time to Kathleen. I insist you take it." He slapped the envelope into Matthew's hands. "I hope this will help you establish your clinic."

With unsteady fingers, Matthew withdrew the check, and his mouth fell open. "This is not the fee I agreed on. In fact, it's more than double."

"A fraction of what it's worth to have my wife back. Consider it an investment in my daughter's future." James winked at him. "Now let's get Deirdre and tell Katie the good news."

EPILOGUE

JUNE 1923

DEIRDRE SAT AT THE DRESSING TABLE in her childhood bedroom and ran a brush through her hair, a bubble of anticipation rising within her—not only for the wonderful festivities ahead, but for the little surprise she had planned for Matthew. A fitting one, given that today three new members of the O'Leary family were to be christened: Brianna and Gil's son, Theodore James; Maggie and Adam's daughter, Katie Annabelle; and Colleen's bundle of joy, Madeline Deirdre.

She smiled at the lovely tribute her sister had given her and Matthew in naming her daughter after them.

"Madeline is the closest girl's name to Matthew I could find," Colleen had told them.

The fact that she'd held off with Madeline's christening until Deirdre and Matthew could come back to attend meant the world to both of them.

As much as Deirdre had grown to love her new life in Toronto as Mrs. Matthew Clayborne, she had to admit she missed Irish Meadows and her family. But thanks to Uncle Victor, now a full partner in Matthew's clinic, they were able to schedule a two-week holiday here.

Other than being slightly upset at having to leave Patches with Mrs. Potts, Phoebe had been more excited about the trip than anyone. She'd packed her bag a full week in advance of their trip. The changes in that precious child reminded Deirdre every day that she'd made the right decision. Deirdre's bedroom door flew open, and Phoebe rushed in, carrying a large box topped with an enormous pink bow.

"Mama, I have a present for you." She puffed as she set the box on the bed.

Deirdre pulled the sash of her robe tighter and rose from the vanity. "A present for me? What for? It's not Christmas, and it's not my birthday."

Phoebe giggled. "It's from Papa. He said it's 'cause he loves you."

A thrill tingled up Deirdre's spine, and she didn't even try to hide the wide smile that bloomed.

Matthew appeared in the open doorway, his smile matching hers. "Well, Mrs. Clayborne, aren't you going to open it?"

"Maybe I should wait until I can open it in private?" She winked at him.

His gaze grew more intense as he crossed toward her. "Although I admire your thinking on the matter, I believe you'll want to open this sooner rather than later."

"Please, Mama. I want to see the dress." Phoebe clapped a hand over her mouth. "I wasn't supposed to tell you."

Deirdre laughed. "It's okay. I already guessed it might be clothing." She glanced at Matthew. "But I already have an outfit for today."

"I'm pretty sure you'll change your mind once you see it."

Something about the gleam in his eyes set Deirdre's nerves to buzzing. With trembling fingers, she pulled off the bow and opened the lid. Under a layer of tissue, a most beautiful white satin material peeked out. Gingerly, she lifted the dress from the wrappings and gaped at the lace bodice.

"What is this, Matthew?" she whispered. "It looks like . . . a wedding dress."

"Correct." His grin widened.

"I don't understand."

"We're getting married, Mama. And I'm going to be a flower girl." Phoebe laughed and twirled until her dress billowed out around her.

Deirdre sank onto the mattress, the dress clutched to her chest. "But we're already married."

Not long after they'd returned to Toronto, Mrs. Potts had taken ill, requiring surgery and a lengthy convalescence. Deirdre had been looking after Phoebe during the day, but with Mrs. Potts out of the house, and Matthew working long hours to get the clinic started, the nights became problematic. Aunt Maimie had offered to take Phoebe until Matthew could hire someone, but Deirdre had felt the most practical solution was for her to marry Matthew sooner than intended and move into his home. After some persuasion, Matthew had finally seen the merit of her idea and had arranged a quick, private ceremony, one she knew he regretted more than she. The small disappointment of not having her family present paled with the happiness she'd found at becoming Matthew's wife.

"Phoebe, would you get the second part of the present, please?" Matthew's eyes never left Deirdre's face.

"Okay, Papa." The girl dashed from the room.

Matthew came to sit beside Deirdre. "When we got married in the rectory with only Victor and Maimie as witnesses, I vowed I'd make it up to you. Today is that day."

"Oh, Matthew." Tears choked her airway.

He reached over to take her face in his hands. "Will you marry me again, Deirdre, in front of your whole family?" Moisture shimmered in the blueness of his eyes.

"I'll marry you again every day if you ask," she breathed.

He pulled her face to his and kissed her so tenderly that the tears she'd been suppressing slipped down her cheeks. When at last he lifted his head, he brushed the moisture from her cheeks with his thumbs.

"What about the christenings?" she asked weakly.

He smiled. "They're actually scheduled for next Saturday. When we get back from our honeymoon."

At her thunderstruck look, he laughed. "Your parents felt we deserved a little time to ourselves, and they've graciously given us a week at the Vanderbilt Hotel in Manhattan."

She blinked, torn between happiness at having time alone with Matthew and disappointment at missing the time with her family.

"However, I told them that, knowing my wife, she wouldn't want to be away from Phoebe or her family for that long, so I compromised on two nights."

She flung her arms around him. "I love you so much."

He laughed again. "Good, then let's go get married. Reverend Filmore is waiting."

"So are your attendants." Brianna breezed into the room with Colleen, Maggie, and Phoebe right behind her. They carried flowers and two more boxes.

"Your husband has thought of everything, and whatever he forgot, we remembered." Brianna bustled over to the bed. "Now if you'll excuse us, Doctor, we need to help the bride get ready."

Two hours later, dressed in his best suit and tie, Matthew stood at the front of St. Rita's church. His stomach tensed in anticipation as the attendants and Phoebe came down the aisle. When the music swelled, and Deirdre and James appeared in the doorway, his breath caught in his lungs at her incredible beauty. Awed gasps and murmurs arose as she walked down the aisle, and Matthew gave silent thanks to Brianna for choosing the perfect dress.

The satin gown hugged Deirdre's figure perfectly. Under a sheer veil, she positively glowed, gliding toward him on James's arm.

When they reached the front, James stopped to lift her veil and kissed her cheek before handing her over to Matthew.

Deirdre's eyes shone brighter than the candles that flickered on the altar. She gave her bouquet to Brianna to hold and slipped her hand into his. He still couldn't believe she loved him, that she belonged to him. That he would have the privilege of spending his life with her.

Matthew was so focused on the absolute love radiating from her face that he barely heard Reverend Filmore's words, finally tuning in when the time came for his vows.

He swallowed hard and looked deeply into her eyes. "I, Matthew Edward Clayborne, take you, Deirdre Bridget O'Leary, to be my wedded wife. To have and to hold from this day forward, for better and for worse, for richer and for poorer, in sickness and in health, to love, honor, cherish, and protect, 'til death do us part, according to God's holy ordinance."

Deirdre squeezed his hand, and her lips trembled.

When the reverend invited Deirdre to say her vows, she hesitated. Then she turned and held out her hand to Phoebe, who was sitting in the front row with Kathleen and James. Beaming, Phoebe rushed over to Deirdre's side.

Deirdre glanced at Reverend Filmore. "I think Phoebe should be up here with us since she's as much a part of this ceremony as we are."

Matthew had never loved Deirdre more than at that moment.

Deirdre locked eyes with him and spoke the same vows. A hushed silence descended over the room. Their faithful promises of love took on even greater significance uttered in this holy place.

Matthew stared down into his beloved's face, until at last Reverend Filmore pronounced them man and wife and gave him permission to kiss the bride.

Matthew readily complied, capturing his wife's lips in the most reverent of kisses.

At a tug on his suit jacket, he looked down at Phoebe, then scooped her up in his arms. A burst of applause broke out over the church, and Reverend Filmore introduced Dr., Mrs., and Miss Clayborne to the congregation.

As they made their way back down the aisle, Matthew raised his eyes to the rafters of the church and offered his most profound thanks to God for allowing such love into his life.

And for changing him enough to receive it.

A few hours later, Matthew stood on the balcony at Irish Meadows and surveyed the throngs of people. The house overflowed with love and laughter and happiness. His heart swelled with satisfaction, watching Deirdre flit from person to person, greeting everyone with a hug and a smile. Though she insisted she hadn't minded the simple ceremony in Toronto, Matthew was grateful he'd managed this surprise for her in the parish where she'd grown up.

"There you are." Deirdre came up beside him at the stone railing and laid a hand on his arm. "You seem pensive. Is everything all right?"

He smiled down at her. "Everything is perfect. I never thought I could be this happy."

"Me either," she whispered and rose up to kiss his lips. "Thank you. This was exactly how I'd always hoped my wedding day would be." She grinned. "Well, with one exception."

Matthew frowned. "What exception?"

"Actually, I planned to tell you after the christening, but the wedding changed all that."

His heart gave a hard lurch. "Tell me what?"

"That I'll need to take some time off from the clinic in about six months."

He counted ahead to December and tried to make sense of her statement. "Do you want to spend Christmas here?"

"That would be lovely, but I'm afraid I won't be able to travel then." A gleam of mischief in her eye was the only indication the situation wasn't grave.

Then she burst out laughing. "What I'm trying to tell you, my love, is that you're going to be a father again."

He stared at her, eyes widening as her meaning finally became clear. "We're having a baby?"

"Yes," she said softly. "We are."

His throat thickened, and he gathered her close against his chest, silly tears blurring his vision. "Why didn't you tell me sooner?"

"For one thing, I didn't know for sure until a few days before we left, and then I thought you might use it as an excuse to postpone the trip. I'm afraid I was a little selfish."

He ran a finger down her cheek. "You are the bravest, most *unselfish* woman I know, and I am humbled by your love."

"You're happy, then?" Deirdre asked in a hushed voice.

"Ecstatic. I feel like I've been given another chance to do fatherhood better this time."

She snuggled against his shoulder with a sigh. "God has been so good to us, Matthew. He knew what I needed when I was headed down a path that may not have been right for me."

"Me too. I was so sure I wasn't made for love or marriage. I thank God every day for the bossy woman who barged into my practice, determined to help her mother no matter what the crotchety doctor said."

Deirdre's eyes twinkled. "You certainly were crotchety, and slightly arrogant, I might add."

"Unfortunately, I can't deny the truth of your assessment." He chuckled and kissed her again.

She reached up to caress his cheek. "Well, Dr. Clayborne, would you care to dance with your wife one more time before we start our honeymoon?"

He wrapped his arms around her. "I most certainly would, Mrs. Clayborne."

James O'Leary stood beside the piano in his parlor and surveyed the room before him. Other than a few close friends and neighbors, the majority of the people gathered for the celebration were family members—his children and grandchildren.

His chest puffed out with pride. What a fine-looking group they were, and more important, they were all kind, respectable, morally upright citizens. People he would like to spend time with even if they weren't related.

James straightened at the sight of his wife walking toward him, leaning heavily on her cane. Tears stood out in her bright eyes.

He rushed to support her weakened side. "Katie, you need to sit down. I think you've overdone it."

Ever since the stroke had felled his indomitable wife, James's world hadn't been the same, forever worried that he could lose her.

Her smile eased a fraction of his concern. "I'm all right, James. Though I won't refuse the offer of a seat."

He guided her to the sofa near the fireplace, which two of his grandchildren quickly vacated. He sat beside her, still not satisfied she was okay.

Kathleen placed a hand over his. "Deirdre just told me the most wonderful news." Her face glowed. "She and Matthew are expecting."

A jolt of emotion squeezed James's chest. "A strange time to announce such a thing—at their wedding."

"You know very well they were married months ago."

He scowled. "In a rectory. In a foreign country. That doesn't count."

Kathleen laughed. "You're such a fraud, my darling. Everyone thinks you're intimidating, but you're nothing but a marshmallow."

James kept his lips from twitching. "So we've another grandchild on the way. You don't think Deirdre regrets giving up her dream?"

"One's dreams have a habit of changing over time." Kathleen smiled and looked across the room. "I think she's very happy. As are all our children."

He followed her gaze to Connor and Josephine, standing close together, involved in a seemingly intimate conversation—perhaps discussing their recent engagement.

Until Connor had met Josephine Miller, Irish Meadows had been his sole passion. The fact that he'd been willing to give up his inheritance for her spoke volumes and had cemented James's support of their union.

"You're not still having reservations about Jo, are you?"

Katie's anxious question brought James out of his thoughts.

"No, my dear. They seem well-suited. And Josephine's talent with the horses has been an added bonus."

"We're so blessed, James." Katie's whisper held a hint of tears.

"We are indeed, my love." He raised her hand to his lips. "Most of all, I'm blessed to have you."

She smiled. "Next week we celebrate the christening of three more grandchildren. What did we do to deserve such a wonderful family?"

He caressed her fingers, his mind drifting. "I've been thinking of my parents quite often of late. Coming to this country with nothing but the clothes on their back. Hoping to give their children a better life. They'd be so proud of the legacy we've created." He swallowed the rise of emotion in his throat.

"They most certainly would."

James leaned over and kissed his wife, who understood him as no other. Then he lifted his head to scan the room filled with his offspring—the future generations of O'Learys—and warmth spread through his chest. God had surely provided them with an abundance of blessings.

And no matter what the future might bring, James rested secure in the knowledge that his family would weather the brunt of any storm that might arise, sustained by the faithful promise of God's unfailing love.

And for that, he was most grateful indeed.

ACKNOWLEDGMENTS

Love's Faithful Promise has been a wonderful, albeit bittersweet, journey, since it marks the end of the COURAGE TO DREAM series and the final chapter in the lives of my beloved O'Leary family. I will miss them all!

One of the most enjoyable parts of writing this story was that a portion of the book was set in the city of Toronto, Ontario, not far from my hometown, which afforded me the opportunity to do some historical research in my own area. I visited Toronto's Old City Hall, now used strictly as a courthouse. Back in the early 1900s, it functioned as Toronto's City Hall as well as a courthouse.

I did a great deal of research about World War I, specifically about the soldiers who returned home injured to Canada, and I based my hero, Dr. Matthew Clayborne, on a cumulation of historical doctors I read about. (I also pictured him looking a lot like Matthew Crawley from *Downton Abbey*, who served in World War I!) In addition, I loosely based the military hospital in my book on the Christie Street Veterans' Hospital, originally the National Cash Register Company Factory, which was converted to the Toronto Military Orthopaedic Hospital in 1919.

I want to thank the wonderful team at Bethany House for all their hard work on my behalf. In particular, thank you to Dave Long, Charlene Patterson, and Sharon Hodge for their excellent editorial input. Thank you also to Noelle Buss, Amy Green, and Stacey Theesfield for their help in promoting my books. Your support and encouragement are greatly appreciated!

Once again, I owe a huge debt of gratitude to my wonderful critique partners, Sally Bayless and Julie Jarnagin, who helped me make this story shine! I appreciate your friendship and support.

And of course, I have to thank my family—my husband, Bud, and my children, Leanne and Eric—for their continued love and encouragement.

I am so grateful to be a part of the Bethany House team of authors. I feel blessed to be able to share my stories with you all and hope to again in the future!

To learn more about my books, please check out my website at www.susanannemason.com.

Warmest wishes,
Susan

About the Author

Susan Anne Mason describes her writing style as "romance sprinkled with faith." She loves incorporating inspirational messages of God's unconditional love and forgiveness into her characters' journeys.

Susan lives outside Toronto, Ontario, with her husband, two children, and two cats. She loves red wine and chocolate, is not partial to snow even though she's Canadian, and is ecstatic on the rare occasions she has the house to herself. In addition to writing, Susan likes to research her family history online and occasionally indulges in scrapbooking.

Learn more about Susan and her books at www.SusanAnne Mason.com.

You May Also Enjoy . . .

More Historical Fiction

Stella West has quit the art world and moved to Boston to solve the mysterious death of her sister, but she is in need of a well-connected ally. Fortunately, magazine owner Romulus White has been trying to hire her for years. Sparks fly when Stella and Romulus join forces, but will their investigation cost them everything?

From This Moment by Elizabeth Camden
elizabethcamden.com

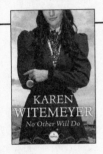

When the women's colony of Harper's Station is threatened, founder Emma Chandler is forced to admit she needs help. The only man she trusts enough to ask is Malachi Shaw, whose life she once saved. As Mal returns the favor, danger mounts—and so does the attraction between them.

No Other Will Do by Karen Witemeyer
karenwitemeyer.com

When disaster ruins Charlotte Ward's attempt to restart a London acting career, her estranged daughter, Rosalind, moves her to a quiet village where she can recover. There, Rosalind gets a second chance at romance, and mother and daughter reconnect—until Charlotte's troubles catch up to her.

A Haven on Orchard Lane by Lawana Blackwell

◆ BETHANYHOUSE